Dear Readers,

It delights me to see my original three LONG, TALL TEXANS in print again. When I began the series, I had no idea that it would become so popular. Since these heroes and heroines are among my own favorites, it is a special pleasure to see them all together in one book.

In answer to many requests, yes, there will be future books in this series! Thank you all for your response to the LONG, TALL TEXANS, and for your kindness to me over the years.

Your friend,

Diana Palmer

Diana Palmer

LONG, TALL TEXANS

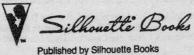

Published by Silhouette Books

America's Publisher of Contemporary Romance

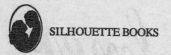 SILHOUETTE BOOKS

LONG, TALL TEXANS

Copyright © 1994 by Harlequin Enterprises B.V.

ISBN 0-373-48320-1

The publisher acknowledges the copyright holders of the individual works as follows:

CALHOUN
Copyright © 1988 by Diana Palmer
JUSTIN
Copyright © 1988 by Diana Palmer
TYLER
Copyright © 1988 by Diana Palmer

Printed in U.S.A.

CONTENTS

The Long, Tall Texans series
from Silhouette Romance

CALHOUN

Diana Palmer

To Mary Wheeler at Micro Pro—
thanks a million!

Chapter One

Abby couldn't help looking over her shoulder from time to time as she stood in line at the theater ticket counter. She'd escaped by telling Justin that she was going to see an art exhibit. Calhoun, thank God, was off somewhere buying more cattle, although he was certain to be home later this evening. When he found out where his ward had been, he'd be furious. She almost grinned at her own craftiness.

Well, it took craftiness to deal with Calhoun Ballenger. He and Justin, his older brother, had taken Abby in when she'd been just fifteen. They would have been her stepbrothers, except that an untimely car accident had killed their father and Abby's mother just two days before the couple were to have gotten married. There hadn't been any other family, so Calhoun had proposed that he and Justin assume responsibility for the heartbroken teenager, Abigail Clark. And they did. It was legal, of course; technically Abby was Calhoun's ward. The problem was that she couldn't make Calhoun realize that she was a woman.

Abby sighed. That was a problem, all right. And to make it even worse, he'd gone crazy on the subject of protecting her from the world. For the past four months it had been a major ordeal just to go out on a date. The way he stood watch over her was getting almost comical. Justin rarely smiled, but Calhoun's antics brought him close to it.

Calhoun's attitude didn't amuse Abby, though. She was desperately in love with Calhoun, but the big blond man still looked upon her as a child. And despite her frequent attempts to show Calhoun that she was a woman, she couldn't seem to get through his armor.

She shifted restlessly. She had no idea of how to attract a man like Calhoun in the first place. He wasn't as much of a rounder now as he had been in his youth, but she knew that he was frequently seen in nightclubs in San Antonio with one sophisticated beauty or another. And here was Abby, dying of love for him. She wasn't sophisticated or beautiful. She was a rather plain country girl, not the sort to immediately draw men's eyes, even though her figure was better than average.

After brooding over the problem, she had come up with a solution. If she could manage to get sophisticated, he might notice her. Going to a strip show wasn't exactly the best first step, but in Jacobsville it was a good start. Just being seen here would show Calhoun that she wasn't the little prude he thought she was. *When* he found out about it—and eventually he would hear she'd attended the show.

Abby smoothed the waistline of her pretty gray plaid skirt. She was wearing a pale yellow blouse with it, and her long, wavy brown hair was in a neat chignon. Her hair, when it was loose, was one of her best assets. It was thick and silky. And her eyes weren't bad. They were big, quiet grayish-blue eyes, and she was blessed with a peaches-and-cream complexion and a perfect bow of a mouth. But without careful makeup she was hopelessly plain. Her breasts were bigger than she wanted them to be, her legs longer than she would have liked. She had friends who were small and dainty, and they made her feel like a beanpole. She glanced down at herself miserably. If only she were petite and exquisitely beautiful.

At least she did look older and more sophisticated than usual in her burgundy velour jacket, and her blue-gray eyes sparkled as she thought about what she was doing. Well, it wasn't so bad for a woman to go to a male dance revue, was it? She had to get educated somehow, and God knew Calhoun wasn't about to let her date any men who knew the score. He saw to it that her only escorts were boys her own age, and he screened every one and made casual remarks about how often he cleaned his guns and what he thought about "fooling around before marriage." It wasn't really surprising to Abby that few of her dates came back.

She shivered a little in the cold night air. It was February, and cold even in south Texas. As she huddled in her jacket, she smiled at another young woman shivering in the long line outside the Grand Theater. It was the only theater in Jacobsville, and there had been some opposition to having this kind of entertainment come to town. But in the end there had been surprisingly few complaints, and there was a long line of women waiting to see if these men lived up to the publicity.

Wouldn't Calhoun just die when he found out what she'd done? She grinned. His blonde-streaked brown hair would stand on end, and his dark eyes would glare at her furiously. Justin would do what he always did—he'd go out and dig postholes while Calhoun wound down. The two brothers looked a lot alike, except that Justin's hair was almost black. They both had dark eyes, and they were both tall, muscular men. Calhoun was by far the handsomer of the two. Justin had a craggy face and a reticent personality, and although he was courteous to women, he never dated anybody. Almost everybody knew why— Shelby Jacobs had thrown him over years ago, refusing to marry him.

That had been when the Ballengers had still been poor, before Justin's business sense and Calhoun's feel for marketing had skyrocketed them to success with a mammoth feedlot operation here in south Texas. Shelby's family was rich, and rumor had it that she thought Justin was beneath her. It had certainly made him bitter. Funny, she mused, Shelby seemed like such a wonderful woman. And her brother, Tyler, was nice, too.

Two more ladies got their tickets, and Abby dug out a ten-dollar bill. Just as she got to the ticket counter, though, her wrist was suddenly seized and she was pulled unceremoniously to one side.

"I thought I recognized that jacket," Calhoun murmured, glaring down at her with eyes that were dark and faintly glittering. "What a good thing I decided to come home through town. Where's my brother?" he added for good measure. "Does he know where you are?"

"I told him I was going to an art exhibit," Abby replied with a touch of her irrepressible humor. Her blue-gray eyes twinkled up at him, and she felt the warm glow she always felt when Calhoun came close. Even when he was angry, it was so good to be near him. "Well, it is an art exhibit, sort of," she argued when he looked skeptical. "Except that the male statues are alive..."

"My God." He stared at the line of amused women and abruptly turned toward his white Jaguar, tugging at her wrist. "Let's go."

"I'm not going home," she said firmly, struggling. It was exciting to challenge him. "I'm going to buy my ticket and go in there—Calhoun!" she wailed as he ended the argument by simply lifting her in his hard arms and carrying her to the car.

"I can't even leave the state for one day without you doing something insane," Calhoun muttered in his deep, gravelly voice. "The last time I went off on business, I came home to find you about to leave for Lake Tahoe with that Misty Davies."

"Congratulations. You saved me from a weekend of skiing," Abby murmured dryly. Not for the world would she have admitted how exciting it was to have him carry her, to feel his strength at such close quarters. He was as strong as he looked, and the subtle scents of his body and the warmth of his breath on her face made her body tingle in new and exciting ways.

"There were two college boys all set to go along, as I remember," he reminded her.

"What am I supposed to do with my car?" she demanded. "Leave it here?"

"Why not? God knows nobody would be stupid enough to steal it," he replied easily, and kept walking, her slight weight soft and disturbing in his hard arms.

"It's a very nice little car," she protested, talking more than usual because the feel of his chest was unnerving her. His clean-shaven chin was just above her, and she was getting drunk on the feel of him.

"Which you wouldn't have if I'd gone with you instead of Justin," he returned. "Honest to God, he spoils you rotten. He should have married Shelby and had kids of his own to ruin. I hate having him practice on you. That damned little sports car isn't safe.''

"It's mine, I like it, I'm making the payments and I'm keeping it," she said shortly.

He looked down at her, his dark eyes much too close to hers. "Aren't we brave, though?" he taunted softly, deliberately letting his gaze fall on her mouth.

She could barely breathe, but he wasn't going to make her back down. Not that way. She didn't dare let him see the effect he had on her. "I'm almost twenty-one," she reminded him. He looked into her eyes, and she felt the impact of his glance like a body blow. It made her feel like a lead weight. And there was a sudden tautness about his body that puzzled her. For seconds that strung out like hours, he searched her eyes. Then abruptly he moved again.

"So you keep telling me," he replied curtly. "And then you go and do something stupid like this."

"There's nothing wrong with being sophisticated," she mumbled. "God knows how I'll ever get an education. You seem to want me to spend the rest of my life a virgin."

"Hang out in this kind of atmosphere and you won't stay in that sainted condition for much longer," he returned angrily. She disturbed him when she made such statements. She had been talking like that for months, and he was no nearer a solution to the problem than he had been at the beginning. He quickened his pace toward the car, his booted feet making loud, angry thuds on the pavement.

Calhoun was still wearing a dark suit, Abby noticed. His thick dark-blond hair was covered by his cream dress Stetson. He smelled of Oriental cologne, and his dark face was clean-shaven. He was a handsome brute, Abby thought.

Sexy and overpoweringly masculine, and she loved every line of him, every scowl, every rugged inch. She forced her screaming nerves not to give her away and attempted to hide her attraction to him, as usual, with humor.

"Aren't we in a temper, though?" she taunted softly, and his dark expression hardened. It was exciting to make him mad. She'd only realized that in the past few weeks, but more and more she liked to prod him, to see his explosive reactions. She loved the touch of his hands, and provoking him had become addictive. "I'm a big girl. I graduated from the trade school last year. I have a diploma. I'm a secretary. I'm working for Mr. Bundy at the feedlot sales office—"

"I remember. I paid for the trade school courses and got you the damned job," he said tersely.

"You sure did, Calhoun," she agreed, her mischievous gaze darting up at him as he opened the passenger door of the vehicle and put her on the smooth leather seat, slamming the door once she was settled. He went around the gleaming hood and got in under the steering wheel. There was muted violence in the way he started the powerful white car, shot away from the curb and drove down the main town's street.

"Abby, I can't believe you really wanted to pay money to watch a bunch of boys take their clothes off," he muttered.

"It beats having boys try to take mine off," she returned humorously. "You must think so, too, because you go nuts if I try to date anybody with any experience."

He frowned. That was true. It upset him to think of any man taking advantage of Abby. He didn't want other men touching her.

"I'd beat a man to his knees for trying to undress you, and that's a fact," he said.

"My poor future husband," she sighed. "I can see him now, calling the police on our wedding night..."

"You're years too young to talk about getting married," he said.

"I'll be twenty-one in three months. My mother was twenty-one when she had me," she reminded him.

"I'm thirty-two, and I've never been married," he replied. "There's plenty of time. You don't need to rush into marriage before you've had time to see something of the world," he said firmly.

"How can I?" she asked reasonably. "You won't let me."

He glared at her. "It's the part of life that you're trying to see that bothers me. Male strip shows. My God."

"They weren't going to take all their clothes off," she assured him. "Just most of them."

"Why did you decide to go tonight?"

"I didn't have anything else to do," she sighed. "And Misty had been to see this show."

"Misty Davies," he muttered. "I've told you I don't approve of your friendship with that flighty heiress. She's years older than you and much more sophisticated."

"No wonder," she replied. "She doesn't have an overbearing guardian who's determined to save her from herself."

"She could have used one. A woman who treats her body cheaply doesn't invite a wedding ring."

"So you keep saying. At least Misty won't faint of shock on her wedding night when her husband takes his clothes off. I've never seen a man without a stitch on. Except in this magazine that Misty had—" she began, warming to her subject.

"For God's sake, you shouldn't be reading that kind of magazine!" He looked outraged.

Her eyebrows went up suddenly, and her eyes were as round as saucers. "Why not?"

He searched for words. "Well . . . because!"

"Men ogle women in those kind of magazines," she said reasonably. "If we can be exploited, why can't men?"

He finally gave in to ill temper. "Why can't you just shut up, Abby?"

"Okay, Calhoun, I'll do that very thing," she agreed. She studied his hard, angry profile, and almost smiled at the way she'd gotten him ruffled. He might not be in love with her, but she certainly did have a knack for getting his attention.

"All this sudden fascination with male nudity," he grumbled, glaring at her. "I don't know what's gotten into you."

"Frustration," she replied. "It comes from too many nights sitting home alone."

"I've never tried to stop you from dating," he said defensively.

"Oh, no, of course you haven't. You just sit with my prospective dates and make a big deal of cleaning your gun collection while you air your archaic views on premarital sex!"

"They're not archaic," he said curtly. "A lot of men feel the way I do about it."

"Do tell?" She lifted her eyebrow. "And I suppose that means that you're a virgin, too, Calhoun?"

His dark eyes cut sideways at her. "Do you think so, Abby?" he asked, in a tone she'd never heard him use.

She suddenly felt very young. The huskiness in his deep voice, added to the faint arrogance in his dark eyes, made her feel foolish for even having asked. Of course he wasn't a virgin.

She averted her eyes. "Foolish question," she murmured softly.

"Wasn't it, though?" He pressed on the accelerator. For some reason, it bothered him to have Abby know what his private life was like. She probably knew more than he'd given her credit for, especially if she was hanging around with Misty Davies. Misty frequented the same kind of city hot spots that Calhoun did, and she'd seen him with one or two of his occasional companions. He hoped Misty hadn't talked to Abby about what she'd seen, but he couldn't count on it.

His sudden withdrawal puzzled Abby. She didn't like the cold silence that was growing between them any more than she liked thinking about his women. "How did you know where I was?" she asked to break the rigid silence.

"I didn't, honey," he confessed. The endearment sounded so natural coming from him that she'd never minded him using it, though she disliked its artificiality when other men did. "I happened to come home through Jacobsville. And who should I see in line—in front of all the lurid posters—but you?"

She sighed. "Fate. Fate is out to get me."

"Fate may not be the only one," he returned, but his voice was so low that she couldn't hear.

He turned onto the road that led past the feedlot to the big Spanish house where the Ballengers lived. On the way they passed the Jacobs's colonial-style house, far off the road at the end of a paved driveway, with purebred Arabian horses grazing in sprawling pastures dotted with oak trees. There wasn't much grass—the weather was still cold, and a few snow flurries had caused excitement the day before. Big bales of hay were placed around the property to give the horses adequate feed, supplemented with blocks of vitamins and minerals.

"I hear the Jacobses are having financial problems," Abby remarked absently.

He glanced at her. "Since the old man died last summer, they're close to bankrupt, in fact Tyler's borrowed all he can borrow. If he can't pull it together now, he never will. The old man made deals Ty didn't even know about. If he loses that place, it's going to be damned hard on his pride."

"Hard on Shelby's, too," she remarked.

He grimaced. "For God's sake, don't mention Shelby around Justin."

"I wouldn't dare. He gets funny, doesn't he?"

"I wouldn't call throwing punches at people funny."

"I've seen you throw punches a time or two," she reminded him, recalling one particular day not too long before when one of the new cowhands had beaten a horse. Calhoun had knocked the man to his knees and fired him on the spot, his voice so cold and quiet that it had cut to the bone. Calhoun didn't have to raise his voice. Like Justin, when Calhoun lost his temper he had a look that made words unnecessary.

He was an odd mixture, she thought, studying him. So tenderhearted that he'd go off for half a day by himself if he had to put down a calf or if something happened to one of his men. And so hotheaded at times that the men would actually hide from his anger. In temperament, he was like Justin. They were both strong, fiery men, but underneath there was a tenderness, a vulnerability, that very few people ever saw. Abby, because she'd lived with them for so many years, knew them better than any outsider ever could.

"How did you get back so fast?" she asked to break the silence.

He shrugged. "I guess I've got radar," he murmured, smiling faintly. "I had a feeling you wouldn't be sitting at home with Justin watching old war movies on the VCR."

"I didn't think you'd be back before morning."

"So you decided you'd go watch a lot of muscle men strip off and wiggle on the stage."

"Heaven knows I tried." She sighed theatrically. "Now I'll die ignorant, thanks to you."

"Damn it all," he laughed, taken aback by her reactions. She made him laugh more than any woman he'd ever known. And lately he'd found himself thinking about her more than he should. Maybe it was just his age, he thought. He'd been alone a long time, and a woman here and there didn't really satisfy him. But Abby wasn't fair game. She was a marrying girl, and he'd better remember that. No way could he seduce her for pleasure, so he had to keep the fires banked down. If he could.

Justin was in his study when they got back, frowning darkly over some figures in his books. When he looked up, his craggy face was devoid of expression, but his dark eyes twinkled when he glanced from Calhoun's irritated expression to Abby's furious one.

"How was the art show?" he asked her.

"It wasn't an art show," Calhoun said flatly, tossing his Stetson onto the coffee table. "It was a male strip show."

Justin's pencil stopped in midair as he stared at Abby. His shock was a little embarrassing, because Justin was even more old-fashioned and reactionary than Calhoun about such things. He wouldn't even talk about anything intimate in mixed company.

"A what?" Justin asked.

"A male revue," Abby countered, glaring at Calhoun. "It's a kind of . . . variety show."

"Hell," Calhoun retorted, his dark eyes flashing. "It's a strip show!"

"Abby!" Justin scolded.

"I'm almost twenty-one," she told him. "I have a responsible job. I drive a car. I'm old enough to marry and have children. If I want to go and see a male variety show—" she ignored Calhoun's instantly inserted "strip show" "—I have every right."

Justin laid his pencil down and lit a cigarette. Calhoun glared at him, and so did Abby, but he ignored them. The only concession he made to their disapproval was to turn on one of the eight smokeless ashtrays they'd bought him for Christmas.

"That sounds like a declaration of war," Justin remarked.

Abby lifted her chin. "That's what it is." She turned to Calhoun. "If you don't stop embarrassing me in front of the whole world, I'll move in with Misty Davies."

Calhoun's good intentions went up in smoke. "Like hell you will," he countered. "You're not living with that woman!"

"I'll live with her if I want to!"

"If you two would..." Justin began calmly.

"Over my dead body!" Calhoun raged, moving closer. "She has parties that last for days!"

"...just try to communicate..." Justin continued.

"She likes people! She's a socialite!" Abby's eyes were almost black now as she clenched her fists by her side and glared up at Calhoun.

"...you just might..." Justin went on.

"She's a featherbrained, overstimulated eccentric!" Calhoun retorted.

"...*COME TO AN UNDERSTANDING!*" Justin thundered, rising out of his chair with blazing eyes.

They both froze at the unfamiliar sound of his raised voice. He never shouted, not even when he was at his angriest.

"Damn, I hurt my ears," Justin sighed, putting his palm to one while he glared at his brother and Abby. "Now, listen, this isn't getting you anywhere. Besides that, any minute Maria and Lopez are going to come running in here thinking someone's been murdered." Just as he finished speaking, two robed, worried elderly people appeared, wide-eyed and apprehensive, in the doorway. "Now see what you've done," Justin grumbled.

"What is all this noise about?" Maria asked, pushing back her long salt-and-pepper hair and glancing worriedly around the room. "We thought something terrible had happened."

"*¡Ay de mí!* Another rumble." Lopez shook his head and grinned at Abby. "What have you done now, *niñita?*"

She glared at him. "Nothing," she said tersely. "Not one thing—"

"She went to a male strip show," Calhoun volunteered.

"I did not!" she protested, red faced.

"What is the world coming to?" Maria shook her head, put her hands to it and went out mumbling in Spanish, followed by a chuckling Lopez. The couple, married more than thirty years, had been with the family for two generations. They were family, not just cook and former horse wrangler.

"But, I didn't!" Abby called after them. She darted a speaking glance at Calhoun, who was perched on a corner of Justin's desk looking elegant and imperturbable. "Now see what you've done!"

"Me?" Calhoun asked coolly. "Hell, you're the one with the lurid curiosity."

"Lurid?" She gaped at him. "Go ahead, tell me you've never been to a female strip show."

Calhoun got up, looking uncomfortable. "That's different."

"Oh, sure it is. Women are sex objects but men aren't, right?"

"She's got you there," Justin said.

Calhoun glared at both of them, turned on his heel and left the room. Abby gazed after him smugly, feeling as if she'd won at least a minor victory. There was little consolation in her triumph, though. Calhoun had been harder to get along with than a bone-dry snake at a poison water hole lately. She didn't know how or what, but she was going to have to do something about the situation, and soon.

Chapter Two

Abby arranged to miss breakfast the next morning. Calhoun's attitude irritated her. He didn't want her himself, but he was so possessive that she couldn't get near another man. His attitude was frustrating at best. He had no idea how she felt, of course. She was careful to hide her feelings for him. A man like Calhoun, who was rich and moderately handsome, could have any woman he wanted. He wouldn't want a plain, unsophisticated woman like Abby. She knew that, and it hurt. It made her rebellious, too. She didn't want to spend the rest of her life grieving for a man she could never have. It was far better to look in other directions. But how could she, when Calhoun refused to let go?

She drove several miles from the ranch to the office at the mammoth feedlot in the small red British sports car she'd talked Justin into cosigning for when she'd graduated from the local vocational school. Because of the attention Calhoun and Justin paid to hygiene, there wasn't as much odor as most feedlots generated, which surprised a lot of visiting cattlemen. Abby had once gone with Calhoun to tour some other feedlots and had come out with a new respect for the one back home. The Ballenger brothers' operation was a little more expensive to run, but there were hardly any cattle deaths here because of disease. And that was a prime consideration. A rancher who contracted with the feedlot to fatten his cattle for slaughter didn't want to lose the animals to disease.

Since Abby was early, the office was deserted. There were three other women who worked here, all married, and they helped keep records on the various herds of feeder cattle being fattened for ranches all over the country. There were contracts to sort and file, records on each lot of cattle to keep, and ongoing vaccination and management reports. There was the constant hum of the heavy equipment used to feed the cattle and to remove waste to underground storage to be used later to fertilize pastures where grain was grown. The phones rang constantly and the computers had to be programmed. There was a payroll department, as well as a salesman, a staff veterinarian and a number of cowboys who moved cattle in and out and saw to feeding them and maintaining the machinery that kept it all going. Abby hadn't realized until she'd come to work here how big the operation was.

The sheer size of it was staggering, even for Texas. Fenced areas filled with steers stretched to the horizon, and the dust was formidable, as was the smell, which was inevitable even when sanitary management practices were employed.

The Ballengers didn't own a packing plant—that wasn't legal, just as it wasn't legal for packers to own custom feedlots. But the brothers did own a third of their feeder cattle, and the other two-thirds were custom fed. Abby had grown up hearing terms like profit margin, break-even prices and ration formulation. Now she understood what the words meant.

She put her purse under her desk and turned on her computer. There were several new contracts waiting to be filled in for new lots of four-footed customers.

The feedlot took in feeder cattle weighing six hundred to seven hundred pounds and fed them up to their slaughter weight of one thousand to eleven hundred pounds. The Ballengers had a resident nutritionist and an experienced stockman who handled the twice-daily feeding routine with its highly automated machinery. They had the feeding down to such a fine art that the Ballenger operation was included in the top five percent of feedlots nationally. And that was a real honor, considering all the things that could go wrong, from falling cattle prices to unexpected epidemics to drought.

Abby was fascinated by the workings of it all. There were thousands of bawling steers and heifers out there. There were always big cattle trucks coming and going and men yelling and herding and vaccinating and dehorning, and the noise could get deafening despite the sound-proofed office walls. Visiting cattlemen came to see their investments. Those who didn't come were sent monthly progress reports. Daily records were kept on everything.

Abby fed the first contract into her electronic type-writer, trying to decipher the spidery scrawl of Caudell Ayker, the feedlot office manager. He was second only to Calhoun in the chain of command, because Calhoun's name went in as manager. He and Justin owned the feed-lot jointly, but Justin held the lion's share of the stock. Justin preferred money management to meeting with clients, so Calhoun did most of the day-to-day management on the feedlot. That was one reason Abby loved the job. It meant she got to see a lot of Calhoun.

When Calhoun walked in the door in a dashing pale tan suit, Abby hit the wrong key, covering the contract with a flock of Xs. She grimaced, backspacing to correct her mistake, and then discovered that she couldn't do it. The correction was too little, too late. Irritated, she ripped the paper out of the machine, put a clean sheet in and started all over again.

"Having problems this morning, honey?" Calhoun asked with his usual cheerful smile, despite the way they'd parted in anger the night before. He never carried grudges. It was one of his virtues.

"Just the usual frustrations, boss," she answered with a blithe smile.

He searched her eyes. They had such a peculiar light in them lately. He found her more and more disturbing, especially when she wore close-fitting suits like the blue one she had on today. It clung lovingly to every line of her tall, slender body, outlining the thrust of her high breasts, the smooth curve of her hips. He took a slow breath, trying to hide his growing attraction to her. It was odd how she'd managed to get under his skin so easily.

"You look nice," he said unexpectedly.

She felt color blush her cheeks, and she smiled. "Thank you."

He hesitated without knowing why, his dark eyes caressing her face, her mouth. "I don't like your hair like that," he added quietly. "I like it long and loose."

She was having a hard time breathing. Her eyes worked up his broad chest to his face and were trapped by his steady gaze. Like electricity, something burst between them, linking them, until she had to drag her eyes down again. Her legs actually trembled.

"I'd better get back to work," she said unsteadily, fiddling with the paper.

"We both had," he replied. He turned and walked into his office without knowing how he got there. Once inside, he sat down behind his big oak desk and stared through the open door at Abby until the buzz of the intercom reminded him of the day's business.

Things went smoothly for a little while, but it was too much to expect that the serenity would last. Just before lunch, one of the cattlemen who had feeder steers in the lot came by to check on them and got an eyeful of Abby.

"You sure are a pretty little thing," the man said, grinning down at the picture she made in her neat blue knit suit and white blouse with her hair in a French twist and a minimum of makeup on her pretty face. He was about Calhoun's age.

She flushed. The man wasn't as handsome as Calhoun, but he was pleasant-looking and he seemed harmless. "Thank you," she said demurely, and smiled at him, just as she smiled at other customers. But he took it as an invitation.

He sat down on the corner of her desk, giving her a purely masculine scrutiny with his pale blue eyes. "I'm Greg Myers," he introduced himself. "I just stopped in on my way to Oklahoma City, and I thought I'd take Calhoun to lunch if he's in. But I think I'd rather take you instead." He lowered his voice, then reached out unexpectedly and touched Abby's cheek, ignoring her indrawn breath. "You pretty little thing. You look like a tea rose, ripe for the picking."

Abby just gaped at him. All her reading and imagining hadn't prepared her for this kind of flirtation with an experienced man. She was out of her depth and frankly stunned.

"Come on, now," Myers drawled, caressing her cheek. "Say you will. We'll have a nice long lunch and get to know each other."

While Abby was searching for the right words to extricate herself from the unwelcome situation, Calhoun came out of his office and stood directly behind Mr. Myers, looking suddenly murderous.

"I'm afraid you'll have to settle for me," Calhoun said tersely. "Abby's my ward, and she doesn't date older men."

"Oops." Myers stood up, grinning sheepishly. "Sorry, old son, I didn't know."

"No harm done," Calhoun said carelessly, but his eyes were dark and cold and dangerous-looking. "Let's go. Abby, I'll want the latest progress report on his cattle when we get back."

Only a few months before, Abby might have had some snappy reply to that, or she might have jumped back at Calhoun for acting so possessive. But now she just looked at him, feeling helpless and hungry and awash on a wave of longing because he was acting jealous.

He seemed to stop breathing, too. His dark eyes searched hers, aware of her embarrassment, her confusion. He let his gaze fall to her mouth and watched her lips part suddenly, and his body reacted in a way that shocked him.

"Lunch. Now." Calhoun ushered the other cattleman to the door. "If you'll get in the car, I'll just get my hat and be right with you," he told the man with a glued-on smile and a pat on the shoulder. "That's right, you go ahead...." He turned to Abby, his expression unreadable. "I want to talk to you." Calhoun took her arm and pulled her up, leading her into his office without a word.

He closed the door, and the way he looked at her made her feel threatened and wildly excited all at the same time.

"Mr. Myers is waiting...." she faltered, disturbed by the darkness of his eyes as they met hers.

He moved toward her, and she backed up until his desk stopped her, her eyes riveted to his. Maybe he was going to make a declaration!

His chin lifted then, and it was anger that glinted in his dark eyes, not possessiveness. "Listen," he said curtly, "Grey Myers has had three wives. He currently has at least one mistress. He's forgotten more than you've had time to learn. I don't want you to learn that kind of lesson with a professional Romeo."

"I'm going to learn it with someone eventually," she said, swallowing hard. Her body felt odd, taut and tingling all at once, because his was close enough that she could feel its warm strength.

"I know that," he said impatiently, and his face hardened. "But I'd just as soon you didn't join a queue. Myers is no serious suitor. He's a playboy with a smooth manner, and he'd have you screaming for help five minutes after you were alone with him."

So that was it. More big-brother responsibility. He wasn't jealous, he was upset because his protective instincts had been aroused. She stared at the steady rise and fall of his chest in dull acceptance. *Stupid me,* she thought miserably, *wishing for a star again.*

"I wasn't trying to lead him on," she said finally. "I just smiled at him, like I smile at everyone—even you. I guess he thought I was sending out smoke signals, but I wasn't, honestly."

His face relaxed. "No harm done." And then he moved. One long, powerful arm slid behind her, bringing his lips within an inch of hers. She almost moaned at the minty warmth of his breath on her mouth. Her gaze dropped to his mouth, curiously tracing every hard line of the thin upper lip and the more chiseled lower one. Her heart throbbed. Her breath seemed to stop altogether, and for one long instant she felt the full weight of his chest against her soft breasts in a contact that was shocking. She looked up at him with wide, stunned eyes.

Then he moved back, the hat he'd been reaching for in one hand, his eyes frankly amused at the look on her face. So she'd never thought of him that way, had she? It irritated him to think that she didn't feel the new and very unwelcome attraction he was discovering for her. It was just as well that he had a business function tonight; it would keep his overimaginative brain away from Abby.

"Were you expecting something?" he asked coldly. "I just wanted my hat." He watched a shadow pass across her eyes before she mumbled something and lowered her gaze. He put his Stetson on his thick blonde-streaked hair and tilted it over one eye. "I hired you to work here, not to send out signals, intentional or otherwise, to clients."

"I hate you," she said suddenly, sick of his accusations and his hateful remarks.

"Sure you do. What else is new?" He tapped her chin with a long finger. "Get busy."

While she was still struggling with her composure he opened the door and went out without a backward glance.

Abby hardly got anything done for the next hour. She couldn't remember a time when she'd felt so turned around, so confused. She was sure she hated Calhoun, but in an hour he'd be back, smiling, and then she'd forgive him. That was what made her so miserable, the knowledge that he could commit murder and she'd still love him. Damn this hateful attraction!

She took a half-hour break and went to the canteen and had a sandwich that she didn't taste. She was barely back at her desk when Mr. Myers returned—with Justin instead of Calhoun.

She handed the progress reports to Justin, who herded Mr. Myers into his brother's office, kept him there a scant ten minutes and then herded him out again. Abby kept her head down and didn't even say hello. That was just as well, because Mr. Myers didn't look in her direction.

Justin gave Abby a curious look afterward. "That's unusual," he remarked. "Calhoun called me out of a board meeting to have lunch and talk over that contract with Myers. Then he waltzed off and left me there. What's going on?"

Abby cleared her throat. "Why, Justin, I have no idea," she said, even managing a smile. Justin lifted an eyebrow, shrugged and went back into Calhoun's office without another word. Abby stared after him, curious herself about Calhoun's behavior. Then it occurred to her that maybe he just didn't like Greg Myers, which led to the unpalatable thought that perhaps they'd fallen out over a woman. Maybe one of Myers's mistresses . . . She turned back to her typewriter. She hated even thinking about that side of Calhoun's life.

Justin was quiet for the rest of the afternoon, but he had plenty to say when Calhoun came in just before quitting time. The door was half-open, and Abby, who was the last of the office group to leave, got an earful as she was straightening up her desk.

"This has got to stop," Justin was telling his brother. "One of the office girls told me that Myers got friendly with Abby just before you cleared out. It's gotten to the point that Abby can't even smile at a man without having you come down on her head like Judgment. She's almost twenty-one. It isn't fair to expect her to live like a recluse."

"I wasn't," Calhoun said curtly. "I just warned her off him. My God, you know his reputation!"

"Abby's no fool," came the reply. "She's a level-headed person."

"Sure, she's proved that," Calhoun said with biting sarcasm. "Going to a strip show—"

"It was not!" Abby called through the open door. "It was a male variety show."

"My God, she's standing out there listening!" Calhoun jerked the door all the way open, glaring at her. "Stop eavesdropping! It isn't polite!"

"Stop talking about me behind my back, then," she returned, picking up her purse. "I wouldn't have gone out with a man like Grey Myers even to spite you, Calhoun. I know a line when I hear one."

Calhoun glared at her. "I'm not sure it's a good idea, your working here."

Her eyebrows went up. "Really? Why?"

"The place is full of men," Calhoun muttered, and Justin had to smother a grin.

Abby lifted her eyebrows and smiled. "Why, so it is," she gushed. "Lovely, unshaven men who smell of cattle and cow chips. Sooo romantic," she sighed.

Justin had turned away. Calhoun's dark eyes were glittering.

"Myers didn't smell of cow chips," he reminded her.

She arched her eyebrows at him. "How interesting that you noticed," she said in a theatrical whisper.

He looked as if he might throw something at her. "Will you cut that out?" he muttered.

She sighed. "Suit yourself. I was just trying to help. God forbid that I should be seduced by some strange, sweet-smelling man."

"Go home!" Calhoun roared.

"My, my, what a nasty temper we're in," she said demurely. She reached for her purse, glancing back at him. "I'll have Maria make you a nice bowl of razor-blade soup, just to keep your tongue sharp."

"I won't be home for supper, thank God," Calhoun said coldly. "I've got a date," he added, for no other reason than to irritate her. He didn't like the idea of her knowing how much Myers's flirting had upset him. He didn't want her to know that he'd been so violently jealous that he couldn't even trust himself to have lunch with the man and had had to call Justin to intervene.

But Abby didn't know that, and she was sure that it was just Calhoun being overprotective as usual. It hurt her to hear about where he was going. Abby felt as if she were being choked to death. If only she were beautiful and blond, if only she could cope! But she managed to hide her emptiness. "That's great, Calhoun, you just enjoy yourself while I sit home alone. I'll never get a date as long as you're two steps behind me."

"Dream on," Calhoun told her. "Hell will freeze over before you'd go out with a man like that."

"There's a little town called Hell, you know," Abby told him. "It does snow there...."

"If I were you I'd go home, Abby," Justin said, eyeing his brother. "It's Friday night. You might find a nice movie to watch. Come to think of it, I just bought a new war movie. You can watch it with me if you want to."

She smiled. Justin really was nice. "Thanks. I might do that, since my watchdog doesn't want me out after dark," she added with a glare at Calhoun. "I'll bet Elizabeth the First had a guardian just like you!"

Justin caught Calhoun's arm in the nick of time, and Abby took off running, her heart in her throat. It was odd how Calhoun, usually so easygoing, had turned explosive lately. She did goad him, of course, but she couldn't help it. Fighting him was the only way she could stay sane and hide her feelings for him. If she ever started batting her eyelashes and sighing over him, he'd probably shoot her off the place like a bullet.

She started her car and drove home, all the fury dying into misery as she left the feedlot behind. What good was pretending? Her heart was broken, because Calhoun was going out with one of his women and she didn't qualify for that title. She never would. She'd grow old with Calhoun patting her on the head. Once or twice she'd almost thought he felt something for her, that he'd begun to notice her. But if he had, he certainly wouldn't be running all over the place with other women. And he wouldn't ignore Abby unless she started a fight or got into trouble. She was his responsibility, of course. His headache. To him she was anything but a warm, attractive woman whom he might love eventually. That she'd never be.

By the time she got to the house, she felt sick all over, but a plan was beginning to form in her mind. If Calhoun thought she was giving in that easily, he was in for a shock. She could have a good time, too, even if she didn't have a date. By golly, she'd get out and find herself one!

Chapter Three

Abby ate a solitary meal. Justin was called to the phone shortly after they got home, and he told Maria to put his dinner on a tray so he could eat it while he watched the movie he'd bought. Calhoun had come home to change for his date, and Abby had made a beeline for her room and stayed there until after he'd left. She didn't even care how it looked; she was sick at the thought of Calhoun with some faceless blonde. That was when she knew she had to break out, even if just for the evening.

She hadn't started out to rebel. But she couldn't sit home and watch the movie with Justin. She'd never hear a word of it; she'd just brood about Calhoun.

So she got dressed in slacks and a blouse and brushed her hair. Then she called Misty.

"How do you feel about helping me rebel?" she asked the older girl.

Misty laughed huskily. "You're lucky my date canceled out. Okay. I'm game. What are we rebelling against?"

"Calhoun caught me at the revue last night and dragged me home," Abby told her. "And today he... Well, never mind, but he set me off again. So tonight I thought I'd like to sample that new dance bar in Jacobsville."

"Now that is an idea worthy of you, Abby. I'll pick you up in fifteen minutes."

"I'll be ready."

Abby ran downstairs, giving no thought at all to how Calhoun was going to react to this latest rebellion. Well, he had his woman, damn him. Horrible pictures of his bronzed body in bed with the faceless blonde danced in front of Abby's eyes. No, she told herself, she wasn't going to let Calhoun's actions hurt her like that. She was going to get out and live!

She poked her head into the living room. Cigarette smoke drifted in front of a screen on which men in uniforms were blowing each other up.

"I'm going out with Misty," she told Justin.

He glanced up from where he was sitting. His long legs were crossed over the coffee table, and he had a snifter of brandy in one hand and a cigarette in the other. "Okay, honey," he said agreeably. "Stay out of trouble, will you? You and Calhoun are hell on the digestion lately, and he doesn't seem to need much excuse to go for your throat."

"I'll behave. Misty and I are just going to that new dance place. I'll be good, honest I will. Good night."

"Good night."

He went back to the bullets and bombs, and she closed the door with a sigh. Justin was so nice. He never tried to hog-tie her. Now why couldn't Calhoun be like that? She felt murderous when she considered Calhoun's possessiveness. She was entitled to a life that didn't revolve around him. There was just no sense in wearing her heart out on his taciturn indifference. None at all!

Misty came ten minutes later. Thank God, Calhoun didn't reappear. With a sigh of relief, Abby ran out to Misty's little sports car, all smiles, her breaking heart carefully concealed from her all-too-perceptive girlfriend.

It was Friday night, and the Jacobsville Dance Palace was booming. It had a live Western band on the weekends, and while it did serve hard liquor, it wasn't the kind of dive Calhoun had forbidden her to frequent. Not that she cared one whit about his strictures, of course.

Abby glanced apprehensively toward the doorway, across the crowded room where cigar and cigarette smoke made a gray haze under bright lights. The band's rhythm shook the rafters. Couples danced on the bare wood floor, the men in Western gear, the women in jeans and boots.

"Calhoun won't know you're here, I tell you." Misty laughed softly. "Honestly, it's ridiculous the way he dogs your footsteps lately."

"That's what I keep telling him, but it does no good at all," Abby replied miserably. "I just want to get out on my own."

"I'm doing my best," Misty assured her. "Any day now I'll have some new apartment prospects for us to look at. I've got a real estate agent helping."

"Good." Abby sipped her drink, trying not to notice the blatant stare she was getting from the man at the next table. He'd been eyeing her ever since she and Misty had walked in, and he was giving her the willies. He looked about Calhoun's age, but he lacked Calhoun's attractive masculinity. This man was dark headed and had a beer belly. He wasn't much taller than Abby, but what he lacked in height he made up in girth. He had a cowboy hat pulled low over his small eyes, and he was obviously intoxicated.

"He's staring at me again," Abby muttered. She lifted her gin and tonic to her lips, wondering at how much better it tasted every time she took a sip. She hated gin, but Misty had convinced her that she couldn't sit at the table drinking ginger ale.

"Don't worry," Misty patted her arm. "He'll give up and go away. There's Tyler! Hi, Ty!"

Tyler Jacobs was tall and rangy-looking. He had green eyes and an arrogant smile, and Abby was a little afraid of him. But he didn't carry his wealth around on his shoulders as some rich men did, and he wasn't a snob, even though the town of Jacobsville took its name from his grandfather.

"Hello, Misty. Abby." Tyler pulled out a chair and straddled it. "What are you doing here? Does Calhoun know?" he asked quietly.

Abby shifted restlessly in the chair and raised her glass to her lips again. "I am perfectly capable of drinking a drink if I want to," she said, enunciating carefully because her tongue suddenly felt thick. "And Calhoun doesn't own me."

"Oh, my God," Tyler sighed. He gave Misty a rueful glance. "Your doing, I gather?"

Misty blinked her long false lashes at Tyler, and her blue eyes twinkled. "I provided transportation, that's all. Abby is my friend. I'm helping her to rebel."

"You'll help get her killed if you aren't careful. Where's Calhoun?" he asked Abby.

"Out with one of his harem," she said with a mocking smile. "Not that I mind, as long as he's out of my hair for the evening," she added carelessly.

"He dragged her out of line at the male revue last night at the Jacobsville theater," Misty explained. "We're getting even."

Tyler's eyes widened. "You tried to see a male strip show? Abby!"

Abby glared at him. "Where else do you expect me to get educated? Calhoun wants me to wear diapers for the rest of my life. He doesn't think I'm old enough to go on dates or walk across the street alone."

"You're like a kid sister to him," Tyler said, defending his friend. "He doesn't want you to get hurt."

"I can get hurt if I like," Abby grumbled. Her eyes closed. She was feeling worse by the second, but she couldn't let on. Tyler was as bad as the Ballenger brothers. He'd have her out of here like a shot if he thought she was sick.

"What are you drinking?" Tyler asked, staring at her glass.

"Gin and tonic," she replied, opening her eyes. "Want some?"

"I don't drink, honey," Tyler reminded her with a slow smile. "Well, I've got to pick up Shelby at the office. She had to work late tonight. Watch out for Abby, Misty."

"Of course I will. Sure you won't stay and dance with me?" Misty asked.

Tyler got up, his eyes worried as they trailed over Abby's wan face. "Sorry. I don't usually have to get Shelby, but her car was in the shop today and they didn't finish with it."

"Lucky Shelby, to have a brother like you," Abby mumbled. "I'll bet you don't have a kamikaze pilot fly behind her when she goes to work, or a gang of prizefighters to walk her home after dark, or a whole crew of off-duty policemen to fend off her suitors...."

"Oh, boy," Tyler sighed.

"Don't worry," Misty told him. "She's fine. She's just miffed at Calhoun, that's all. Although how anybody could get upset at a dishy man like that being so protective—"

"Dishy isn't a word I'd use to describe Calhoun if he finds Abby like that and thinks you're responsible for it," Tyler cautioned. "Have you ever seen him get angry?"

Misty pushed back her curly hair uncomfortably. "Justin's temper is worse," she reminded him.

Tyler lifted an eyebrow. "Don't be so sure. They're cut from the same cloth." He touched Abby's shoulder. "Don't drink any more of that." He gestured toward her drink.

"Whatever you say, Ty," Abby said, smiling. "Good night."

"Good night."

He waved and left them there.

"I wonder what he was doing here," Misty said, puzzled. "Since he doesn't drink."

"He may have been looking for somebody," Abby murmured. "I guess a lot of cattlemen congregate around here on the weekends. This stuff is pretty good, Misty," she added, taking another sip.

"You promised you wouldn't," she was reminded.

"I hate men," Abby said. "I hate all men. But especially I hate Calhoun."

Misty chewed her lower lip worriedly. Abby was starting to tie one on, and that wasn't at all what Misty had had in mind. "I'll be back in a minute, honey," she promised, and got up to go after Ty. She had a feeling she was going to need his help to get Abby to the car, and now was the time to do it.

The minute she left, the burly, intoxicated man who'd been watching Abby for the past hour seized his opportunity. He sat down next to her, his small, pale eyes running hungrily over her.

"Alone at last," he drawled. "My gosh, you're a pretty thing. I'm Tom. I live alone and I'm looking for a woman who can cook and clean and make love. How about coming home with me?"

Abby gaped at him. "I don't think I heard you?"

"If you're here with a girlfriend, you've got to be out looking for it, honey." He laughed drunkenly. "And I can sure give it to you. So how about it?" He put his pudgy-fingered hand on her arm and began to caress it. "Nice. Come here and give old Tom a kiss...."

He pulled her toward him. She protested violently, and in the process managed to knock her drink over onto him. He cursed a blue streak and stood up, holding her by the wrist, homicide in his drunken eyes.

"You did that on purpose," he shot at her. "You soaked me deliberately! Well, let me tell you, lady, no broad pours liquor on me and gets away with it!"

Abby felt even sicker. He was hurting her wrist, and there was a deathly hush around them. She knew that most people didn't involve themselves in this kind of conflict. She couldn't fight this man and win, but what else was she going to do? She wanted to cry.

"Let her go."

The voice was deep, slow, dangerous and best of all, familiar. Abby caught her breath as a tall, heavily built blond man came toward her, his dark, deep-set eyes on the man who had Abby's wrist. He was in a gray vested suit and a dressy cream-colored Stetson and boots, but Abby knew the trappings of civilized company wouldn't save this ruddy cretin if he didn't turn her loose. Abby had seen Calhoun lose his temper, and she knew how hard he could hit when he did.

"What's she to you?" the drunken cowboy demanded.

"My ward."

Calhoun caught the smaller man's wrist in a hard, cruel grasp and twisted. The man groaned and went down, holding his hand and cursing.

"Hey, you can't do that to Tom!" one of the man's cronies protested, standing up. He was almost Calhoun's size, and a lot rougher-looking.

"Want to make something out of it, sonny?" Calhoun asked in a soft drawl that was belied by the dark glitter in his eyes.

"You bet I do!"

The younger man threw a punch, but he was too slow. Calhoun's big fists put him over a table. He reached down and picked up the Stetson that the man's blow had connected with and looked around the room as he ran his fingers through his thick, silky blond hair.

"Anybody else?" he invited pleasantly.

Eyes turned the other way, and the band started playing again. Then Calhoun looked down at Abby.

She swallowed. "Hi," she said, and tried to smile. "I thought you were out on a date."

He didn't say a word, but his glittering eyes told her every single thing he was feeling. He wouldn't admit for a minute that his dinner date was strictly business, or that he'd expected something like this after the argument he and Abby had had. She was giving him fits, but he didn't let his expression show how concerned he really was.

"Did you see Misty?" she asked hopefully.

"Luckily for her, no," he said in a tone that could have boiled ice water. "Get your purse."

She fumbled on the chair beside hers for it, weak and shaky. He had a gift for intimidating people, she thought, watching him slam his Stetson over his eyes at a slant. The men who were picking themselves up off the floor didn't seem anxious to tangle with him twice. It was amazing, she thought, how unruffled he looked for a man who'd just been in a fight.

He caught her arm and propelled her out of the bar and into the night air. Misty and Ty were standing just outside, both looking faintly apprehensive.

"It wasn't all my fault, Cal," Misty began in a subdued tone.

Calhoun eyed her coldly. "You know what I think of this so-called friendship. And I know the reason behind it, even if she doesn't."

Abby was puzzled by that remark. The cold, level look in Calhoun's dark eyes and the uncomfortable flush in Misty's pretty face didn't add up.

"I'd better go get Shelby," Ty said quietly. "I was going to offer to take Abby home, but under the circumstances I'm a bit relieved that you came along," he told Calhoun.

"If Justin finds out you were in the same room with her, there'll be hell to pay," Calhoun agreed. "But thanks all the same." He turned Abby toward his Jaguar. "I assume you rode into town with your girlfriend?" he added.

"We came in Misty's car," Abby murmured. She felt weary and a little sick. Now she really looked like a child, with all the concerned adults making a fuss over her. Tears burned in her eyes, which she was careful to keep hidden from the angry man beside her.

"Honest to God," he muttered as he put her into the passenger seat and went around to get into the driver's seat. "I don't know what the hell's wrong with you lately. Last night I find you in line at a male strip show, and tonight you're getting drunk and eyeing strange men in bars!"

"I was not eyeing that lewd creature," she said unsteadily. "And you can't say I was dressed to invite his kind of comment. I'm not wearing anything that's the least bit immodest!"

He glanced at her. "You were in a bar unescorted. That's all the invitation that kind of man needs!"

She felt his gaze on her, but she wouldn't look at him. She knew she'd cry if she did. She clasped her hands firmly in her lap and stared out the window instead as he started the car and headed for home.

It was a long ride, over deserted paved roads and dirt ones that led past the huge feedlot and then uphill to the house, which sat on a level plain about three miles away.

"Do you want me to carry you?" he asked stiffly as he helped her out of the car and she stumbled.

She pushed away from him as if she'd touched hot coals. "No, thank you." He was making her more nervous than ever tonight. The scent of him filled her nostrils, all leathery and spicy and clean. She averted her eyes and walked as straight as she could toward the kitchen door. "Are you going to sneak me in the back way so that Justin doesn't see me?" she challenged.

"Justin told me where to find you," Calhoun said as he put the key in the lock and opened the back door. "He's still watching his war movie."

"Oh." She walked through the door he was holding open for her. "I thought you were out on a date."

"Never mind where I was," he said curtly. "My God, I really must have radar."

She flushed. Thank God he couldn't see her face. She felt odd tonight. Frightened and nervous and a little unsure of herself. The gin had taken away some of her inhibitions, and she had to be careful not to let Calhoun see how vulnerable she felt when he came close to her.

She went in ahead of him, barely noticing the huge, spotless kitchen with its modern conveniences, or the hall, or the mahogany staircase she began to climb. Behind the closed living room door, bombs were going off in a softly muted way, indicating that Justin's war movie was still running.

"Abby."

She stopped, her back to him, trying not to show how nervous she felt. He was behind her, much too close, and she could smell the fresh, clean scent of his body and the spicy cologne he wore.

"What's wrong, honey?" he asked.

His tone broke her heart. He used it with little things—a newborn kitten, or a filly he was working for the first time. He used it with children. He'd used it with Abby the day her mother had died in the wreck. It had been Calhoun who'd found her and broken the news to her and then held her while she cried. It was the tone he used when something was hurt.

She straightened, trying hard to keep her back straight and her legs under control. "That man..." she began, unable to tell him he was breaking her heart because he couldn't love her.

"Damn that drunken—" He turned her, his strong hands gentle on her upper arms, his dark eyes blazing down into hers. He was so big, and none of it was fat. He was all muscle, lean and powerful, all man. "You're all right," he said softly. "Nothing happened."

"Of course not," she whispered miserably. "You rescued me. You always rescue me." Her eyes closed, and a tear started down her cheek. "But hasn't it occurred to you that I'm always going to land in trouble if you don't let me solve my own problems?" She looked up at him through a mist. "You have to let go of me," she whispered huskily, and her eyes reflected her heartbreak. "You have to, Calhoun."

There was a lot of truth in what she said, and he didn't really know how to respond. He worried about her. This strange restlessness of hers, this urge to run from him, wasn't like Abby. She was melancholy, when for the past five years or more she'd been a vibrant, happy little imp, always laughing and playing with him, teasing him, making him laugh. She couldn't know how somber the house had been when she'd first come to live with him and Justin. Justin never laughed anyway, and Calhoun had come to be like him. But Abby had brought the sunshine. She'd colored the world. He scowled down at her, wondering how she did it. She wasn't pretty. She was plain, and she was serious a good bit of the time. But when she laughed... When she laughed, she was beautiful.

His hands contracted. "I wouldn't mind if you'd go to conventional places," he muttered. "First I catch you in line to watch a bunch of nude men parade around a stage, and the very next night you're drinking gin and tonic in a bar. Why?" he asked, his deep voice soft with curiosity and concern.

She shifted. "I'm just curious about those things," she said finally.

He searched her eyes quietly. "That isn't it," he replied, his own gaze narrowing. His hands shifted, gentle on her arms, Abby could feel their warmth through the fabric. "Something's eating you alive. Can't you tell me what it is?"

She drew in her breath. She'd almost forgotten how perceptive he was. He seemed to see right through to the bone and blood sometimes. She let her gaze drop to his chest, and she watched its lazy rise and fall under his gray vest. He was hairy under his shirt. She'd seen him once in a while on his way to or from the shower, and it had been all she could do not to reach out and run her hands over him. He had thick brown hair across his tanned chest, and it had golden tips where it curled. There was a little wave in his thick blond hair, not much, but enough that it was unruly around his ears. She let her gaze go up, feeding on him, lingering just above his dimpled chin at the thin but sensuous curve of his upper lip and the faintly square, chiseled fullness of his lower lip. He had a sexy mouth. His nose was sexy, too. Very straight and imposing. He had high cheekbones, and thick eyebrows on a jutting brow that shadowed his deep-set eyes. He had black eyes. Both the Ballengers did. But Calhoun was something to look at, and poor old Justin was as rangy-looking as a longhorn bull by comparison.

"Abby, are you listening to me?" Calhoun murmured, shaking her gently because her faintly intoxicated stare was setting his blood on fire.

Her eyes levered up to his, finding darkness in them, secrets, shadows. Her lips parted on a hopeless sigh. When Misty had told her last week about seeing him with some ravishing blonde up in Houston, it had knocked her for a loop, bringing home the true hopelessness of her situation. Calhoun liked sophisticated women. He'd never look twice at drab little Abby. Once Abby had faced that unpalatable fact, she'd been on a one-way road to misery. She'd been looking for an escape, last night and tonight, but she couldn't find one. Wherever she turned, Calhoun was there, hounding her, not realizing how badly he was hurting her.

"What did you say?" she asked miserably.

His chest rose and fell roughly. "It's hopeless trying to talk to you in this condition. Go to bed."

"That's just where I was headed," she said.

She turned and started up the staircase ahead of him, her eyes burning with tears that she was too proud to let him see. Oh, Calhoun, she moaned inwardly, you're killing me!

She went into her room and closed the door behind her. She almost locked it, but realized that would be a joke and a half. Locking a door against Calhoun was a hilarious idea. He'd as soon come looking for a lady vampire as to look at Abby with amorous intent. She started laughing as she went into the bathroom to bathe her face, and she almost couldn't stop.

Chapter Four

Abby managed to get into the silver satin night gown, but she couldn't seem to fasten it in the front. The gown hung open over her full, firm breasts. She looked at herself in the mirror as she passed it, fascinated by the sophistication the unbuttoned state lent her. She looked oddly mature with the pink swell of her breasts blatantly revealed and her long hair tangled around her face. Then she laughed at her own fancy and stretched out on top of the pale pink coverlet on her canopied bed.

The whole room was decorated in shades of pink and white with blue accents. She loved it. The Ballengers had let her choose her own colors, and these were what she favored. Very feminine colors, even if she wasn't a sophisticated blonde. She shifted restlessly on the cover, and the bodice of her gown came completely away from one breast. Her eyes closed. What did it matter, she thought as she drifted off to sleep. There was no one to see her.

No one except Calhoun, who eased the door open with an expression of concern in his dark eyes. He saw something that knocked the breath out of him.

Abby was barely conscious. She didn't even open her eyes when he came into the room. It was just as well, because he knew he wouldn't be lucid if he had to speak. He'd never thought of Abby as a woman, but the sight of her in that silky drift of silver fabric, with one exquisite breast completely bare and her slender body outlined to its best advantage, shot through him like fire.

He stood frozen in the doorway, facing for the first time the fact that Abby was an adult. No sane man who saw her lying there like that could ever think of her as a child again. And even as the thought formed he realized why he hadn't been himself lately, why he'd deliberately antagonized her, why he'd been so overprotective. He...wanted her.

He closed the door absently behind him and moved closer to her. God, she was lovely! His face hardened as he stared down at her, helplessly feeding on the sensuous nudity she wasn't even aware of.

He wondered if she'd ever let any of her dates see her like this, and a murderous rage stiffened his tall form. He hated the thought of that. Of another man looking at her, touching her, putting his mouth on that soft swell and searching for a tip that he could make hard with the warm pressure of his open mouth....

He shook himself. This wouldn't do. "Abby," he said tersely.

She stirred, but only to shift on the bed so that the whole damned bodice fell open. He actually trembled at the sweetness of her pretty pink breasts with their delicate mauve tips relaxed in sleep.

He muttered something explosive and forced himself to bend over her, to pull the fabric together and fasten it. His hands shook. Thank God she wasn't awake to witness his vulnerability.

She moaned when his hard knuckles came into contact with her skin, and she arched slightly in her sleep.

His lips parted on a rough breath. Her skin was like silk, warm and sensuous. He gritted his teeth and caught the last button. Then he scooped her up in his arms and stood holding her propped on one knee while he tore the covers loose and stripped back the colorful pink patterned top sheet over the soft blue fitted one.

Her eyes blinked and opened lazily. She searched his hard face, smiling faintly. "I'm asleep," she whispered, nuzzling close. Her sweet scent and the feel of her soft body in his arms overwhelmed him.

"Are you?" he asked, his voice deeper, huskier than he wanted it to be. He laid her down on the sheet, cupping the back of her head in his hand while he drew a pillow under it, his mouth just above hers.

Her hands were around his neck. He drew them down and pulled the covers up over her with a feeling of relief.

"I never had anybody tuck me in before," she mumbled drowsily.

"Don't expect a bedtime story," he murmured, his deep voice lazy with forced humor. "You're too young for the only ones I know."

"I guess I am. Too young for everything. Much too young." She sighed heavily, as her eyes closed. "Oh, Calhoun, I wish I was blond...."

"Now what brought that on?" he asked, but she was asleep again. He looked down at her softly flushed sleeping face, his eyes narrow and dark and thoughtful. After a minute he turned and went out, flicking off the light behind him.

Justin was coming out of the living room when Calhoun got back downstairs.

"Did you bring Abby home?" Justin asked his brother.

"Yes. She's in bed. Dead drunk," Calhoun added with a faintly amused smile. He'd already taken off his Stetson, along with his jacket and vest.

Justin's dark eyes narrowed. "What's wrong with you? Your lip is cut."

"A slight altercation in the local bar and dance hall," Calhoun said sardonically. He went to the brandy bottle and poured himself half a snifterful. He swirled it, staring into the glass. "Want one?"

Justin shook his head and lit a cigarette instead, ignoring Calhoun's pointed glare of disapproval.

"What were you fighting about?"

Calhoun sipped his brandy. "Abby."

Justin turned, his dark eyebrows arching. "Abby?"

"Misty Davies took her to a bar."

"Last night a nude revue, tonight a bar." Justin stared at his cigarette. "Something's eating our girl."

"I know. I just don't know what. I don't like what Misty's doing, either, but I can't tell Abby."

Justin cocked his head as he drew on the cigarette. "She's trying to get back at you through Abby, I gather."

"Got it in one." Calhoun raised the brandy snifter mockingly before he drained it. "She came on to me hard, and I turned her down. My God, as if I'd be crazy enough to seduce Abby's best friend."

"Misty should have known that. Is Abby all right?"

"I guess," Calhoun said, not adding that he'd put her to bed himself or that she was the reason he was drinking, something he rarely did. "Some red-faced jackass was manhandling her."

Justin whirled. "And?"

"I think I knocked one of his teeth out."

"Good for you. All the same, she needs watching."

"I'll say amen to that. Shall we flip a coin?" Calhoun asked with pursed lips.

"Why should I interfere when you're doing such a good job of looking out for her interests?" Justin asked, smiling faintly. His smile faded as he searched the younger man's troubled eyes. "You do remember that Abby turns twenty-one in three months? And I think she's already been apartment-hunting with Misty."

Calhoun's face hardened. "Misty will corrupt her. I don't want Abby passed around like an hors d'oeuvre by some of Misty's sophisticated boyfriends."

Justin's eyebrows arched. That didn't sound like Calhoun. Come to think of it, Calhoun didn't *look* like Calhoun. "Abby's our ward," he reminded his brother. "We don't own her. We don't have the right to make her decisions for her, either."

Calhoun glared at him. "What do you want me to do, let her be picked up and assaulted by any drunken cowboy who comes along? Like bloody hell I will!"

He turned on his heel and walked out of the room. Justin pursed his thin lips and smiled softly to himself.

Abby woke the next morning with a headache and a feeling of impending doom. She sat up, clutching her head. It was seven o'clock, and she had to be to work by 8:30. Even now, breakfast would be underway downstairs. Breakfast. She swallowed her nausea.

She got out of bed unsteadily and went into the bathroom to wash her face and brush her teeth. She managed that and felt much better. As she started to get out of her gown, she noticed that the buttons were fastened. Odd. She was sure she'd left the thing unbuttoned. Oh, well, she must have gotten it buttoned and climbed in under the covers sometime before dawn.

It was Saturday, but ordinarily the feedlot stayed open. The cattle still had to be looked after, and the paperwork had to be done no matter what day it was. Abby had gotten used to the long work week, and it was just routine not to have her Saturdays free. She could get off at noon sometimes if she needed to go somewhere. But that hadn't been her habit in recent months. She was hungry for the sight of Calhoun, and he was there most weekends.

She got into a pale gray suit with a blue silk print blouse and put her hair into a French twist. She used a little makeup—not much—and slid her nylon-encased feet into tiny stacked high heels. Well, she was no ravishing beauty, that was for sure, but she wouldn't disgrace herself. She was going down with all flags flying. Calhoun would be mad as fury, and she couldn't let him see how pale she was.

The Ballenger brothers were both at the table when she got downstairs. Calhoun glanced at her, his gaze odd and brooding, as she sat between him and Justin.

"It's about time," he said curtly. "You look like hell, and it serves you right. I'll be damned if I'll have you passing out in bars with that Davies woman!"

"Please, Calhoun, not before I eat," Abby murmured. "My head hurts."

"No wonder," he shot back.

"Stop cussing at my breakfast table," Justin told him firmly.

"I'll stop when you do," Calhoun told his brother, just as firmly.

"Oh, hell," Justin muttered, and bit into one of Maria's fluffy biscuits.

Ordinarily that byplay would have made Abby smile, but she felt too dragged-out to care. She sipped black coffee and nibbled at buttered toast, refusing anything more nourishing.

"You need to take some aspirins before you go to work, Abby," Justin said gently.

She managed to smile at him. "I will. I guess gin isn't really my drink."

"Liquor isn't healthy," Calhoun said shortly.

Justin's eyebrows lifted. "Then why were you emptying my brandy bottle last night?"

Calhoun threw down his napkin. "I'm going to work."

"You might offer Abby a lift," Justin suggested with a strangely calculating expression.

"I'm not going directly to the feedlot," Calhoun said. He didn't want to be alone with Abby, not after the way he'd seen her the night before. He could hardly look at her without remembering her lying across that bed....

"I'm not through with breakfast," Abby replied, hurt that Calhoun didn't seem to want her company. "Besides," she told Justin with a faint smile, "I can drive. I didn't really have all that much to drink."

"Sure," Calhoun replied harshly, dark eyes blazing. "That's why you passed out on your bed."

Abby knew she'd stopped breathing. Justin was pouring cream into his second cup of coffee, his keen eyes on the pitcher, not on the other occupants of the room. And that was a good thing, because Abby looked up at Calhoun with sudden stark knowledge of what he'd seen the night before and had her fears confirmed by the harsh stiffening of his features.

She blushed and started, almost knocking over her cup. So she had gone to sleep on the covers. Calhoun found her with her bodice undone, he'd seen her—

"Never mind breakfast. Let's go," Calhoun said suddenly, his lean hand on the back of her chair. "I'll take you to the feedlot before I do what I have to. You're not fit to drive.''

Justin was watching now, his gaze narrow and frankly curious as it went from Abby's red face to Calhoun's taut expression.

That look was what decided Abby that Calhoun was the lesser of the two evils. She couldn't tell Justin what had happened, but he'd have it out of her in two seconds if she didn't make a run for it. Calhoun must have realized that, too.

He took her arm and almost pulled her out of the chair, propelling her out of the room with a curt goodbye to his brother.

''Will you slow down?'' she moaned as he took the steps two at a time. ''My legs aren't long enough to keep up with you, and my head is splitting.''

''You need a good headache,'' he muttered without a glance in her direction. ''Maybe it will take some of the adventure out of your soul.''

She glared at his broad back in silence as she followed him to the Jaguar and got into the passenger seat.

He started the car and reversed it, but he didn't go toward the feedlot. He went down the driveway, turned off onto a ranch road that wasn't much more than a rut in the fenced pastures and cut off the engine on a small rise.

He didn't say anything at first. He rested his lean hands on the steering wheel, studying them in silence, while Abby tried to catch her breath and summon enough nerve to talk to him.

''How dare you come into my room without knocking,'' she whispered after a long minute, her voice sounding husky and choked.

''I did knock. You didn't hear me.''

She bit her lower lip, turning her gaze to the yellowish-brown pastures around them.

"Abby, for God's sake, don't make such an issue out of it," he said quietly. "Would you rather I'd left you like that? What if Justin had come to wake you, or Lopez?"

She swallowed. "Well, I guess they'd have gotten an eyeful," she said, her voice unsteady. After a minute, her face flushed, she turned toward him and asked plaintively, "Calhoun...I wasn't uncovered all the way, was I?"

He looked into her eyes and couldn't quite manage to look away. She was lovely. He reached out involuntarily and touched the side of her neck, his fingers tender and exquisitely arousing.

"No," he managed, watching the relief shadow her eyes as he told the lie with a straight face. "I buttoned you back up and tucked you in."

She let out a hard breath. "Thank you."

His fingers moved up to her cheek. "Abby, have you ever let a man see your breasts?" he asked unexpectedly.

She couldn't handle a remark that intimate. She dropped her eyes and tried to catch her breath.

"Never mind, tenderfoot," he chided softly. "I can guess."

"You mustn't talk like that," she whispered.

"Why?" he mused, tilting her chin up so that her shocked eyes met his. "You're the one trying to grow up, aren't you? If you want me to treat you like an adult, Abby, then this is part of it."

She shifted nervously. He made her feel so gauche it was ridiculous. She twisted her purse out of shape, afraid to meet the dark eyes that were relentlessly probing her face.

"Don't," she pleaded breathlessly, and her eyes closed.

"Are you really afraid of me?" he asked, his voice deeper, silkier.

He touched her mouth with a lean forefinger and she actually jumped, her eyes flashing open, all her hidden hungers and fears lying vulnerable there. And that was when his self-control fell away. She was hungry for him. Just as hungry as he was for her. Was that why she'd been so restless, because she'd become attracted to him and was trying to hide it? He had to know.

She couldn't answer him. She felt as if he were trying to see inside her mind. "I'm not afraid of you. Can't we go?"

"What are you trying to do?" he whispered, leaning closer, threatening her lips with his. "Block it out? Pretend that you aren't hungry for my mouth?"

Her heart went wild at the soft question. If he didn't stop, she was going to go in headfirst. He could be playing, and to have him tease her without meaning it would kill her. Her fingers touched his shoulder, pushed experimentally against the hard muscle under the soft fabric of his suit. They trembled there as her eyes suddenly tangled with his and her mouth echoed the faint tremor of her body.

He stared at her. It was a kind of exchange that Abby had never experienced before. A level, unblinking, intense look that curled her toes and made her heart race. Very adult, very revealing. His dark eyes held hers, and his lean fingers traced up and down her soft throat, arousing, teasing. His hard mouth moved closer to hers, hovering above it so that she could feel his warm, minty breath on her parted lips, so that she was breathing him.

"Cal...houn," she whispered, her voice breaking on a hungry sob.

She heard his intake of air and felt his hand curl under her long hair, powerful and warm, cradling her nape to tilt her head up.

"This has been coming for a hell of a long time, baby," he whispered as his head bent and he started to give in to the hunger that had become a fever in his blood. "I want it as much as you do...."

He leaned even closer, but just as his hard mouth started down over hers, before his lips touched her pleading ones, the sound of an approaching vehicle broke them apart like an explosion.

Calhoun felt disoriented. He looked in the rearview mirror and saw one of the ranch trucks coming up behind, but it took a moment to register. He was having trouble breathing. His body felt rigid, like drawn cord.

He glanced at Abby. She'd moved away and the realization that she was trembling brought home the total shock of what he'd been about to do. Damn it, she'd knocked him for a loop without even trying. That made him mad, and so, ironically, did the fact that she'd given in so easily. It infuriated him even more that he'd been about to kiss her. He didn't want complications, damn it, and Abby was the biggest he'd ever faced. Was she vulnerable because she wanted him or just because she'd suddenly discovered that she was a woman and wanted to experiment?

"We'd better get to work," he said tersely, starting the Jaguar. He drove down the path, waving to the men in the vehicle behind them. He cut off at the next dirt road, and minutes later they were at the feedlot. "Go on in. I've got to drive over to Jacobsville and talk to our attorney for a few minutes," he said as coolly as he could. That was a bald-faced lie, but he needed time to get hold of himself. He was as tense as a boy with his first woman, and he was losing his sense of humor. He didn't want Justin to see him like this and start asking embarrassing questions.

"All right," Abby said, her voice faltering.

He glanced at her with narrowed eyes. She'd give the show away all by herself if she went inside looking like that. "Nothing happened," he said shortly. "And nothing will," he added, his voice cold, "if you can manage to stop looking at me like a lovesick calf!"

A sob tore from her throat. Her wide, hurt eyes sought his and quickly fell away. She opened the door and got out, closing it quietly behind her. She straightened and walked toward the office without looking back.

Calhoun almost went after her. He hadn't wanted to say that to Abby, of all people, but he was off balance and terrified of what he might do to her if she kept looking at him that way. He couldn't make love to her, for God's sake. She was a child. She was his ward. Even as he told himself that, a picture formed in his mind of Abby lying on the bed with her breasts bare. He groaned and jerked the car into gear, sending it flying down the road.

Abby didn't know how she got through the day. It was impossible to act as if nothing had happened, but since Justin knew she had a hangover he didn't question her pale complexion or her unusually quiet demeanor. And Calhoun didn't come back to the office. That was a godsend. Abby didn't think she could have borne seeing him after what he'd said to her.

"You need a diversion," Justin remarked later in the day, just about quitting time. "How about a steak in Houston? I've got to meet a man and his wife to talk about a new lot of stocker calves, and I'd hate to go alone."

He was smiling, and Abby warmed to his gentle affection. Justin wasn't the cold creature most people thought him. He was just a sad, lonely man who should have married and had several children to spoil.

"I'd like that very much," Abby said honestly. It would be nice to go out to dinner, especially if it meant she could avoid Calhoun. Of course, it was Saturday night. He wasn't usually home on Saturday nights anyway, but it would be so much better if she didn't have to dread seeing him.

"Good," Justin said, rising. "We'll get away about six."

Abby wore a soft burgundy velour dress. It had a slightly flared knee-length skirt and bishop sleeves, and a neckline that was V-shaped and not at all suggestive. She wore black accessories with it and, because it had turned cold, her heather-colored wool cape.

"Very nice," Justin said, smiling. He had on dark evening clothes and looked elegant and sophisticated, as he always did on the rare occasions when he dressed up.

"I could return the compliment," Abby said. She clutched her purse, sending a restless look down the hall.

"He won't be home," Justin told her, intercepting her worried glance. "I gather the two of you had another falling-out?"

She sighed. "The worst yet," she confessed, unwilling to tell him any of the details. She looked up at him. "Calhoun acts as if he hates me lately."

Justin searched her eyes quietly. "And you don't know why," he mused. "Well, give it time, Abby. Rome wasn't built in a day."

She blinked. "I don't understand."

He laughed softly and took her arm. "Never mind. Let's get going."

Houston was big and sprawling and flat as a pancake, but it had a very special personality and Abby loved it. At night it was as colorful as Christmas, all jewel lights and excitement.

Justin took her to a small, intimate dinner club where they met the Joneses, Clara and Henry. They owned a small ranch in Montana where they raised stocker calves to supply to feedlots. They were an older couple but full of fun, and Abby liked them instantly. She and Clara talked fashion while Justin and Henry talked business. Abby was really having a good time until she glanced across the room and saw a familiar face on the cozily intimate dance floor.

Calhoun! Her eyes widened as she followed his blond head through the crowd until there was a clear space. Then she saw the ravishing blonde with him. He was holding the woman, who was at least his own age, with both hands at her waist, and she was curled up against him as if they'd been dancing together for years. They were smiling at each other like lovers.

Abby felt sick. She could almost feel herself turning green. If Calhoun had worked at it for years, he couldn't have hurt her any worse. Coming on the heels of the insulting remark he'd made just a few hours earlier, it was a death blow. This was his kind of woman, Abby realized. Sleek, beautiful, sophisticated. This was one of his shadowy lovers. One of the women he never brought home.

"What's wrong, Abby?' Justin asked suddenly. But before she could answer he followed her gaze to the dance floor, and something in his dark eyes became frightening, dangerous.

"Isn't that Calhoun?" Henry Jones grinned. "Well, well, let's get him over here, Justin, and see what he thinks of our proposition." Before anyone could stop him, he got up and headed for the dance floor.

"Mrs. Jones, shall we go to the powder room?" Abby asked with a pale but convincing smile.

"Certainly, dear. Excuse us, won't you, Justin?" the white-haired woman asked politely, and started out of the restaurant ahead of Abby.

Justin unexpectedly caught Abby's upper arm and drew her back. "Don't panic," he said quietly. "I'll get you out of here as soon as I can. Do you want a drink?"

She looked up, almost in tears at his unexpected understanding. "Could I have a piña colada with just a little rum?" she asked.

"I'll order it. Keep your chin up."

She smiled at him softly. "Thanks, big brother," she said gently.

He grinned. "Any time. Get going."

She glanced away in time to catch Calhoun's dark eyes. She nodded her head at him and turned away with no apparent haste.

Ten minutes later, she and Mrs. Jones returned to find Calhoun about to leave the table, the blonde still clinging to his arm. He looked up at Abby. His face was unreadable, but there was something in his expression that disturbed her. She wasn't about to let it show, though. Lovesick calf, indeed. She'd show him, by gosh.

She smiled. "Hi, Calhoun!" she said easily, sliding into the chair next to Justin's. "Isn't this a nice place? Justin decided I needed a night on the town. Wasn't that sweet of him?" She picked up her piña colada and took a big sip, relieved to find that it had barely enough rum to taste and even more relieved that her hand didn't shake and betray her shattered nerves.

"She's a big girl now," Justin told his brother, leaning back in his chair arrogantly and daring Calhoun to say a word. His cool smile and level, cold stare had a real impact, even on his brother.

But Calhoun didn't look any too pleased at the implication of the remark, especially when Justin slid an arm around Abby's shoulders. In fact, Calhoun seemed almost ready to leap forward and shake his brother loose from Abby.

"I'm tired," the blonde sighed, nuzzling her face against Calhoun's arm. "I need some sleep. Eventually," she teased gently, with a meaningful look at Calhoun's rigid expression.

Abby lifted her chin, looking straight at him. "Enjoy yourself, big brother," she said with forced gaiety. She even managed a smile. Thank God for Justin. She lifted her glass, took a sip of her drink and winked at the blonde, who smiled at her, obviously thinking Abby was a relative and no threat even if she wasn't.

Calhoun was trying to find his voice. The sight of Abby with his brother was killing him. He hadn't even considered that possibility. And while Justin might not be a playboy, he was a mature, very masculine man, and he had, after all, attracted a beauty like Shelby Jacobs.

Calhoun hadn't meant to ask the blonde out. She was a last-ditch stand against what he was feeling for Abby, and a very platonic one at that. He didn't even want her physically; she was just someone to talk to and be with who didn't threaten his emotions. But he'd never thought Abby might see him with her. It cut him to the bone, embarrassed him. Did Abby care? Try as he might, he couldn't find the slightest hint of jealousy in her face. She was wearing more makeup than usual, and that dress suited her. She looked lovely. Had Justin noticed?

"I said, I'd really like to go home, Cal," the blonde drawled, laughing. "Can we, please? I've had a long day. I'm a model," she added. "And we had a showing this afternoon. My feet are killing me, however unromantic that sounds."

"Of course," Calhoun said quietly. He took her arm. "I'll see you later," he told Justin.

"Sure you will," Justin mused, his tone amused and unbelieving, and he smiled at the blonde, who actually blushed.

Calhoun noticed then how Abby reacted to the remark. She lowered her eyes, but her slender hand was shaking as it held the piña colada. He felt murderous. He wanted to pick her up and carry her out of here, out of Justin's reach.

But Justin had his arm around Abby, and he tightened it. "We may be late," Justin told his brother. "So don't wait up if you beat us home. I thought I might take Abby dancing," he added with narrowed eyes and the arrogant smile Calhoun hated.

"Yes, I'd like that," Abby told him, smiling.

Calhoun felt his throat contracting. He managed a smile, too, but not a normal one. "Good night, then," he said tautly. He hardly heard what the others said as he escorted the blonde out of the restaurant.

"It's all right," Justin told Abby, his voice quiet. "They've gone."

She looked up, her eyes full of tears. "You know, don't you?"

"How you feel, you mean?" he asked gently. He nodded. "Just don't let him see it, honey. He's still got a wild streak, and he'll fight it like hell even if he feels what you do. Give him time. Don't hem him in."

"You know a lot about men," she said, sniffing into the tissue she took from her purse.

"Well, I am one," he replied. "Dry your eyes, now, and we'll take the long way home. That ought to give him hell. He hated the very idea of your being out with me."

"Really?"

He smiled at her expression. "Really. Chin up, girl. You're young. You've got time."

"What do I do in the meantime? He's driving me crazy."

"You might consider looking for that apartment," he said. "I hate to see you move out, but it may be the only answer eventually."

"I'd already decided that." She wiped her eyes. "But he hates the idea of my rooming with Misty."

"So do I," he remarked honestly. "Did you know that she made a pass at Calhoun and he turned her down?"

"Can't I trust anybody?" she moaned. "Aren't there any women who don't like him?"

"A few, here and there," he mused, his dark eyes twinkling. "I think you might do better to find a room in somebody's house. But that's your decision," he added quietly. "I'm not going to tell you what to do. You're old enough to decide alone."

"Thanks, Justin," she said gently. She smiled. "You'll make some lucky girl a nice husband one day."

His expression hardened, and the humor went out of his dark eyes. "That's a mistake I won't make," he said. "I've had my fill of involvement."

"You never asked about Shelby's side of it," Abby reminded him. "You wouldn't even listen, Calhoun said."

"She said it all when she gave me back the ring. And I don't want to discuss it, Abby," he cautioned, his eyes flashing warning signals as he rose. "I talk to no one about Shelby. Not even you."

She backed down. "Okay," she said gently. "I won't pry."

"Let's go," he said, reaching for the check. "We'll take two hours getting home, and I hope Calhoun has kittens when we get there."

"I doubt he'll notice," Abby said miserably. "She was very pretty."

"Looks don't count in the long run," he replied. He looked at Abby. "Odd, isn't it, how embarrassed he was when you saw him with her?"

She turned away. "I'm tired. But it was a lovely dinner. Thank you."

He lifted an eyebrow. "Don't thank me. I had a good time. It beats watching movies at home, anyway." He chuckled gently.

Abby wanted to ask him why he never dated anyone and whether he was still carrying a torch for Shelby Jacobs after six years. Calhoun had said he was, but Justin was a clam when it came to his private life. And Abby wasn't about to pry any further. She wasn't that brave, not even with a piña colada inside her.

Chapter Five

Abby was miserable by the time they got home. She'd done nothing but think of Calhoun and the model. Justin had been kind, talking as if she were really listening to him. But she was reliving those few tempestuous minutes in Calhoun's Jaguar, when he'd come so close to kissing her and then had insulted her so terribly. She didn't understand his hot-and-cold attitude or his irritability. She didn't understand anything anymore.

Justin parked his elegant black Thunderbird in the garage, and Abby was surprised to find Calhoun's Jaguar already there.

"Well, well, look who's home," Justin murmured, glancing at Abby. "I guess he felt like an early night."

"Maybe he was exhausted," Abby said coldly.

Justin didn't comment, but he seemed highly amused and smug about something.

Calhoun was in the living room with the brandy bottle when they got home. He was down to his white shirt-sleeves, which he'd rolled up to his elbows. His shirt was almost completely open in front, and Abby had to bite her lip to keep from staring helplessly at the broad expanse of his muscular chest. He was the most sensuous man she'd ever known, so powerful and tall and huge. Just the sight of him made her body tingle.

"So you finally brought her home," Calhoun shot at his brother. "Do you know what time it is?"

"Sure," Justin said imperturbably. "It's two o'clock in the morning."

"What were you doing?"

Justin cocked an eyebrow. "Oh, riding around. And things. Night, Abby," he said, and winked at her before he turned and went up the staircase.

Abby felt as if she'd been poleaxed. Now why had Justin said that? It had made Calhoun look frankly murderous. She cleared her throat.

"I think I'll go up, too." She started to turn, only to have her arm caught in a viselike grip by huge warm fingers and be pulled into the living room.

Calhoun slammed the door behind her, his chest heaving with rough breaths. His dark eyes were really black now, glittering, dangerous, and his sensuous mouth was a thin, grim line.

"Where were you?" he demanded. "And doing what? Justin's thirty-seven, and he's no boy."

She stared at him blankly. The sudden attack had knocked the wind out of her for a minute, but then her temper came to the rescue.

"That blonde you were out with was no schoolgirl, either," she replied as calmly as she could, even though her knees were shaking under her. She leaned back against the door for support.

His heavy brows drew together. "My private life is none of your business," he said defensively.

"Of course not," she agreed. "You've already said that you didn't want me hanging around you like a lovesick calf, and I'm doing my best not to," she added, although it hurt terribly to try to make light of that hurtful remark.

His heavy shoulders made a jerky movement as he looked at her and away again, as if her answer made him uncomfortable. "Justin's too old for you."

"Bullfeathers," she replied, lifting her chin. "You've objected to every other man I've ever gone out with, but you can't object to your own brother. Justin would never hurt me, and you know it."

He did know it, but that didn't help. He was dying at the thought of Abby and Justin together.

"Oh, for God's sake!" he burst out, lost for words.

She took a steadying breath, though her heart was still doing a tango in her chest. "Why should it matter to you what I do?" she challenged him. "And you're a fine one to sit in judgment on other people! My gosh, Calhoun, everybody in the world knows what a playboy you are!"

He glared at her, trying to keep his temper. "I'm not a playboy," he said tersely. "I may date women occasionally—"

"Every night," she returned. Even though she knew her assertion wasn't completely true, she was too angry to split hairs. "Not that I mind," she added with a cold smile. "I don't care who you go out with, as long as you stop poking your nose into my business. I'll date whom I please, Calhoun, and if you don't like it, you know what you can do!"

He started to tell her what she could do, but before he could get the words out she'd jerked the door open and gone out and up the staircase.

"If you stay out until two o'clock in the morning again, with or without Justin, I'll take a tree limb to you!" Calhoun yelled up the stairs.

Abby made a sound that almost drove him crazy. He muttered something obscene and went back into the living room, slamming the door so hard it shook the room.

Damn women! He could have screamed at the effect she was having on him lately. She was ruining his love life, ruining his business life. All he did was think about her damned pretty breasts....

Abby cried herself to sleep. It had been a rotten evening altogether, and every time she thought of Calhoun kissing that model she got sicker. She hated him. She hated every bone in his body, and she most especially hated his possessiveness. She had to find an apartment. She had to get away. After tonight it was going to be just plain horrible trying to stay in the same house with Calhoun until her birthday.

The next morning she slept late. She usually got up and went to church, but this time she played hooky. She didn't want to risk running into Calhoun.

But as it was, there was nothing to worry about. When she finally went downstairs at lunchtime, wearing jeans and a beige knit top, her hair in a ponytail, Calhoun was nowhere in sight.

"Good morning," Justin said from the head of the table, smiling faintly. "How did it go last night?"

"Don't ask," she groaned. She sat down and glanced nervously at the door. "Is he here?"

He shook his head and filled his cup with coffee then passed the carafe to Abby. "He's still asleep," he said. That was surprising, because Calhoun was usually up early. Justin actually grinned then. "What happened?"

"He thinks I should be in before two o'clock in the morning, even if he isn't," she said calmly. "And you're too old for me," she added with a faint grin, eyeing him.

He chuckled. "What else?"

"He's going crazy, Justin," she said. "I don't know what's gotten into him lately. It can't be his love life—his model seemed to be more than willing," she added cattily.

Justin looked at her, but he didn't reply. He poured cream into his coffee. "Oh, I almost forgot. Misty phoned. Something about having an apartment she wanted you to look at today if you want to go with her."

"Yes, I think I do," she murmured with a cold glance at the staircase.

"You know I don't approve of Misty as your prospective roommate," Justin told her honestly. "But it's your decision."

"You're a nice man."

"I'm glad you think so. Obviously my brother thinks I'm as big a rake as he is." He chuckled.

"Thank God you aren't," she sighed. "One in the family is enough!"

"If you're going out, you'd better wear a jacket," Justin warned. "I stepped out to get the paper and almost froze in place."

Abby sighed again. "And they keep saying spring is just around the corner."

She finished her breakfast and called Misty to tell her she'd be right over. Then she returned to her room to get her burgundy velour jacket. She was looping the last button when she turned to the open door and found Calhoun standing there, looking at her broodingly.

He'd just showered. He was bare chested, and his blond hair was damp. But Abby's eyes stopped at his brawny chest in helpless appreciation of the sheer masculinity of him. He leaned idly against the doorjamb, and muscles rippled under the wedge of thick brown hair that ran down into the wide belt around his slender hips. He didn't smile, and his dark eyes had heavy circles underneath them. He looked as tired as Abby felt.

"Where are you going now?" he asked coldly.

"Out to look at apartments," she said carelessly. "In a little over two and a half months I'll be needing one."

"How does Justin feel about that?" he asked, his eyes narrowing angrily.

"Justin isn't the one who's trying to keep me in a cage," she replied. She was tired of the whole thing, of his unreasonable anger and even of Justin playing cupid. "Look, Justin just took me out for a meal. He didn't park the car and try to make love to me. He isn't that kind of man, and you should be ashamed of yourself for thinking he is. Justin's like a brother to me. Just... as you are," she finished, averting her eyes. "I don't have romantic thoughts about either one of you."

"And that's a damned lie," he said in a cold tone. He jerked away from the door, slamming it behind him, bringing her shocked eyes to him as he advanced toward her. "I'm no more your brother than I'm your great-uncle."

She backed up into a chair, swerved and made it to the wall. He looked dangerous, and she didn't know how to handle this lightning mood switch.

"That's what you want me to be," she said accusingly, pressing against the cold wall. "You want me to be a kid sister and not get in your way or make eyes at you—"

"My God, I don't know what I want anymore," he ground out as he placed his big hands on either side of her head, his body too close, too sensuous, too deliciously masculine. The scent of him filled her nostrils, excited her senses. She could see the tiny golden tips of the hair on his chest now, glittering in the light. Glittering...like the dark, intent eyes that caught hers and held them.

"Calhoun, I have to go," she said, her voice faltering.

"Why?" he asked.

She could see him breathing. His chest rose and fell roughly, as if he were having a hard time getting air in and out. She felt that way herself. He was too close, and her vulnerability was going to start showing any minute. She couldn't bear to have him see her weakness and make fun of it.

"Stop it," she whispered huskily, closing her eyes. "Damn you, stop...oh!"

He had her mouth under his so smoothly and easily that her heart seemed to stop beating. He wasn't gentle, either. It was as if the feel of her soft body under his made him wild, made him hungry.

In fact, he was starving for her. He leaned down so that his hips and thighs were fully against her, so that his bare chest was against the velour of her jacket. He didn't like not being able to feel her breasts, so he snapped open the buttons of the jacket and pushed the material aside. He felt her gasp as her breasts pressed against him, and he groaned, marveling at the warm softness of her. Nudging her lips apart, he nipped sensuously at the lower one. That was arousing, too, and he wanted her. He wanted her mouth as he wanted her soft, sweet young body. His tongue pushed into her mouth, past her lips, tangling with her own, and he groaned and gave her his full weight, pressing her against the wall.

Abby was frightened. She hadn't expected anything quite so adult, and she'd never been kissed by anyone who had any expertise. Calhoun was experienced, and he was kissing her as if she knew all the answers, too. But she didn't. The feel of his body in such unfamiliar intimacy was embarrassing, and his mouth was doing shocking things to her own. She pushed at his chest, afraid of his lack of control.

"No!" she whimpered.

He barely heard her. His mind was spinning, his body in torment. He managed to lift his head, breathing roughly, and look down at her. But the passion and delight he had expected to see in her pale eyes was missing. They were wide, but not with desire. With...fear!

He scowled. Her hands were on his chest, but they were pushing, not caressing, and she was crying.

"Abby," he whispered gently. "Honey..."

"Let me...go," she sobbed brokenly. "Oh, let me go!" She pushed again, harder.

This time he flexed his hands against the wall and pushed away from her, leaving her cold, empty. She moved past him, putting half the length of the room between them. So that—that!—was what passion felt like. She shivered a little at the memory. Her mouth hurt where his had ground against it, and her breasts were sore from the hard pressure of his chest. He hadn't even tried to be gentle. She stared at him accusingly, her eyes bright with tears as she drew her jacket closer and shivered.

Calhoun felt as if he'd been hit in the head with a hammer. Her reaction hadn't been anything like what he'd expected. He'd almost kissed her once before, and she'd been yielding then, willing. But now she looked as if she hated him.

"You hurt me," she whispered shakily.

He was lost for words. Concerned, he stared at her, his dark eyes quiet on her wan face. She looked as if she had never experienced a man's passion. Was that possible?

Could any woman be that unawakened in this day and age?

"Haven't you ever been kissed?" he asked softly.

"Of course I have," she replied stiffly. "But not . . . not like that!"

His eyebrows went up. At last he was catching one. "My God," he said huskily. "Abby, adults kiss that way!"

"Then I don't want to be an adult," she returned, coloring. "Not if I have to be mauled like that!"

He watched her turn and leave the room, and he was powerless to stop her. Her reaction had floored him completely. He'd expected her to know a little about lovemaking, at least, but she seemed totally innocent. She'd never known a deep kiss or the intimacy of a man's body.

It should have pleased him, but he found it irritating that she thought he'd mauled her. By God, he should have let her go out with Myers. Then she'd know what it was to be mauled!

He left the room and closed the door, his expression thunderous as he heard her footsteps going down the staircase and then her muffled goodbye to Justin.

Calhoun went back to his own room. He was breathing roughly, and his heart wouldn't beat properly. He felt hot all over. Frustrated. Furious. Damn Abby and her soft body. It was driving him out of his mind!

He went into the bathroom and turned on the shower. Well, it was a good thing she didn't like his kisses, because hell would freeze over before she ever got another one.

Abby was blissfully unaware of Calhoun's thoughts. She climbed into her car and started it with hands that were still trembling. How could Calhoun have hurt her like that if he'd cared anything about her? He'd just proved how little she meant to him. He'd only been interested in his own pleasure, not hers. Well, he could go back to his blondes for all she cared. She was sure she hated him now.

Misty was already dressed and waiting when Abby got to the colonial mansion the older girl shared with her parents. Misty took them to town in her little sports car, and for once Abby didn't mind the wind. It might blow away her misery. Just thinking about Calhoun's rough treatment made her miserable. She loved him and it hurt terribly that he could treat her that way. But she had to pretend that nothing was wrong, so that Misty wouldn't start asking questions that Abby didn't want to answer.

They parked in town and went to the first address on Misty's list. It was an apartment above a sweet shop, on the corner across from the bank. Misty didn't like the place, because there was only one bedroom and she wanted her privacy. Abby deliberately put the implications of that remark in the back of her mind and added that she didn't like the view. It was too close to the center of town, and there was a good deal of traffic on Saturday night.

The second place they went was just right. The room being rented was upstairs in a private house owned by a Mrs. Simpson, who was friendly and bright and welcoming. That turned Misty off completely. She didn't want an old busybody watching out for her. But Abby was rapidly coming to the conclusion that Misty was going to do some entertaining once they were on their own, and her association with the Ballengers made her balk at the thought of Misty's plans.

"I'll take it," she told Mrs. Simpson, "if you don't mind having just me instead of both of us, and if you aren't in a hurry for me to move in. It will be a few weeks...."

"That will work out fine. I'm going off to my sister's for a week or so, anyway." Mrs. Simpson smiled broadly, her blue eyes lighting up. "My dear, I'd be delighted." She leaned forward while Misty was still upstairs grumbling about the lack of privacy. "Your friend seems very nice, mind you, but I'm rather old-fashioned...."

"So am I," Abby whispered, putting her finger to her lips when Misty came downstairs again.

"No, I'm sorry, it won't do," she sighed.

"I have the perfect solution," Abby told her. "I'll take this one, and you take the other one. It'll be great. We can visit each other, and we'll both have our privacy."

Misty raised an eyebrow. "Well...it might be nice at that. But you said you wanted to room with me."

Mrs. Simpson excused herself, asking Abby to phone her later about a date for moving in.

Abby moved with Misty to the door. "Let's face it," she told her friend, "you want to entertain men, and I'll have Calhoun and Justin all over me if they find out about it. I'm sure you don't want them on your case."

Misty shuddered delicately. "Are you kidding? Calhoun, maybe, but not Justin! That man doesn't have a humorous bone in his whole body."

Abby remembered how amused Justin had been about Calhoun's behavior, but she just nodded her head.

"Let's have coffee," Misty suggested. She drove them back into town in her little sports car and parked beside the bank. The two women had just gotten out of the car when Tyler Jacobs and his sister Shelby came around the corner looking somber and disturbed.

Abby greeted them. "Tyler. Shelby. How are you?"

"This isn't a good time to ask," Shelby sighed, but she smiled. She was a dish. Short dark hair framed her elfin face, and she had eyes that were an odd shade of green, almost glassy in color. Her mouth was perfect, and she was tall. She would have made a fortune as a model, but her parents wouldn't have heard of such a profession for their only daughter.

Tyler was like his sister in coloring. He had thick dark hair, almost black, and an olive complexion and the same odd-colored green eyes. He was as big as Calhoun, but slender. Whipcord-lean and dangerous-looking. He wasn't handsome at all, but he had character, and women usually found him irresistible.

Misty turned to see where Abby had gotten to and smiled delightedly at Tyler.

"Well, hello," she drawled. "Fancy seeing you here."

"Hello, Misty," he said, smiling lazily. "You look devastating, as usual. What are you two doing in town on a Sunday?"

"Looking for an apartment to share, originally." Abby sighed. "But we wound up with one each, across town from the other. I'm renting from Mrs. Simpson, and Misty has a neat place overlooking the bank."

"Right up there, in fact." Misty pointed across the street. "It needs decorating, but I can take care of that."

Abby grinned. "I'll bet you can."

"Come and have coffee with us," Shelby invited. "Tyler needs cheering up. We had a bad blow yesterday, and an even worse one today."

Abby looked up at him. He did seem reticent. And moody, which was totally unlike him. "I'm sorry. Can I help?"

"You little doll," he murmured, and touched her hair gently. "No. But thanks for the offer. How's Calhoun?"

Abby averted her eyes. "He's fine, I guess. He and Justin are both at home."

"No problems the other night after Calhoun got you home?" Tyler persisted with a teasing smile.

"Only the usual lecture," Abby said. She managed a shaky smile as all four of them went down the street and entered a small cafeteria.

They were quickly seated, and the waitress brought four cups of coffee and a pitcher of cream.

Shelby cast a glance at Abby and laughed softly. "You devil," she teased.

"I just wanted to see how the other half lived," Abby sighed.

"I did my best to help you," Misty sighed. "On the other hand, weren't you lucky that it was Calhoun and not Justin who came after you? Calhoun is a little more easygoing."

"Not lately, he isn't," Abby said tautly.

At the mention of Justin, Shelby became quiet and shy. Abby felt sorry for her. Justin had never gotten over Shelby's defection. He probably never would, and Shelby had to know that.

"How is Justin?' Tyler asked casually. Too casually.

"He goes to work and comes home and goes to work and comes home," Abby said as they added cream and sugar to their coffee.

Misty yawned. "What an exciting life."

"He's lonely, I suppose," Abby said deliberately. "He never goes anywhere."

"I know somebody else like that," Tyler murmured with a hard glance at Shelby, who shifted restlessly in her seat.

"How's the horse business going?" Abby interrupted, posing the question to Tyler as she sipped her coffee.

"Going bust, I'm afraid," he said heavily. "Dad made some bad investments before he died. So far, I've managed to meet the payments. This month I defaulted." His face hardened. "I'm going to have to sell Geronimo."

"Oh, Tyler, I'm sorry." Abby grimaced. "He was your favorite."

"Mine, too," Shelby said with a sigh. "But we can't keep him and pay off Dad's debts. I don't suppose you'd want him, Abby?"

"I don't ride that well," Misty confessed.

"If I can talk Justin into it I'd like to have him," Abby said gently.

"Thank you, Abby, but that wouldn't be a good idea," Shelby replied. "Justin would go right through the roof if you asked him."

"Like a rocket," Tyler said, smiling at Abby. "No, we'll do it through an agent. We won't have any problems selling him. I'd rather know who he was going to, that's all. Some people want a horse strictly for breeding purposes. They look at dollars and cents, not at the horse itself."

"I've got a cousin in Texas," Misty piped up. "She's trying to hold on to the ranch all by herself. It's a horse ranch," she added. "Does that tell you anything?"

He smiled. "Enough. I'd appreciate it if you'd put her in touch with me."

"I'll give her your number, if you don't mind."

"Fine."

Lights gleamed in Shelby's black hair as she lifted the cup and finished her coffee. Abby wondered at her elfin beauty, and thought it strange that a man like Justin could attract such a lovely woman when he wasn't handsome or even very personable. Then Abby remembered how kind he'd been to her in Houston, and the way he'd supported her with Calhoun. On the other hand, maybe it wasn't so surprising that he could attract her. What was surprising was that he'd ever let her go. It made Abby uncomfortable, thinking about how two people could be so much in love one day and bitter enemies the next. Love didn't last, after all.

"Tyler, we'd better go. I've got to call Barry Holman about those bonds and securities we're selling," Shelby said gently. "I'm sorry. I'd love to stay and talk. We hardly ever see each other these days, and I guess Justin would burn the house to the ground before he'd let me through the front door to visit you."

Tyler sighed. "He holds a grudge longer than any man I've ever known, that's for sure. And without reason."

"No," Shelby pleaded, her green eyes seeking his. "Please don't. Abby owes him her loyalty. Don't put her in the position of having to defend him."

"Sorry," he said, his green eyes glittering with controlled rage. Then he smiled at Abby. "There's a square dance at the dance hall next Friday night. How about going with me?"

Abby hesitated. Justin would be furious, and she didn't like to think about what Calhoun might say or do. He was so unpredictable lately. On the other hand, going out with Tyler would show Calhoun that she wasn't going to make eyes at him any more....

"Don't do it," Shelby pleaded. "Can't you see, it will only make things worse."

"For whom?" Tyler shot back. "Could the situation possibly be any worse for you? My God, you're living like a nun!"

Shelby put her napkin down with calm, steady fingers. "The way I live is no one's concern except my own." She stood up. "Abby, Justin would come down on your head like Judgment. He isn't the man he was. I'd hate to see you caught in the cross fire."

"I'm not afraid of him, Shelby," Abby said gently. "Not much, anyway. I'm trying to get out from under

Calhoun's thumb. Tyler and I would kind of be helping each other.''

"You see," Tyler told his sister. "And here you were thinking I was just doing it to irritate your ex-fiancé.''

"Well, aren't you?" Shelby said challengingly.

He lifted his chin arrogantly. "Maybe.''

"Sometimes I wonder if Mom and Dad didn't find you under a cabbage leaf," Shelby muttered.

"Not a chance," Misty mused, looking him up and down. "He's much too big.''

"Tease," he said, flirting lazily with Misty as he did with most women. But Tyler was deep, like Shelby, and if there was a special woman, nobody knew except himself. He was discreet about his love life.

"Justin used to laugh, you know," Shelby told Abby as they walked out together, with Misty and Tyler talking together ahead of them. "He wasn't always cold and hard and unyielding. Not until I gave him back his ring and made him bitter." She clutched her purse against her breasts. "Abby, don't hurt him," she pleaded, her eyes soft and gentle. "Don't let Tyler hurt him. He hides it, but he's so vulnerable. . . .''

"I know that," Abby said gently. She touched the taller woman's arm, stung by the look in Shelby's eyes. Yes, she was vulnerable, too, and Abby sensed that Shelby was still in love with Justin, even now. . . . "I'm sorry that things have gone so badly for both of you. Justin doesn't have women, you know. If you live like a nun, he lives like a monk. There isn't anyone.''

Shelby's lower lip trembled. She looked away, her head tilting to stop a tear from escaping. "Thank you," she managed huskily.

Abby wanted to say more, but the others were waiting impatiently. "Ready to go?" she called brightly to Misty.

"Okay. Can you keep it under ninety going home? Honest to goodness, I don't think that car knows any legal speeds!"

"I'm a good driver," Misty informed her haughtily. "You just come with me and I'll prove it. So long, Tyler. Shelby."

"I'll pick you up at six on Friday," Tyler told Abby. "Wear something sexy."

She curtsied. "You'd better bring a baseball bat when you come to the door. And pray that Justin doesn't have a long cord for his chain saw."

"Dangerous games, my friend," Misty told Abby as they drove away. "Justin won't like it, and he's pretty frightening when he loses his temper."

"So is Tyler. But they won't come to blows. I'll make sure of it."

"And what will Calhoun say?" Misty added with a quick glance at Abby.

Abby felt herself going pale. She could feel all over again the terrible crush of his mouth, the shattering intimacy of his body. She swallowed. "He won't care," she said coldly.

"Why do it? You're moving out. Isn't that enough of a show of independence for you?"

"No." Abby leaned back against the leather seat and closed her eyes. "But going out with Tyler will be."

Misty sighed and shook her head. "Well, I'll remember you in my prayers. Hang on." She pressed her foot down on the accelerator, and Abby wondered what the Guinness book of world records listed as the top land speed by a wild blonde in a little sports car. Whatever the record was, she thought as she held on for dear life, she'd bet that Misty could break it.

Chapter Six

Calhoun was gone when Abby got home, and she spent a quiet afternoon watching television. Justin was around long enough to ask about the apartment and to approve Abby's choice of lodgings. But then he left to deal with some problem at the feedlot.

Abby dreaded the moment when Calhoun would return, because of what had happened that morning. She couldn't reconcile the man she knew with the stranger who'd been so rough with her. Boys had kissed her before, but lightly and carefully. Calhoun hadn't been careful, and he'd frightened her with his experience. She'd never experienced adult passion before, and she didn't know what it was. But surely a man like Calhoun, with his love life, couldn't have been thrown off balance so completely by a twenty-year-old virgin.

He'd already said he didn't want her making eyes at him, so maybe he was showing her what she'd be inviting if she let him see her interest. She shivered. What a deft and accurate way he'd picked, if that were the case.

Supper was on the table and she and Justin were about to start serving themselves when Calhoun came in. He sat down, looking worn and rumpled, and poured himself a cup of coffee. He didn't speak to Abby, and she kept her head down so that he wouldn't notice her scarlet flush. It wasn't necessary, anyway, because he didn't even look at her. He started talking to Justin about a prospective new feedlot customer he'd found, and he kept the conversation going until they were having a second cup of coffee. Abby felt shut out and ignored. When Calhoun finally got up to leave and looked at her, she felt worse than she had in her life.

There was barely controlled anger in his eyes, mingled with something darker, something she didn't understand. She dropped her eyes and felt her heart race under his cold scrutiny. He acted as if she were the guilty one. Didn't he realize how he'd hurt her? That his treatment of her had been frightening?

"Hey," Justin said softly as the outside door opened and closed.

She looked up, her eyes faintly misty. "He didn't even speak to me," she whispered.

Justin leaned back in his chair and lit a cigarette, exhaling smoke as he watched her. "He's been like that all day," he said. "While you were gone he stared out the window whenever I tried to talk to him. He didn't even hear me. Finally he lit a cigarette and went outside and just walked."

She stared at him. "Calhoun stopped smoking years ago."

He shrugged. "He's gone through a pack already. You keep telling me that there's nothing wrong, but my brother goes from bad to worse. Now either you tell me or I'll beat it out of him. I love him, but I've had enough silence.''

Abby swallowed hard. Justin's tone was unnerving. But she couldn't tell him what Calhoun had done. Justin was unpredictable, and she didn't want him to rake Calhoun over the coals for something that in all honesty she'd helped to provoke.

Then she remembered what she'd said to Calhoun, and suddenly all the pieces of the puzzle fit together. She must have hurt Calhoun's pride with what she'd said and done after he'd kissed her so intimately. The more she thought about it, the worse she felt. For months she'd dreamed of having him kiss her. Then he had, and she'd been too frightened by his experienced bulldozer technique to even respond. She'd behaved like a child.

Justin lifted an eyebrow and waited expectantly. When she didn't say anything, he prodded, ''Well?''

''I said some terrible things to him,'' she confessed finally. ''I was jealous.''

''And hurt,'' he said perceptively.

''And hurt,'' she sighed. Her blue-gray eyes met his dark ones. ''Oh, Justin, he hates me. And I can't even blame him. I hurt his pride so badly that I don't imagine he'll ever talk to me again.''

''Incredible, isn't it, that you could hurt him,'' he mused. ''When women have been trying for years to get through that thick hide and never have.''

''He's been responsible for me for a long time,'' she said quietly. ''I guess it's hard for him to let go.''

''Maybe,'' he said. He took another draw on the cigarette. ''Maybe not. He's acting strangely lately.''

''Maybe he's got the gout or something,'' she suggested with a slight smile.

''Or something.''

She sipped her coffee so that she'd have something to do with her hands. She had to talk to Justin about Friday night, and it was only just dawning on her how difficult it was going to be.

"Justin, I have to tell you something."

His dark eyebrows lifted. "This sounds serious," he said with a faint smile.

"It is. And I hope you won't get mad at me."

His chin lifted. "Is it about the Jacobses?"

"I'm afraid so," she sighed. She looked at her coffee, because his eyes were getting darker by the second. "Tyler asked me to a square dance Friday night, and I said I'd go." She clenched her teeth, waiting for the outburst. When it didn't come, she looked up. He was watching her, but without any particular anger. She continued quickly, "I don't have to let him pick me up here. I can meet him at the dance. In fact, Shelby did her best to stop him from asking me, because she didn't want to upset you."

Something passed across his face, too fleeting to identify. But for one wild second his eyes were soft and quiet and full of wonder. Then it was gone, and he stared down at his glowing cigarette. "Did she?"

"She didn't want Tyler to make any trouble," Abby said gently.

"It's been six years," he said after a minute, his face quiet and oddly gentle. "Six long, empty years. I've hated her, and I've hated the family. I guess I could go on hating them until we're all dead. But it wouldn't change anything. It's all over and done with, a long time ago."

"She's so lovely," Abby said.

Justin winced, and there were memories in his dark eyes, in his taut face. He crushed out his cigarette roughly. "Tyler can pick you up here," he said abruptly, and got to his feet. "I won't give him a hard time."

She looked up as he passed by her chair and then down at her cup, thoughtfully. "She lives like a nun, you know. Tyler says she hasn't dated anyone for years."

Abby thought he stopped then, just for a second, but it might have been her imagination, because he kept walking and he didn't say a word.

What a pity, Abby thought with quiet melancholy, that love could die so violent a death. And the saddest part of it was that in spite of what Justin said, she'd have bet Justin and Shelby were still madly in love, even though it had been six years since they'd broken up. What had Shelby done to make Justin turn against her so vehemently? Surely just being given back his engagement ring wouldn't make a man so vindictive!

Abby got up from the table and went to her room. It was much too early to go to bed, but she didn't relish the idea of staying downstairs and having Calhoun stare holes through her. Avoiding him had suddenly become imperative.

That wasn't too hard. But avoiding the memories that lingered in her room was. The wall where he'd pinned her with his big body and kissed the breath out of her was all too empty. In the end she pushed a bookcase against it, just to keep her mind from replaying the scene.

She went to work as usual for the rest of the week, and so did Calhoun. But there was a difference. There was no soft greeting, no smile, no teasing grin. This Calhoun was more and more like his older brother. The fun had gone out of him, leaving behind a hard, formidable businessman who alternately ignored Abby or chewed her out for any nervous mistakes she made. It was impossible to get near him, even to talk.

By quitting time on Friday, she was a nervous wreck. She looked forward to the square dance like a doomed prisoner coveting an appeal. At least the dance would get her out of the house and take her mind off Calhoun. Not that she expected him to be home on a weekend. He'd probably be up in Houston with his model. Abby gritted her teeth as she thought about that.

Hindsight was a sad thing, Abby reflected, and she'd only begun to realize why Calhoun had been out of control with her in the bedroom. It hadn't been because he was angry or because he was punishing her. He'd been out of control because he'd wanted her. She was almost sure of it now, having asked Misty some subtle but intimate questions about men. Calhoun had wanted her, and she'd stabbed his pride bloody. She could have cried, because she'd had his attention and hadn't even known it. He was well and truly cured now. He didn't speak to her unless he had to, and he avoided her like the plague. She was glad she'd had that room reserved at the boarding house, because she had a feeling she was going to need it any time now.

She dressed in a red-checked full skirt with several crinolines and a perky white blouse with puffy short sleeves and a button front. It was almost March, but it was still cold, and she got out her long tan coat to wear with it. Tyler was due at six, and it was almost that when she went downstairs, her long hair silky and clean around her shoulders, wearing just enough makeup to give her a rosy-cheeked glow. She'd never wished more that she was blond or that she could have a second chance with Calhoun. Just her luck, she thought miserably as she made her way down the staircase, to foul everything up on the first try. Why hadn't she realized that Calhoun felt passion, not anger? Why hadn't she waited to give him a chance to be tender? He probably would have been if she hadn't struggled with him.

She reached the bottom of the staircase just in time to watch Calhoun open the front door for Tyler, because Maria and Lopez had the night off. Abby's heart jumped helplessly at the sight of those broad shoulders and that long back. Calhoun was so big he even towered over Tyler.

Abby's body tensed as she wondered if Justin had told Calhoun she'd be going out with Tyler. But he finally opened the door all the way and let the other man inside.

Tyler, in jeans and a red checked Western shirt and bandanna and denim jacket, looked as Western as a man could get, from his black boots to his black hat. Calhoun was dressed in a similar fashion, except that his shirt was blue. They stared at each other for a long moment before Calhoun broke the silence.

"Justin said you were taking Abby out," he said tersely. "You can wait in the living room if you like."

"Thanks," Tyler said, equally tersely, as he met Calhoun's eyes and glanced away.

"I'm already dressed," Abby said with forced cheerfulness, smiling at Tyler and getting a smile back. She didn't look at Calhoun. She couldn't. It would have been like putting a knife in her heart.

"Then let's go," Tyler replied. "I hear the Jones boys are going to play tonight. You remember Ted Jones, Calhoun; he was in our senior class back in high school."

"I remember him," Calhoun said quietly. There was a smoking cigarette in his hand, and he looked like a stranger.

A minute later, Justin came out of his study, stopping short when he saw the three of them. He and Calhoun were wearing almost identical clothing, and it was odd for Justin to dress up on a Friday night. Unless...

"Where are you off to?" Abby asked the oldest of the three men with a smile.

"The square dance, of course," Justin said, glancing at Tyler. "Not to keep tabs on her, in case you were wondering," he added with a cold smile. "We're meeting a business contact there."

Abby's heart jumped. Calhoun was going to the dance, too. She hated her own helpless pleasure at the thought that she might have at least a few minutes in his arms.

Tyler studied Justin warily. "You aren't meeting Fred Harriman, by any chance?"

Justin's eyebrows arched. "Yes. Why?"

Tyler grimaced. "He just bought our place."

Calhoun caught his breath. "For God's sake, you weren't forced out?"

"I'm afraid so," Tyler replied with a sigh. "Funny, you never think you'll go under. I was sure that I could undo the damage Dad had done, but I was too late. At least it's not a complete loss. We've still got a couple of stallions, and we can hold on to at least the house and an acre or two of land."

"If you need a job, we've got one open at the feedlot," Justin said unexpectedly. "It's not charity, damn it," he added when he saw Tyler's incredulous look and glinting green eyes. "I don't have to like you to know how good you are with livestock."

"That's a fact," Calhoun agreed, raising a cigarette to his chiseled mouth. "The door's open."

Abby, watching them, was struck by the sheer force of so much masculinity at close range. The three of them were like patterns cut from the same rough cloth. Long, tall Texans. She was suddenly proud to be a friend to two of them, even if the third hated her.

"Thanks for the offer, then," Tyler said. He stared at Justin. "I didn't think you went to dances, business or not."

"I don't. Calhoun gets drunk if I don't baby-sit him," he said, grinning at his brother's outraged expression.

"Like hell I do," Calhoun replied. "I remember a night when you tied one on royally and I put you to bed."

Justin pursed his lips. "We all lose our heads occasionally," he said. "Don't we, Abby?" he added with a glance in her direction and then in Calhoun's. Abby flushed, and Calhoun turned his back and headed for the front door, holding it open for the rest of them without another word. Justin only smiled.

"Shelby's going, too," Tyler remarked to Abby as they walked out. "I had to twist her arm, but she needs some diversion. She's working a six-day week for the first time in her life, and it's rough."

Justin didn't say a word, but if that quiet unblinking gaze meant what Abby thought it did, he was listening intently. She wondered just how many fireworks a dance hall could stand. Behind her, Calhoun was glaring at her and at Tyler with a scowl so hot that she would have grown warm if she'd seen it.

The dance hall was jumping. The Jones boys' band was playing a toe-tapping Western medley, and the dance floor was full. Old Ben Joiner, his fiddle in his hand, was calling the dance, his voice rising deep and clear above the music as he told the dancers what to do and when.

"Nice crowd," Tyler remarked. He and Abby had arrived after Justin and Calhoun. The two of them were at a table with a third man who looked pitifully out of place.

"Yes, it is nice. What do the brothers want with Fred Harriman, I wonder?" she asked, thinking out loud as she and Tyler headed toward the table where Shelby was sitting all alone.

"You're in a position to know better than I am," Tyler returned, "but I expect he wants the brothers to feed out his new cattle for him." Tyler glanced at his sister and saw where her big, soulful green eyes were staring. "God, she's got it bad," he said under his breath.

Abby noticed, too, and touched his sleeve. "Justin doesn't date, either. Do you suppose there's any chance for them?"

"Not after what he thinks she did," Tyler replied tersely. "And talking about it won't butter any biscuits. Hi, sis," he said more loudly, smiling at his sister as he pulled out a chair for Abby and then sat down himself.

"Hi," Shelby said with a grin. "Abby, you look gorgeous."

"So do you." Abby sighed. "You don't know what I'd give to be as pretty as you are."

"Oh, go on," Shelby murmured, embarrassed. But she did look pretty, her dark hair coiled on her head with a bow holding it, her green Western-style dress exactly matching her eyes and showing off her beautiful figure.

"I wish things had worked out for you. Your job must be rough," Abby commiserated.

Shelby smiled back. "Oh, I like it," she said. "And at least we've got the house. We'll finish the last details of the sale next week, and then all the gossip will die down and we'll have our privacy back." She picked up her glass of ginger ale and sipped it. "I hope you don't mind my being a third wheel...."

"You go on," Abby replied. "You know Ty and I are just friends. I'm glad to have your company, and I'm sure your brother is, too."

Tyler smiled, but the look he sent her over Shelby's oblivious head wasn't quite platonic.

"Let's get in that next set," Tyler said, pulling Abby up by the hand. "Shelby, order Abby and me a ginger ale, would you?" he asked his sister.

She grinned. "Of course."

Abby stared at Tyler as he led her into the throng of dancers. "I can have a gin and tonic if I want to."

"Not while you're out with me," he said firmly, leading her into place in front of him. "I don't drink. That means you don't drink."

"Spoilsport," she sighed.

He chuckled. "Shame on you. You don't need booze to have a good time."

"I know. But I had looked forward to being treated like an adult," she told him.

"Well, don't give up hope," he said, his voice deep and soft as his lean hand curled around her waist. "The night's still young yet."

Abby smiled, because of course he was just flirting. She let him jostle her around the dance floor, graceful on his feet, expertly leading her through the twists and turns and shuffles and exchanges. Abby was having a great time until she glanced at the table where Justin and Calhoun were sitting. Justin's dark eyes kept darting over to Shelby. Abby was too far away to read his expression. Calhoun, on the other hand, was glaring at Abby and Tyler with enough venom for ten rattlesnakes.

Her heart leaped at the jealousy she saw on his face. Maybe there was still a little hope. The thought perked her up, and she began to smile, and then to laugh. Tyler mistook her response for pleasure in his company, and so did Calhoun. By the time the dance was over, Abby was caught in the middle of a building storm.

It threatened to explode when Calhoun, sick of watching Abby with Tyler, went and asked Shelby to dance.

Shelby was hesitant because Justin had just straightened at his table and looked capable of starting a world war all by himself.

"He won't mind," Calhoun said. "You look lonely sitting here by yourself."

"Oh, Calhoun, don't start anything," she pleaded.

"I won't," he promised. "Now come and dance with me."

Shelby gave in, but her lovely face was troubled.

Abby watched them go onto the dance floor, and her spirits fell. Shelby and Calhoun looked good together, her brunette beauty a perfect foil for his blond good looks. Abby felt plain and unattractive by comparison. She stared at Ty's chest, hopelessly depressed. What if Calhoun had come because of Shelby? What if he was courting her now? She felt sick.

"I feel like I'm sitting on a time bomb," Tyler mused as he watched Calhoun and Shelby and then got a look at Justin's face. "I don't know what Calhoun's up to, but Justin looks dangerous. Even if he hates my sister, he still seems to consider her his personal property. Would you look at that scowl?"

Abby saw Justin's expression and was ashamed of herself for wishing he would get out of his chair and beat the hell out of Calhoun. She flushed with embarrassment. "If Justin was dancing with another woman, how do you think Shelby would feel?" she asked, looking up at him.

He pursed his lips, his green eyes dancing as they searched her face. "I hadn't considered that."

"Calhoun probably thought Shelby was uncomfortable sitting by herself with nobody to dance with," Abby added.

Tyler sighed, his eyes wandering quietly over Abby's distracted expression as she looked toward the other couple on the floor. And all at once a lot of things became clear for him. Foremost was that Abby was jealous. Her eyes weren't any softer than Justin's. If she wasn't already in love with Calhoun, she was well on the way to it. Tyler felt all his chances slipping away, and there wasn't a thing he could do about it.

The evening wore on, and the tension rose. Calhoun seemed to enjoy dancing with Shelby. Abby stuck with Tyler. Justin sat and drank quietly by himself after he finished his business with the other gentleman, who left. The tall man began to look more coldly violent by the minute.

Toward the end of the dance, Calhoun left Shelby long enough to saunter over to Abby, who was sipping ginger ale while Tyler spoke to someone he knew at a nearby table. Abby hadn't been watching Calhoun, because he was making her miserable. He didn't smile at her anymore. He hated her, she was sure of it. So when Calhoun appeared in front of her, Abby grew flustered and nervous and almost spilled her drink.

Calhoun saw the nervous motion, and it gave him hope. "How about dancing one with me?" he asked quietly.

She looked up, her eyes searching his face almost hungrily. "No, I'd better not," she said softly.

He caught his breath at the wounded sound in her voice. "Abby, why not?" he asked.

"It might hurt Shelby's feelings," she said, and turned away, searching the room desperately for Tyler. "I can't imagine where Tyler got to," she added huskily.

Calhoun looked like a radio with the transistors removed. He blinked, doubting that he'd really heard what she'd just said. Shelby might be hurt? Surely she didn't think—It suddenly dawned on him that if Abby was crazy enough to imagine he was getting involved with Shelby, Justin might, too.

He turned toward the table where Justin was sitting like a statue, and whistled under his breath. "Oh, my God," he breathed. "I've done it now."

Abby didn't say another word. She watched Calhoun move through the crowd toward Justin and wondered absently if his life insurance was paid up. Justin looked murderous.

There were two full ashtrays in front of Justin, and one half-empty whisky glass. The older man drank on occasion, but usually not when he was angry. If he did, he limited himself to one drink. The glass was what told Calhoun how angry his older brother was.

Calhoun sat down across from him, leaning back to study the older man. "She was lonely," he told Justin.

Justin drained his glass and rose, his eyes blacker than Calhoun had seen them in a long time. "Then I'll see what I can do about it."

While Calhoun was catching his breath, Justin walked to Shelby's table. He didn't say a word. He looked at the woman until her face colored, then simply held out his hand. She put hers into it. He pulled her onto the dance floor, and they melted into each other to a slow, dreamy tune.

Abby sighed as she watched them. They were stiff, as if there were more than just space between them, but the look on Shelby's face was hauntingly beautiful. His expression was less easily read, hard and rigid. But Abby would have bet that he was as close to heaven as he'd been in six years.

"How about that for a surprise?" Tyler murmured over her head, watching. "My God, look at them. They're like two halves of a whole."

"Why did they ever split up?" she asked him.

"I don't know," he said with a sigh. "I think my father was mixed up in it somehow, and one of his friends. But Shelby never talks about it. All I know is that she gave him back his ring and he's been bitter ever since."

As the music ended, the couple stopped dancing. Justin released Shelby very slowly and abruptly turned and walked out of the dance hall. After a minute, Shelby went back and sat down. Calhoun returned to the table.

Abby, turning to watch Calhoun bend toward Shelby, felt even sicker when she saw Shelby get up and leave the building, holding Calhoun's arm.

She toughed it out for several more dances, but when Calhoun didn't come back, she finally realized that he'd more than likely taken Shelby home. And was still there...

"Can we go home, Ty?" she asked huskily.

"Are you sure that's what you want?" Ty asked, his voice full of sympathy.

"I'm tired," Abby replied, and it was no lie. She really was. She was tired of watching Calhoun in action. First the blonde, now Shelby, and all in one week. But plain little Abby didn't figure in his world. She didn't even matter. She looked up at Ty, her eyes misty with unshed tears. "Do you mind?"

"Of course I mind," he said gently. "But if that's what you want, we'll go."

Abby didn't speak all the way home. It was unlike Calhoun to deliberately start trouble. It was almost as if he were getting back at Justin for something, but for what? Justin hadn't done anything to him.

Tyler walked her up the steps onto the long front porch with its graceful arches and porch furniture.

"Sorry the evening ended so abruptly," Tyler said. "But I hope you had fun."

"I did, honestly," she said, smiling up at him.

He took a deep breath and bent toward her hesitantly. When she didn't resist, he brushed his mouth gently against hers. There was no response, and after a minute he lifted his dark head.

His green eyes searched hers, and he wasn't smiling. "You don't have a clue, do you, honey?" he asked gently. "And I think it's lack of interest more than just lack of experience."

"You think I'm green as grass, too, I guess," she sighed miserably.

He cocked an eyebrow and tweaked her chin with his lean fingers. "So that's how it is." He pursed his lips. "Well, little Abby, with some cooperation from you I could take care of the green part in about five minutes. But I think that's a lesson the man you're mooning over should teach you." He touched his lips to her forehead. "I hope he appreciates his good luck. You're a special girl."

"He doesn't think so, but I'm glad you do." She looked up at him with a faint smile. "I wish it could be you."

His expression hardened for just an instant before the old mocking humor came back. "So do I. Want to go to dinner one night? Just a friendly dinner. I know when a door's being closed, so you won't have any worries on that score."

Her smile grew brighter. "You're a nice man."

"Not always." He touched her cheek gently. "Good night."

"Good night, Tyler. I had a good time."

"So did I."

He took the steps two at a time, and Abby stood quietly, watching him drive off. It was a long time before she turned and went into the house.

She closed the front door and started toward the staircase, only to be stopped in her tracks by an off-key rendition of a Mexican drinking song. Somewhere in the back of her mind she recognized it as one Justin sang on the very rare occasions when he had had too many glasses of whiskey.

Chapter Seven

Abby went all the way inside the house and closed the door. Then she slipped down the hall to the study and peeked in.

Justin was holding a square whiskey glass. It was empty. He was sprawled on the leather sofa with his dark hair in his eyes and his shirt rumpled, one big boot propped on the spotless leather seat, singing for all he was worth. On the coffee table beside him were a smokeless ashtray, a crumpled cigarette pack, a fresh cigarette pack, and half a bottle of whiskey.

"No puedo hacer..." He stopped at the sound of her footsteps and looked up at her with bloodshot eyes.

"Oh, Justin," she moaned.

"Hello, Abby. Want a snort?"

She grimaced at the glass he held up. "It's empty," she told him.

He stared at it. "Damn. I guess it is. Well, I'll fill it up, then."

He threw his leg off the sofa, almost ending up on the floor in the process.

Abby put down her purse and coat and helped him onto the sofa. "Justin, this won't help," she said. "You know it won't."

"She cried," Justin murmured. "Damn it, she cried. And he took her home. I want to kill him, Abby," he said, his eyes blazing, his voice harsh. "My own brother, and I want to kill him because he went off with her!"

She bit her lower lip. She didn't know what to say, what to do. Justin never drank, and he never complained. But he looked as if he were dying, and Abby could sympathize. She'd felt that way, too, when Calhoun had left with Shelby.

"I saw them go," he ground out. He put his face in his lean hands and sighed heavily. "She's part of me. Still part of me after all the years, all the pain. Calhoun knew it, Abby, he did it deliberately...."

"Calhoun loves you," she defended him. "He wouldn't hurt you on purpose."

"Any man could fall in love with her," he kept on. "Shelby's beautiful. A dream walking."

Abby knew how attractive Shelby was. The knowledge didn't help her own sense of failure, her own lack of confidence or her breaking heart.

"Drinking isn't the answer," she said softly. She touched his arm. "Justin, get some sleep."

"How can I sleep when he's with her?"

"He won't be for long. Tyler just went home," she said tautly.

He took a deep breath, letting it out in jerks. His hands came away from his eyes. "I don't know much about women, Abby," he said absently. "I don't have Calhoun's charm, or his experience, or his looks."

She felt a sense of kinship with him then, because she had the same problem. Justin had always seemed so self-assured that she'd never thought of him having the same doubts and fears that she did.

"And I don't have Shelby's assets," Abby confessed. She sat down beside him. "I guess we'd both lose a beauty contest. I wish I was blond, Justin."

"I wish I had a black book." Justin sighed.

She grinned at him, and he grinned back. He poured whiskey into the glass, getting half again as much on the heavy coffee table. "Here," he offered it to her. "To hell with both of them. Have a shot of ego salve."

"Thanks, masked man," she sighed, taking it. "Don't mind if I do."

It tasted horrible. "Can you really drink this stuff and live?" she wondered. "It smells like what you put in the gas tank."

"It's Scotch whiskey," he returned. "Cutty Sark."

"It would cutty a shark all right," she mused, sipping it.

"Not cutty a shark. Cutty Shark. Sark. Hell." He took the glass and finished what little whiskey she'd left. "Now, if you're going to drink Cutty Sark, Abby, you have to learn to sing properly. I'll teach you this song I learned down in Mexico, okay?"

And he proceeded to do just that. When Calhoun walked in the front door about thirty minutes later, there was a very loud off-key chorus coming from the study.

He stared in the door incredulously. Justin was lying back on the sofa, his hair in his eyes, one knee lifted, a whiskey bottle in his hand. Abby was lying against his up-lifted knee, her legs thrown over the coffee table, sipping from a whiskey glass. She looked as disreputable as his brother did, and both of them looked soaked to the back teeth.

"What in hell is going on?" Calhoun asked as he leaned against the doorjamb.

"We hate you," Abby informed him, lifting her glass in a toast.

"Amen." Justin grinned.

"And just as soon as we get through drinking and singing, we're going to go down to the feedlot and open all the gates, and you can spend the rest of the night chasing cows." She smiled drunkenly. "Justin and I figure that's what you do best, anyway. Chasing females, that is. So it doesn't matter what species, does it, old buddy?" she asked Justin, twisting her head back against his knee.

"Nope," Justin agreed. He lifted the whiskey bottle to his lips, rolling backward a little as he sipped it.

"We were going to lock you out," Abby added, blinking, "but we couldn't get up to put on the chain latches."

"My God." Calhoun shook his head at the spectacle they made. "I wish I had a camera."

"What for?" Justin asked pleasantly.

"Never mind." Calhoun unbuttoned his cuffs and rolled up his sleeves. "I'll make some black coffee."

"Don't want any," Abby murmured drowsily. "It would mess up our systems."

"That's right," Justin agreed.

"You'll see messed-up systems by morning, all right." Calhoun grimaced and moved off toward the kitchen.

"We should check his collar for lipstick!" Abby told Justin in a stage whisper.

"Good idea," Justin frowned. He started to sit up, then fell back against the arm of the sofa, cradling the bottle. "In a minute. I have to rest first."

"That's okay," she said. "I'll do it." She yawned. "When he gets back." Her eyes closed.

By the time Calhoun got back, they were both snoring. The whiskey bottle was lying on the floor, with the neck in Justin's lean hand. Calhoun righted it and put it on the table along with Abby's empty glass. The sight of them was as puzzling as it was amusing. Both Justin and Abby were usually the teetotalers at any gathering, and here they were soused. He wondered if his leaving with Shelby had set them off and realized that it probably had. In Justin's case it was understandable. But Abby's state was less easily understood, after the way she'd treated him since he'd kissed her. Unless...

He frowned, his dark eyes quiet and curious as he watched her flushed, sleeping face. Unless she'd finally realized why he'd been rough with her and was regretting her hot words. Was that possible? She'd seemed jealous of the time he'd spent with Shelby at the dance, and here she was three sheets to the wind. Well, well. Miracles did happen, it seemed.

He still wasn't sure about Tyler Jacobs's feelings toward Abby, but at least now he didn't have to worry about Justin's. If just seeing his brother with Shelby had this effect on Justin, he was still crazy about Shelby.

Calhoun lifted Abby and sat her crookedly in a chair while he laid Justin down on the sofa, pulled the older man's big boots off and covered him with one of the colorful serapes that were draped on chairs all over the room. Then he swung Abby up in his arms, balanced her on his knee while he turned off the overhead light, and closed the study door. Justin was going to hate himself in the morning.

Abby stirred as he carried her up the staircase. Her eyes flickered open, and she stared up drunkenly at the hard, quiet face above hers.

"You're with Shelby," she muttered drowsily. "We know you are. We know what you're doing, too." She laughed bitterly, then sighed and broke into the Mexican song Justin had taught her.

"Stop that." Calhoun scowled at her. "My God, you shouldn't use language like that."

"What language?"

"That song Justin taught you," he muttered, topping the staircase and heading down the hall toward her room. "It's vulgar as all hell."

"He didn't say it was."

"Of course he didn't. He wouldn't have taught it to you if he'd been sober. He'll have a heart attack if he hears you singing it when he's back on his feet."

"Want me to teach it to you?" she asked.

"I already know it."

"That isn't surprising," she sighed. She closed her eyes as he walked through the open door into her room and kicked it shut behind him. There were memories in this room, he thought angrily as he headed toward the bed. Abby, half-naked on that pink coverlet. Abby's soft body under his against that far wall—where she'd put a bookcase. He frowned at it. The new furniture arrangement was fairly revealing. Why would she shift the bookcase there unless it bothered her to remember?

He laid her down on the bed and watched her curl up. "No, you don't," he murmured. "You can't go to sleep like that."

She yawned. "Yes, I can."

He pulled off her shoes, and after a moment's hesitation his hard fingers went to her skirt. He removed it and about a hundred layers of full underskirts, and then her panty hose and blouse. Under it all, she was wearing dainty pink lace briefs and a matching bra that was no cover at all over her full, firm breasts.

This, he thought as he looked at her, was a hell of a mistake. But she was the most delicious little morsel. Her body was perfect, the most beautiful he'd seen in his life. And when he realized just how innocent she was, how untouched, his body rippled with pleasure mingled with need.

She sighed then, and her eyes opened. She searched his face, watching where his gaze had fallen. "You undressed me," she said.

"You couldn't sleep in that rig," he replied tautly.

"I guess not." She knew it should bother her that he was seeing her like this, in those wispy pink things she'd been crazy enough to buy at Misty's insistence. But if the way he was staring at her was any indication, he seemed to like what he saw.

"Do you have pajamas or a gown?" he asked after a minute.

"A gown. Under my pillow."

He managed to make his legs move and took out a bit of material that would cover no more of her than her underwear. "You'll freeze to death in this thing," he muttered.

"Misty said it was a sexy outfit," she said drowsily. She moved, her long hair framing her oval face with its delicate flush, her pale blue-gray eyes enormous as they searched the faintly blurred outline of his body. "I thought I'd seduce Ty," she added. "He likes me."

His face hardened. "Like hell you will," he said shortly.

"You did that to Shelby," she accused. "Shame on you, when Justin loves her."

"I didn't touch Shelby," he returned. "I left her at her front door and went back to the dance hall looking for you."

"I wasn't there," she murmured.

"Obviously." He didn't mention that he'd had to fight the urge to go looking for Tyler's car in case he and Abby were parked somewhere. The thought of her with Ty made him want to do something violent.

"Justin is going to beat you up when he can stand up again," she told him gaily.

"I guess he's entitled." Calhoun sighed. "I sure as hell made a mess of things." He sat down beside her, his eyes reluctantly leaving the long, sweet line of her legs and hips and the open seductiveness of her almost-bare breasts. "Do you know how perfect you are?" he said absently.

She was suddenly cold sober. Her eyes opened wide, searching his. "Me?"

"You," he said harshly. "From your legs to your hips to those sweet, pretty brea—" He stopped, hating his own vulnerability. "Come here." He put the gown in her lap and drew her into a sitting position, watching the tips of her firm breasts suddenly harden. He caught his breath.

She looked up at him curiously. "What's wrong?"

"This." He touched her delicately, only the back of his knuckles rubbing softly against her nipples. She pulled away, her breath audible, and he lifted his head to search her shocked eyes.

She looked back at him, relaxed from the alcohol, all her deeply buried longings surfacing without the restraint of a usually protective mind. She touched the back of his hand and intertwined her fingers with his. And then she pulled gently, watching as she drew his hand across her breasts.

"Abby..." he ground out.

"I'm sorry, " she whispered. "About what I said that morning. About how I...reacted." She swallowed, searching for courage. She opened his fingers and pressed them hesitantly just underneath her breast, lifting them so that he could feel the swell against his skin.

"Don't, for God's sake," he groaned.

She moved his hand against her, drowning in the sweetness of his touch, arching toward it. Both her hands went there, pushing his fingers completely over her. "Calhoun," she moaned. She felt so weak that she thought she'd have to lie down again, but she couldn't let go of his hand.

"You aren't sober enough," he whispered roughly, although the feel of her was doing terrible things to his self-control. He was already going rigid with need as he followed her down.

"I'm not sober enough to be afraid," she whispered. Her eyes searched his glittering eyes. "Teach me."

He actually shuddered. "I can't."

"Why?" she asked. "Because I'm plain and unsophisticated, because I'm not blond—" Her voice broke.

So did his control. He leaned down, his smoky breath mingling with hers as his hand cupped her. "Because you're a virgin," he breathed into her mouth as he took it.

She moaned. It was sweet, so sweet. Nothing like that other time, when he'd been rough and hadn't given her enough room to respond. He'd been impatient and demanding, but now he was gentle. His fingers stroked her body from her breasts to her waist to her flat stomach. His mouth teased at hers, probed it, traced it in a silence that was thick with sensual pleasure. Abby felt warm all over, safe and cared-about. She let her lips admit the probing of his tongue, admit him into the sweet darkness of her mouth. She didn't even protest when the kiss grew much deeper, much slower, or when she felt his hand slide under her to find the catch at her back.

The air was cool on her body. He removed the lacy covering that was no covering at all, and his hands were heaven on her hot skin. She moaned, helping him, pressing his fingers against her, drawing them over her hungry body.

"Abby," he groaned against her mouth, half-crazy with the hunger to make love to her completely, to salve the ache that was throbbing through his body.

She opened her eyes, letting her gaze fall lazily to his chest. Her hands went to his shirt, and she worked at the buttons, feeling him tense. But he didn't protest, even though his heartbeat was shaking his big body as it lay beside hers.

"There," she whispered when she could see and touch the thick wedge of hair that ran down to his belt. "I'll bet women love to touch you there," she murmured as she pressed her fingers hungrily against him.

"I've never let a woman touch me like this before," he said huskily. "I didn't like it until now."

Her eyes searched his, and she shifted restlessly on the coverlet, hungry, aching for something without a name, without an image.

"What do you want?" he asked gruffly, searching her eyes. "Tell me. I'll do anything you want me to."

She swallowed, and her lips parted unsteadily. She took his head in her hands and tugged at it, lifting her body. And he understood without her having to put it into words.

"Here?" he whispered tenderly, and put his open mouth completely over the swollen tip of her breast.

She moaned helplessly. It was beyond her wildest imaginings of what passion would feel like. Her body was in control. Her mind could only watch, it couldn't slow down

what was happening. She twisted the cool, thick strands of
his blond hair while he smoothed his warm mouth over her
breasts and stomach, her faint cries encouraging him, her
body welcoming him.

His mouth slid back up to meet hers. And as she opened
her own lips to welcome him, she felt his body slowly cover
her.

Her eyes opened then as his mouth lifted fractionally,
and she watched his face, hard with passion, as his body
fit itself perfectly to her slenderness.

She barely breathed, her eyes wide and full of new
knowledge as she felt him intimately and knew without
words how badly he wanted her.

"Are you afraid this time?" he whispered quietly.

"I should be," she replied. She reached up and touched
his face as he drew his chest slowly, teasingly over her
breasts. Her breath caught, but she traced his eyebrows, his
cheeks, his mouth with fingers that trembled and adored
him.

His big, callused hands slid under her back, lifting her
up into the curve of his body. "I want you, Abby," he
whispered, bending to her mouth as his body shuddered
over hers. "I want you so much...."

She curled her arms around his head and held his mouth
against her eager one. "I want you, too, Calhoun," she
whispered into his mouth.

He almost lost control completely then. He kissed her
until he had to stop for breath, his body shuddering
rhythmically, his knee between her long, soft legs, his hand
low on her hips. He felt her trembling and heard her
whimper. Oddly, it brought him to his senses.

Slowly, so slowly, he rolled onto his side, bringing her
with him, cradling her against his damp body. He slid his

hands to her head, holding her forehead to his throbbing chest.

"Lie still, honey," he whispered raggedly when she began to move again. He caught her hips and stilled them. "Just lie against me and breathe. It will be all right in a minute. Lie still, baby."

Her hands were flat against his chest, trembling there in the thick mat of hair, and she felt his unsteady breathing against her hair. He was as shaken as she was, but why had he stopped? She didn't understand. If he wanted her, then why had he stopped?

"Sweet thing," he breathed when the tremor was almost out of his big arms. "Sweet, precious thing, another few seconds and nothing on earth would have stopped me, did you know?"

She nuzzled her head against him. "Why did you stop?" she asked dazedly.

He tilted her head back on the pillow and smiled into her drowsy eyes. "Don't you know?"

"Because I'm not blond, I guess," she sighed, almost weeping with frustration and disappointment.

"Because you're not lucid," he corrected. He brushed the long, soft hair away from her face. "Abby, you're half lit."

"I want you," she moaned.

"I know. I can see it. Feel it." He hugged her close for a minute, because he was almost in control now. Then he let go and quickly and efficiently slid her into her gown. "Sit up, honey."

She did, and he eased back the covers and helped her get under them. She lay quietly beneath two layers of fabric and blinked at him sleepily. "Calhoun, stay with me," she whispered.

He smiled gently, his dark eyes possessive on her flushed face. "Justin would love finding us in your bed together. He'd probably make me marry you."

"And I guess that would be the end of your world," she replied.

His expression hardened. He drew in a slow breath and touched her cheek gently, thoughtfully. "I've been alone a long time. I like being my own boss, answering to no one. I've been a rounder, and in some ways I still am. I'm a bad marriage risk."

"One woman wouldn't satisfy you, I guess," she murmured, hiding her eyes from him. All her dreams were dead now. Every last one. He wanted her, but not enough for marriage. He was telling her so.

He shrugged, confused and feeling faintly hunted. "One woman never has," he said curtly. "I don't want to be tied."

"God forbid that I should try," Abby said, forcing a smile. "Don't worry, Calhoun, I was just…experimenting. I wondered why you were so rough with me the other morning, and I wanted to see if passion made people rough. I guess it does, because that's how I felt tonight. Thanks for the…the lesson."

He frowned slightly, searching her eyes. "Is that all it felt like. An experiment? A lesson in making love?"

"Tyler said I needed teaching," she said with a yawn, missing the flash of fury in his face. "But I don't anymore." She closed her eyes and turned her face against the pillow. "I'm sleepy."

Calhoun sat watching her, his eyes stormy. She'd used him. That was all she'd wanted. She'd been experimenting, seeing how it felt to be touched. Damn her!

He got up, glaring at the lacy bra he'd removed from her soft breasts just before she'd let him touch them. Let him!

God, she'd helped him! His blood ran hot at the memory
of how uninhibited she'd been with him tonight. Had she
been competing with Shelby, or had it been curiosity
alone? Could she care about him and be hiding it? And
how did he feel? Did he just want her physically, or was it
more than that? Could he bear the loss of his freedom?
Because it would come to that if he took her. Marriage.
Trap.

He tossed the bra onto the chair beside her bed and took
a long last look at her sleeping face. She didn't need to be
blond. She was exquisite. Her long hair was spread out
around her, her lashes were feathering her flushed cheek,
and her parted lips were pink and faintly swollen because
he'd been hungry. She was delicious. Virginal and sweet-
tasting and exquisitely beautiful without her clothes. He
wondered if he'd ever get over the taste of her—if he'd be
able to forget. Hell, would he ever be able to have another
woman, or would the memory of Abby always stand in the
way?

He opened the door and went out, closing it quietly behind him. He should never have touched her in the first
place, he thought furiously.

He had to get away for a while. Far away, so that he
could think things through. Now that he'd touched Abby,
it was going to be the purest kind of hell keeping his hands
off her. And Justin wouldn't like having that sort of love-
play going on, not if it threatened Abby. Calhoun knew
that if he took Abby into his arms again, it wasn't going to
end with a few kisses. He wanted her too badly, and she
was too responsive. He aroused her as no man ever had.
That meant she'd give herself to him with hardly any
coaxing. Calhoun was terrified that he might lose his head
and take her.

He didn't want marriage. He didn't want ties. Abby wouldn't understand that. In her world, lovemaking meant marriage. Maybe in his, too, when the woman was a virgin. He didn't like the noose she was tying around his neck, but he hated the thought of never touching her again almost as much.

She was heaven to love. Her mouth was young and sweet and so eager to learn. Her body was nectar. Just the sight of it made him drunk, not to mention the exquisite feel of it between his hands, under his skin.

Abby, he groaned inwardly as he made his way to his own room. He couldn't have her and he couldn't give her up. He didn't know what in hell he was going to do. Maybe when he got back from wherever he wound up he would have reached a decision.

He sat down at the small desk in a corner of his room and wrote Justin a note telling him he was going away for a few days to check on some stockers in Montana. Justin might think it strange, but Abby wouldn't. He wondered how she was going to feel when she woke up and found him gone. He hoped she wouldn't even remember what they'd done in her bed together. But even if she did, that was going to be one private memory. Abby wouldn't share it any more than he would.

Chapter Eight

Abby groaned the minute the light got to her eyes. She had the world's biggest headache, and nausea sat in the pit of her stomach like acid.

She managed to get on her feet and into the bathroom, where she bathed her face with cold water and pressed a cold cloth against her eyes. She remembered drinking whiskey in the study with Justin. Then Calhoun had taken her to bed, and—

Her head jerked up. In the mirror her eyes looked wild, and her paleness had been eclipsed by a scarlet blush. She'd let Calhoun see her. Worse, she'd let him touch her. She swallowed. Well, at least she remembered that he'd stopped before she'd gone to sleep, so nothing unspeakable had happened, thank God. As more of the details of her eagerness came back, she groaned in embarrassment. She'd never be able to look at him again, although what had happened would make the sweetest of memories to tuck in a corner of her mind for solace in her old age. Calhoun would never settle down or fall in love with her. He'd be forever out chasing his blondes. But this was something of him that Abby would always have. A tiny crumb of loving to live on.

Now she understood what had happened that morning in her room. He hadn't been rough on purpose. He'd wanted her. It gave her the oddest feeling of pride that she could have thrown him that far off balance. She was almost sure that no other woman ever had. Looking back, she thought she must have seemed terribly naive to him for reacting that way to an intimate kiss. But at the time his actions had seemed shocking and frightening. For all her dreams about Calhoun, she hadn't realized what the reality of his lovemaking would be like. Now that she knew, it was like an addiction. She wanted more. But could she afford the risk of letting him that close again?

A sob racked her slender body. Well, she had to get herself together. She had to remember her pride. She held her aching head. She had to remember, most of all, to never accept a drink of whiskey from Justin again! Or from anyone, for that matter. Drowning one's sorrows was vastly overrated. She'd tried it, and now she knew that it only brought hangovers, not oblivion.

She put on a gray slacks suit with a blue blouse, left her hair around her shoulders because she was hurting too much to worry with putting it up, and pulled on a pair of sunglasses. Then she felt her way down the staircase and into the dining room.

Justin was sitting at the table with his head in his hands. He was dressed in jeans and a blue checked shirt, and when he looked up, his eyes looked even worse than Abby's.

"Nice touch," he remarked, noticing the dark glasses. "I wish I had mine, but they're out in the car."

"You look like I feel," Abby said as she sat down, very gently, in the chair beside him, grimacing because even that slight jarring made her head feel like bursting. "How are we going to work today?"

"Beats me," Justin replied. "Calhoun's gone."

Her heart skipped a beat, and she was glad she was wearing dark glasses. "Is he?"

"Skipped town. Gone to Montana to look at stockers, or so he said." He fumbled for a cigarette and lit it. "I'm rather disappointed. I had consoled myself all morning with the thought of beating the hell out of him for last night."

"How selfish," Abby muttered as she tried to pour herself a cup of hot coffee from the carafe. "I ought to get in a lick or two of my own."

"I'll sit on him, you can hit him," Justin offered. He sipped black coffee and smoked quietly.

Abby took one swallow of her coffee and sat back, feeling miserable. "Weren't we singing something?" she thought, frowning. "Oh, yes, I remember...." She launched into a few measures of the song. Justin went white, and Maria came running out of the kitchen, beet red, waving her apron.

A tidal wave of Spanish hit Abby between the eyes, delivered in a scolding, furious tone. "For shame, for shame!" Maria wound up breathlessly, crossing herself. "Where you learn such terrible language?"

Abby stared at her blankly. "Justin taught me," she said.

Justin had his face in his hands. Maria launched into him, and he replied in the same tongue, a little sheepishly. Maria shook her head and stormed out of the room.

"What did I say?" Abby asked him, wide-eyed.

He took a slow breath. "You don't want to know," he said finally. "I think you'd better forget the song, Abby, or we're going to be eating burned meals for a month."

"You taught it to me," she pointed out.

He groaned. "I was sauced. That was a drinking song I learned when I was barely out of school from one of the Mexican boys I used to pal around with. I didn't even remember it until last night, and I never should have taught it to you."

"It's all Calhoun's fault," she said.

"I wonder why he started it?" Justin asked, watching her. "He didn't show any signs of wanting to dance until he saw you and Tyler."

Abby shifted restlessly in her chair. "Well, he doesn't want me," she said miserably. "Not on any permanent basis, anyway. He told me last night that he was a bad marriage risk. He likes variety, you see."

"Most men do, until they find themselves so hopelessly enthralled with one woman that they can't even look at anyone else," Justin said tersely, staring at his coffee.

"Is that why you spend all your time alone?" she asked gently, searching his hard, drawn face. "Because your world begins and ends with Shelby?"

He glared at her. "Abby..."

"Sorry." She sipped the coffee. "It's just that I know how it feels now." She traced the pattern of her lipstick on the edge of the cup. "I feel that way about your stupid, blind brother."

The brief anger left his face, and he smiled gently. "I could pretend to be surprised, but I'm not. You're pretty obvious. On the other hand," he added, tilting his head back, "so is he. In all the years Calhoun's been dating, this is the first time I've ever seen him behave as if he were jealous."

Abby bit her lower lip. "He...wants me," she said. She couldn't look at him as she said it.

"Of course," he replied carelessly, smiling at her shocked expression. "Abby, for a man that's a big part of caring about a woman."

"I guess I don't know very much about men," she said with a sigh. "In fact, I don't know anything. Except that I want to live with him all my life, and have children with him, and look after him when he's sick, and keep him company when he's lonely." She bit her lower lip. "So, that being the case, Justin, I think I'd better get out while I still can. Before something happens and Calhoun winds up trapped." She looked up at Justin, her fear plain in her eyes. "You understand, don't you?"

He nodded. "I think you're very wise, Abby. If he cares enough, he'll come after you. If he doesn't...you might save both of you a lot of heartache by heading off trouble." He shrugged. "But I'll miss having you around."

"I'll come back and visit." She sipped more coffee, and as she began to feel a little better she took off her dark glasses. "Can I still have my twenty-first birthday party here?"

"Sure," he said readily.

"You may not approve of my guest list," she added gently.

He took a deep breath. "Tyler Jacobs will be on it, I gather."

"And Shelby." He glared at her, and she smiled hesitantly. "Justin, I can't very well invite him and not her. How would it look?"

"Calhoun might—" He stopped short.

Abby lifted her chin. "I have to stop caring what Calhoun does, and so do you. And if you don't like Calhoun paying attention to Shelby, why not do something about it?'' she added impishly. "You might get her drunk and teach her that terrible song."

He almost smiled. "I did once," he said, his dark eyes softening at the memory. "The night we got engaged." Then he flinched and got up from the table. "I've got to try and go to work. How about you? Can you make it?"

"Of course I can." She stood up, feeling as wobbly as he looked. She glanced at him ruefully. "Shall we flip a coin and see who drives?"

He chuckled. "I think I'd better. I've got more practice at it than you have. Come on."

They muddled through the day, and at the end of it Abby called Mrs. Simpson and asked if she could go ahead and move in later that week. The older woman was delighted and promised to have the room ready. Then, with a heavy heart, Abby began to pack up her things, getting ready to say goodbye to the only home she'd known for the past five and a half years. Worst of all was the realization that once she left it she'd probably never see Calhoun again. Although she hadn't mentioned it to Justin yet, she'd decided to quit her job at the feedlot, too. The prospect of seeing Calhoun every day, knowing that he wanted her but had no love for her, would tear her heart out.

Justin and two of the cowhands helped her get her possessions over to Mrs. Simpson's house. Since the room was furnished, she hadn't tried to take furniture with her, but she had plenty of clothes and records and books to carry. Her stereo and her color television went with her, along with her memorabilia. It was easier to think about living elsewhere with her belongings around. But after having a home of her own, even if she had shared it with the brothers, it was hard to adjust to a small apartment in someone else's house.

She gave notice at the feedlot the very next day. It was hard, but Justin seemed to understand. He didn't say a word. He just smiled.

But Calhoun didn't understand. He came back unexpectedly in the middle of the following week, and when Abby came back from lunch it was to find him sitting on the corner of her desk, looking worn and smoking like a furnace.

She stared at him with eyes that adored him. It had only been a few days. A little over a week. But she'd ached for him. To be without him was like having part of her body cut away, and she didn't know how she was going to manage to hide her feelings from him.

He was wearing a beige suit with a striped shirt, and his blond hair gleamed clean and thick in the light from the office window. He scowled over his cigarette.

She straightened the skirt of her pale blue dress nervously, waiting for him to look up. Then he did, and she saw the darkness of his eyes, the faint shadows under them.

He looked at her for a long time, oblivious to the noise around them, the ringing telephones, the buzz of printers. He looked at her until she felt uncomfortably warm and she blushed.

"You've moved out," he said without preamble.

"Yes," she replied huskily.

"And you've put in your notice here."

She took a deep breath, moving a little closer. He smelled of spice and soap, and she stared unconsciously at his mouth, remembering its exquisite sweetness on her lips. "I . . . I'm going to work for George Brady and his father," she said. "At the insurance office. I'm used to working with forms, so it won't be so unfamiliar."

"Why?" he ground out.

She smoothed her lower lip with her tongue, looking up at him with soft, wounded eyes.

"Here," he muttered, catching her arm. He pulled her into his office and closed the door behind them, frowning down at her. He didn't let go even then. His fingers were warm and firm through her soft sleeve, and their touch made her tingle.

"You know I can't stay in the house anymore," she whispered. "You know why."

"Are you that afraid of me?" he asked quietly.

She shifted restlessly, letting her eyes slide down to his firm jaw. "I'm afraid of what could happen."

"I see."

It was embarrassing to talk to him about it, but he had to know how vulnerable she was. It wasn't anything he hadn't guessed. She studied his patterned red tie carelessly.

"I suppose I sound conceited," she added. "But...but if you—" Her eyes closed. "I'm vulnerable," she whispered. Her lower lip trembled, and she bit it. "Oh, Calhoun, I'm so vulnerable—"

"Don't you think I know?" he said under his breath, and the eyes that met hers were dark with emotion. "Why do you think I left?"

She couldn't look at him anymore. She felt naked. "Well, I'm saving you from any more complications," she said tightly. "I won't be around."

He couldn't seem to breathe. His cigarette had burned out, and it hung in his hand, as dead as he felt. "Is that what you want?"

She straightened. "Tyler's taking me to dinner tonight," she said out of the blue, just to let him see that she wasn't going to try to hang on to him or act lovesick. "He's got a job, too, by the way. He's going to manage old man Regan's ranch for him. In no time at all he'll be settled and able to take on more responsibilities.''

Calhoun's heart felt like lead in his chest. Was she saying what he thought she was? Was she implying that she might marry Tyler?

"You don't love him," he said harshly.

She looked up. "I don't need to," she replied quietly. "Love isn't anything. It's just an emotion that blinds people to reality."

"Abby!" he burst out. "You can't believe that?"

"Look who's talking." She glared at him. "You're the one who said it was for the birds, aren't you? You've never let your emotions get in the way of a good time!"

He took a slow, steadying breath, and his dark eyes searched hers in the static silence that followed. "Maybe that was true a few years ago," he admitted, his voice deep and slow and measured. "I've never had any trouble attracting women, and I had a sizable appetite back then. But I learned that sex by itself has very little flavor, and it didn't take long to realize that most of those women were trading their bodies for what I could give them." He laughed bitterly. "How would that appeal to you, tidbit? Being traded a few kisses and a night in bed for a car or a coat or some expensive jewelry, so that you never could be sure that it was you or your wallet they really wanted?"

She'd never heard him talk like this. He never had, at least not to her. She searched his face, finding cynicism and faint mockery in his smile, in his hard eyes.

"You're very attractive," she replied. "Surely you know that."

His big shoulders rose and fell. "Plenty of men are," he said without conceit. "But I'm rich with it. My money has appeal."

"Only to a certain type of woman," she reminded him. "One who doesn't want ties or emotional liabilities. One with mercenary tendencies who could walk away from you if you lost everything, or if you were sick or old." She smiled gently. "I suppose you liked that, too. You could be independent and still enjoy yourself."

He frowned a little, watching her. "I haven't had a woman since the night you went to the strip show," he said quietly.

She didn't want to hear about his love life. She turned her head. "You had dates...."

"Well, my God, I can date women without seducing them!"

"It's none of my business." She started to reach for the doorknob, but his big, warm hand engulfed hers, sensuously caressing her fingers as he moved closer, drowning her in the clean cologne-rich scent of him.

"Make it your business," he said tautly.

She looked up at him slowly, searchingly. But there was nothing readable in his face or his eyes or even the set of his head. It was like trying to learn from stone. "I don't understand," she said, her voice faltering.

"I don't like bridles," he said shortly. "I don't like the thought of ropes around me, or a ring through my nose. I hate the thought of marriage." He grimaced, but his eyes held hers. "But you're in my blood," he breathed. "And I don't know what to do about it."

"I won't sleep with you," she said with quiet pride. "And yes, I want to." She laughed bitterly. "More than I want to breathe."

"Yes. I knew that when I left." He touched her hair, smoothing it, tracing its length down to her shoulder with a possessive touch that made her tremble. "I know all too well how you feel about me. I suspected it the night you went to that bar with Misty and you whispered that you wished you were blond...." His dark eyes lanced up to her shocked ones. "And the night of the square dance cinched it. I did a lot of thinking while I was away. I managed to put two and two together at last."

She felt as if he'd cut the ground from under her feet. Stark naked. She'd thought her secret was safe, and now it wasn't.

"You don't need to deny it," he added when he saw her expression. "There's no reason to. I'm not going to make fun of you or try to embarrass you. But I told you the night I left how I felt. I'm twelve years older than you. I'm a rounder, and I haven't ever tried abstinence. You're even my ward. If I had any sense I'd let you go and wave you off, laughing. You're a complication I don't want or need."

"Thanks," she said shortly. Her face was flaming. It was embarrassing to have him see right through her, when she hadn't realized how transparent she must be to an experienced man.

"That's what my mind is telling me," he added, laughing with faint mockery as he moved closer. "Now let me show you what my body says—"

She opened her mouth to protest, but his lips covered hers before she could speak. His kiss was warm and slow, and when his hands went to her hips and pulled them against his and he let her feel the blatant hunger of his body, she gave in.

"So soft," he whispered as he brushed his lips over her mouth. "So sweet. I dream about kissing you. I dream about your body and the way you are with me when I make love to you. I want you more than I've ever wanted a woman in my life."

"That's...physical," she protested.

"That's all I can offer you," he replied. His lips moved to her eyelids, closing them with kisses. "Now do you see, Abby? I've never loved anyone. I've never wanted that. All you can have of me is this."

She swallowed. What a bitter, hopeless relationship that would be. She loved him with all her heart, and all he had to offer her was his body.

He tasted the tears before he saw them. His blond head lifted, and he winced at the sight of her drenched blue-gray eyes. "Oh, God, don't," he breathed, wiping the wetness away with his thumbs.

"Let me go, please," she pleaded, pushing at his broad, hard chest.

"You want something I can't give you."

"I know that now," she whispered. She bit on her lower lip to stop it from trembling, and stared at his tie. "I guess I was never cut out to be a mercenary blonde," she said with an attempt at humor, feeling his body stiffen as she made the remark. She looked up then, with drenched eyes that couldn't hide her hunger for his heart. "But I would have loved you so—"

"Abby," he groaned. His mouth silenced her, ardently, roughly. He wrapped her up in his hard arms, kissing her with such force that her head bent back against his arms, and still he didn't stop, couldn't stop. He began to tremble faintly, the hunger a living thing in him, torturously sweet.

But Abby couldn't bear the bitter mockery of a kiss that screamed of pity and desire. She twisted her mouth from under his and buried her face in his jacket, her hands gripping the fabric as she shook with frustrated need.

"I'm young," she whispered after a minute. "I'll get over you."

"Will you?" His voice sounded odd. His big hands were in her hair, holding her head to him. They were just a little unsteady, and the chest under her forehead was shuddering with the force of his heartbeat.

"I'll have to," she said. She took a slow, soft breath. "It was enough that you and Justin have taken care of me all these years," she murmured. "I can't expect anything more from you. I shouldn't have. It was...just proximity, and a huge crush, and...and curiosity, that's all. I didn't mean—"

"Stop it," he said harshly. He pulled her closer, enfolding her in his big arms, holding her, rocking her. "My God, stop it. Am I laughing at you? Am I making fun of how you feel, or trying to shame you for it? I never should have said that to you at the feedlot that day about hating the way you looked at me. I didn't mean it. I wanted you so badly all I could think about was getting you out of the car before I lost my head." He laughed coldly. "And a hell of a lot of good it did. I lost it anyway, that morning in your room, and scared the hell out of you."

"I didn't understand what intimacy was until then," she confessed quietly.

"And the way I was holding you made you all too aware of what I wanted," he added with a faint laugh.

She flushed. "Yes."

He smoothed her hair, noticing the way her body was resting against his, so trustingly, even though he was just as aroused now as he had been the morning he'd mentioned. "And now it doesn't frighten you, does it?" he whispered, tilting her eyes up to his.

She searched his face softly. "No. Nothing about you frightens me or embarrasses me."

He touched her cheek, her mouth, and his powerful legs trembled at the contact with hers. "Not even knowing how badly I want you?"

She shook her head. "Not even that. I—" She dropped her gaze.

"You—" He made her look at him. "Say it," he whispered. "Say the words. I want it all."

She should have denied how she felt. Or run. Something. "I love you," she whispered with faint anguish in her tone.

His eyes caressed her face. "Such big eyes," he breathed. "So soft. So full of secrets." He bent and drew his mouth tenderly against hers. "You're very special to me, Abby. Part of my life. I wish I could give you what you want. I wish I could give you back those words and offer you a future. But that would cheat us both ultimately. Marriage should be a joint commitment, with a foundation of shared love." He sighed bitterly. "I . . . don't know how to love. Justin and I were raised by our father, Abby. Our mother died when I was born. We never had a woman's touch, and until your mother came along, Dad went from one woman to another like a bee to pollen." He toyed with a strand of her hair. "I don't understand commitment, because I never got a good look at it. The only thing I know about love is that it doesn't last. Look at Justin. See what happened to him because it all went wrong."

"At least he took the chance," she said gently. "And it does last. Or didn't you see how Justin and Shelby looked at each other while they were dancing?"

"Is that your idea of a perfect relationship?" he asked with a cold laugh. "A little love, followed by years of hating each other?"

"What's your idea of perfection, Calhoun?" she replied. "A succession of one-night stands and a lonely old age at the end of the road, with no family, no one to love you, nothing to leave behind?"

He scowled down at her. "At least I won't die of a broken heart," he said.

"No," she replied. "You won't." She pushed at his chest, but he wouldn't move. "Let me go, please."

"Why?"

"Because I've got a lot of work to get through."

"And a date with Tyler," he added mockingly.

She glanced up. "Tyler is solid, capable, very masculine and a good marriage risk. He isn't afraid of commitment. He'll make a good husband."

"You aren't marrying Tyler," he said shortly.

"Not unless he asks me," she agreed.

"You aren't marrying him even if he does."

"How do you plan to stop me?" she asked curiously.

"Guess."

She cocked her head, staring up at his stubborn face. "Why bother? You don't want me, except in bed. I want someone who can love me."

He shifted restlessly. "Maybe love can be taught," he said uncomfortably. He stared down at her hands on his chest. "Maybe you could teach me how."

She didn't feel as if her feet were touching the floor anymore. Could she possibly have heard him say that?

"I'm only twenty," she reminded him, "and your ward, and you don't want commitment—"

His mouth covered hers in midsentence, tenderly probing, pushing at it, savoring it. "Kiss me, Abby," he whispered into her mouth.

"I don't want—" she tried to protest.

"Love me, baby," he breathed.

Her arms slid under his jacket and around him. She pressed close, holding him, giving him her mouth with all the wonder and generosity of her love for him. She felt his lips smile against hers, heard his soft breathing, and then he increased the pressure of his mouth and his arms and she went under in a maze of stars.

A long time later, he groaned and his mouth slid to her throat, his arms contracting as he tried to breathe. "That," he whispered roughly, "was a mistake."

She could hardly get her own breath, and she knew it was much harder for him. She smoothed his cool, thick hair, gently soothing him, comforting him as he fought for control.

Her lips pressed light, undemanding kisses to his cheek, his temple, his closed eyelids. He stood very still, giving her that freedom with a sense of wonder at how it felt to be caressed so tenderly.

His eyes opened when she stopped. "That was a nice touch," he whispered, cupping her face in his warm hands. "Have you been talking to Misty again, or did you just think it might calm me down?"

"I read it in a book," she confessed, lowering her flushed face.

"Reading about it and doing it are pretty different, aren't they?" he asked gently.

"Yes." She was still trying to breathe properly. Her fingers toyed with a button on his patterned shirt. He was warm, and she loved the feel and smell and closeness of his body towering over her.

"I've never made love to a virgin," he whispered. His mouth touched her forehead with breathless tenderness. "I'd have to hurt you a little, maybe, at first."

She felt waves of embarrassment wash over her at the vivid pictures in her mind. His big, nude body over hers in bed, covering her, his hands holding her...

"Does it always hurt?" she asked shyly.

"Not for a man," he whispered, lifting his eyes to hers. "Not for you, either, if I could keep my head long enough to arouse you properly."

Her heart was going like a trip hammer. "H... how... would you?"

He kissed the very tip of her nose. "Go out with me and I'll show you."

"On a date?" she whispered.

"Um hmm." He nuzzled his cheek against hers. "Tomorrow night. I'll take you to Houston. We'll wipe out the bad memory of that last time there. We'll dance and walk." He brushed his mouth over her ear. "Remember, I have an apartment there," he said slowly.

She closed her eyes. "No. I won't go to your apartment."

"It isn't the last century," he whispered. "We could be alone. We could make love."

Her face flamed. "No," she repeated.

"Abby..."

She pulled away from him, hating her own inhibitions and his attitude, as well. If he'd loved her, it might have been different. But he didn't. He wanted her. And after that first time, she'd be just like every other woman he'd slept with. She'd be just another one of Calhoun Ballenger's conquests, an ache that he'd satisfied and forgotten. A used toy.

"I have work to do," she said, and tried to smile. "And...I don't think I'll go to Houston with you, thanks all the same."

He realized only then what she thought. He'd made it sound as if he was going to round off the evening with a night in bed. He'd made it sound cheap, and that hadn't been his intention at all. He'd meant that he'd make love

"She mentioned something about it," Abby told him. "She's a nice landlady."

He got in, started the car and pulled out onto the road. "Do you miss the big house?"

"I miss the brothers," she said quietly, fingering her small purse. "It's hard getting used to my own company. There was always something going on at home."

"Can I ask why you moved out?" he persisted, glancing in her direction.

She smiled at him. "No."

His eyebrows arched wickedly. "Don't tell me. Calhoun wrestled you down on the desk and tried to ravish you."

Her face turned scarlet. She cleared her throat. "Don't be absurd."

He chuckled. "It isn't absurd, considering the way he was watching you dance with me that night at the bar."

"He was too busy dancing with Shelby to notice," she murmured. "Justin went home and got drunk afterward," she added, neglecting to mention her own participation.

"Shelby cried all night." He sighed. "Hell of a thing, isn't it, Abby, the way they still care about each other. Six years, and they're as far apart now as they were then."

"And both of them dying inside," she added. She thought about herself and Calhoun and hoped that she wasn't going to end up like Shelby, grieving for a man she could never have. She forced a bright smile. "W[here] are we going?"

"To that new Greek restaurant." h[...] [th]e food is really good. Have you[...]

"No. I'm looking forward to t[...] [Th]e conversation was back on safe t[...] [fr]om the disturbing subject of Calh[...]

to her, very light love, and then he'd take her home. He hadn't meant—!

"Abby, no!" he burst out. "I didn't mean what you think!"

She opened the door. "I have to go." She went out, and he followed her, intent on having things out. But as he reached for her, Justin came in with two businessmen. Abby escaped into the bathroom, shaking, broken inside by hopelessness and rejection. Calhoun not only didn't love her. Now he didn't even respect her.

to bed, very tight lovely evening in a nice fashion. He ...

"Abby, no," he muttered. "I don't know what you ...

She opened the door. "I have to go," she was out, and ...

... As he went into the bathroom shower, "I won't ride ...

...

Chapter Nine

Abby was grateful that business kept Calhoun occupied for the next two days. She could hardly bear the thought of seeing him when he knew so well how she felt about him. And now that he'd reduced their relationship to a strictly physical one, some of the joy had gone out of life for her. She hadn't expected that he'd actually proposition her. But if inviting her to his apartment wasn't a proposition, what was it?

She managed to avoid him when he was in the office that Thursday and Friday, since things stayed hectic. Abby was training a new secretary, and Calhoun seemed reluctant to discuss their private lives around the other woman. She was a year older than Abby, bright and quick-witted. And, unfortunately, already stuck on Calhoun. She had a habit of sighing and batting her long eyelashes every time he passed her desk. Abby was glad Friday was her last day. Having to watch Calhoun with a potential new con-

quest—the girl was blond and very pretty—was bearable.

There was a small farewell party for Abby late afternoon. Justin and Mr. Ayker and the wome worked in the office had taken up a collection to bu a beautiful cardigan in a pale yellow shade. There cake, too, and Justin made a brief speech about how uable she'd been to them and how they hated losing Calhoun wasn't there. Abby left with mingled relief a disappointment. Apparently she wasn't even going to g to say goodbye to him. Well, that suited her. She didn care if he was glad to be rid of her. Not one bit.

She cried all the way to Mrs. Simpson's house becau she didn't care.

Tyler was right on time to take her to dinner. He looke good dressed up. He was wearing a navy blazer with ta slacks, a white shirt and a natty blue striped tie. He look elegant and very masculine. His green eyes danced as Ab came downstairs in a gray crepe dress with a full skirt a a low, crosscut bodice with fabric buttons. Her hair neatly styled, and she looked elegant and sexy.

"You look pretty," he commented with a slow smi

She curtsied. "So do you. Good night, Mrs. S son," she called out. "I'll be in by midnight!"

Mrs. Simpson came to the doorway, grinning. " that no good-looking woman tries to take Ty awa you," she teased.

"No chance of that," he replied carelessly, smilin t Abby. "This dishy lady is enough for me. Goo s. Simpson."

Good night," the older woman replied. "Ha r walked her out to his white Ford, opening "I like your landlady. Her husband use id you know that?"

* * *

Meanwhile, Calhoun was pacing in Justin's study at the house, his dark eyes black, his hands linked behind his back, scowling.

"Will you stop?" Justin muttered as he tried to add figures and ignore the distraction of his restless brother. "Abby's not our responsibility anymore. She's a grown woman."

"I can't help it. Tyler's been around. He's no boy."

"So long as Abby isn't interested in him, none of that will matter."

Calhoun stopped pacing and glared at him. "And what if she is? What if she's throwing herself at him on the rebound?"

Justin laid down his pencil. "Rebound from whom?" he asked, lighting a cigarette.

Calhoun rammed his hands into his pockets and stared out the dark window. "From me. She loves me," he said quietly.

"Yes," Justin replied, and for once his tone was sympathetic.

Calhoun hadn't realized how much Justin knew. He turned, his dark eyes curious, wary. "Did she tell you?"

Justin nodded. He took a draw from the cigarette, watching it instead of his brother. "She's young, but that could be an advantage. She isn't cynical or world-weary or promiscuous like most of your women. And she hasn't got a mercenary bone in her body."

"She'd want marriage," Calhoun replied tautly. "Happily ever after. I don't know if I could adjust to being married."

Justin looked up. "How are you going to take to a life without Abby in it?"

For an instant, Calhoun looked hunted. He stared at the carpet. "And what if it doesn't last?" he replied harshly. "What if it all falls apart?"

Justin blew out a cloud of smoke. "Love lasts. And if you're worried about being faithful to her," he added with a pointed stare, "you may find that fidelity isn't all that difficult."

Calhoun's dark eyes snapped. "Oh, sure. Look at you. Happily ever after. Your perfect relationship fell apart," he said, hurting and striking out because of it. "And how many women have you consoled yourself with in the past six years?"

Justin stared at him for a long moment, his eyes narrow and glittering. He smiled then, faintly. "None."

Calhoun didn't move. He hadn't expected that answer, despite Justin's clamlike attitude toward his private life.

"I had an old-fashioned idea that sex came after marriage with a woman like Shelby," Justin said quietly. "So I held back. After she broke it off, I found that I wasn't capable of wanting anyone else." He turned away, oblivious to Calhoun's shocked expression. "These days I find my consolation in work, Calhoun. I've never wanted anyone but Shelby since the day I met her. God help me, I still don't."

The younger man felt as if he'd been hit by a two-ton weight. His heart ran wild. Justin's words echoed in his mind. He couldn't even feel desire for the ravishing blonde Abby had seen him with in Houston. He hadn't felt it with anyone since that night he'd brought Abby home from the bar and seen her naked to the waist. Was that what he had to look forward to? Would he end up like Justin, imprisoned in desire for the one woman he couldn't have, alone for the rest of his life because he was incapable of wanting another woman?

"I didn't realize," Calhoun said quietly. "I'm sorry."

Justin shrugged. "One of those things," he said philosophically. He sat down behind his desk. "You may not believe in marriage, but you may find that a relationship can tie you up properly without a ring or a legal paper. And I'll throw your own question right back at you," he added, cocking his head at his brother. "How many women have you had since you noticed Abby?"

Calhoun's face grew hard and remote. He glared at Justin, then turned and left the room.

Justin lifted an eyebrow and chuckled softly to himself as he bent over his figures again.

Abby had a nice supper with Tyler, and the moussaka she sampled was delicious, like the elegant baklava they had for dessert and the faintly resinous wine they drank with their meal. But while she was listening to Ty talk about his new job, she was thinking about the empty future, about living without Calhoun. She'd gotten used to listening for his step in the hall late at night as he went to his room, to seeing him across the table, to watching television with him, to being near him at work. Life was so empty now, so cold. She felt as if she'd never know warmth again.

"The only bad part of it is that I'm going to get loaned out," Tyler was telling her resignedly as he drank a demitasse of Greek coffee after dessert. "Old man Regan has a daughter in Arizona who's coping with a dude ranch and two of her nephews for the summer. I'm going to be sent out there to get the place in shape, I gather, while my assistant looks after things here." He grimaced. "I hate dude ranches. And I don't much care for the woman trying to run this one. Apparently she thought she could and talked Regan into it, but she seems to be losing her shirt."

Abby glanced at him. "What's she like, do you know?"

"I don't have a clue. She's probably one of those feminists who think men should have the children and women should earn the living. I'll be damned if she'll tell me how to do my job."

Abby could see the fireworks already, and she smiled behind her cup at the mental image. Tyler was so much like Justin and Calhoun, a reactionary, a holdover from the old West. It would be fascinating to see how he coped with a modern woman.

He took her home minutes later, bending to kiss her cheek at the door of Mrs. Simpson's house. "Thanks for keeping me company," he grinned. "I enjoyed it."

"So did I." She smiled up at him. "You're a nice man. Someday you'll make some lucky girl a nice husband."

"Marriage is for—"

"The birds," she finished for him, sighing. "You and Calhoun ought to do an act together. You've got the chorus down pat."

"No man wants to get married," he told her. "Men get corralled."

"Oh, sure they do," she agreed. "By greedy, grasping, mercenary women."

"I'd marry you in a minute, Abby," he said. He was smiling, but he didn't sound as if he were joking. "So if Calhoun slips the noose, you just throw it my way. I won't even duck."

"You doll." She reached up and kissed his firm jaw. "I'll remember that. Good night, Ty."

"Good night. I'll give you a call next week, okay?"

"Okay."

She waved at him and then used her key and went inside. She climbed the stairs lazily, relaxed from the resinated wine and worn out from her long week of avoiding

It was the longest Saturday of Abby's life. She tried to sleep late, but she couldn't. She went downstairs and had breakfast with Mrs. Simpson and then she went back to her room and forced herself to watch television. Having Saturdays free was still new. At the feedlot, she'd always worked them. Now she had the whole weekend off, and she didn't know what to do with herself.

Time dragged all day long. She went for a ride just to give herself something to do and wound up in town shopping for a new dress to wear on her date with Calhoun.

She came out with a pretty red patterned silk skirt and matching sweater. It brought out her tan and made her look sophisticated. She thought about having her hair cut, but she'd gotten used to its length. She experimented with different hairstyles for an hour, only to brush it out and leave it around her shoulders afterward.

She was dressed and ready at 4:30. She tried to get interested in a book while she waited. Those thirty minutes were going to be agony.

Apparently Calhoun felt the same way, because he showed up twenty minutes early.

She forced herself not to run to let him in, but she was breathless all the same as she looked up into his dark, quiet eyes.

"Hi," she said.

He smiled slowly, gazing approvingly not only at her outfit but at her hairdo as well. "Hi," he replied lazily.

He was wearing a charcoal-gray suit with pale gray tooled leather boots and a pearl Stetson. He looked handsome that Abby could hardly believe he was really her out on a date. It was so new, so unreal.

"Are you sure you want to take me out?" she asked quietly, her eyes troubled as they met his. "You feel sorry for me—?"

Calhoun. So it was a surprise to find the telephone ringing in her room, where she had her own private extension.

She put down her purse and sat on the bed to answer it. "Hello?"

A deep, familiar voice that made her pulse leap said, "Hello."

"Calhoun?" she asked softly.

"I can't sit up and wait for you anymore," he said. "So I thought I'd make sure you got home all right."

"I did."

"Where did you go?"

She lay back on the bed, her head on the pillow. "To the new Greek place."

"Ummm," he murmured, sounding as if he were stretched out on his own bed. "I've been there for business dinners a time or two. Did you try the moussaka? It's delicious."

"Yes, that's what I had, and some of that resinated wine. It's very strong."

He paused. "Did you come straight home?"

She almost smiled at his concern. "Yes, I came straight home. He didn't even try to seduce me."

"I don't remember accusing him of it."

She touched the receiver gently. "Is everything all right at the house?"

"I guess so." There was a pause. "It's lonely."

"It's lonely here, too," she said.

Another pause. "I didn't mean what you thought I did," he said quietly. "I wouldn't take you to bed on a bet. You aren't the kind of woman to be used and thrown aside. I'm ashamed of you for thinking I could treat you like that after all these years."

Her heart ran away. She clutched the receiver closer to her ear. "But you said—"

"I said we could go to the apartment and be alone," he interrupted. "And that we could make love. I meant we could make a few memories and then I'd take you home." He sighed. "I'd probably do it bent double, but I never had any intention of taking advantage of the situation."

"Oh."

"So now that we've cleared that up, how about dinner tomorrow night?" he asked.

She hesitated. "Calhoun, wouldn't it be better if we just didn't see each other again?" she asked quietly, even though it broke her heart to say the words.

"I've looked out for you, watched over you and ordered your life for years," he replied. "Now you're grown, and things have happened between us that I never expected. We can't go back to the relationship we had, and we can't be intimate. But there has to be a way that we can keep each other," he said heavily. "Because I can't quite put you out of my life, Abby. I hate like hell going past your room at night and knowing you aren't in it. I hate watching television alone and sitting at a table alone when Justin has business dinners. I hate the feedlot because there's going to be another woman at your desk."

"She's blond," she reminded him.

"She isn't you," he said shortly. "Are you going to come with me or not?"

"I shouldn't...."

"But you will," he returned.

She sighed, smiling. "Yes."

"I'll pick you up at five."

"Five?"

"We're going to Houston, remember?" he laughed softly.

"Dining and dancing."

"Just that, if it's what you want," he said gent won't even touch you unless you want it."

"That apartment," she asked hesitantly. "Ha you... have you taken a lot of women there?"

He didn't answer her immediately. "While I was away those few days, I moved. I changed apartments," he said. "This one is across town from the one I had. And I've never taken a woman there."

She wondered at the switch, wondered why he'd bothered. Surely it couldn't be to protect her from the memory of his old life, in case one day she did go there with him?

"I see," she murmured.

"No, I don't think you do," he replied, his voice deep and soft. "Not yet, anyway. I'd better let you get to sleep. It's late."

She didn't want him to hang up. She searched for something to say, something to keep him on the line, but her mind was blank.

"You and Justin never came to blows over Shelb guess," she asked then, because it had just occurred t that Justin had threatened to punch Calhoun the m after the square dance.

"Justin and I had a long talk," he replied. "N expect it to do any good. He's too set in his way and he won't let Shelby get near him."

"Maybe someday he'll listen."

"Maybe." He sighed. "Five tomorrow. D

As if she could! She touched the receiver touching him. "Good night."

"Good night, sweetheart," he said so went dead.

She floated into her nightgown an nothing but the endearment, that u word, until sleep finally claimed her

He put his thumb gently against her lips, silencing her.
"I wouldn't take you to the post office out of pity," he replied. "Are you getting cold feet?" he added softly.

She grimaced and stared at his jacket. "Yes."

"I won't hurt you," he said, his voice quiet and deep. "I won't rush you or embarrass you."

She bit her lower lip. "It's just that it's . . . new."

"You'll get used to it." He moved restlessly. "Are you ready to go? I'm early, but I was afraid I'd get held up if I didn't leave while I could."

"Yes. I'll just get my purse."

She got her purse and her black velvet blazer, as well, and let him escort her out to the Jaguar. She got more nervous by the minute, which was absurd considering how long she'd dreamed of going anywhere with him. She could hardly talk, and her hands shook.

"How do you like living with Mrs. Simpson?" Calhoun asked on the way to Houston.

She smiled. "I like it very much." Her fingers toyed with the handle of her purse. "I miss the house sometimes. It's different, living alone."

He glanced at her, his eyes narrow. "Yes." He turned his eyes back to the road, frowning as he pulled a cigarette from the pack in his pocket and stuck it in his mouth. He reached for the car lighter, noticing her curious stare. "I'm nervous," he said without thinking, and then he laughed at his own confession. "That's one for the books, isn't it, Abby, with my reputation?"

She felt warm all over. She smiled, her eyes carefully lowered. "I'm nervous, too," she said.

"I'm not a virgin," he reminded her as he put the lighter against the cigarette.

"Rub it in," she sighed miserably.

"Don't make it sound like leprosy," he teased as he replaced the lighter in its hole beside the ashtray in the dash. "Frankly, I've had my fill of experienced women telling me what to do in bed."

She stared at him, torn between curiosity and jealousy. "Do women really do that?"

His eyebrows arched. He hadn't realized how innocent she really was. "Don't you go to movies?"

"I tried," she recalled. "You never would let me in to see the really good ones."

He whistled softly. "Well, well." His eyes brushed her slender body, then returned to the road. "You'll take a lot of teaching, won't you, tidbit?" he murmured.

She shifted against the seatbelt. "Which would probably bore you to death."

"I don't think so," he mused. "After all—" he lifted the cigarette to his firm lips "—I could customize you."

She gaped at him. "Now I've heard everything!"

"Tell me you'd hate being my lover, Abby," he challenged softly, glancing her way.

She couldn't. But she couldn't quite admit the truth, either. She averted her face, burning with subdued irritation at his soft, predatory laughter.

They went to the same club where she'd seen him with the blonde, but this time was different. There seemed to be no barriers after the first few awkward minutes.

"I've never had rice made like this," Abby remarked as she enjoyed the small portion that came with her roast beef au jus.

"With scallions, you mean? It's unique. Like you," he added, and she looked up to find his eyes steady on her face. Intent. Unblinking.

She gazed back at him. He made her feel giddy when he looked at her that way. Her whole body tingled.

And she wasn't the only one affected. His heart was doing a tango in his chest at the way she was watching him, at her pleasure in his company. He even liked the way he felt himself, nervous and a little uncertain.

They finished their meal, and the dessert that followed it, in silence. As they lingered over a second cup of coffee, he finally spoke. "Want to dance?" he asked softly.

She swallowed. Her eyes traveled slowly over his big body, and just the thought of being pressed against him on the dance floor frightened her. She'd drown in pleasure, and he'd know it. He'd see how helpless she was, how vulnerable.

"I—don't know," she stammered finally, and swallowed the last spoonful of her apple pie.

"Are you really afraid to let me hold you in front of a roomful of people, Abby?" he asked with narrowed eyes.

She lifted her own gaze. "Yes."

"Why?" he persisted.

Well, why not be honest, she thought fatalistically. "Because I want you," she whispered softly, watching his expression become taut. "And because you'll be able to see how much."

Her lack of guile floored him. He couldn't remember a single woman in his past being quite so straightforward about such things. He took a slow breath and reached across the table for her hand, turning it over to trace the palm tenderly with a long forefinger.

"I want you just as badly," he said, watching her hand instead of her eyes. "And you'll be able to feel how much, as well as see it. And I still want to dance with you."

She was so hungry for him that her body was pulsing softly. Even having him know every thought in her mind, being vulnerable, didn't seem to matter anymore. She worshiped him with her eyes, and he looked up and caught her in the act.

"Let's stop pretending," he said quietly. "Come here."

He got up, drawing her with him. He led her to the small dance floor, where a band was playing a lazy tune, and when he pulled her close, she went without a murmur.

"Have you ever noticed how perfectly we fit together?" he asked against her hair as they moved to the music. His hand at her back contracted, bringing her even closer, and the sound of his voice at her ear was deliciously exciting. "I like the way you feel against me."

She could tell that, because his body was beginning to react in a totally masculine way to her softness. She stiffened a little, but the caressing motion of his fingers on hers relaxed her.

"It's all right," he whispered. "I won't hurt you."

"I know that." She closed her eyes, drowning in his nearness, in the music, in the magic.

He shuddered, a barely perceptible stiffening of his big body, and his hand pressed her against him for one wild second. "This is stupid," he said tautly.

"I tried to tell you that," she whispered shakily as her fingers contracted helplessly in his and she looked up into his eyes.

His jaw clenched. Everything she felt was in those worshipful eyes, in her face, in her body so soft against his. His mind whirled; he was floating. She wanted him.

"For God's sake," he groaned. "Let's get out of here."

Her gaze searched his hard, dark face, the eyes that blazed down into hers. He looked impossibly mature and experienced, and she knew she was out of her league. But she wanted to lie in his arms and let him love her. She wanted nothing in life more than to be alone with him now.

"I…" She swallowed. "I don't know how…I've never had to…about precautions, I mean…"

He bent, brushing his hard mouth against her soft one briefly, silencing her. "Are you scared?"

"Yes."

His nose nuzzled hers. "But you'd give yourself to me anyway."

She clenched her teeth. "Yes."

"And hate me afterward."

Her slender shoulders lifted and fell. "No."

Her expression touched him. "Do you love me that much?"

She lowered her eyes, but he tilted her chin up again and there was something new in his look, in his scrutiny of her face.

"Do you love me that much?" he whispered again.

Her eyes closed. "Yes!" she breathed.

His hand slid up her back into her long, thick hair and pulled her forehead against him, pressed it there as they moved to the rhythm of the music. "Precious," he said in a tone that could have burned water. She hardly heard him over the wild beating of her heart. His lips smoothed her forehead, brushing it tenderly.

"I won't make you pregnant," he whispered. "Come with me."

As if she had a choice, she thought shakily as she let him lead her off the dance floor. She'd never been so helpless in her life. All she could do was look at him with helpless need, love radiating from her oval face like fire from an open hearth.

He paid the bill and drew her out into the cold night air, tucked her in the car and drove across town without saying a single word.

Chapter Ten

Calhoun had a penthouse apartment with a private elevator and a view of Houston that was breathtaking. It was furnished in tans and browns, with African carvings and weavings mingled with Western paintings and Indian rugs. It was an apartment that was welcoming despite its purely masculine ambience.

"Do you like it?" Calhoun asked, watching her from the closed door.

"Very much," she said, smiling. "It suits you."

He came into the room, his eyes never leaving her face. "How about something to drink? I can make coffee."

She shifted her eyebrows. "Coffee?"

His dark eyes narrowed. "Just because you got drunk with Justin doesn't mean you can expect the same courtesy here."

She shifted restlessly, her purse clutched against her waist. "Well, I didn't mean to get drunk with Justin."

to her, very light love, and then he'd take her home. He hadn't meant—!

"Abby, no!" he burst out. "I didn't mean what you think!"

She opened the door. "I have to go." She went out, and he followed her, intent on having things out. But as he reached for her, Justin came in with two businessmen. Abby escaped into the bathroom, shaking, broken inside by hopelessness and rejection. Calhoun not only didn't love her. Now he didn't even respect her.

Chapter Nine

Abby was grateful that business kept Calhoun occupied
for the next two days. She could hardly bear the thought
of seeing him when he knew so well how she felt about
him. And now that he'd reduced their relationship to a
strictly physical one, some of the joy had gone out of life
for her. She hadn't expected that he'd actually proposition her. But if inviting her to his apartment wasn't a
proposition, what was it?

She managed to avoid him when he was in the office that
Thursday and Friday, since things stayed hectic. Abby was
training a new secretary, and Calhoun seemed reluctant to
discuss their private lives around the other woman. She
was a year older than Abby, bright and quick-witted. And,
unfortunately, already stuck on Calhoun. She had a habit
of sighing and batting her long eyelashes every time he
passed her desk. Abby was glad Friday was her last day.
Having to watch Calhoun with a potential new con-

quest—the girl was blond and very pretty—was just unbearable.

There was a small farewell party for Abby late Friday afternoon. Justin and Mr. Ayker and the women who worked in the office had taken up a collection to buy her a beautiful cardigan in a pale yellow shade. There was a cake, too, and Justin made a brief speech about how valuable she'd been to them and how they hated losing her. Calhoun wasn't there. Abby left with mingled relief and disappointment. Apparently she wasn't even going to get to say goodbye to him. Well, that suited her. She didn't care if he was glad to be rid of her. Not one bit.

She cried all the way to Mrs. Simpson's house because she didn't care.

Tyler was right on time to take her to dinner. He looked good dressed up. He was wearing a navy blazer with tan slacks, a white shirt and a natty blue striped tie. He looked elegant and very masculine. His green eyes danced as Abby came downstairs in a gray crepe dress with a full skirt and a low, crosscut bodice with fabric buttons. Her hair was neatly styled, and she looked elegant and sexy.

"You look pretty," he commented with a slow smile.

She curtsied. "So do you. Good night, Mrs. Simpson," she called out. "I'll be in by midnight!"

Mrs. Simpson came to the doorway, grinning. "Mind that no good-looking woman tries to take Ty away from you," she teased.

"No chance of that," he replied carelessly, smiling down at Abby. "This dishy lady is enough for me. Good night, Mrs. Simpson."

"Good night," the older woman replied. "Have fun."

Tyler walked her out to his white Ford, opening the door for her. "I like your landlady. Her husband used to work for Dad. Did you know that?"

"She mentioned something about it," Abby told him. "She's a nice landlady."

He got in, started the car and pulled out onto the road. "Do you miss the big house?"

"I miss the brothers," she said quietly, fingering her small purse. "It's hard getting used to my own company. There was always something going on at home."

"Can I ask why you moved out?" he persisted, glancing in her direction.

She smiled at him. "No."

His eyebrows arched wickedly. "Don't tell me. Calhoun wrestled you down on the desk and tried to ravish you."

Her face turned scarlet. She cleared her throat. "Don't be absurd."

He chuckled. "It isn't absurd, considering the way he was watching you dance with me that night at the bar."

"He was too busy dancing with Shelby to notice," she murmured. "Justin went home and got drunk afterward," she added, neglecting to mention her own participation.

"Shelby cried all night." He sighed. "Hell of a thing, isn't it, Abby, the way they still care about each other. Six years, and they're as far apart now as they were then."

"And both of them dying inside," she added. She thought about herself and Calhoun and hoped that she wasn't going to end up like Shelby, grieving for a man she could never have. She forced a bright smile. "Where are we going?"

"To that new Greek restaurant," he told her. "They say the food is really good. Have you ever had Greek food?"

"No. I'm looking forward to trying it," she said, and the conversation was back on safe territory again and away from the disturbing subject of Calhoun.

* * *

Meanwhile, Calhoun was pacing in Justin's study at the house, his dark eyes black, his hands linked behind his back, scowling.

"Will you stop?" Justin muttered as he tried to add figures and ignore the distraction of his restless brother. "Abby's not our responsibility anymore. She's a grown woman."

"I can't help it. Tyler's been around. He's no boy."

"So long as Abby isn't interested in him, none of that will matter."

Calhoun stopped pacing and glared at him. "And what if she is? What if she's throwing herself at him on the rebound?"

Justin laid down his pencil. "Rebound from whom?" he asked, lighting a cigarette.

Calhoun rammed his hands into his pockets and stared out the dark window. "From me. She loves me," he said quietly.

"Yes," Justin replied, and for once his tone was sympathetic.

Calhoun hadn't realized how much Justin knew. He turned, his dark eyes curious, wary. "Did she tell you?"

Justin nodded. He took a draw from the cigarette, watching it instead of his brother. "She's young, but that could be an advantage. She isn't cynical or world-weary or promiscuous like most of your women. And she hasn't got a mercenary bone in her body."

"She'd want marriage," Calhoun replied tautly. "Happily ever after. I don't know if I could adjust to being married."

Justin looked up. "How are you going to take to a life without Abby in it?"

For an instant, Calhoun looked hunted. He stared at the carpet. "And what if it doesn't last?" he replied harshly. "What if it all falls apart?"

Justin blew out a cloud of smoke. "Love lasts. And if you're worried about being faithful to her," he added with a pointed stare, "you may find that fidelity isn't all that difficult."

Calhoun's dark eyes snapped. "Oh, sure. Look at you. Happily ever after. Your perfect relationship fell apart," he said, hurting and striking out because of it. "And how many women have you consoled yourself with in the past six years?"

Justin stared at him for a long moment, his eyes narrow and glittering. He smiled then, faintly. "None."

Calhoun didn't move. He hadn't expected that answer, despite Justin's clamlike attitude toward his private life.

"I had an old-fashioned idea that sex came after marriage with a woman like Shelby," Justin said quietly. "So I held back. After she broke it off, I found that I wasn't capable of wanting anyone else." He turned away, oblivious to Calhoun's shocked expression. "These days I find my consolation in work, Calhoun. I've never wanted anyone but Shelby since the day I met her. God help me, I still don't."

The younger man felt as if he'd been hit by a two-ton weight. His heart ran wild. Justin's words echoed in his mind. He couldn't even feel desire for the ravishing blonde Abby had seen him with in Houston. He hadn't felt it with anyone since that night he'd brought Abby home from the bar and seen her naked to the waist. Was that what he had to look forward to? Would he end up like Justin, imprisoned in desire for the one woman he couldn't have, alone for the rest of his life because he was incapable of wanting another woman?

"I didn't realize," Calhoun said quietly. "I'm sorry."

Justin shrugged. "One of those things," he said philosophically. He sat down behind his desk. "You may not believe in marriage, but you may find that a relationship can tie you up properly without a ring or a legal paper. And I'll throw your own question right back at you," he added, cocking his head at his brother. "How many women have you had since you noticed Abby?"

Calhoun's face grew hard and remote. He glared at Justin, then turned and left the room.

Justin lifted an eyebrow and chuckled softly to himself as he bent over his figures again.

Abby had a nice supper with Tyler, and the moussaka she sampled was delicious, like the elegant baklava they had for dessert and the faintly resinous wine they drank with their meal. But while she was listening to Ty talk about his new job, she was thinking about the empty future, about living without Calhoun. She'd gotten used to listening for his step in the hall late at night as he went to his room, to seeing him across the table, to watching television with him, to being near him at work. Life was so empty now, so cold. She felt as if she'd never know warmth again.

"The only bad part of it is that I'm going to get loaned out," Tyler was telling her resignedly as he drank a demitasse of Greek coffee after dessert. "Old man Regan has a daughter in Arizona who's coping with a dude ranch and two of her nephews for the summer. I'm going to be sent out there to get the place in shape, I gather, while my assistant looks after things here." He grimaced. "I hate dude ranches. And I don't much care for the woman trying to run this one. Apparently she thought she could and talked Regan into it, but she seems to be losing her shirt."

Abby glanced at him. "What's she like, do you know?"

"I don't have a clue. She's probably one of those feminists who think men should have the children and women should earn the living. I'll be damned if she'll tell me how to do my job."

Abby could see the fireworks already, and she smiled behind her cup at the mental image. Tyler was so much like Justin and Calhoun, a reactionary, a holdover from the old West. It would be fascinating to see how he coped with a modern woman.

He took her home minutes later, bending to kiss her cheek at the door of Mrs. Simpson's house. "Thanks for keeping me company," he grinned. "I enjoyed it."

"So did I." She smiled up at him. "You're a nice man. Someday you'll make some lucky girl a nice husband."

"Marriage is for—"

"The birds," she finished for him, sighing. "You and Calhoun ought to do an act together. You've got the chorus down pat."

"No man wants to get married," he told her. "Men get corralled."

"Oh, sure they do," she agreed. "By greedy, grasping, mercenary women."

"I'd marry you in a minute, Abby," he said. He was smiling, but he didn't sound as if he were joking. "So if Calhoun slips the noose, you just throw it my way. I won't even duck."

"You doll." She reached up and kissed his firm jaw. "I'll remember that. Good night, Ty."

"Good night. I'll give you a call next week, okay?"

"Okay."

She waved at him and then used her key and went inside. She climbed the stairs lazily, relaxed from the resinated wine and worn out from her long week of avoiding

Calhoun. So it was a surprise to find the telephone ringing in her room, where she had her own private extension.

She put down her purse and sat on the bed to answer it. "Hello?"

A deep, familiar voice that made her pulse leap said, "Hello."

"Calhoun?" she asked softly.

"I can't sit up and wait for you anymore," he said. "So I thought I'd make sure you got home all right."

"I did."

"Where did you go?"

She lay back on the bed, her head on the pillow. "To the new Greek place."

"Ummm," he murmured, sounding as if he were stretched out on his own bed. "I've been there for business dinners a time or two. Did you try the moussaka? It's delicious."

"Yes, that's what I had, and some of that resinated wine. It's very strong."

He paused. "Did you come straight home?"

She almost smiled at his concern. "Yes, I came straight home. He didn't even try to seduce me."

"I don't remember accusing him of it."

She touched the receiver gently. "Is everything all right at the house?"

"I guess so." There was a pause. "It's lonely."

"It's lonely here, too," she said.

Another pause. "I didn't mean what you thought I did," he said quietly. "I wouldn't take you to bed on a bet. You aren't the kind of woman to be used and thrown aside. I'm ashamed of you for thinking I could treat you like that after all these years."

Her heart ran away. She clutched the receiver closer to her ear. "But you said—"

"I said we could go to the apartment and be alone," he interrupted. "And that we could make love. I meant we could make a few memories and then I'd take you home." He sighed. "I'd probably do it bent double, but I never had any intention of taking advantage of the situation."

"Oh."

"So now that we've cleared that up, how about dinner tomorrow night?" he asked.

She hesitated. "Calhoun, wouldn't it be better if we just didn't see each other again?" she asked quietly, even though it broke her heart to say the words.

"I've looked out for you, watched over you and ordered your life for years," he replied. "Now you're grown, and things have happened between us that I never expected. We can't go back to the relationship we had, and we can't be intimate. But there has to be a way that we can keep each other," he said heavily. "Because I can't quite put you out of my life, Abby. I hate like hell going past your room at night and knowing you aren't in it. I hate watching television alone and sitting at a table alone when Justin has business dinners. I hate the feedlot because there's going to be another woman at your desk."

"She's blond," she reminded him.

"She isn't you," he said shortly. "Are you going to come with me or not?"

"I shouldn't...."

"But you will," he returned.

She sighed, smiling. "Yes."

"I'll pick you up at five."

"Five?"

"We're going to Houston, remember?" he laughed softly.

"Dining and dancing."

"Just that, if it's what you want," he said gently. "I won't even touch you unless you want it."

"That apartment," she asked hesitantly. "Have you . . . have you taken a lot of women there?"

He didn't answer her immediately. "While I was away those few days, I moved. I changed apartments," he said. "This one is across town from the one I had. And I've never taken a woman there."

She wondered at the switch, wondered why he'd bothered. Surely it couldn't be to protect her from the memory of his old life, in case one day she did go there with him?

"I see," she murmured.

"No, I don't think you do," he replied, his voice deep and soft. "Not yet, anyway. I'd better let you get to sleep. It's late."

She didn't want him to hang up. She searched for something to say, something to keep him on the line, but her mind was blank.

"You and Justin never came to blows over Shelby, I guess," she asked then, because it had just occurred to her that Justin had threatened to punch Calhoun the morning after the square dance.

"Justin and I had a long talk," he replied. "Not that I expect it to do any good. He's too set in his ways to bend, and he won't let Shelby get near him."

"Maybe someday he'll listen."

"Maybe." He sighed. "Five tomorrow. Don't forget."

As if she could! She touched the receiver as if she were touching him. "Good night."

"Good night, sweetheart," he said softly, and the line went dead.

She floated into her nightgown and into bed, hearing nothing but the endearment, that unexpected, beautiful word, until sleep finally claimed her.

It was the longest Saturday of Abby's life. She tried to
sleep late, but she couldn't. She went downstairs and had
breakfast with Mrs. Simpson and then she went back to
her room and forced herself to watch television. Having
Saturdays free was still new. At the feedlot, she'd always
worked them. Now she had the whole weekend off, and
she didn't know what to do with herself.

Time dragged all day long. She went for a ride just to
give herself something to do and wound up in town shopping for a new dress to wear on her date with Calhoun.

She came out with a pretty red patterned silk skirt and
matching sweater. It brought out her tan and made her
look sophisticated. She thought about having her hair cut,
but she'd gotten used to its length. She experimented with
different hairstyles for an hour, only to brush it out and
leave it around her shoulders afterward.

She was dressed and ready at 4:30. She tried to get interested in a book while she waited. Those thirty minutes
were going to be agony.

Apparently Calhoun felt the same way, because he
showed up twenty minutes early.

She forced herself not to run to let him in, but she was
breathless all the same as she looked up into his dark, quiet
eyes.

"Hi," she said.

He smiled slowly, gazing approvingly not only at her
outfit but at her hairdo as well. "Hi," he replied lazily.

He was wearing a charcoal-gray suit with pale gray
handtooled leather boots and a pearl Stetson. He looked
so handsome that Abby could hardly believe he was really
taking her out on a date. It was so new, so unreal.

"Are you sure you want to take me out?" she asked
unexpectedly, her eyes troubled as they met his. "You
don't feel sorry for me—?"

He put his thumb gently against her lips, silencing her. "I wouldn't take you to the post office out of pity," he replied. "Are you getting cold feet?" he added softly.

She grimaced and stared at his jacket. "Yes."

"I won't hurt you," he said, his voice quiet and deep. "I won't rush you or embarrass you."

She bit her lower lip. "It's just that it's . . . new."

"You'll get used to it." He moved restlessly. "Are you ready to go? I'm early, but I was afraid I'd get held up if I didn't leave while I could."

"Yes. I'll just get my purse."

She got her purse and her black velvet blazer, as well, and let him escort her out to the Jaguar. She got more nervous by the minute, which was absurd considering how long she'd dreamed of going anywhere with him. She could hardly talk, and her hands shook.

"How do you like living with Mrs. Simpson?" Calhoun asked on the way to Houston.

She smiled. "I like it very much." Her fingers toyed with the handle of her purse. "I miss the house sometimes. It's different, living alone."

He glanced at her, his eyes narrow. "Yes." He turned his eyes back to the road, frowning as he pulled a cigarette from the pack in his pocket and stuck it in his mouth. He reached for the car lighter, noticing her curious stare. "I'm nervous," he said without thinking, and then he laughed at his own confession. "That's one for the books, isn't it, Abby, with my reputation?"

She felt warm all over. She smiled, her eyes carefully lowered. "I'm nervous, too," she said.

"I'm not a virgin," he reminded her as he put the lighter against the cigarette.

"Rub it in," she sighed miserably.

"Don't make it sound like leprosy," he teased as he replaced the lighter in its hole beside the ashtray in the dash. "Frankly, I've had my fill of experienced women telling me what to do in bed."

She stared at him, torn between curiosity and jealousy. "Do women really do that?"

His eyebrows arched. He hadn't realized how innocent she really was. "Don't you go to movies?"

"I tried," she recalled. "You never would let me in to see the really good ones."

He whistled softly. "Well, well." His eyes brushed her slender body, then returned to the road. "You'll take a lot of teaching, won't you, tidbit?" he murmured.

She shifted against the seatbelt. "Which would probably bore you to death."

"I don't think so," he mused. "After all—" he lifted the cigarette to his firm lips "—I could customize you."

She gaped at him. "Now I've heard everything!"

"Tell me you'd hate being my lover, Abby," he challenged softly, glancing her way.

She couldn't. But she couldn't quite admit the truth, either. She averted her face, burning with subdued irritation at his soft, predatory laughter.

They went to the same club where she'd seen him with the blonde, but this time was different. There seemed to be no barriers after the first few awkward minutes.

"I've never had rice made like this," Abby remarked as she enjoyed the small portion that came with her roast beef au jus.

"With scallions, you mean? It's unique. Like you," he added, and she looked up to find his eyes steady on her face. Intent. Unblinking.

She gazed back at him. He made her feel giddy when he looked at her that way. Her whole body tingled.

And she wasn't the only one affected. His heart was doing a tango in his chest at the way she was watching him, at her pleasure in his company. He even liked the way he felt himself, nervous and a little uncertain.

They finished their meal, and the dessert that followed it, in silence. As they lingered over a second cup of coffee, he finally spoke. "Want to dance?" he asked softly.

She swallowed. Her eyes traveled slowly over his big body, and just the thought of being pressed against him on the dance floor frightened her. She'd drown in pleasure, and he'd know it. He'd see how helpless she was, how vulnerable.

"I—don't know," she stammered finally, and swallowed the last spoonful of her apple pie.

"Are you really afraid to let me hold you in front of a roomful of people, Abby?" he asked with narrowed eyes.

She lifted her own gaze. "Yes."

"Why?" he persisted.

Well, why not be honest, she thought fatalistically. "Because I want you," she whispered softly, watching his expression become taut. "And because you'll be able to see how much."

Her lack of guile floored him. He couldn't remember a single woman in his past being quite so straightforward about such things. He took a slow breath and reached across the table for her hand, turning it over to trace the palm tenderly with a long forefinger.

"I want you just as badly," he said, watching her hand instead of her eyes. "And you'll be able to feel how much, as well as see it. And I still want to dance with you."

She was so hungry for him that her body was pulsing softly. Even having him know every thought in her mind, being vulnerable, didn't seem to matter anymore. She worshiped him with her eyes, and he looked up and caught her in the act.

"Let's stop pretending," he said quietly. "Come here."

He got up, drawing her with him. He led her to the small dance floor, where a band was playing a lazy tune, and when he pulled her close, she went without a murmur.

"Have you ever noticed how perfectly we fit together?" he asked against her hair as they moved to the music. His hand at her back contracted, bringing her even closer, and the sound of his voice at her ear was deliciously exciting. "I like the way you feel against me."

She could tell that, because his body was beginning to react in a totally masculine way to her softness. She stiffened a little, but the caressing motion of his fingers on hers relaxed her.

"It's all right," he whispered. "I won't hurt you."

"I know that." She closed her eyes, drowning in his nearness, in the music, in the magic.

He shuddered, a barely perceptible stiffening of his big body, and his hand pressed her against him for one wild second. "This is stupid," he said tautly.

"I tried to tell you that," she whispered shakily as her fingers contracted helplessly in his and she looked up into his eyes.

His jaw clenched. Everything she felt was in those worshipful eyes, in her face, in her body so soft against his. His mind whirled; he was floating. She wanted him.

"For God's sake," he groaned. "Let's get out of here."

Her gaze searched his hard, dark face, the eyes that blazed down into hers. He looked impossibly mature and experienced, and she knew she was out of her league. But she wanted to lie in his arms and let him love her. She wanted nothing in life more than to be alone with him now.

"I..." She swallowed. "I don't know how...I've never had to...about precautions, I mean..."

He bent, brushing his hard mouth against her soft one briefly, silencing her. "Are you scared?"

"Yes."

His nose nuzzled hers. "But you'd give yourself to me anyway."

She clenched her teeth. "Yes."

"And hate me afterward."

Her slender shoulders lifted and fell. "No."

Her expression touched him. "Do you love me that much?"

She lowered her eyes, but he tilted her chin up again and there was something new in his look, in his scrutiny of her face.

"Do you love me that much?" he whispered again.

Her eyes closed. "Yes!" she breathed.

His hand slid up her back into her long, thick hair and pulled her forehead against him, pressed it there as they moved to the rhythm of the music. "Precious," he said in a tone that could have burned water. She hardly heard him over the wild beating of her heart. His lips smoothed her forehead, brushing it tenderly.

"I won't make you pregnant," he whispered. "Come with me."

As if she had a choice, she thought shakily as she let him lead her off the dance floor. She'd never been so helpless in her life. All she could do was look at him with helpless need, love radiating from her oval face like fire from an open hearth.

He paid the bill and drew her out into the cold night air, tucked her in the car and drove across town without saying a single word.

Chapter Ten

Calhoun had a penthouse apartment with a private elevator and a view of Houston that was breathtaking. It was furnished in tans and browns, with African carvings and weavings mingled with Western paintings and Indian rugs. It was an apartment that was welcoming despite its purely masculine ambience.

"Do you like it?" Calhoun asked, watching her from the closed door.

"Very much," she said, smiling. "It suits you."

He came into the room, his eyes never leaving her face. "How about something to drink? I can make coffee."

She shifted her eyebrows. "Coffee?"

His dark eyes narrowed. "Just because you got drunk with Justin doesn't mean you can expect the same courtesy here."

She shifted restlessly, her purse clutched against her waist. "Well, I didn't mean to get drunk with Justin."

unless I tell you how." He moved down then, drawing his open mouth lazily over her lips until he managed to get between them. "That's it," he whispered. "Just relax."

He was doing the most sensuous things to her mouth. It amazed her, the sensations he aroused so effortlessly. Her breath was already coming in gasps, and she felt her body tautening as what he did to her mouth began to affect the entire length of her.

"God, you're sweet to kiss," he whispered into her parted lips. "Come here, Abby."

He abruptly rolled over onto his back and turned her with him so that she was above him, looking down into his dark, dancing eyes.

"That's better," he murmured. "Do you feel less

"I'll bet the pair of you could hardly walk the next morning."

"We sort of leaned on each other," she confessed. She searched his hard face. "He was afraid you were going to use your experience to take Shelby away from him. He didn't come right out and say so, but it was implied."

"As if I could hurt him like that," he said curtly. His dark eyes wandered quietly over her face, tracing every soft line. "Did you care that I danced with her?"

She turned toward the window. "I like the scenery," she said, trying to change the subject, trying to breathe normally.

"Yes, I like it, too," he said finally. "I wanted something with a view of the city. And I have to spend a lot of time here on business, so that makes it a good investment."

She heard his steps coming closer, and she could feel his warmth at her back, smell the clean, spicy scent of him.

Her pulse jumped as his lean hands caught her waist and pulled her against his big body. She heard his breath and felt it in her hair as he wrapped her up in his arms from behind, rocking her lazily as they watched the city lights spread out below them.

He inhaled the floral scent of her body and the clean, shampooed softness of her hair all at the same time. He bent his head and brushed his mouth against her neck through her silky hair.

"I miss you," he said softly. "You haunt me."

"You'll get used to not having me around," she said sadly. "After all, up until five and a half years ago, you and Justin had the house all to yourselves."

"And then you moved in," he mused, linking his lean hands in front of her. "We got used to running feet and laughter, to music in the living room and movies on television and teenage girls in and out and hot-rodding young men speeding up the driveway."

"You were both very tolerant for old bachelors," she said. "Looking back, I guess I really cramped your style."

He stiffened a little, because it was true. She had at first. But now it hurt to look back, to remember his furtive affairs, his hidden amours. It hurt to think that there'd ever been a woman in his arms except Abby.

"A woman in the dark is just a body," he said softly. "And I never gave my heart, Abby."

"Do you have one?" she asked.

He turned her gently, putting her hand on his chest, over his white silk shirt, against hard, warm muscle and thick hair. "Feel it beat," he whispered.

"That isn't what I meant."

"I know." He looked down at her hand, feeling his body tauten at the light touch. He moved her fingers across his chest to a hard male nipple and held her palm there, letting her feel.

She glanced up at him, her blue-gray eyes wide and searching as he stroked her hand against the hardness.

"That happens to women," she whispered.

"And to men." He gently pulled her closer, his hands moving into her hair as he bent his head. "Unbutton my shirt. I'm going to show you how to touch me."

Her heartbeat sounded and felt unnaturally loud in the stillness of the room. But she didn't protest. Her fingers fumbled with the buttons, and eventually she had the shirt out of his slacks and away from his broad, bronzed chest with its thick covering of hair.

He smiled at her faint embarrassment. "Here. Like this." He pulled her hands against him in long, sensual strokes and watched their slender gracefulness as he drew

them down to the wide belt around his slender hips. But when he tried to move them past it, she froze.

He searched her soft eyes quietly, sensing the turmoil in her heart. "You're very innocent," he said, his voice unusually deep and slow. "You've never touched a man intimately, have you?"

She traced a tiny pattern on his chest. "I've never done anything intimate with a man in my life, except with you."

He was incredibly pleased to hear that. His chin lifted. "I need more than a few chaste kisses," he said softly.

She flushed, staring at the heavy rise and fall of his chest. "I'm sorry."

He bent abruptly and lifted her, cradling her against him as he turned and walked down the hall with her.

He went through an open d

them down to the wide belt around his slender hips. But when he tried to move them past it, she froze.

He searched her soft eyes quietly, sensing the turmoil in her heart. "You're very innocent," he said, his voice unusually deep and slow. "You've never touched a man intimately, have you?"

She traced a tiny pattern on his chest. "I've never done anything intimate with a man in my life, except with you."

He was incredibly pleased to hear that. His chin lifted. "I need more than a few chaste kisses," he said softly.

She flushed, staring at the heavy rise and fall of his chest. "I'm sorry."

He bent abruptly and lifted her, cradling her against him as he turned and walked down the hall with her.

He went through an open door, and she turned her head to find a huge king-size bed with a cream-and-chocolate quilted cover over it in a darkened room.

"Calhoun, no," she whispered, raising her eyes to his in the dimness of the heavily curtained room.

"I won't even undress you," he breathed, brushing her lips with his. "We're going to make a little love, and then I'll take you home. There won't be a risk. I give you my word on it."

"But you want me," she whispered in protest when he slid her onto the coverlet and stretched out beside her, his body so close that she could feel how aroused he was.

"Of course I want you," he said gently, smiling as he lay poised above her, his lean hands smoothing back her long, soft hair. "But there's no risk involved, as long as you don't do anything to knock me off balance."

She searched his dark face, loving every inch of it. "How could I do that?" she whispered.

"By doing anything I don't invite," he murmured deeply. "Don't touch me, or move against me, or kiss me unless I tell you how." He moved down then, drawing his open mouth lazily over her lips until he managed to get between them. "That's it," he whispered. "Just relax."

He was doing the most sensuous things to her mouth. It amazed her, the sensations he aroused so effortlessly. Her breath was already coming in gasps, and she felt her body tautening as what he did to her mouth began to affect the entire length of her.

"God, you're sweet to kiss," he whispered into her parted lips. "Come here, Abby."

He abruptly rolled over onto his back and turned her with him so that she was above him, looking down into his dark, dancing eyes.

"That's better," he murmured. "Do you feel less threatened on top?"

She colored faintly, and he laughed. Then he drew her mouth down over his and opened it, and the laughter stopped.

She felt his hands moving her, lifting her. She was beside him, then over him, and he had her hips, bringing them down completely over his.

"Don't do that," he whispered when he felt her tautness. "Just lie still and let me feel your body over mine."

She felt shaky. She trembled as his tongue began to probe gently around her lips and past them, teasing its way into the sweet darkness of her mouth.

She caught her breath, and he heard it. His dark eyes opened, looking up at her.

"They call it a soul kiss," he said softly. "It's intimate and wildly arousing and very, very suggestive. Let me kiss you that way."

She felt her legs tremble where they touched his. "You . . . you're already wildly aroused," she whispered unsteadily.

"I'm going to make you that way, too," he murmured. He turned her slowly so that she was on her back. His long, powerful leg insinuated itself between hers.

She stiffened as she felt his big, muscular body spread over hers, pushing her down into the mattress. His masculinity was blatant now. The intimacy was shocking, and the sensations it caused were a little frightening.

He saw her fear, and his hands slid into her hair, caressing as he let his weight down on her slender body, his elbows catching a little of it as he moved.

"I won't hurt you," he said softly. "Lie very still for me, Abby. I want to show you what passion is."

"I already know...oh!" She clenched her teeth. Her nails bit into the fine fabric of his jacket, and her eyes widened in shock when he moved against her. She felt him in a way that turned her face blood red with embarrassed knowledge, and a tiny cry forced its way out of her throat.

His mouth covered hers. His tongue teased, probed, withdrew, probed again and began a taunting invasion that was every bit as intimate as his huge, softly moving body on hers. She moaned. She grasped him. She bit at his firm, chiseled lower lip. Her tongue shyly grasped him. She bit at his firm, chiseled lower lip. Her tongue shyly encountered his and began to fence with it. She began to shudder, and so did he, and just when she was going under for the third time he slid away from her and gathered her against his side, holding her cheek to his shoulder while the trembling grew.

"Calhoun." Her voice broke.

"It's all right," he whispered. "I'll make it bearable."

His big hands found her jacket and eased it off. He unfastened the sweater where it buttoned over one shoulder, and levered it up lazily, unfastening the hooks of her lacy bra and tugging the whole of her upper covering over her head and moved it aside.

She started to cover herself, but his mouth was suddenly on her breasts, and what he did to them was too sweet, too addictive to protest.

She gave in, arching toward his mouth, drowning in his ardor. He knew exactly what to do, how to arouse her to a fever pitch. She let him, welcomed him, her body fluid in his hands, her voice softly inciting him.

He sat up for just a minute, long enough to strip off his jacket and shirt. Then he was poised over her, vibrantly male with his hair-roughened chest bare and muscular, his eyes glittering with desire as they caressed her own bareness.

"I can't stop you," she whispered shakily, tears stinging her eyes as she watched him come to her. "I don't want to stop you."

"I want to hold you like this," he whispered, levering his chest over her bare, aroused breasts, rubbing softly against her body. "Isn't it sweet, Abby? Skin against skin. Breast to breast in the darkness, mouth to aching mouth... Kiss me, sweetheart. Open your mouth and kiss me until you can't bear the wanting any longer."

She did. Her arms held him, trembling, her body welcomed the crush of his. The mattress moved under them and the air washed over her body while his mouth fed on hers, seduced hers, intimate and ardent and tender.

His mouth lifted seconds later, and he looked into her eyes in the faint light from the hall. "I don't think I can stop," he whispered, his voice oddly husky.

"I don't want you to stop," she moaned. "Oh, Calhoun, please, please... please!"

His mouth slid down to her breast, taking it inside. His hand went to the fastening of her skirt and loosened it. His lean fingers slid onto the soft skin of her belly, pressing there, savoring the soft skin.

"The . . . risk," she whispered shakily.

"Of a child?" he murmured against her breasts. He nuzzled her soft skin with his cheek, his eyes closed, the scent of her all around him, in his blood. His hand slid under her hips, lifting them hungrily into the hard contours of his own, holding her there with undisguised passion. "For the first time in my life, I'm not afraid of the consequences, Abby."

His mouth was over hers again, and she wasn't quite sure she'd heard him. Her mind was on fire, her body was burning. Her legs moved helplessly against his. She wanted him. She wanted all of him. She moaned as she tried to get closer, to absorb him, possess him. She felt savage and wild. She wanted to join with him, to be a part of the massive, muscular body that was slowly driving her mad.

Her arms reached up, her fingers tangled in his thick blond hair as she moved her hips sensually under his in movements that made him cry out.

"Abby—!" he bit off, shuddering.

"I love you," she sobbed.

His mouth was over hers, and he began to remove her skirt with unsteady hands. It was going to happen. Here, now, she was going to know him in every way there was.

But in the middle of her feverish pleas, there was the sudden, unexpected pealing of the doorbell.

He paused, his body racked by shudders. "Oh, my God," he said, choking.

"Don't answer it," she whispered tearfully.

He lifted his head, pushing back sweaty hair. He was gasping for breath, his body vibrating with frustrated need, driving urgency. He shuddered. "I can't get up," he whispered with a hollow laugh. He pushed away from her and lay on his stomach, groaning, his lean hands speared into the pillow, crushing it.

Abby didn't know what to do. She knew better than to touch him. She lay there, not moving, sanity coming back slowly. She concentrated on trying to breathe while her heartbeat shook her.

The doorbell kept ringing. After a moment, Calhoun managed to sit up. He looked a little foggy as he got to his feet, but he was breathing almost normally.

"Are you all right?" she whispered shyly.

"I'm all right," he said softly. "Are you?"

At least he wasn't angry. "Yes," she replied, her tone equally soft.

He took a steadying breath and got to the door. Unexpectedly he switched on the light and turned to look at her, his eyes narrow, full of possession and something violent, dark, hungry.

Her breasts were mauve and peach, exquisitely formed, taut with arousal. Where he'd pulled her skirt down, he could see the graceful curve of her hips below her small waist.

"God, I could die looking at you," he said huskily. "I've never seen a woman so perfect."

She flushed, but the intensity of his delight in her was overwhelming. She sat up slowly, watching his gaze move to the firm thrust of her breasts, and she felt herself go hot with pride and pleasure.

He looked up then, catching the light in her eyes. "You belong to me now," he said. "As surely as if I hadn't stopped. We'll work out the details later, but there won't be anyone else for me from this night on. I'll never touch another woman until I die." And with that quiet, terse statement, he turned and left the room.

Abby wasn't sure she hadn't dreamed the whole thing. She got into her clothes in a daze, shaking with pent-up emotion. She wanted to cry and scream and laugh and dance.

He was talking to someone. His voice was curt and almost angry. Frowning, Abby stepped out into the hall, her mouth swollen, her hair in tangles, her silk skirt hopelessly wrinkled. As she went into the living room, she recognized Calhoun's guest. It was the blonde from the restaurant, the one he'd taken out the night Abby had gone to dinner with Justin.

"So that's why you didn't have time for me," the older woman said when she saw Abby. "My God, she's barely out of school!"

"Abby, go back into the bedroom," Calhoun said.

"Yes, Abby, go and hide," the blonde added viciously, although tears were visible in her big eyes.

But Abby didn't. She went quietly to Calhoun and slid her hand trustingly into his.

"I love him with all my heart," Abby told the other woman. "I guess you probably do, too, and I'm sorry. But I'd rather die than lose him."

The blonde looked at her for a long moment, and then at Calhoun. "It would have served you right if she hated you, as many hearts as you've broken," she cried, her lower lip trembling. "But that won't ever happen, any more than you'll ever love any one of us. Not even she can reach that stone you call a heart!" She turned to Abby. "You'll never have all of him." She laughed bitterly. "All he can give you is his body, and he'll soon get tired of yours and go off to conquer new worlds. Men like him don't settle down, honey, so if you're looking for happy endings, you'd better run like hell."

She gave Calhoun a final, bitter glance and was gone as quickly as she'd arrived.

Calhoun closed the door, his face hard, unyielding.

"I'm sorry you had to hear that," he said quietly.

"So am I." Abby searched his eyes sadly, wondering if the other woman was right about his lack of feeling. Perhaps she should run. But how could she, when she loved him?

His eyes narrowed as he saw the indecision and fear in hers. "You don't trust me, do you?" he asked. "You think she might be right, that you can't have a future with me."

"You said yourself that you didn't want to be tied," she replied. "I understand." She dropped her eyes. "Maybe I'm too young for marriage anyway. I've never been out on my own at all. I've hardly even dated. Maybe what I feel for you is just a crush and my first taste of desire."

She didn't really mean what she'd just told him, but it gave him an out if he wanted one. He'd wanted her in the bedroom, and perhaps he'd said things he didn't really mean. She didn't want him to feel obligated just because they'd almost gone too far.

But Calhoun didn't realize that she was trying to save him from himself. He took her words at face value and felt their impact as if they were bullets. She was telling him that she wasn't sure she loved him, and at the worst possible moment. When she'd put her slender hand so trustingly in his, he'd known for the first time what he felt for her. His feelings went deeper than lust, and they wouldn't fade. But now he was afraid to tell her, to put the emotion into words. She was admitting that she might have mistaken infatuation and desire for something lasting. She was young, all right, and inexperienced. He might be taking advantage of a natural step in her progression to womanhood. What if he risked his heart and she kicked it aside when she got through this phase? She was young, and she'd bounce back. But Calhoun had never loved before, and the thought of being rejected terrified him.

He stared down at her with bitter realization darkening his eyes to black. He'd fallen into the trap that he'd swore he'd never be taken by. Now here they were, almost lovers, and she was telling him that it was all a mistake. He felt as if she'd hit him in the chest with an ax.

"Would you take me home, please?" she asked without looking at him.

He straightened. "Of course."

He turned toward the bedroom, and she sat on the sofa, reaching for the purse she'd tossed there when they'd first arrived. She sat twisting and turning it, listening to his quick, sharp movements in the bedroom while he dressed. Her eyes closed in mingled shame and embarrassment. It had only just occurred to her how many liberties she'd allowed him, how close they'd come to making love completely. She hadn't had the presence of mind to think of stopping, and neither had he. If that woman hadn't interrupted them—

Her face went hot. He'd been undressing her. He wouldn't have stopped at all, he hadn't had any intention of denying himself. And afterward, how would it have been? She'd have been eaten up by guilt and sorrow, and he'd have felt obligated to marry her because she'd been a virgin. He'd have been well and truly trapped.

She didn't take seriously anything Calhoun had said in the semidarkness of his bedroom, because men didn't think when they were engulfed by passion. Even though she was innocent, she knew that much. He'd wanted her for a long time, and tonight had been his one chance to get her into bed. He'd almost taken her. He knew she loved

him, and it didn't even seem to bother him that he was
taking advantage of something she couldn't help.

Calhoun came into the living room minutes later, pale
and strained but neatly dressed. He'd even combed his
thick blond hair. After one quick glance, she didn't look
at him again. She stood up.

He opened the door for her, noticing her unnatural
stiffness. "I don't know what to say, Abby," he said quietly. "I don't know how she traced me here."

"It doesn't matter," she replied, looking only as high as
his chin. "It would be unrealistic to expect that we'd never
run across any of your discarded lovers."

His dark eyes flashed fire. He reached beside her and
slammed the door before she could get out, forcing her
shocked eyes up to his angry ones.

"And that's what you think you would have been if she
hadn't interrupted us?" he asked coldly.

She ground her teeth together to keep from breaking
down. "You weren't going to stop," she said.

"I *couldn't* stop," he corrected. "Any more than you
could. If you want to know, it was a first. I've always been
able to pull back before."

"Should I be flattered?" she asked on a trembling
laugh. "Because I'm not. Bodies are cheap."

"Yours isn't," he returned. "Yours is young and sweet
and exquisitely formed. Innocent, when I've never had
innocence in my life. I might have been half out of my
head, but I'd have managed to make you want me back
and I wouldn't have hurt you."

"And after you were through?" she probed, lifting her
pained eyes.

He touched her swollen lips with a cool forefinger.
"That would have taken all night," he said softly. "And

by then you wouldn't have had any doubts left about where we stood with each other. I'd have made sure of it."

She flushed. "I'd have been another conquest...."

He drew her against him, sighing heavily as he smoothed her long, dark hair and felt her body shake with soft sobs.

"It's just frustration, sweetheart," he whispered at the top of her head. "You wanted me and I wanted you, and neither of us had fulfillment, that's all. It passes."

Her curled fingers pressed against him while tears ran down her pale cheeks. "I hate you," she cried.

He only smiled, because he understood. He kissed her hair gently. She was so very young. Too young, probably. He drew in a slow, sad breath and wondered how he was going to live without her.

"You've got to see Maria about your birthday party," he said after a few minutes. "She's going to hire a caterer. And you'll have to provide a guest list for us. I can have one of the women at the office send out the invitations."

She drew back, sniffing, and he pulled out a handkerchief and mopped her face. "You don't have to do that," she mumbled.

"We want to." He touched the handkerchief to her red eyes. "I won't come near you until then, Abby," he added to her surprise. His dark gaze was quiet and unblinking, and it did wild things to her pulse. "I won't call you, or take you out, or see you until then."

"Because of tonight?" she asked with what dignity she still possessed.

"In a way." He put the handkerchief away and searched her face. "You're afraid of giving in to me, aren't you?"

She moved restlessly.

"Aren't you?" he persisted.

She bit her lower lip. "Yes."

"Why?"

"I won't have you forced into a marriage you don't want," she said warily. "Calhoun, you aren't a marrying man. You even told me so."

He brushed his mouth against hers, and he nuzzled her nose with his, teasing her lips, playing with her mouth.

"Abby, I told you not so long ago that my playboy days were over, and I meant it," he said softly. "I haven't lived like a recluse, but in the past few years, I've settled down. And if you want the truth," he added, resting his forehead on hers, "I haven't thought of any other woman since the night I found you bare-breasted on your bed, little one. You've been in my bed every night since then, a vision that haunts me from dawn to dusk."

Her heart jumped straight up. He'd never lied to her. He wasn't doing it now, she knew.

"Me?" she whispered.

He smiled gently. "You." He brushed her mouth lazily with his. "And if you'd given yourself to me in my bedroom a few minutes ago," he whispered, "we'd have been on our way to get a marriage license by morning."

"Because of your conscience?" she asked.

He chuckled softly. "Because of my body," he breathed. "Lovemaking is addictive. The way I want you, little Abby, I'd have you pregnant by the end of the first week."

She flushed wildly and hid her face from him, feeling his chest shake with laughter.

"Did you hear what I said," he whispered, "when you warned me about the risk?"

Her heart ran wild. "Yes."

His mouth bit at hers. "Didn't it seem an odd response for a philandering playboy to make?"

"You wanted me—"

"God, I still do!" he breathed. "But a man interested in nothing but a good time is sure as hell not interested in making babies, Abby."

"Stop that!" she whispered.

He smiled against her mouth, delighting in her innocence, in her reaction. He wasn't worried anymore. Now, at last, he knew why she'd said what she had in front of his visitor. She'd been offering him a way out. But he didn't want one. He wanted Abby. He wanted a future.

"I'll take you home now," he said gently. "And you can have until your birthday to think about me and miss me and want me. And then, if you can't stand it anymore, I'll give you a birthday present you'll never forget."

"What?" she asked breathlessly.

He covered her open mouth with his own. "Me," he breathed into it.

Chapter Eleven

Abby pondered that odd remark for the next few lonely weeks. What had Calhoun meant, that they were going to become lovers? Or had he meant something quite different?

He'd taken her home after that last, passionate kiss, and he hadn't made another single personal remark to her. He'd talked about the feedlot, about things at the house, even about the weather. And he'd left her at Mrs. Simpson's with a warm, secretive smile, contenting himself with a chaste but breathlessly tender kiss on her forehead.

As he'd promised, he hadn't called or come visiting. She hadn't seen him or heard from him since that night. It had been hard going, too. She'd stopped by Misty's a time or two, pretending to be happy so that her friend wouldn't ask too many questions. Tyler had asked Abby out again, but she'd refused without really understanding why. She wanted only the memory of Calhoun. If it was all she could ever have of him, it would be more than a lot of lonely women had.

She enjoyed her work at the insurance office, and her bosses were good to her. She settled in without any problem, but she went home to a lonely room, and as the days went by she was almost frantic with the need to see Calhoun.

She'd gone to the Ballenger house to talk to Maria about the party, and she'd left a list of guests for Justin, but to her disappointment both the brothers had been away at the time. She'd managed to get nothing out of Maria, either, except for a careless remark that everything was fine at home and the brothers seemed to be very happy. Which did nothing for Abby's self-esteem, especially since she missed Maria's wicked, conspiratorial smile.

The night of the party, Abby drove herself to the Ballenger house. She felt starved for the sight of Calhoun. All her memories and all her fantasies only made it worse.

She was wearing a long electric-blue gown that enhanced her blue-gray eyes and emphasized her exquisite figure. It had soft fabric straps and a crisscross bodice, a fitted waist and a long, narrow skirt. She wore her hair up in a braided coiffure with wispy little curls hanging beside her ears and curling on her forehead. She looked mature and sophisticated. She might not be beautiful, but she felt it tonight, and her face radiated with a glow that only the anticipation of seeing Calhoun could give her.

Maria opened the door and hugged her impulsively. "So lovely," the older woman sighed. "Everything has worked out so nicely, even the band was on time. Your guests have started arriving. The Jacobses are in the living room with Justin."

Abby winced, but Maria shook her head.

"No, it is all right," she said quickly. "Señor Justin and Señor Tyler have been talking cattle, and Señorita Shelby—" Maria smiled sadly. "Her soft eyes feed on Señor Justin like dry flowers welcoming rainfall. It breaks my heart."

"And mine," Abby said gently. "I'll go and keep her company."

She walked into the living room and smiled at Shelby, who was wearing a long green velvet skirt with a simple chemise top in white silk. She looked exquisitely lovely. Justin and Tyler, in dark suits, rose as she entered the room, both pairs of masculine eyes gazing appreciatively at her dress.

"Happy birthday, honey," Justin said gently, and went forward to brush his hard mouth against her cheek. "And at least a hundred more."

"I'll second that," Tyler grinned, his green eyes dancing as he bent and kissed her softly on the mouth. "You look delicious."

"Thank you both," she replied.

"I remember my own twenty-first birthday," Shelby sighed after she'd hugged Abby and congratulated her. "It was very special." Her eyes went helplessly to Justin, who stood very still and looked at her, his dark eyes full of emotion.

Abby could have cried. She hadn't understood before, but now she knew how devastating it could be to want someone that much. She looked around the room. There were several other people there, friends from school, who waved and lifted their glasses in her direction. She smiled back, but her heart was getting heavier by the second.

"Justin, where's Calhoun?" she asked finally.

Justin took a draw from his cigarette and dragged his gaze away from Shelby. Abby had asked the question he'd dreaded ever since she'd walked in the door. "I don't know if he's going to make it, honey," he hedged, because he didn't know where in hell Calhoun was either. She looked devastated, so he improvised. "He said to tell you happy birthday and—Abby!"

She couldn't help it. She burst into tears, shaking with the disappointment. "I'm sorry..." she sobbed.

"Shelby, take her into the study, please," Justin said.

"Of course." Shelby put a gentle arm around her. "Abby, please don't cry. I know Calhoun would have been here if he could have."

"I'll be all right in a minute," Abby told Justin as they passed him and a quietly curious Tyler. "I'm sorry. It's been a long week," she added with a faint smile.

"I'll knock him through a wall for this," Justin said coldly. "I swear to God I will."

"No, you won't," Abby sniffed. "As Shelby said, I'm sure he had a good reason." She laughed coldly. "Probably a blond one..." Tears fell hotly again, and Shelby quickly got her out of the room, across the hall and into the study.

"Now sit down." Shelby helped her to the burgundy leather sofa. "I'll get you a brandy. Is that all right?"

"I hate him," Abby said, burying her face in her hands. "I hate him so much!"

"Yes, I know." Shelby smiled wryly and poured brandy into a snifter. She gave the glass to Abby, and watched her take a sip and grimace at the harsh taste.

Her blue-gray eyes lifted to Shelby's green ones. "I haven't even seen him in weeks," she said brokenly. "He hasn't called or come to see me. I didn't know why then, but now I do. He was letting me down easy. He knows how I feel, and he doesn't want to hurt me...."

"If it means anything, I know how you feel, too," Shelby said gently, her eyes soft and sad.

"Yes, I'm sure you do." Abby touched the older woman's hand. "Justin never looks at anyone else. Calhoun said once that he supposed Justin would die loving you."

"And hating me, all at once," Shelby sighed. "Justin thinks I slept with someone else. He believed my father and a crony of his, and I've never been able to make him listen. As if I could have let any other man touch me, ever!"

Abby stared at her, momentarily distracted. "Oh, Shelby," she whispered.

Shelby grimaced. "Stubborn, proud, hardheaded man." Her eyes lifted. "I'd die for him."

"I hope it works out someday."

The older woman sighed. "Miracles still happen occasionally." She searched Abby's eyes. "Will you be all right now?"

Abby finished the brandy. "Of course I will. I don't care if Calhoun misses my party. I can have a perfectly good time without him. After all, I was only his ward and now I'm not anymore. He's just another man." She got up, smoothing her hair. "I'd better fix my makeup."

She went to the mirror and repaired her lipstick and powder, but there was very little she could do about her red eyes. Then she followed Shelby out the door.

The band was good. They played a succession of dreamy waltzes and country-and-western songs, which their lead singer belted out in a smooth baritone. Abby danced every dance, some with Justin, some with Tyler, and a lot with old school friends. But still Calhoun didn't make an appearance. Abby grew more vivacious by the minute to cover up her misery.

She was dancing much too close to Tyler in a lazy two-step, when she felt eyes on her back. Without looking, she knew Calhoun had arrived. He'd spoiled her party by not showing up until it was almost over, and she hated him. Having settled that in her mind, she kept her eyes closed and kept dancing.

"Calhoun's here," Tyler murmured into her hair.

"So what?" she said icily.

His eyebrows arched. He glanced at Calhoun, who was thunderously angry, and then at Justin, who was heading toward his younger brother with an expression that would have made a lesser man than Calhoun back off.

"Abby, Justin's going toward Calhoun with blood in his eye."

"Good," she muttered. "I hope he kills him."

"Abby!"

She bit her lower lip. "I don't care."

"You don't care like hell," Tyler replied curtly. He stopped dancing and held her by the arms. "Stop it. If you want him, for God's sake, show him that you do. Don't pout and hem and haw until you lose him."

"You don't understand," she began.

"Abby, look at Shelby and Justin," he said quietly. "Is that how you want to end up?"

She searched Tyler's face and then looked over to the doorway, where Justin and Calhoun were talking in terse monosyllables. "All right," she said wearily.

He smiled. "Good girl. Go on."

She hesitated, but then she walked away. Tyler watched her go, a faint sadness in his own eyes. That was quickly erased when Misty Davies wandered over in a frothy gold party dress and asked him to dance.

Justin stopped talking when Abby came near. He glared at Calhoun. "Tell it to Abby," he said shortly. "She's been having a hell of a good time, though, all by herself."

Justin smiled faintly at them and wandered off to talk to another of the guests, leaving a cold-eyed Calhoun and a fuming Abby staring at one another.

"Thank you for coming," she said with faint hauteur. "I'm having a lovely time."

"How could you think I'd willingly treat you like that?" he asked quietly. "Turn my back on you, deliberately arrive late, embarrass you with your guests... Oh, God, don't you know me better than that?"

He disconcerted her. She looked up at him helplessly. "What happened?"

"I ran the Jaguar into a ditch and damned near wrecked it," he said with a mocking smile. "I was going too fast, and I took a curve where there'd been an oil spill that I didn't know about."

Her face went white. She saw a graphic mental picture of him lying in a ditch, dead. It erased all her stupid suspicions and left her shaking.

Without a word, she pressed hard against him. She held him, trembling, oblivious to her surroundings, to everything but Calhoun.

"You're trembling," he said, faintly surprised. His big hands went to her back, where it was bare over the deep plunge of her dress. "I'm all right, honey."

She held him tighter, fighting tears. The trembling grew worse, and she couldn't seem to stop.

"For God's sake...!"

He drew her out of the room, one big arm supporting her, and into the study. He locked the door behind them, shutting out the music and muffled conversation and other party sounds. His dark eyes looked down into her wild, pale ones.

"I wouldn't have missed your party on purpose, little one," he said gently.

That was the old Calhoun, she thought wildly. Her guardian. Her protector. The kind, caring older man who looked after her and kept her safe. But he didn't look or sound like a lover, and she supposed that he'd used those weeks to good advantage, getting her out of his system. She felt sick and shaken, and she wanted nothing more than to go home and cry herself to sleep.

"No, I'm…I'm sure you wouldn't have," she said, her voice husky. She forced a smile. "It was kind of you and Justin to let me have the party here."

His dark eyes narrowed. He leaned back against the door, elegant in his evening clothes, the white silk of his shirt emphasizing his high cheekbones, his blond hair and dark skin, his powerful build. "You sound strange," he said. "You look strange."

"I've had a long week, that's all." She was beginning to sound like a broken record. "I'm enjoying my new job. I like it very much. We stay busy. And—"

"Stop it," he said softly.

Her eyes closed, tears burning them. Her hands at her sides tautened into fists and she fought for control. "I'm sorry."

"Come here, Abby," he said in a tone that she remembered, deep with tenderness, soft with sensuality.

She opened her eyes. "I don't want pity," she whispered.

His chin lifted. "What do you want?"

She lowered her gaze to his highly polished shoes. "The moon," she said wearily.

He moved forward abruptly. One big, lean hand caught hers and pried it open. He placed something in it and curled her fingers around it. She frowned. Something small and thin and metallic…

She opened her hand. It was a ring, a very simple circle of gold without any flourishes or frills. It was a wedding ring.

He bent, lifting her. He carried her to the burgundy sofa and put her down on it. Then he knelt on the carpet beside her, his lean hands on her waist, his blond hair gleaming like the golden ring in the soft light from the ceiling.

"I love you," he said softly, holding her gaze as he said it.

Her eyes searched his, getting lost in their dark, unblinking intensity. "W-what?"

"I love you," he repeated. "I didn't know it until the night I almost made love to you, and even then I wasn't sure that I could settle down." He laughed faintly, watching her with eyes that adored her. "But I'm sure now. These past few weeks have been the purest hell I've ever known. A dozen times I've almost stormed over to your apartment at three in the morning to get into bed with you. I've thought about kidnapping you from work and carrying you off into the mountains. But I promised to give you time, and I have. Now I've run out of it. If you don't marry me, so help me, I'll ravish you where you sit."

"I'll marry you," she whispered. "But—"

"But what?" he whispered back.

Her lips parted as she let her shoulders droop, so that the silky fabric of her dress fell and revealed all of her breasts except the hard tips. "But wouldn't you ravish me anyway?"

His breath caught. "As if I needed asking..."

His hands finished the job, stripping the fabric to her waist. He sat looking at the soft, pretty swell of her breasts, watching her breathe for a long moment before he drew her toward him and bent his head.

She began to tremble when she felt his mouth on her soft, heated skin. Her hands cradled his head and she wept softly, kissing his hair, whispering to him. "I love you," she murmured. "I'm sorry I...made a fuss. I thought you were out with some woman, that you didn't want me.... Oh, Calhoun!"

His mouth had opened, taking almost all of one perfect breast inside to taste, to caress with his tongue. His lean hand was at her back, searching for a zipper, and in the next instant she was on the carpet under him, her body bare from the neck down except for her briefs and her stockings.

"I was in Houston buying a ring. Buying two rings. Your engagement ring had to be sized. It's a yellow diamond." He kissed her hungrily. "I got caught in traffic, and since I knew I was going to be late, I rushed back...too fast. But it's all right now, isn't it, sweetheart?" He eased his hands down her body, feeling her tremble. "Abby, suppose we make love right here?" he murmured, stroking her gently with his warm, hard fingers.

"Someone might come in," she whispered breathlessly.

He smiled as he bent. "I locked the door," he breathed into her open mouth. "I'm hungry."

"I'm hungry, too."

His nose nuzzled hers. "Or we could go up to my bedroom," he murmured huskily. "And lock the door. Even Justin wouldn't disturb us there."

"The guests..."

"They'll never miss us. They're too busy enjoying themselves. I want you, Abby. I want you for the rest of my life, until I die. And if I get you pregnant..." He lifted his head, searching her warm, soft eyes. "Would you mind having my child?"

She touched his mouth with aching tenderness. "I love you," she said. "I want to have lots of babies with you."

He actually shuddered. "You're very young."

She smiled. "All the better." She traced his heavy eyebrows with her finger. "I can play with them."

He smoothed back her hair, his eyes full of wonder. "Abby...I never dreamed how sweet it would be to belong to someone. To have someone of my own. And a family." He touched her breasts tenderly. "Ever since the first time I touched you, I've felt as if there'd never been a woman for me. You make it all new and exciting. You make me feel whole."

"You make me feel the same way." She reached up to find his mouth with hers, kissing him slowly, tenderly. "Justin won't like it if we go upstairs together."

"He won't see us," he whispered and smiled wickedly. "Where's your sense of adventure?"

"I'm nervous—"

"We'll be married by tomorrow afternoon. I've already got the license. All we need is a blood test, and we can have that in the morning.

"You rake," she said accusingly.

"Reformed rake."

"All right," she breathed.

He searched her eyes quietly. "I need you badly. But I can wait if you want me to."

"You don't want to," she said.

He smiled. "I've felt married to you since that night in my apartment, Abby. A piece of paper and a few solemn words aren't going to tie me to you any more firmly than I am right now. I love you, honey," he said softly. "That's the beginning and the end of my life, wrapped up in those words."

She pressed against him. "I love you so."

He helped her into her dress and led her out the back door, around through the guest bedroom and to the rear staircase. Then he picked her up, laughing softly, and carried her upstairs. He'd just made it to the landing and was turning the corner toward his own room when they ran headfirst into Justin and almost went down on the floor with the impact.

Abby gasped. Calhoun actually turned blood red. Justin's eyebrows went up expressively. Then they just stared at each other.

"Tired of dancing?" Justin asked after a minute, his lips pursed mischievously.

Calhoun cleared his throat. "We were going to..."

"...talk," Abby improvised.

Justin's dark eyes went over Abby's face, reading all the telltale signs there. Then he glanced toward Calhoun and stared him down.

"Oh, what the hell," Calhoun muttered darkly. "You know damned good and well where we were going and why. But there's something you don't know. I love Abby. We're getting married tomorrow. The license is in my pocket."

"And the ring," Abby added, faintly embarrassed at being caught in such a compromising situation.

"Congratulations," Justin said pleasantly. "I couldn't be happier for both of you. And if I might just add, it's about time."

Calhoun shifted Abby. "Thank you."

"You'll be a lovely brother-in-law," Abby agreed.

"The very best," Calhoun added.

Justin smiled. "It won't work. I'm not going anywhere, and neither are you."

"Damn it, Justin!" Calhoun ground out.

"Twenty-four hours is just overnight," Justin continued. "Then you can both go to Houston and have a honeymoon in that penthouse apartment you bought."

"Listen here . . ." Calhoun began.

"Abby, you tell him how you really feel about this," Justin said, staring at her.

She grimaced, her hands linked around Calhoun's neck. She sighed. "Well, I love him," she said finally.

"I thought you wanted to," Calhoun said softly, searching her embarrassed face. "I'd never have forced you."

"Oh, I know that," she said, her eyes worshipful. "But I couldn't refuse you."

He smiled ruefully. "You're one of a kind," he said gently. "And I love you."

"I love you, too," she whispered, smiling.

He kissed her softly. "I guess we'd better wait, since Justin is going to stand there until he takes root."

"I guess we had," Abby murmured.

Calhoun put Abby on her feet. "Well, let's go downstairs and dance, Abby," he said. "Then we can sing that terrific drinking song that Justin taught you."

Justin glared at him, looking uncomfortable. "You started that."

Calhoun's eyebrows lanced upward. "All I did was dance with Shelby."

Justin stared at him coldly. "And if you hadn't been my brother, I'd have broken your jaw for it."

There was a faint sound behind them, and Justin turned to find Shelby standing two steps behind him.

"Go ahead, Shelby, get an earful," Justin said icily. "Does it please you that after six years I still feel murderous when another man touches you?"

"That works both ways, Justin," Shelby said quietly. "Or didn't you know that it would kill me to see you with another woman?"

She turned and stormed off downstairs. Justin stared after her, shocked.

"Why don't you carry her upstairs?" Calhoun asked his brother with pursed lips. "Then Abby and I could stand on the landing and block your way."

Justin said something in Spanish that Abby was glad she didn't understand and stomped off downstairs.

Calhoun glanced at Abby's questioning face and grinned. "I'll tell you after we're married," he whispered in her ear.

And he did tell her two days later as they lay together in the big soft bed at his penthouse, sated and close in each other's arms as the sun drifted lazily through the blinds.

"What did Justin say to you the night you started to carry me upstairs?" she asked drowsily.

"He said that if he ever took Shelby to bed it would be on a desert island with mines on the beach." he chuckled. "Poor Justin," he added quietly. "To love like that and not even have a memory to live on."

She lifted her eyes to his, her hand lazily stroking his thick, hair-matted chest. "What do you mean?"

"Justin never slept with Shelby," Calhoun said softly. "And since the engagement broke off, he's never slept with anyone else."

She caught her breath.

"It isn't so incredible, Abby," he mused, rolling over to look down into her soft eyes. The covers had long since been thrown off, and his dark gaze slid over her nudity with possession and exquisite memories of the night before. "I couldn't touch anyone else after I kissed you."

"That's very profound," she whispered, trembling as his lean hand stroked gently over her taut breasts and down over her belly to the silken softness of her thighs.

"It's that," he agreed, bending to brush his lips across her mouth. "Have I hurt you too badly, or is it all right if we make love again?"

She flushed, remembering their first time, the softness of his voice whispering to her to lie still after he'd realized how difficult it was going to be. And then he'd bridled his own needs so that he could rouse her all over again. The pain had been minimal, because the savage hunger he'd kindled in her had surpassed pain or fear or even thought. She'd given everything he'd asked in the end, her body so completely his that he could have done anything to her.

"I'm all right now," she whispered, adoring his hard face with her eyes. "You made it all right."

"You were very much a virgin, Mrs. Ballenger," he said with faint traces of satisfied delight. "And it wasn't the easiest initiation."

She traced his chin. "I love you. And any way you loved me would have been all right."

He kissed her softly. "You make me feel humble."

"You make me feel wild," she gasped, arching as his hand moved. Her eyes widened as it moved again. "Yes...do...that..."

He smiled through his own excitement as she responded to him. He enjoyed her innocence as he'd never imagined he could. He held back this time, drawing out his possession until she was crying with her arousal, until she was almost in torment from the need. And then he eased down, tenderly, coaxing her to bank down her own fires and settle into a new and achingly sweet rhythm that brought with it a fulfillment beyond her wildest dreams, beyond even his experience.

Afterward, he cradled her against his hard, damp body, trembling as he held her, stroked her. She'd gone with him every step of the way, and she was exhausted. So was he. She made an adventure of lovemaking, an exquisite expression of shared love. It was something he'd never known in a woman's arms. Whispering softly, he told her that.

She smiled as she lay nestled against him. "I don't have anyone to compare you with," she whispered. "But on a scale of ten, I'd give you a twenty."

Calhoun laughed softly, closing his eyes and sighing contentedly as he felt her snuggle close to him, her body fitting perfectly against his.

"Abby, how would you feel about living in the old Dempsey place?" he asked unexpectedly.

She opened her eyes. "That big Victorian house that you and Justin bought last year? It's been remodeled and furnished, hasn't it? I thought you were going to use it for offices."

"I'd thought about it," he told her. "But I want to live there with you."

"There, and not with Justin?" she asked softly.

He touched her hair. "It will make life hell for him if we're under the same roof."

"Yes, I know. To see how happy we are will only point out what he's lost." She smiled. "I'll live with you wherever you say."

He searched her eyes gently. Then he folded her up against him and drew the sheet over their damp bodies. "I love you, Abby," he said drowsily.

"I love you, too." She slid her arm across his broad chest and sighed contentedly. It was spring, and soon the pastures would be dotted with wildflowers and seed would begin sprouting everywhere. She closed her eyes, thinking

about the long horizons and lazy summers and the promise of children playing around her skirts while she sat in the
circle of Calhoun's arm and watched the cattle graze. It
sounded like the most exciting kind of future to share—
with a long, tall Texan at her side.

*　*　*　*　*

JUSTIN

Diana Palmer

To the editors at Silhouette Books,
with love

Chapter One

It was a warm morning, and the weatherman had already promised temperatures into the eighties for the afternoon. But the weather didn't seem to slow down the bidders, and the auctioneer standing on the elegant porch of the tall white mansion kept his monotone steady even though he had to periodically wipe streams of sweat from his heavily jowled face.

As he watched the estate auction, Justin Ballenger's black eyes narrowed under the brim of his expensive creamy Stetson. He wasn't buying. Not today. But he had a personal interest in this particular auction. The Jacobs's home was being sold, lock, stock, and barrel, and he should have felt a sense of triumph at seeing old Bass Jacobs's legacy go down the drain. Oddly enough, he didn't. He felt vaguely disturbed by the whole proceeding. It was like watching predators pick a helpless victim to the bone.

He kept searching the crowd for Shelby Jacobs, but she was nowhere in sight. Possibly she and her brother, Tyler, were in the house, helping to sort the furniture and other antique offerings.

A movement to his left caught his eye. Abby Ballenger, his sister-in-law of six weeks, stood beside him.

"I didn't expect to see you here," she remarked, smiling up at him. She'd lived with him and Calhoun, her almost-stepbrothers, since the tragic deaths of their father and her mother. Their parents were to have been married, so the brothers took Abby in and looked after her. And just weeks before, she and Calhoun had married.

"I never miss an auction," he replied. He looked toward the auctioneer. "I haven't seen the Jacobses."

"Ty's in Arizona." Abby sighed, and she didn't miss the sudden glare of Justin's dark eyes. "He didn't go without a fight, either, but there was some kind of emergency on that ranch he's helping to manage."

"Shelby's alone?" The words were almost wrenched from him.

"Afraid so." Abby glanced up at him and away, barely suppressing a smile. "She's at the apartment she's rented in town." Abby smoothed a fold of her gray skirt. "It's above the law office where she works..."

Justin's hard, dark face went even tauter. The smoking cigarette in his hand was forgotten as he turned to Abby, his whipcord-lean body towering over her. "That isn't an apartment, for God's sake, it's an old storeroom!"

"Barry Holman is letting her convert it," Abby said, her guileless pale eyes the picture of innocence under her dark hair. "She doesn't have much choice, Justin. With the house being sold, where else can she afford to live on what she makes? Everything had to go, you know. Tyler and Shelby thought they could at least hold onto the house and property, but it took every last dime to meet their father's debts."

Justin muttered something under his breath, glaring toward the big, elegant house that somehow embodied everything he'd hated about the Jacobs family for the past six years, since Shelby had broken their engagement and betrayed him.

"Aren't you glad?" Abby baited him gently. "You hate her, after all. It should please you to see her brought to her knees in public."

He didn't say another word. He turned abruptly, his expression as uncompromising as stone, and strode to where his black Thunderbird was parked. Abby smiled secretively. She'd thought that he'd react, if she could make him see how badly this was going to hurt Shelby. All these long years he'd avoided any contact with the Jacobs family, any mention of them at home. But in recent months, the strain was beginning to tell on him. Abby knew almost certainly that he still felt something for the woman who'd jilted him, and she knew Shelby felt something for Justin, too. Abby, deliriously happy in her own marriage, wanted the rest of the world to be as happy as she was. Perhaps by nudging Justin in the right direction, she might make two miserable people happy.

Justin had only found out about the estate sale that morning, when Calhoun mentioned it at the office at their joint feedlot operation. It had been in the papers, but Justin had been out of town looking at cattle and he hadn't seen the notice.

He wasn't surprised that Shelby was staying away from the auction. She'd been born in that house. She'd lived in it all her life. Shelby's grandfather, in fact, had founded the small Texas town of Jacobsville. They were old money, and the ragged little Ballenger boys from the run-down cattle ranch down the road weren't the kind of friends Mrs. Bass Jacobs had wanted for her children, Tyler and Shelby.

But she'd died, and Mr. Jacobs had been friendly toward the Ballengers, especially when Justin and Calhoun had opened their feedlot. And when the old man found out that Shelby intended to marry Justin Ballenger, he'd told Justin he couldn't be more pleased.

Justin tried never to think about the night Bass Jacobs and young Tom Wheelor had come to see him. Now it all came back. Bass Jacobs had been upset. He told Justin outright that Shelby was in love with Tom and not only in love, the couple had been sleeping together all through the farce of Shelby's "engagement" to Justin. He was ashamed of her, Bass lamented. The engagement was Shelby's way of bringing her reluctant suitor into line, and now that Justin had served his purpose, Shelby didn't need him anymore. Sadly, he handed Justin Shelby's engagement ring and Tom Wheelor had mumbled a red-faced apology. Bass had even cried. Perhaps his shame had prompted his next move, because he'd promised on the spot to give Justin the financial backing he needed to make the new feedlot a success. There was only one condition—that Shelby never know where the money came from. Then he'd left.

Never one to believe ill of anyone without hard evidence, Justin phoned Shelby while Bass was still starting his car. But she didn't deny what Justin had been told. In fact, she confirmed all of it, even the part about having slept with Wheelor. She'd only wanted to make Tom jealous so he'd propose, she told Justin. She hoped he hadn't been too upset with her, but then, she'd always had everything she wanted, and Justin wasn't rich enough to cater to her tastes just yet. But Tom was...

Justin had believed her. And because she'd pushed him away the one time he'd tried to make love to her, her confession rang with the truth. He'd gone on a legendary bender afterward. And for the past six years, no other woman had ever gotten close enough to make a dent in his heart. He'd been impervious to all the offers, and there had been some. He wasn't a handsome man. His dark face was too craggy, his features too irregular, his unsmiling countenance too forbidding. But he had wealth and power, and that drew women to him. He was too bitter, though, to accept that kind of attention. Shelby had hurt him as no one else in his life ever had, and for years all he'd lived for was the thought of vengeance.

But now that he saw her brought to her knees financially, it was unsatisfying. All he could think of was that she was going to be hurt and she had no family, no friends to comfort her.

The apartment above the law office where she worked was tiny, and it didn't sit well with him that it was in such proximity to her bachelor boss. He knew Holman by reputation, and rumor had it that he liked pretty women. Shelby, with her long black hair, slender figure and green, sparkling eyes, would more than qualify. She was twenty-seven now, hardly a girl, but she didn't look much older than she had when she and Justin became engaged. She had an innocence about her, still, that made Justin grind his teeth. It was false; she'd even admitted it.

He paused at the door to the apartment, his hand raised to knock. There was a muffled noise from inside. Not laughter. Tears?

His jaw tautened and he knocked roughly.

The noise ceased abruptly. There was a scraping sound, like a chair being moved, and soft footsteps that echoed the quick, hard beat of his heart.

The door opened. Shelby stood there, in clinging faded jeans and a blue checked shirt, her long dark hair dishev-

eled and curling down her back, her green eyes red-rimmed
and wet.

"Did you come to gloat, Justin?" she asked with quiet
bitterness.

"It gives me no pleasure to see you humbled," he replied, his chin lifted, his black eyes narrow. "Abby said
you were alone."

She sighed, dropping her eyes to his dusty, worn boots.
"I've been alone for a long time. I've learned to live with
it." She shifted restlessly. "Are there a lot of people at the
auction?"

"The yard's full," he said. He took off his hat and held
it in one hand while the other raked his thick, straight
black hair.

She looked up, her eyes lingering helplessly on the hard
lines of his craggy face, on the chiseled mouth she'd kissed
so hungrily six years ago. She'd been so desperately in love
with him then. But he'd become something out of her
slight experience the night they became engaged, and his
ardor had frightened her. She'd fought away from him,
and the memory of how it had been with him, just before
the fear became tangible, was formidable. She'd wanted so
much more than they'd shared, but she had more reason
than most women to fear intimacy. But Justin didn't know
that and she'd been too shy to explain her actions.

She turned away with a groan of anguish. "If you can
bear my company, I'll fix you a glass of iced tea."

He hesitated, but only for an instant. "I could use that,"
he said quietly. "It's hot as hell out there."

He followed her inside, absently closing the door behind him. But he stopped dead when he saw what she was
having to contend with. He stiffened and almost cursed out
loud.

There were only two rooms in the makeshift apartment. They were bare except for a worn sofa and chair, a scratched coffee table and a small television set. Her clothes were apparently being kept in a closet, because there was no evidence of a dresser. The kitchen boasted a toaster oven and a hot plate and a tiny refrigerator. This, when she was used to servants and silk robes, silver services and Chippendale furniture.

"My God," he breathed.

Her back stiffened, but she didn't turn when she heard the pity in his deep voice. "I don't need sympathy, thank you," she said tightly. "It wasn't my fault that we lost the place, it was my father's. It was his to lose. I can make my own way in the world."

"Not like this, damn it!" He slammed his hat down on the coffee table and took the pitcher of tea out of her hands, moving it aside. His lean, work-roughened hands held her wrists and he stared down at her with determination. "I won't stand by and watch you try to survive in a rattrap like this. Barry Holman and his charity be damned!"

Shelby was shocked, not only by what he was saying, but by the way he looked. "It's not a rattrap," she faltered.

"Compared to what you were used to, it is," he returned doggedly. His chest rose and fell on an angry sigh. "You can stay with me for the time being."

She blushed beet red. "In your house, alone with you?"

He lifted his chin. "In my house," he agreed. "*Not* in my bed. You won't have to pay me for a roof over your head. I do remember with vivid clarity that you don't like my hands on you."

She could have gone through the floor at the bitter mockery in the words. She couldn't meet those black eyes or challenge the flat statement without embarrassing them both. Anyway, it was so long ago. It didn't matter now.

She looked at his shirt instead, at the thick mat of black hair under the white silk. He'd let her touch him there, once. The night of their engagement, he'd unbuttoned it and given her hands free license to do what they liked. He'd kissed her as if he'd die to kiss her, but he'd frightened her half out of her mind when the kisses went a little too far.

Until that night, he'd never tried to touch her, or gone further than brief, light kisses. His holding back had first disturbed her and then made her curious. Surely Justin was as experienced as his brother, Calhoun. But perhaps he'd had hang-ups about the distance between their social standing. Justin had been barely middle class at the time, and Shelby's family was wealthy. It hadn't mattered to her, but she could see that it might have bothered Justin. And especially after she jilted him, because of her father's treacherous insistence.

She'd gotten even with her father, though. He'd planned for her to marry Tom Wheelor, in a cold-blooded merger of property, and Justin had gotten in the way. But Shelby had refused Tom Wheelor's advances and she'd never let him touch her. She'd told Bass Jacobs she wouldn't marry his wealthy young friend. The old man hadn't capitulated then, but just before his death, when he realized how desperately Shelby loved Justin, he'd felt bad about what he'd done. He hadn't told her that his guilt had driven him to stake Justin's feedlot, but he'd apologized.

She looked up then, searching Justin's dark eyes quietly, remembering. It had been hard, going on without him. Her dreams of loving him and bearing his sons had died long ago, but it was still a pleasure beyond bearing just to look at him. And his hands on her wrists made her body glow, tingle with forbidden longings, like the warm threat of his powerful, cologne-scented body. If only her father hadn't interfered. Inevitably, she'd have been able to explain her fears to Justin, to ask him to be gentle, to go slow. But it was too late now.

"I know you don't want me anymore, Justin," she said gently. "I even understand why. You don't need to feel responsible for me. I'll be all right. I can take care of myself."

He breathed slowly, trying to keep himself under control. The feel of her silky skin was giving him some problems. Unwillingly, his thumbs began to caress her wrists.

"I know that," he said. "But you don't belong here."

"I can't afford a better apartment just yet," she said. "But I'll get a raise when I've been working for two months, and then maybe I can get the room that Abby had at Mrs. Simpson's."

"You can get it now," he said tersely. "I'll loan you the money."

She lowered her eyes. "No. It wouldn't look right."

"Only you and I would know."

She bit her lower lip. She couldn't tell him that she hated the thought of being in this place, so near Barry Holman, who was a nice boss but a hopeless womanizer. She hesitated.

Before she could say yes or no, there was a knock on the door. Justin let her go reluctantly and watched her move toward the door.

Barry Holman stood there, in jeans and a sweatshirt, blond and blue-eyed and hopeful. "Hi, Shelby," he said pleasantly. "I thought you might need some help moving...in.'' His voice trailed away and he saw Justin standing behind her.

''Not really,'' Justin said with a cold smile. ''She's on her way over to Mrs. Simpson's to take on Abby's old room. I'm helping her move, although I knew she appreciated the offer of this—'' he looked around distastefully ''—apartment.''

Barry Holman swallowed. He'd known Justin for a long time, and he was just about convinced that the rumors he'd heard were true. Justin might not want Shelby himself, but he was damned visible if anybody else made a pass at her.

''Well,'' he said, still smiling, ''I'd better get back downstairs then. I had some calls to make. Good to see you again, Justin. See you early Monday morning, Shelby.''

''Thanks anyway, Mr. Holman,'' she said. ''I don't want to seem ungrateful, but Mrs. Simpson offers meals as well, and it's peaceful there.'' She smiled. ''I'm not used to town living, and Mrs. Simpson has the room free right now...''

''No hard feelings, you go right ahead.'' Barry grinned. ''So long.''

Justin glared after him. ''Lover boy,'' he muttered. ''Just what you need.''

She turned, her eyes soft on his face. ''I'm twenty-seven,'' she said. ''I want to marry and have children eventually. Mr. Holman is very nice, and he doesn't have any bad habits.''

''Except that he'll sleep with anything that wears skirts,'' he replied tersely. He didn't like thinking about Shelby having another man's children. His black eyes searched over her body. Yes, she was getting older, not that she looked it. In eight or ten years, children might be a risk for her. His expression hardened.

"He's never said anything improper to me." She faltered, confused by the way he was looking at her.

"Give him time." He drew in a slow breath. "I said I'll loan you enough to get the room at Mrs. Simpson's. If you're hell-bent on independence, you can pay me back at your convenience."

She had to swallow her pride, and it hurt to let him help her when she knew how bitter he was about the past. But he was a caring man, and she was a stray person in the world. Justin's heart was too big to allow him to turn his back on her, even after what he thought she'd done to him. Quick, hot tears sprang to her green eyes as she remembered what she'd been forced to say to him, the way she'd hurt him.

"I'm so sorry," she said unexpectedly, biting her lip as she turned away.

The words, and the emotion behind them, surprised him. Surely she didn't have any regrets this late. Or was she just putting on an act to get his sympathy? He couldn't trust her.

She got herself back together and brushed at the loose hair at her neck as she poured the tea into two glasses filled with ice. "I'll let you lend me the money, if you really don't mind," she said, handing him his glass without looking up. "I don't like the idea of living alone."

"Neither do I, Shelby, but it's something you get used to after a while," he said quietly. He sipped his tea, but he couldn't pry his eyes away from her soft oval face. "What is it like, having to work for a living?"

She didn't react to the mockery in the words. She smiled. "I like it," she said surprisingly, and lifted her eyes to his.

"I had things to do, you know, when we had money. I belonged to a lot of volunteer groups and charities. But law offices cater to unhappy people. When I can help them feel a little better, it makes me forget my own problems."

His black brows drew together as he sipped the cool, sweet amber liquid. The glass was cold under his lean fingers.

She searched his black eyes. "You don't believe me, do you, Justin?" she asked perceptively. "You saw me as a socialite; a reasonably attractive woman with money and a cultured background. But that was an illusion. You never really knew me."

"I wanted you, though," he replied, watching her. "But you never wanted me, honey. Not physically, at any rate."

"You rushed me!" she burst out, coloring as she remembered that night.

"Rushed you! Up until that night, I hadn't even kissed you intimately, for God's sake!" His black eyes glittered at her as he remembered her rejection and his own sick certainty that she didn't love him. "I'd kept you on a pedestal until then. And all the time, you were sleeping with that boy millionaire!"

She threw up her hands. "I never slept with Tom Wheelor!"

"You said you did," he reminded her with a cold smile. "You swore it, in fact."

She closed her eyes on a wave of bitter regret. "Yes, I said it," she agreed wearily, and turned away. "I'd almost forgotten."

"And all the post mortems accomplish nothing, do they?" he asked. He put down the glass and pulled out a cigarette, lighting it without removing his eyes from her stiff expression. "It doesn't matter anymore. Let's go. I'll run over to Mrs. Simpson's and you can see about the room.''

Shelby knew that he'd never give an inch. He hadn't forgotten anything and he still despised her. She felt as if the world was sitting on her thin shoulders as she got her purse and followed him to the door. She didn't look at him as they left.

Chapter Two

Justin tucked a wad of bills into Shelby's purse when he stopped the Thunderbird on the side of the road near Mrs. Simpson's house. She tried to protest, but he simply smoked his cigarette and ignored her.

"I told you earlier that the money was between you and me," he said quietly, his dark eyes challenging as he cut the engine. He turned in the bucket seat, his long legs stretched out as he touched the power-window switch on the console panel. It was a rural road, and sparsely traveled. He had stopped under a spreading oak tree. He hooked his elbow on the open window to study Shelby narrowly. "I meant it. If you want to look on it as a loan, that's up to you."

She chewed on her lower lip. "I'll be able to pay you back one day," she said doggedly, even though she knew better. With what she made, it was going to be a struggle to eat and pay the rent. New clothes might become impossible.

"I'm not worried about it."

"Yes, but I am." She looked up, all her misgivings in her green eyes. "Oh, Justin, what am I going to do?" she moaned. "I'm alone for the first time in my life. Ty's in Arizona, I have no family..." She got a grip on herself, averting her eyes. "It's just panic," she said tightly. "Just fear. I'll get used to it. I'm sorry I said that."

He didn't speak. He'd never seen Shelby helpless. She'd always been poised and calm. It was new and faintly disturbing to see her frightened.

"If things get too rough," he replied quietly, "you can move in with me."

She laughed hollowly. "That would do our reputations a world of good."

He blew out a cloud of smoke. "If gossip bothers you all that much, we can get married." He said it carelessly, but his eyes were sharp on her face.

She knew she wasn't breathing. She looked at him as the old wounds opened with a vengeance. "Why?" she asked.

He didn't want to answer her. He didn't want to admit, even to himself, that he was still vulnerable. He shrugged. "You need a place to stay. I'm tired of living alone. Since Abby and Calhoun moved out, the damned house is like a mausoleum."

"You feel sorry for me," she accused.

He took another draw from the cigarette. "Maybe I do. So what? Right now you don't have many options. Either you borrow from me to afford Mrs. Simpson's boarding house, or you marry me." He studied the tip of the cigarette. "Of course, you can always go back to that converted storeroom over Barry Holman's office and show him that you're available—"

"You stop that," she muttered. She shifted restlessly. "Mr. Holman isn't that kind of man. And you have no reason to feel possessive about me."

"Haven't I?" His black eyes searched hers. "But I am, just the same. And I remember your saying the same thing about me. We were engaged once, Shelby. That kind of involvement doesn't go away."

"Some involvement," she said with a tired sigh. "I never could decide why you wanted to marry me."

"You were a feather in my cap," he said coldly, lying through his teeth. "A rich sophisticate. I was just a country boy with stars in my eyes, and you took me for a hell of a ride, lady. Now it's my turn. I've got money and you haven't." His dark eyes narrowed. "And don't think I want to marry you out of some lingering passion."

He hadn't forgotten. It was in his eyes, his whole look. He'd marry her and make her hunger for a love he'd never felt, couldn't feel for her. He held her in contempt because he thought she'd slept with Tom Wheelor, and that was the biggest joke of all. She was still a virgin, and wouldn't it throw a stick into his spokes to find that out the hard way?

"No." She sighed, belatedly answering his question. "I'm not stupid enough to think you still want me, after what I did to your pride." She lifted her eyes to study the proud, arrogant set of his dark head, his eyes shadowed by the Stetson he always wore. "I used to think you cared for me a little, even though you never said you did."

That was the truth. She'd never really been sure why he wanted to marry her. Except for that one night, he hadn't been wild to try to get her into bed, and he'd never seemed emotionally involved, either. But she'd been so in love with him that she had not realized how relatively uninvolved he'd seemed until after their engagement had been broken.

He ignored her remarks. "If you want security, I can give it to you," he said quietly. "I've got money now, although I'll never be in the same class as your father was. He had millions."

She closed her eyes on a wave of shame. She had her father and her own naïveté to thank for Justin's bitterness. But Justin wanted revenge and she'd be a fool to deliver herself on a silver platter to him. "No, Justin. I can't marry you," she said after a minute. Her hand reached for the door handle. "It was a crazy idea!" She averted her face so that all he could see of it was her profile.

He put his hand over hers briefly, holding it, and then withdrew his fingers almost as quickly. His expression hardened. "It's a big house," he said. "With Calhoun and Abby living down the road, there's only Lopez and Maria living with me. You wouldn't need to work if you didn't want to, and you'd have security."

He was offering her heaven, except that it was impersonal on his part. More than anything else, he felt sorry for her. But under the pity was a darker need; she could feel it. Something in him wanted revenge for her rejection six years ago. His pride wanted restitution. Well, didn't she owe him that, she wondered bitterly, after what her father had cost him? And she'd be near him. She'd have meals with him. She could sit with him in the evenings while he watched television. She could sleep under the same roof. Her hungry heart wanted that, so badly. Too badly.

"I don't guess you'd...I don't suppose you'd ever want a..." She couldn't even say it. *A child*, she was thinking, although God only knew how she'd manage to deal with what had to happen to produce one.

"I won't want a divorce," he said, misunderstanding her thoughts. His eyes narrowed. "I'm not exactly Mr. America, in case you haven't noticed. And I don't want a woman I have to buy, unless it's on my terms."

That sounded suspiciously like a dig at her, because she'd refused him for what he thought was a lack of money. Her eyes lifted to his. "Do you still hate me, Justin?" she asked; she needed to know.

He stared at her without speaking for a long moment, quietly smoking his cigarette. "I'm not sure what I feel."

That reply was honest enough, even if it wasn't a declaration of undying love. There were so many wounds between them, so much bitterness. It was probably an insane thing to do, but she couldn't resist the temptation.

She stared at his cigarette instead of at him. "I'll marry you, then, if you mean it."

He didn't move, but something inside him went wild at the words. She couldn't know how many nights he'd spent aching for just the sight of her, how desperately he wanted her near him. But he could never trust her again, and that was the hell of it. She was just a stray person, he told himself. Just someone who needed help. He had to think of her that way, and not want the moon. She might even play up to him out of gratitude, so he'd have to be on his guard every minute. But, oh, God, he wanted her so!

"Then we don't need to see Mrs. Simpson until we've had time to make plans." He started the car, pulled out onto the road and turned the Thunderbird toward the feedlot and his house. His hands had a perceptible tremor. He gripped the steering wheel hard to keep Shelby from seeing how her answer affected him.

If Maria and Lopez were shocked to see Shelby with Justin, they didn't say anything. Lopez vanished into the kitchen while Maria fussed over Shelby, bringing coffee and pastries into the living room where Justin sprawled in his armchair and Shelby perched nervously on the edge of the sofa.

"Thank you, Maria," Shelby said with a warm smile.

The Mexican woman smiled back. "It is my pleasure, *señorita*. I will be in the kitchen if you need me, *señor*," she added to Justin before she went out, discreetly closing the door behind her.

Shelby noticed that Justin didn't comment on Maria's obvious conclusions. Perhaps Maria thought he might want to wrestle her down onto the sofa, but Shelby knew better. Justin had done that once, and only once. And she'd been so frightened that she'd reacted stupidly. She'd never forgiven herself for that. Justin had probably thought she found his ardor distasteful, and that was the last thing it had been.

She sighed, lowering her eyes to his black boots. They weren't working boots; they were the ones he wore when he dressed up. He had such big feet and hands. She smiled, remembering how it had been when they'd first started dating. They'd been like children, fascinated with each other's company, both of them a little shy and reserved. It had never gone beyond kisses except the night they got engaged.

"I said, do you want some coffee?" Justin repeated pointedly, holding the silver coffeepot over a cup he'd just filled.

"Oh. Yes, thank you." She took it black, and apparently he remembered her preference, because he didn't offer her any cream or sugar. He poured his own cup full, put a dash of cream in it and sat back with the china cup and saucer balanced on his crossed knee.

Shelby glanced at him and wondered how she could contemplate living under the same roof with him. He was so unapproachable. Obviously he wanted revenge. She'd be a fool to give him that much rope to hang her with.

On the other hand, if she was living with him, she had a better chance than ever of changing his mind about her. All she really had to do to prove her innocence was to get him into bed. But that was the whole problem. She was scared to death of intimacy.

"Why the blush?" he asked, watching her.

She cleared her throat. "It's warm in here," she said.

"Is it?" He laughed mirthlessly and sipped his coffee. "In case you wondered, you'll have your own room. I won't expect any repayment for giving you a home."

The blush went scarlet. She had to fight not to fling her cup at him. "You're making me sound like a charity case."

"I'll bet that rankles," he agreed. "But Tyler can't help you and hold down a job at the same time. And you'll never make it on what Holman pays you, with all due respect to him. Secretaries in small towns don't make much."

"I'm not mercenary," she said defensively.

"Sure," he replied. He sipped his coffee without another word.

"Listen, Justin, it was all my father's idea, that fake engagement to Tom Wheelor—"

"Your father would never have done that to me," he interrupted coldly, and his eyes went black, threatening as he leaned forward. "Don't try to use him for a scapegoat just because he's dead. He was one of the best friends I had."

That's what you think, she mused bitterly. Obviously it wasn't going to do any good to talk to him. Just because her father had put on a show of liking him was no reason to put the man on a pedestal. God only knew why Justin had such respect for a man who'd caused him years of bitter humiliation.

"You'll never trust me again, will you?" she asked softly.

He studied her lovely face, her pale green eyes staring at him, her gaze burning into his soul. "No," he replied with the honesty that was as much a part of him as his craggy face and thick black hair. "There's too much water under the bridge. But if you think I'm nursing a broken heart, don't. I found you out just a little too soon. My pride suffered, but you never touched my heart."

"I don't imagine any woman ever got close enough to do that," she said, her voice soft. She traced the rim of the china cup. "Abby told me once that you haven't dated anyone for a long time."

"I'm thirty-seven years old," he reminded her. "I sowed my wild oats years ago, even before I started going with you." He finished his coffee and put the cup down. His black eyes met hers in a direct gaze. "And we both know that you've sown yours, and who with."

"You don't know me at all, Justin," she said. "You never did. You said I was a status symbol to you, and looking back, I guess I was, at that." She laughed bitterly. "You used to take me around to your friends to show me off, and I felt like one of those purebred horses Ty used to take to the steeplechase."

He stared at her over his smoking cigarette. "I took you around because you were pretty and sweet, and I liked being with you," he said heavily. "That was a lot of garbage about wanting you for a status symbol."

She leaned back wearily. "Thank you for telling me," she said. "But I guess it doesn't matter now, does it?" She finished her coffee and put the cup down. "Are we going to have a church wedding?" she asked.

"Aren't we a little old for that kind of ceremony?" he asked.

"I can see you're still eating live rattlesnakes to keep your venom potent," she said without flinching. "I want a church wedding."

He dusted the long ash from his cigarette into an ashtray. "It would be quicker to go to a justice of the peace."

"I'm not pregnant," she reminded him, averting her self-conscious face. "There's no great rush, is there?"

She was tying him up in knots. He glared at her. "All right, have your church wedding. You can stay at Mrs. Simpson's until we're married, just to keep everything discreet." His dark eyes narrowed as he got up and crushed out his cigarette. "There's just one thing. Don't you come down that aisle in a white dress. If you dare, I'll walk out the front door of the church and keep going."

She lifted her chin. "Don't you know what every woman in the congregation will think?"

The soft accusation in her green eyes made him feel guilty. He was still hurt by Shelby's affair with Tom Wheelor. He'd wanted to sting her, but he hadn't counted on the wounded look in her eyes.

"You can wear something cream-colored," he muttered reluctantly.

Her lower lip trembled. "Take me to bed." Her eyes dared him, even though she went scarlet and shuddered at her own boldness. "If you think I'm lying about being innocent, I can prove I'm telling the truth!"

His black eyes cut back to hers, unblinking. "You know as well as I do that it takes a doctor to establish virginity. Even an experienced man can't tell."

Her face colored. She could have told him that in her case, it would be more than normally evident, and that her doctor could so easily settle all his doubts. She started to, despite her embarrassment at discussing such an intimate subject, but before she could open her mouth, there was a quick knock at the door and Lopez came in with a message for Justin.

"I've got some cattle out in the road," he told Shelby. "Come on. I'll run you over to Mrs. Simpson's first. You can call Abby and make plans for the wedding. She'll be glad to help with the invitations and such."

She didn't even argue. She was too drained. They were going to be married, but he was going to see to it that she was publicly disgraced, like an adultress being paraded through the streets.

Her teeth ground together as they went out to the car. Well, she'd get around him somehow. She wasn't going to wear anything except a white gown to walk down that aisle. And if he left her standing there, all right. Maybe he didn't even mean what he'd said. She had to keep believing that, for the sake of her pride. He didn't know, and she'd hurt him badly. But, oh, how different things had been six years ago.

Shelby had known the Ballengers all her life. Ty, her brother, and Calhoun, Justin's brother, were friends. That meant that she naturally saw Justin from time to time. At first he'd been cold and very standoffish, but Shelby had thought of him as a challenge. She'd started teasing him gently, flirting shyly. And the change in him had been devastating.

They'd gone to a Halloween party at a mutual friend's, and someone had handed Shelby a guitar. To Justin's amazement, she'd played it easily, trying to slow down enough to adjust to the rather inept efforts of their host, who was learning to play lead guitar.

Without a word, Justin had perched himself on a chair beside her and held out his hand. Their host, with a grin that Shelby hadn't understood at the time, gave the instrument to Justin. He nodded to Shelby, tapped out the meter with his booted foot and launched into a rendition of *San Antonio Rose* that brought the house down.

After the first shock wore off, Shelby's long, graceful fingers caught up the rhythm and seconded him to perfection. He looked into her eyes as they wound to a finish, and he smiled. And at that moment, Shelby gave him her heart.

It wasn't a sudden thing, really. She'd known for years how kind he was. He'd just taken Abby in and given her a home when the girl's mother and Mr. Ballenger had died in a tragic car wreck. Justin was always around when someone needed a helping hand, and there wasn't a more generous or harder working man in Jacobsville. He had a temper, too, but he controlled it most of the time, and his men respected him because he didn't ask them to do anything he wasn't willing to do himself. He was the boss, along with Calhoun, but Justin was always the first to arrive and the last to leave when there was a job to be done. He had many admirable qualities, and Shelby was young and impressionable, and just at the right age to fall hopelessly in love with an older man.

After that night, she seemed to see Justin everywhere. At the restaurant where she had lunch with a friend on Tuesdays and Thursdays, at social events, at charity bazaars, where she went riding on trails that wound near the Ballenger property. It didn't occur to her to wonder why such a reclusive, hard-working man suddenly had so much free time and spent it at places she was known to frequent. She was in love, and every second spent with Justin fed her hungry heart.

She hadn't thought he was interested in her at first. They had a lot in common, despite their very different backgrounds, and he seemed to enjoy talking to her.

Then, very suddenly, everything changed. They were walking down the trail, near where they'd tied their horses, and Justin had suddenly stopped walking to lean against a tree. He didn't say a word, but the expression in his eyes spoke volumes. He had a smoking cigarette in one hand, but he held out the other one to Shelby.

Shelby didn't know what to expect when she took it. Her heart was hammering and she looked at his mouth and wanted it obsessively. Perhaps he knew that, but he didn't take advantage of it.

He pulled her closer. Only their hands were touching. Then, his black eyes searching her soft green ones, he bent slowly, giving her all the time in the world to pull back, to hesitate, to show him that she didn't want him.

But she did. She stood very still as his hard lips brushed hers, her eyes open, watching him. He lifted his head and searched her eyes.

He dropped the cigarette and ground it out under his boot while her heart went crazy. His arms slid around her, bringing her against him but not intimately. He bent again and kissed her with tenderness and respect, with soft wonder. She kissed him back the same way, her arms around his shoulders, her mind sinking into layers of pleasure.

He drew back a minute later and let her go without a word. He took her hand in his and they started walking.

"Do you want a big wedding, or will a civil service do?" he asked as easily as if they were discussing the weather.

And just that quickly they were engaged. That night they went back to her house and told her father. Although his first expression was explosive, they didn't see it. He turned away long enough to compose himself, and then he made happy conversation and welcomed Justin into the family. Justin took Shelby home to share the news with Calhoun and Abby, but Abby was spending the night with a girl-friend and Calhoun had flown to Oklahoma to see a man on business.

They'd had the house to themselves. Shelby remembered so vividly how they'd laughed and toasted their future happiness. Then he'd drawn her to him and kissed her in a very different way, and she'd blushed at the intimacy of his tongue probing delicately inside her lips.

"We're going to be married," he'd whispered with open delight at her innocence. "I won't hurt you."

"I know." She buried her face in his white silk shirt. "But it's so new, being like this with you."

"It's new for me, too," he breathed. His chest rose and fell heavily. He moved her hands a little to the side of the buttons on his shirt and pressed them hard against him while he flipped buttons out of buttonholes and then guided her fingers to the thick mat of hair that covered his muscular, suntanned chest.

"Now," he breathed. "Touch me, Shelby."

She was shocked at this new intimacy, but when he bent and took her mouth under his, she forgot the shock and relaxed against him. Her fingers curled, liking the feel of him, the smell of him that lingered like spice in her nostrils.

"Harder," he whispered roughly. He pressed her hands closer and when she looked up, there was an expression in his eyes that she'd never seen in the weeks they'd been going together. Something wild and out of control was visible there. She trembled a little at that glimpse of desire she hadn't expected to find in such a controlled man.

Then his hand went under her nape, lifting her up to his mouth, and he took her lips in brief, biting kisses that had an unexpected, unbelievable effect on her. She moaned helplessly, frightened at the new sensations.

But to Justin, a moan had a totally different meaning. He thought she was as immersed in pleasure as he was, and his mouth grew suddenly invasive, insistent. His hands dropped to Shelby's slender hips and suddenly lifted her against him into an embrace that shocked her senseless.

She knew very little about men and intimacy, but the changed contours of Justin's hard body told her graphically what he was feeling. He groaned into her mouth as he moved against her in blatant arousal.

She struggled, but he was strong and half out of his mind with unbridled passion. He didn't realize that she was trying to get away until she dragged her mouth away from his and pushed at him, begging him to stop.

He lifted his head, breathing roughly, his eyes black with frustration.

"Shelby..." he ground out in agony.

"Let me go!" she moaned. "Please...Justin, don't!"

"I'll stop before we go all the way," he whispered against her mouth, and bent to kiss her again. Her protests muffled under his warm, drugging mouth, he lifted her off the floor and carried her to the sofa, putting her down gently, full-length, on its soft cushions.

He shuddered with unbearable need, his mouth rough as it pressed against hers. His body slid over her, pushing her into the cushions, heavy and hard and intimate. She felt his sudden loss of control with real fear. She knew what could happen, and that they were engaged. He might not try very hard to stop.

"Justin!"

"I'm not going to take your chastity, Shelby," he breathed into her mouth. His brows drew together in agonized pleasure as his hands slid over her hips. "Oh, God, honey, don't hold back with me. Let me love you. Kiss me back..."

The words died against her soft mouth. He kissed her with growing hunger, his loss of control evident in the urgent movement of his hips against hers, his hands suddenly searching as they moved over her soft breasts. Then his knee moved between her legs and she panicked.

She began to fight him, afraid of the unfamiliar intimacy that was beyond her experience. She pushed at him. All at once, he seemed to feel her resistance. He lifted his head, his eyes blazing with black hunger, and just stared at her for an instant, disoriented. Then when he saw the rejection, felt it in the stiffness of her body, he suddenly tore away from her and got to his feet. By the time she was able to breathe again, he was standing several feet away smoking a cigarette. Several tense minutes passed before he turned around again to pour brandy into two snifters. He gave her one and smiled mockingly at the way she avoided touching him.

He turned away from her to stare out the window while he sipped his brandy. His back was ramrod stiff. "We'll sleep together when we're married," he said. "I hope you know that I don't plan on separate rooms."

"I know." She sipped her own drink with shaking hands, wanting to explain, but his attitude was hardly welcoming. "Justin... I'm a virgin."

"Don't you think I knew that?" he asked tersely. He looked at her and his expression was a cold and totally unreadable mask, hiding emotions she couldn't even guess at. "My God, we're going to be married. Do I have to stop touching you altogether until the ring's on your finger?"

She started to speak and lowered her eyes to her glass. She stiffened. "Perhaps... it might be wiser."

"Considering my lack of control, I suppose you mean." He said it icily, in a tone she'd never heard him use. He drank his brandy and after a while, the anger seemed to go

out of him, to Shelby's relief. He didn't apologize, but he
went to her and took her hand gently, smiling at her as if
nothing at all had happened. They drank brandy, and he
taught her a Mexican drinking song as the aftereffects of
the evening and the potency of the aged brandy began to
work on them. Maria and Lopez had chanced to come
home then from a party and Justin had taken Shelby
home. Maria had been raging at him in Spanish, and
Shelby only found out later that the song he'd been teaching her wasn't one she could ever sing in public.

She'd looked forward to the wedding with joy and also
with apprehension. Justin's passion had unsettled her and
made her doubt her ability to match him. He was experienced and she wasn't, and she was more afraid than ever
of having him make love to her when he was totally out of
control.

But there was no cause for alarm, because there was no
more heated lovemaking. The most ardent move he made
for days afterward was to kiss her cheek or hold hands with
her, and all the while, those black eyes wandered over her
with the strangest searching expression. She relaxed and
began to enjoy his company again, losing her nervousness
since he wasn't making any more demands on her.

Then, suddenly, her father had put an end to it. Give up
Justin, he'd demanded, or watch him lose everything he
had. Justin would end up hating her, her father had said.
He'd blame her for making him poor and their marriage
wouldn't stand a chance. His pride alone would kill it.

She'd been very young and unworldly, and her father
was an old hand at getting what he wanted. He'd enlisted
aid from Tom Wheelor, who was motivated by the thought
of a beneficial merger. And she'd done what her father
asked and lied to Justin, admitted to having an affair with

Tom, to wanting wealth and position, things that Justin couldn't give her.

So long ago, she thought. So much pain. She'd only been protecting Justin, trying to spare him the agony of losing everything he and his family had worked so long and so hard to achieve. But in the process, she'd sacrificed her own happiness. She had only herself to blame for Justin's cold attitude. And not only did she blame herself for her betrayal, but she also hadn't been honest with him about the reasons she'd been afraid to let him touch her.

Now he was going to marry her out of pity, not out of love. And, too, there was always his wish for revenge. She didn't know how she was going to live with him, but only proximity was going to change his mind about her. And living with him would be so sweet. Even though she couldn't be the kind of woman he needed, it was all of heaven to be near him. Maybe one day she'd find the courage to tell him the truth about herself, to make him understand.

All her doubts were back. But she'd given her word to go through with the wedding, and she couldn't back down now. She was going to have to make the best of it, and hope that Justin's thirst for revenge wasn't prompting his decision to marry her.

Chapter Three

Abby was enlisted to help Shelby with the wedding preparations. Shelby had always liked the Ballenger brothers' ward. Abby seemed to understand so well what was going on between Justin and his ex-fiancé.

"I don't imagine Justin is making it easy for you," Abby said while they addressed envelopes for the invitations that they'd just picked up from the printer.

Shelby brushed back a strand of dark hair, sighing gently. "He feels sorry for me," she said with a faint smile. "And maybe he's bent on revenge. But I'm afraid that's all he's got to give me."

"He seemed to be coming around pretty well the night we all went to that square dance and Calhoun spent most of it dancing with you," Abby recalled, tongue in cheek. It was easy to laugh about the past now, although she and Justin had been devastated at the time.

Shelby cleared her throat. "Justin had enough to say to me when we danced. Afterward, I guess he gave Calhoun the devil, if his expression was anything to go by. He was mad."

"Mad!" Abby laughed. Her blue-gray eyes searched Shelby's. "He went home and got drunk. Worse," she confessed ruefully, "he got me drunk, too. When Calhoun got back from taking you home, we were sprawled on the sofa together trying to figure out a way to get up and lock him out of the house."

Shelby's eyes glistened with amused light. "Abby!"

"Oh, it gets even better," she added. "Justin taught me this horribly obscene Spanish drinking song..."

Shelby blushed, remembering the first time she'd heard that song. "He taught it to me, too, the night we got engaged, and we were just starting to sing it when Maria came in and was furious."

Abby finished one of the envelopes and put an invitation in it, sealing it absently while she studied Shelby's reflective expression. "Justin never got over you, you know."

Shelby's eyes lifted. "He never got over what I did, you mean. He's so unbending, Abby. And I can't blame him for the way he feels. At the time, I lacerated his pride."

"Why?"

The other woman only smiled. "I thought I was saving him, you see," she said quietly. "My father didn't want a cowboy for a son-in-law. He had a rich man all earmarked for me, a financially advantageous marriage. But I wouldn't play along, and when he found out I'd agreed to marry Justin, he set out to destroy the relationship." She turned a sealed envelope in her hands. "I never realized how ruthless my father could be until then. He threatened to ruin Justin if I didn't go along." She smoothed the envelope as she remembered the bitterness. "I didn't believe him, so I called his bluff. The bank foreclosed on the feedlot and the Ballenger boys almost lost everything."

"It was a long time ago," Abby said, touching her hand gently. "The feedlot is prosperous now. In fact, it was then. Wasn't it?"

"My father promised that if I went along with his proposition, he'd pull a few strings and talk the bank out of putting the place on public auction. Justin told me about the bankruptcy proceedings," she added. "He was devastated. He even talked about calling off the engagement, so I figured I was going to lose him anyway and it might as well be to his advantage. At the time," she added, remembering how distant Justin had been, how standoffish, "I remember thinking that he'd changed his mind about marrying me. I was pretty reserved." She didn't enlarge on that, but she remembered clearly the way Justin had reacted when she'd struggled away from him on the sofa. But surely that hadn't hurt his pride. He must have been pretty experienced.

Abby leaned forward. "What did your father do?"

"He produced Tom Wheelor, my new fiancé, and took him to meet Justin. He told Justin," she continued dully, "that I'd only been dating him to make Tom propose, because Tom was rich and Justin wasn't. He made out that it was all my fault, that I was the culprit. Justin believed him. He believed that I'd deliberately led him on, just to get Tom jealous enough to marry me. And then Dad told Justin that Tom and I were lovers, and Tom confirmed it."

Abby lifted her eyes. "You weren't," she said with certainty.

Shelby smiled. "Bless you for seeing the truth. Of course we weren't. But in order to save Justin's fledgling business, I had to go along with my father's lie. So when Justin called me and asked me for the truth, I told him what

I'd been coached to say." She lowered her gaze to the carpet. "I told him that I wanted money, that I'd never wanted him, that it was all a game I'd been playing to amuse myself while I brought Tom in line." Her eyes closed. "I don't think I'll ever be able to forget the silence on the line, or the way he hung up, so quietly. A few weeks later, all the talk of bankruptcy died down, so I guess Dad convinced the bank that the Ballengers were a good risk. Tom Wheelor and I went around together for a while, to convince Justin, and then I went to Europe for six months and did my best to get myself killed on ski jumps all over Switzerland. Eventually I came back, but something in me died because of what my father did. He realized it at last, just before I lost him. He even apologized. But it was much too late."

"If you could just make Justin listen..." Abby sighed.

"He won't. He can't forgive me, Abby. It was like a public execution. Everybody knew that I'd jilted him for a richer man. You know how he hates gossip. That destroyed his pride."

Abby grimaced. "He must have realized that your father didn't approve of him."

"Oh, that was the beauty of it. My father welcomed Justin into the family with open arms and made a production about how proud he was going to be of his new son." She laughed bitterly. "Even when he went to Justin with Tom, my father played his part to perfection. He was almost in tears at the callous way I'd treated poor Justin."

"But why? Just for a merger? Didn't he care about your happiness?"

"My father was an empire builder," she said simply. "He let nothing get in the way of business, especially not the children. Ty never knew," she added. "He'd have been furious if he'd had any inkling, but it was part of the bargain that I couldn't tell Ty, either."

"Haven't you ever told Ty the truth?"

"It didn't seem necessary," Shelby replied. "Ty is a loner. It's hard even for me to talk to him, to get close to him. I think that may be why he's never married. He can't open up to people. Dad was hard on him. Even harder than he was on me. He ridiculed Ty and browbeat him most of our childhood. He grew up tough because he had to be, to survive his home life."

"I never knew. I like Ty," Abby said with a smile. "He's a very special man."

Shelby smiled back. She didn't tell Abby that Ty had been infatuated with her. And on top of losing his entire heritage and having to go to work for someone else, losing his chance with Abby was just the last straw. Ty had left for Arizona and his new job without a voiced regret. Perhaps the change would do him good.

Mrs. Simpson brought in a tray of cake and coffee and the three women sat and talked about the wedding until Abby had to leave. Shelby hadn't told anyone what Justin had said about her dress. But the next day she went into Jacobsville to the small boutique that one of her childhood playmates now owned, and the smart linen suit she bought to be married in was white.

That didn't worry her, because she knew she could prove to Justin that she was more than entitled to the symbolic white dress. Then she went for her premarital examination.

Dr. Sims had been her family doctor for half her life, and the tall, graying man was like family to all his patients. His quiet explanation after the examination, after the blood test was done by his lab, made her feel sick all over. And even though she protested, he was quietly firm about the necessity.

"It's only a very minor bit of surgery," he said. "You'll hardly feel it. And frankly, Shelby, if it isn't done, your wedding night is going to be a nightmare." He explained it in detail, and when he finished, she realized that she didn't have a choice. Justin might swear that he was never going to touch her in bed, but she knew it was unrealistic to assume that they could live together without going too far. And with the minor surgery, some pain could be avoided.

She finally agreed, but she insisted that he do only a partial job, so that there was no doubt she was a virgin. Doctor Sims muttered something about old-fashioned idiocy, but he did as she asked. He murmured something about the difficulty she might still encounter because of her stubbornness and that she might need to come back and see him. She hadn't wanted to argue about it, but it was important for Justin to believe her. This was the only proof she had left. The thing was, she hadn't counted on the prospect of such discomfort, and it began to wear on her mind. Had she done the right thing? She wanted Justin to know, without having to be told, that she was innocent. But that prospect of being hurt was just as frightening as it had been in the past—more so.

The wedding was the social event of the season. Shelby hadn't expected so many people to congregate in the Jacobsville Methodist church to see her get married. Certainly there were more spectators than she'd included on her list.

Abby and Calhoun were sitting in the family pew, holding hands, the tall blond man and the dark-haired woman so much in love that they radiated it all around. Beside them was Shelby's green-eyed, black-haired brother, Tyler, towering above everyone except Calhoun. There were neighbors and friends, and Misty Davies, Abby's friend, on the other side of the church. Justin was nowhere in sight, and Shelby almost panicked as she remembered his threat to leave if she wore a white dress.

But when the wedding march struck up, the minister and Justin were waiting for her at the altar. She had to bite her lower lip hard and grip her bouquet of daisies to keep from shaking as she walked down the aisle.

She and Justin had decided not to have a best man or a matron of honor, or much ceremony except for the actual service. There were plenty of flowers around the altar, and a candelabra with three unlit white candles. The minister was in his robes, and Justin was in a formal black suit, very elegant as he waited for his bride to join him.

When she reached him, and took her place at his side, she looked up. Her green eyes caught his black ones and her expression invited him to do what he'd threatened, to walk out of the church.

It was a tense moment and for one horrible second, he looked as if he were thinking about it. But the moment passed. He lifted his cold eyes to the minister and he repeated what he was told to say without a trace of expression in his deep voice.

He placed a thin gold band on her hand. There had been no engagement ring, and he hadn't mentioned buying one. He'd bought her ring himself, on a trip to town, and he hadn't asked if she wanted him to wear one. Probably he didn't want to.

They replied to the final questions and lit two candles, each holding a flame to the third candle, signifying the unity of two people into one. The minister pronounced them man and wife. He invited Justin to kiss his bride.

Justin turned to Shelby with an expression she couldn't read. He looked down at her for a long moment before he bent his head and brushed a light, cool kiss across her lips. Then he took her arm and propelled her down the aisle and outside into the hall, where they were surrounded seconds later by well-wishers.

There was no time to talk. The reception was held in the fellowship hall of the church, and punch, cake and canapés were consumed while Shelby and Justin were each occupied with guests.

Someone had a camera and asked them to pose for a photograph. They hadn't hired anyone to take pictures of the wedding, an oversight that Shelby was secretly disappointed at. She'd hoped for at least a photograph of them together, but perhaps this one would do.

She stood behind Justin and smiled, feeling his arm draw her to his side. Her eyes lifted to his, but it was hard to hold the smile as those black eyes cut into hers.

The instant the camera was gone, he glared at her. "I said any color except white."

"Yes, Justin, I know you did," she said calmly. "And think how you'd have felt if I'd insisted that you wear a blue dress instead of a black suit to be married in."

He blinked, as if he wasn't quite sure he'd heard right. "A white dress means—" he began indignantly.

"—a first wedding," she finished for him. "This is mine."

His eyes kindled. "You and I both know there's an implied second reason for wearing white, and you aren't entitled to it." He noticed something darken her eyes and his own narrowed. "You told me you could prove it, though, didn't you, Shelby?" He smiled coldly. "I just might let you do that before we're through."

She blushed and averted her eyes. For an instant, she felt cowardly, thinking about how difficult it was going to be if he wasn't gentle, if he treated her like the scarlet woman he thought she was. It didn't bear consideration, and she shivered. "I don't have to prove anything to you."

He laughed, the sound of it like ice shattering. "You can't, can you? It was all bravado, to keep me guessing until we were married."

Her eyes lifted to his. "Justin..."

"Never mind." He pulled out a cigarette and lit it. "I told you, we won't be sharing a bed. I don't care about your chastity."

She felt an aching sadness for what might have been between them and she looked at him, her eyes soft and quietly adoring on his craggy features. He was so beautiful. Not handsome, but beautifully made, for a man, from his lithe, powerful build to his black eyes and thick black hair and olive complexion. He looked exactly the way a man should, she decided.

He glanced down at her, caught in that warm appraisal. His cigarette hovered in midair while he searched her eyes, holding them for so long that her heart went wild in her chest. She let her eyes fall to his chiseled mouth, and she wanted it suddenly with barely contained passion. If only she could be the uninhibited woman she wanted to be, and not such a frightened innocent. Justin intimidated her. He had to be at least as worldly as Calhoun. She'd disappoint him, anyway, but if only she could tell him the truth and ask him to be gentle. She shivered at the thought of telling him something so intimate.

It was a blessing that Ty chose that moment to say his goodbyes, sparing Shelby the embarrassment of having Justin mock her for her weakness.

"I've got to catch a plane back to Arizona," he told his sister as he bent his head to brush her cheek with his lips. "My temporary lady boss is scared stiff of men."

Shelby's eyes brightened. "She's what?"

Ty looked frankly uncomfortable. "She's nervous around men," he said reluctantly. "Damn it, she hides behind me at dances, at meetings . . . it's embarrassing."

Shelby had to fight down laughter. Her very independent brother didn't like clinging women, but this one seemed to be affecting him very strangely. His temporary boss was the niece of his permanent boss. She lived in Arizona, where she was trying to cope with an indebted dude ranch. Ty's boss in Jacobsville had sent him out to help. He'd hated it at the beginning, and he still seemed to, but maybe the mysterious Arizona lady was getting to him.

"Maybe she feels safe with you?" Shelby asked.

He glowered at her. "Well, it's got to stop. It's like having poison ivy wrap itself around you."

"Is she ugly?" Shelby persisted.

"Kind of plain and unsophisticated," he murmured. "Not too bad, I guess, if you like tomboys. I don't," he added doggedly.

"Why don't you quit?" Justin asked. "You can work for Calhoun and me, we've already offered you a job."

"Yes, I know. I appreciated it, too, considering how strained things were between our families," Ty said honestly. "But this job is kind of a challenge and that part I like."

Justin smiled. "Come and stay when you get homesick."

Ty shook his outstretched hand. "I might, one day. I like kids," he added. "A few nieces and nephews wouldn't bother me."

Justin looked murderous and Shelby went scarlet. Ty frowned, and Justin thanked God that Calhoun and Abby joined them in time to ward off trouble. He didn't want to think about kids. Shelby sure wouldn't want his, not if the way she'd reacted to him the one time he'd been ardent with her was any indication. She was repulsed by him.

"Isn't this a nice wedding?" Calhoun asked Ty, joining the small group with his arm around a laughing Abby. "Doesn't it give you any ideas?"

Ty smiled at Abby. "It does that, all right. It makes me want to get an inoculation, quick," he murmured dryly.

"You'll outgrow that attitude one day," Calhoun assured him. "We all get chopped down at the ankles eventually," he added, and ducked when Abby hit his chest. "Sorry, honey." He chuckled, brushing a lazy kiss against her forehead. "You know I didn't mean it."

"Can we give you a lift to the airport, or did you rent a car?" Abby asked Ty.

"I rented a car, but thanks all the same. Why don't you two walk me out to it?" He kissed Shelby again. "Be happy," he said gently.

"I expect to," she said, and smiled in Justin's direction.

Ty nodded, but he didn't look convinced. When he followed Abby and Calhoun out of the fellowship hall, he was preoccupied and frowning thoughtfully.

The reception seemed to go on forever, and Shelby was grateful when it was finally time to go home. Justin had sent Lopez to fetch Shelby's things from Mrs. Simpson's house early that morning. The guest room had been prepared for Shelby. Maria had questioned that, but only once, because Justin's cold eyes had silenced her. Maria understood more than he realized, anyway. She, like everyone else on the property, knew that despite his bitterness, Justin still had a soft spot for Shelby. She was alone and impoverished, and it didn't surprise anybody that Justin had married her. If he felt the need for a little vengeance in the process, that wasn't unexpected, either.

"Thank God that's over," Justin said wearily when they were alone in the house. He'd tugged off his tie and jacket and unbuttoned the neck of his shirt and rolled up the sleeves. He looked ten years older than he was.

Shelby put her purse on the hall table and took off her high heels, smoothing her stockinged feet on the soft pile of the carpet. It felt good not to be two inches taller.

Justin glanced at her and smiled to himself, but he turned away before she could see it. "Do you want to go out for supper or have it here?"

"I don't care."

"I suppose it would look odd if we went to a restaurant on our wedding night, wouldn't it?" he added, turning to give her a mocking smile.

She glared at him. "Go ahead," she invited. "Spoil the rest of it, too. God forbid that I should enjoy my own wedding day."

He frowned as she turned and started up the staircase. "What the hell are you talking about?"

She didn't look at him. She held onto the railing and stared up at the landing. "You couldn't have made your feelings plainer if you'd worn a sign with all your grievances painted on it in blood. I know you hate me, Justin. You married me out of pity, but part of you still wants to make me pay for what I did to you."

He'd lit a cigarette and he was smoking it, propped against the doorjamb, his face quiet, his black eyes curious. "Dreams die hard, honey, didn't you know?" he asked coldly.

She turned around, her green eyes steady on his. "You weren't the only one who dreamed, Justin," she said. "I cared about you!"

His jaw tautened. "Sure you did. That's why you sold me out for that boy millionaire."

She stroked the banister absently. "Odd that I didn't marry him, isn't it?" she asked casually. "Very odd, wouldn't you say, when I wanted his money badly enough to jilt you."

He lifted the cigarette to his mouth. "He threw you over, I guess, when he found out you wanted the money more than you wanted him."

"I never wanted him, or his money," she said honestly. "I had enough of my own."

He smiled at her. "Did you?" Surely she didn't expect him to believe she was unaware of how much financial trouble her father had been in.

"You won't listen," she muttered. "You never would. I tried to tell you why I broke off the engagement—"

"You told me, all right! You couldn't stand for me to touch you, but I knew that already." His eyes glittered dangerously. "You pushed me away the night we got engaged," he added huskily. "You were shaking like a leaf and your eyes were as big as saucers. You couldn't get away from me quick enough."

Her lips parted on a slow breath. "And you thought it was revulsion, of course?" she asked miserably.

"What else could it have been?" he shot back, his eyes glaring. "I didn't come down in the last rain shower." He turned. "Change your clothes and we'll have supper. I don't know about you, but I'm hungry."

She wished she could tell him the truth. She wanted to, but he was so remote and his detached attitude intimidated her. With a sigh, she turned and went up the staircase numbly, wondering how she was going to live with a man she couldn't even talk to about intimacy.

They had a quiet wedding supper. Maria put everything on the table and she and Lopez went out for the evening, offering quiet congratulations before they left.

Justin leaned back in his chair when he'd finished his steak and salad, watching Shelby pick at hers.

He felt vaguely guilty about their wedding day. But in a way, he was hiding from her. Hiding his real feelings, hiding his apprehension about losing her a second time. It had wrung him out emotionally six years before. He didn't think he could bear it a second time, so he was trying to protect himself from becoming too vulnerable. But her sad little face was getting to him.

"Damn it, Shelby," he ground out, "don't look like that."

She lifted her eyes. There was no life in them anymore. "I'm tired," she said softly. "Do you mind if I go to bed after we eat?"

"Yes, I mind." He threw down his napkin and lit a cigarette. "It's our wedding night."

She laughed bitterly. "So it is. What did you have in mind, some more comments on my scarlet past?"

He frowned slightly. She didn't sound like Shelby. That edge to her voice was disturbing. His eyes narrowed. She'd lost her father, her home, her entire way of life, even her brother. She'd lost everything in recent weeks, and married him because she needed a little security. He'd given her hell, and now she looked as if today was the last straw on the camel's back. He hadn't meant for it to be that way. He didn't want to hurt her. But he couldn't seem to keep quiet; there were so many wounds.

He sighed heavily. His black eyes searched her wan face, remembering better times, happier times, when he could look at her and get drunk on just the sight of her smile.

"Are you sure you want to keep on working?" he asked quietly, just to change the subject, to get the conversation on an easier level.

She stared down at her plate. "Yes, I'd like to," she said. "I've never really done any work before, except society functions and volunteer work. I like my job."

"And Barry Holman?" he asked, his smile a challenge.

She got up. She was still wearing her white skirt with a pale pink blouse, and she looked feminine and elegant and very desirable. Her long hair waved down to her shoulders, and Justin wanted to get up and catch two handfuls of it and kiss her until she couldn't stand up.

"Mr. Holman is my boss," she said. "Not my lover. I don't have a lover."

He got up, too, moving closer, his eyes narrow and calculating, his body tense with years of frustrated desire. "You're going to have one," he said curtly.

She wouldn't back away. She wouldn't give him the satisfaction of watching her run. She lifted her face proudly, even though her knees felt weak and her heart was racing madly. She was afraid of him because of their past, because he wanted revenge. She was afraid because he thought she was experienced, and even with that minor surgery, she knew that it wasn't going to be the easiest time of her life. Justin was deceptively strong. She knew the power in that lean, hard body, and to be overwhelmed by it in passion was a little scary.

He watched the fear flicker in her eyes, and understood it instantly. "You're off base, honey," he said quietly. "Way off base. I'd never hurt you in bed, not for revenge or any other reason."

Her lower lip trembled on a stifled sob and tears welled in her eyes. She lowered her gaze to his broad chest, missing the faint shock in his face at her reaction. "Maybe you wouldn't be able to help it," she whispered.

"Shelby, are you really afraid of me?" he asked huskily.

Her thin shoulders shifted. "Yes. I'm sorry."

"Were you afraid with him?" he asked. "With Wheelor?"

She opened her mouth to speak and just gave up. What was the use? He wasn't going to listen. She turned away and went toward the staircase.

"Running won't solve anything," he said shortly, watching her go with mingled feelings, the foremost of which was anger.

"Neither will trying to talk to you," she replied. She turned at the bottom of the staircase, her green eyes bright with unshed tears and returning spirit. "Do your worst. Make me pay. I'm fresh out of things I care about. I've got absolutely nothing left to lose, so look out, Justin. I'm not going to live up to your idea of a society wife. I'm going to be myself, and I'm sorry if it destroys any of your old illusions."

He eyed her quietly. "Meaning what?"

"No affairs," she replied, picking the thought out of his mind. "Despite what you think of me, I'm not starved for a man."

"That much I'd believe," he said shortly. "My God, I get more warmth out of an ice cube than I ever got from you!"

She felt the impact of those words like daggers against her bare skin. She should have realized that he thought her frigid, but it had never really registered before.

"Maybe Tom Wheelor got more!" she threw at him.

His black eyes splintered with rage. He actually started toward her before he checked himself with the iron control that he kept on his temper.

Shelby saw that movement, and thanked God that he stopped when he did. She lifted her chin. "Good night, Justin. Thank you for a roof over my head and a place to live."

His eyelids flickered as she started up the staircase. Looking at her he recalled years of dreams, of remembered delight in just being with her, frustration at having to hold back only to lose her anyway. He still cared. He'd lied to protect his pride, but he cared so much. And he was losing her, all over again.

He wanted to tell her that he hadn't meant to accuse her of being frigid. He'd wanted her to distraction, and she hadn't wanted him. That had hurt far more than having her break their engagement, especially when he'd found out that Tom Wheelor was her lover. It had damned near killed him. And here she was throwing it in his teeth, hitting him in his most vulnerable spot. He'd always wondered if she found him revolting physically. That was what made him believe that she'd meant what she told him about not wanting him, about wanting Tom Wheelor instead—that reluctance in her to let him get close to her.

And she was different now. She wasn't the shy, introverted young woman he'd known six years ago. She was oddly reckless; high-spirited and uninhibited when she forgot herself. But he couldn't bend. He couldn't make himself bend enough to tell her what was in his heart, how much he still wanted her, because he didn't dare trust her again. She'd hurt him too badly. He watched her go up the staircase, his eyes black and soft and full of hunger. He didn't move until she was out of sight.

Chapter Four

Shelby had hoped beyond hope that Justin might still love her. That he might have married her not so much out of pity as out of love. But her wedding day had convinced her that what little emotion had been left in him after years of bitterness was all gone. He still blamed her for what he thought she'd done with Tom Wheelor, and he thought she was frigid.

She didn't know how to deal with her own fears and his anger. Her marriage was going to be as empty as her life had been. There would be no black-headed little babies to nurse, no soft, sweet loving in the darkness, no shared delight in making a life together. There would be only separate bedrooms and separate lives and Justin's hunger for vengeance.

The black depression that she'd taken to bed on her wedding night got worse. Justin tolerated her presence, but he was away more often than not. At meals, he spoke to her only when it was necessary, and he never touched her.

He was like a polite host instead of a husband. And day by miserable day, Shelby began to feel a new recklessness. While Justin was away one weekend, she went on a white-water rafting race with Abby's friend Misty Davies. She tried her hand at skydiving. She joined a fencing class. She went back to the old, more reckless days of her adolescence. Justin had never really known her, she thought sometimes. He seemed surprised by the things she enjoyed and a time or two he acted as if her life-style bothered him. Well, what had he expected her to do, she fumed, stay at home and arrange flowers? Perhaps that was the image he had of her, that she was a pretty socialite with beauty and no brains.

She'd kept working after the wedding, but Barry Holman insisted that she take a few days off. It wasn't right, he said, for her to work through her honeymoon. She wanted to laugh at that, and tell him that her husband didn't want a honeymoon. Justin had come home from his latest trip and had gone straight to the feedlot office with an abrupt and coolly polite greeting. After a few bored hours, Shelby phoned the office, just to see how things were going. She liked her job. She missed working terribly. It was something to do; it helped keep her mind off her marriage and her own inadequacies.

When she called, the poor temporary secretary, Tammy Lester, answered the phone, obviously half out of her mind trying to cope with an impatient, frustrated Barry Holman. So Shelby dressed in a cool white and red summery dress and white high heels and went to work.

The old sedan she drove broke down halfway there and she had to have it towed in to the dealer car lot where she had her mechanical work done.

Once Shelby was at the dealership, as fate would have it, she noticed Abby's little sports car was there and up for sale. The sight of the car brought back memories. Shelby had driven one like it during six of the blackest months in her life, the time she'd spent in Switzerland after she'd given back Justin's ring. She'd loved that car, but she'd wrecked it accidentally. The wreck hadn't dampened her enthusiasm for fast cars, though. Now she wanted one—it appealed to the wild streak in her that had never totally disappeared. It wasn't a suicidal streak; she just loved a challenge. She liked sports cars and the exhilaration of driving in the fast lane.

Justin didn't know that Shelby had a wild streak, because he'd accepted the illusion of what she appeared to be rather than wondering what was beneath the surface. Well, he was in for a few shocks, she decided, starting now.

Because the dealer knew that Shelby had just married Justin, he didn't even ask for a cosigner on the note. He sold her the car outright, with payments she could afford on her own salary.

She parked the vehicle right outside the office, delighting in its new paint job. Abby had had it painted red with white racing stripes just before she traded it for something more sedate. The new colors suited Shelby very well. She sighed over it, delighted that she could afford it and even manage the payments by herself. All her life she'd depended on her father's money. There was something challenging and very satisfying about taking care of herself financially. She was sorry now that she'd panicked at being on her own and rushed into marrying Justin. She'd hoped for something more than a roof over her head, but that wasn't going to happen. Justin was taking care of her, just as he'd taken care of Abby, and if he had any lingering desire for her, it didn't show. After he'd accused her of being frigid, she'd kept out of his way altogether. If only she wasn't so repressed, she could have told him what the problem was and how frightened she was of intimacy. But it was hopeless. Justin would probably be as embarrassed as she was to talk about it, anyway. So things would just have to rock along as they had been, until one of them broke the silence.

When she got to the office, Barry Holman was pacing the floor while the temporary secretary cried. They both turned as Shelby put her purse in the top drawer of the desk and smiled.

"Can I help?" she asked.

The woman at her desk cried even harder. "He yells," she wailed, pointing at Barry Holman, who looked furiously angry from his blond head to his big feet.

"Only at incompetents!" he flashed back.

"Now, now," Shelby soothed. "I'm here. I'll take care of everything. Tammy, why don't you make Mr. Holman a cup of coffee while I straighten out whatever's fouled up, then I'll show you how to update the files and you can keep busy with that. Okay?"

Tammy smiled, her soft brown eyes quiet. "Okay."

She got up and Shelby sat down. Her dark brows lifted as Barry Holman glanced at her uncomfortably.

"It's your vacation," he said. "You shouldn't be here."

"Why not? Justin is working, why shouldn't I?"

He frowned. "Well . . ."

"Tell me what needs to be done, and then I'll show you my new car." She grinned. "It was Abby's, and they let me buy it without even a cosigner."

"Naturally, considering your husband's credit line," he mused. She gave him a strange look, but he ignored it, delighting in his good fortune. "Here, this is what's giving Tammy fits."

He produced two scribbled pages of notes on a legal pad that he wanted transcribed and put into English instead of abbreviations and scrawls, and fifty copies run off with different salutations on each.

"Simple, isn't it?" he said. He glared toward the back of the office. "She cried."

Shelby wanted to. It was an hour's work just to translate his handwriting. But she knew how to use the computer's word-processing program, and Tammy had three simplified tutorials spread out on the desk, none of which would explain the program to a person who'd never used a computer.

"She asked me what these were for." Barry Holman sighed, picking up one of the diskettes in its jacket. He looked up. "She thought they were negatives."

Shelby had to bite her lower lip. "She's never had any computer training," she reminded him.

"That's no excuse for not having a brain," he returned hotly.

"Mr. Holman!" Tammy exclaimed, glaring at him as she came back with three cups of black coffee on a tray. "That was unkind and unfair."

"Didn't they tell you at the temporary-services agency that computer experience was necessary to do this job?" he grumbled.

"I have computer experience," Tammy replied with hauteur. "I play games on my brother's Atari all the time."

Mr. Holman looked as if *he* wanted to cry. He ground his teeth together, went back into his office and closed the door.

"I guess I told him." Tammy grinned wickedly.

There was a loud, feverish, furious, *"Damn!"* from the vicinity of Mr. Holman's office. Shelby and Tammy exchanged amused glances.

"They didn't tell me about the computer," Tammy confided. "They asked if I had office skills, and I do. I type over a hundred words a minute and take dictation at ninety. But I don't read Sanskrit," she whispered, pointing at the scribbling on the legal sheets.

Shelby burst out laughing. It felt so good to laugh, and she thanked God for this job, which was going to save her sanity. She shook her head and, putting the books aside, she began to explain the computer's operation to Tammy.

After work, she took the long route home. Mr. Holman had relaxed after lunch, and he was tolerating Tammy much better now. In fact, he hadn't even growled when Shelby had mentioned that it might be economical to have two secretaries in the office because of the backlog of filing and updating the computer's entries. He'd talked about taking on an associate, and if he hired Tammy full time, he could do it.

Shelby turned the small sports car onto the highway sharply, delighting in its rack-and-pinion steering and easy handling. She gunned it up and up and up, loving the speed, loving the freedom and the wind tearing through her long hair. She felt reckless. As she'd told Justin, she had nothing left to lose. She was going to enjoy her life from now on. Justin could just do his worst.

There was a slow car in front, and she didn't even brake. She surged around it and barely got back into her lane as a white car sped in the opposite direction. She thought it looked familiar, but she didn't look in the rearview mirror. It was going toward the feedlot. She passed the turnoff, increasing her speed. She wasn't ready to go home to her cell just yet.

Calhoun was muttering a prayer as he pulled up in front of the feedlot. That was Abby's old car, and it had been Shelby at the wheel. He'd barely recognized her in that split second, her face laughing with pleasure at the speed, her hair flying in the wind. She made Abby's friend Misty Davies look like a safe driver by comparison.

Justin looked up from his desk as Calhoun came in and closed the door behind him. "It's almost time to go home," he remarked, glancing at his Rolex. "I didn't think you were coming back today from Montana."

Calhoun grinned. "I missed Abby. Speaking of Abby," he added, perching himself lazily on the edge of his brother's desk, "a wild woman driving her sports car just came within an inch of running me down."

"Didn't Abby sell it?" Justin remarked.

"She certainly did. I insisted."

"I see." Justin smiled faintly. He leaned back with his cigarette smoking in his lean fingers. "I gather that some other fool's wife is driving it?"

"You could put it that way. She was doing eighty if she was doing a mile." His dark eyes narrowed. "Are you sure you want Shelby to have it?"

There was a shocked silence. "What do you mean, do I want Shelby to have it?" Justin sat up abruptly. "Are you telling me Shelby was driving that sports car?"

"I'm afraid so," Calhoun said quietly. "You didn't know?"

Justin's expression became grim. Shelby wasn't happy and he knew it. Her most recent behavior was already worrying him, although he was careful to keep his misgivings from Shelby. But purchasing a sports car was going too far. He was going to have to talk to her. He'd avoided confrontations, letting her settle in, keeping his distance while he tried to cope with the anguish of having Shelby in his house when she backed away the minute he came into the room. But this was too much.

He couldn't let her kill herself. He got up from the desk without even looking at Calhoun, plucked his hat off the hat rack and started for the door. "Was she going toward the house?" he asked curtly.

"The opposite direction," Calhoun told him. His eyes narrowed. "Justin, what's going on between the two of you?"

The older man looked at him, black eyes glittering. "My private life is none of your business."

Calhoun folded his arms. "Abby says Shelby is running wild, and that you're apparently doing nothing to stop her. Are you that hell-bent on revenge?"

"You make it sound as if she's suicidal," Justin said coldly. "She's not."

"If she was happy, she wouldn't be like this," the younger man persisted. "You've got to stop trying to live in the past. It's time to forget what happened."

"That's damned easy for you to say." Justin's black eyes flashed. "She threw me over and slept with another man!"

Calhoun stared at him. "You don't have my track record, but you're no more a saint than I am, big brother. Suppose Shelby couldn't accept the women in your past?"

"It's different with men," the older man said irritably.

"Is it?"

"She was mine. I was so damned careful never to put a foot wrong with her. I held back and gritted my teeth to keep from scaring her, and she flinched away from me every time I touched her. And all the while she was sleeping with that pasty-faced boy millionaire. How do you think I felt?" he blazed. "And then she told me that I was too poor to suit her expensive tastes, she wanted somebody rich."

"She didn't marry him, did she?" Calhoun returned. "She left for Europe and went wild, just as she's going wild now. She was in a wreck in Switzerland, Justin. In a sports car," he added, watching the horror grow in his

brother's eyes, "just like the one she's driving now. She
was grieving for you. Even her father realized that, at
last."

Justin fumbled a cigarette into his mouth and lit it.
"Nobody ever told me that."

"When would you ever listen to anything about her?"
Calhoun replied. "It's only in the past few months that
you've calmed down enough to talk about anything connected with the Jacobses."

"I wanted her," Justin ground out. "You can't imagine how I felt when she broke it off."

"Yes, I can," Calhoun replied. "I was there. I know
what it was like for you. But you never even considered
that Shelby might have had a reason. She tried to explain
it once, to tell you why she broke off the engagement. You
wouldn't even listen."

"What was there to listen to?" Justin asked impatiently. "She'd already told me the truth, in the beginning."

"I never believed it," Calhoun replied. "And neither
would you have, if you hadn't been in love for the first
time in your life and so damned uncertain about your own
ability to keep Shelby. You were always worried about
losing her to another man. Even to me. Remember?"

It was hard to argue with the truth. Justin knew he'd
been possessive about Shelby. Hell, he still was. But how
could he help it? She was a beautiful woman, and he was
a plain, unworldly man. He'd never been able to understand why Shelby had stayed with him as long as she had.

"Even now," Calhoun continued quietly, "it seems to
me that you're trying your best to make her leave you."

Justin smiled mockingly. "What do you expect me to
do, tie her in the cellar?" he asked reasonably. "I can't
make her stay if she doesn't want to. Hell—" he laughed

coldly "—I can't even touch her. She flinched away from me the one time I tried to make love to her," he said bluntly, remembering. His eyes went blacker and he looked away. "I can't get near her. She's afraid of me that way."

"How interesting," Calhoun said, choosing his words, "that such an experienced woman of the world could be afraid of sex. Isn't it?"

Justin frowned. "What do you mean?"

Calhoun didn't answer him. He was smiling a little when he started out the door, but Justin couldn't see the smile. "I've got to get home. See you, big brother." And before Justin could reply, he was gone.

Justin took a minute to get his temper under control. He went out the door behind Calhoun without a word to his secretary, his eyes narrow with concern. Calhoun had delayed him too long. Suppose Shelby wrecked that little car?

He went up and down the road, but he didn't see any sign of the sports car. Later, he went to the house, and almost went down on his knees with relief when he found it parked at the steps.

He had to force himself to behave normally when his hands were almost shaking from fear that he might find her in a ditch somewhere. He walked into the house, tossing his hat onto the hat rack, and went into the dining room, where Shelby was sitting in a chair halfway down the long cherry-wood table, talking to Maria about some new recipe.

She looked toward the doorway, but when she saw him, all the laughter and animation went out of her like a light that was suddenly turned off. She was wearing a red and white dress and her hair was down around her shoulders in a pretty, dark, waving tangle. The wind, he thought absently, tearing through her hair in the convertible.

"I've traded cars," she said defiantly. "How do you like it? It was Abby's. You don't even have to cosign with me, I can make the payments from my salary."

Justin glanced at Maria, who knew the look and made herself scarce. He sat down at the head of the table, lit a cigarette and leaned back in the chair to stare intently at Shelby. "The last thing in the world you need is a sports car. You already drive too damned fast."

She searched his dark eyes, reading the thinly veiled concern. "Somebody saw me in the car this afternoon," she guessed.

He nodded. "Calhoun."

"I thought it was him." She studied her hands in her lap, turning the thin gold band on her wedding finger. "I like speed," she said hotly.

"I don't like funerals," he shot back. "I don't intend having to go to yours. You'll take that sports car back tomorrow or I'll take it back for you."

"It's mine!" she cried. Her green eyes flashed angrily. "And I won't take it back!"

He took a long draw from his cigarette. In his reclining position, his white silk shirt was drawn taut over tanned muscles. His chest was thick with hair that peeked out through the unfastened top buttons of his shirt. His jacket was off, his sleeves rolled up. He looked devastatingly masculine, from his disheveled black hair to his sensuous mouth.

"I'm not going to argue about it, honey," he replied. Through a veil of smoke, his black eyes searched hers. "Calhoun told me you wrecked a car overseas."

She flushed. "That was an accident."

"You aren't going to have any accidents here," he said. "I won't let you kill yourself."

"For heaven's sake, Justin, I'm not suicidal!" she protested. She lifted her coffee cup to her lips and took a fortifying sip of the black liquid.

"I didn't say you were," he agreed. He moved his ashtray on the tablecloth, watching it spin around. "But you need a firmer hand than you've been getting."

"I'm not Abby," she said. Her finely etched features grew hard as she looked at him. "I don't need a guardian."

He looked back, black eyes searching, quiet. "And while we're on the subject, I don't like you working for Barry Holman."

She blinked. She felt suddenly as if control of her own life was being taken away from her. "Justin, I didn't ask how you liked it," she reminded him. "I told you before we married that I wanted to keep on working."

"There's more than enough to do around here," he said. He tapped an ash into the ashtray. "You can manage the house."

"Maria and Lopez do that very nicely, thank you," she replied. She stiffened. "I don't want to stay home and swirl around the house in silk lounge pajamas and throw parties, Justin, in case you wondered. I've had my fill of charity work and flower arranging and social warfare."

He was looking at the cigarette, not at her. "I thought you might miss those things. In the old days, you never had to lift a finger."

She studied her neat hands in her lap, pleating the thin silky fabric of the red and white dress. "My father saw me as a parlor decoration," she said tautly. "He would have been outraged if I'd tried to change my image."

He frowned slightly. "Were you afraid of him?"

"I was *owned* by him," she replied. She sighed, raising her eyes to Justin's. The curiosity there puzzled her, but at least they were talking for a change instead of arguing. "He wasn't the easiest man to live with, and he had terrible ways of getting even when Ty and I disobeyed."

"He kept you pretty close to home," he recalled. "Although he trusted you with me."

"Did he really?" she laughed hollowly. "Justin, you were the second man I ever dated and the first I ever went out with alone. You look shocked. Did you think my father let me live the life of a playgirl? He was terrified that some fortune hunter might seduce me. I lived like a recluse while he was alive."

Justin wasn't sure he understood what he was hearing. His head tilted a little and his eyes narrowed. "Would you like to run that by me again?" he asked. "You hadn't been out with a man alone until you went with me?"

"That's it," she agreed. "I didn't get out of my father's sight until after I broke the engagement and went to Switzerland." She smiled sadly. "I guess the freedom was too much, because I ran wild. The sports car was just an outlet, a way of celebrating. I never meant to wreck it."

"How badly were you hurt?" he asked.

"I broke my leg and cracked two ribs," she said. "They said I was lucky."

He finished his cigarette and crushed it out. "I didn't realize you were that sheltered," he said quietly. He was only beginning to understand how innocent she'd been in those days. If she'd only dated one other man, then very likely her first taste of intimacy had been with him. He thought about that, and felt himself go taut. He'd expected her to have a little experience, even though he'd known she was virginal. But if she'd had none, it was easy to understand why his ardor would have frightened her so.

"I couldn't talk about things like that with you," she confessed. "I was young and hopelessly naive."

He stared at her narrowly, his black eyes glittering. "I frightened you the night we got engaged, didn't I?" he asked suddenly. "That was why you pulled back—not because I disgusted you."

She caught her breath audibly. "You never disgusted me!" she burst out, hurting for him. "Oh, Justin, no! You didn't think that?"

"We didn't know very much about each other, Shelby," he said, his voice deep and measured. "I suppose we both had false ideas. I saw you as a sophisticated, elegant society woman. And while I knew you were innocent, I thought you'd had some experience with men. If I'd had any idea of what you've just told me, I damned sure wouldn't have been that demanding with you."

She went red and averted her eyes. She couldn't find the right words. Amazing, that they were married and she was twenty-seven years old, and this kind of talk could still embarrass her.

"I was afraid you couldn't stop," she murmured evasively.

He sighed heavily and lifted his coffee cup to his lips, draining it. "So was I," he said unexpectedly. "It was touch and go for a few seconds, at that. I'd gone hungry for a long time."

"I didn't think men had to, these days," she said softly. "I mean, society is so permissive and all."

"Society may be permissive. I'm not," he said flatly. His black eyes flashed at her. "I never was, in the way you mean. A gentleman doesn't seduce virgins—or take advantage of women who don't know the score. That leaves party girls." He held the cup in his big, lean hands, smoothing over it with his thumb. "And just to be frank, honey, the type never appealed very much to me."

Her soft eyes searched over his hard features, lingering on his chiseled mouth.

"I guess you never lacked offers, all the same," she said, letting her gaze fall to her lap again.

"I'm rich." There was cool cynicism in the words. "Sure, I get offers." He studied her face calculatingly. "In fact, Shelby, I had one while I was in New Mexico last week, wedding ring and all."

Her teeth clenched. She didn't want him to see that it bothered her, but it was hard to hide. "Did you?"

He put the cup down. "You're as possessive about me as I am about you," he said then, surprising her gaze up to lock with his in a slow, electric exchange. "You don't like the thought of other women making eyes at me, do you, Shelby?"

She crossed her legs. "No," she said honestly.

He smiled mockingly as he lit another cigarette. "Well, if it's any comfort, I froze her out. I won't cheat on you, honey."

"I never thought you would," she replied. "Any more than I'd cheat on you."

"That would be the eighth wonder of the world," he remarked with deceptive softness, "considering your hang-ups. We've been married for almost two weeks, and you still look like a sacrificial lamb every time I come near you."

She drew in a slow, steadying breath. "Yes, I know," she said miserably. She smiled bitterly. "I'm aware of my own failings, Justin. I guess you won't believe it, but you can't possibly blame me any more than I blame myself for what I am."

He scowled. He hadn't meant to put her on the defensive. His pride was stung and he was striking out. But he didn't want to hurt her anymore. He'd done enough of that already.

"I didn't mean it like that," he said on a weary breath. "It's the way things happened, that's all." He looked his age for a minute, his expression bleak, his dark eyes haunted. "You savaged my pride, Shelby. It's taken a long time to put it behind me. I guess I haven't, just yet."

"I didn't get off scot-free, either," she murmured. Her thin shoulders slumped. "I've had my share of grief over what I did."

"Why?" he asked shortly.

She closed her eyes and winced. "I did it for your sake," she whispered.

He let out an angry breath. "Well, that's a new tack, at least." He ground out the half-finished cigarette and got to his feet. "I've got some paperwork to do before Maria gets supper on the table." He paused beside her chair, watching the way she stiffened as he got close to her. He reached down and caught a handful of her long hair, dragging her head back so that he could see her eyes. "Fear," he ground out, searching them. "That's all I ever see in your eyes when I come near you. Well, don't sweat it, honey. You won't be called on to make the supreme sacrifice. I'm not desperate!"

He let her go and moved past her with anger in every line of his powerful body, without another word or a backward glance.

Shelby felt the tears come and she didn't stop them. He didn't know why she was afraid, and she couldn't tell him. He just assumed that she withdrew because she didn't want him. Nothing was further from the truth. She did, desperately. But she wanted him controlled and gentle, and she remembered how it had been when he wasn't.

She got up from the table and went up to her room to spend a few quiet minutes before they ate getting herself back together again. It was so hard to talk to him, to get around his growing impatience. Her rejection was doing terrible things to him, and even now she felt protective. She wanted to give him what he wanted, to erase those hard lines from his face. But she was so frightened of the demands he might make on her.

If only she could tell him. But her sheltered background made it too embarrassing to explain why she was the way she was. Until she could find a way to make him understand, it was going to put an even worse strain on their marriage.

Chapter Five

If Shelby had hoped to find Justin less angry over dinner, she was doomed to disappointment. He sat at the head of the table like a stone man, barely speaking through the meal. She couldn't talk to him. She didn't know what to say.

Afterward, he went out the door without a word and Shelby felt a sense of utter desperation. If only she could go to him and put her arms around him, explain how she felt, why she was the way she was. But would he believe her, with their past?

Misery wrapped around her like a blanket. She got her purse and went out to her car. If Justin thought she was going to sit around by herself for what was left of the evening, he could just think again.

She started the sports car, revved the engine, backed out and roared away. The wonderful thing about the little car was the delicious feel of its controlled speed. She loved the straight road, the sense of freedom she felt with the wind in her long hair, the exhilaration of being alone with her thoughts.

Justin hated her, but that was nothing new. He always had. She'd hurt him and he was never going to forgive her. She didn't know why she'd agreed to marry him; it was never going to work out. She'd been a fool to go through with it in the first place, so she had only herself to blame for her present misery.

She was so deep in thought that she didn't notice the stop sign until she was on it, and the loud baritone of a truck's horn made her blood freeze.

A huge transfer-trailer truck was barreling down the highway. Shelby's little car wasn't going to be fast enough to beat that mammoth vehicle across the intersection, and it was touch and go if she'd be able to stop at all.

With her heart in her throat, and the numb certainty of death stiffening her body, she hit the brake. The car went into a spin, the squeal of tires terrible in the later afternoon stillness, her face frozen with terror as she lost control and the sky went around and around and around . . .

The car spun into the deep ditch and leaned drunkenly sideways, but amazingly it didn't turn over. Shelby sat, shaken but unhurt, nausea bitter in her throat and the world spinning around her. There was the sound of another car screeching to a halt. A door opened. There was the sound of running feet and then, suddenly, a man's anguished shout.

"Shelby!" The man's face was familiar, but somehow unfamiliar. It was hoarse and choked and blackly furious. "Answer me, damn it, are you all right?"

She felt her seat belt being forced away from her with hands that were lean and brown and shaking. She felt those same hands running over her body, searching for blood or broken bones, exquisitely gentle.

"Are you all right?" Justin asked huskily. "Do you hurt anywhere? For God's sake, sweetheart, answer me!"

"I...I'm fine," she whispered numbly. "The door...?"

"It won't open, the frame's sprung. Easy does it, now." He carefully reached down to get her under the armpits and with formidable strength he lifted her clear of the car. When she was on the ground, swaying, he picked her up with exquisite tenderness and carried her up from the ditch. The truck driver had stopped down the road and was coming toward them, but Justin didn't seem to see him. His expression was rigid with control, but he couldn't stop his arms from trembling under her slender body.

That fact finally registered in Shelby's dazed mind. She looked up then and saw his face, and her breath fluttered. He was flour-white, only his eyes alive and glittering blackly in that set, haunted face. He looked down at her, his arms convulsively dragging her against his chest.

"You little fool...!" he choked.

As long as she lived, she knew she'd never forget the horror she saw in his eyes. She reached up to hold him, her only thought to remove that look from his eyes.

"It's all right, Justin," she murmured softly. His reaction fascinated her. She'd never seen him shaken before. It made her feel protective, that tiny chink in his cool armor.

"I'm fine, Justin," she whispered. Her eyes searched his, amazed at the vulnerability there. She touched his mouth, her soft fingers caressing as they slid up into his thick, dark hair. "Darling, I'm all right, really I am!" She pulled his mouth down and put hers softly against it, loving the way he let her kiss him, even if it was only out of shock—which, in fact, it was. For several seconds she savored the newness of it, then something stirred in her slender body, and her mouth pushed upward, hungry for a harder, deeper contact than this. It had been years since they'd kissed, since they'd really kissed. She moaned softly and he seemed to come out of his trance. His arm contracted, and his hard mouth opened hungrily against hers on a wild, shattered groan.

His mouth hurt as it dragged against hers while he muttered something violent and unintelligible against her soft lips. He pulled back with evident reluctance as the truck driver came running down the highway toward them.

"Is she all right?" the man asked, panting from the long run he'd had. "My God, I was sure I'd hit her...!"

"She's all right," Justin answered tersely. "But that damned car won't be when I can lay my hands on my rifle."

The truck driver sighed with pure relief. "Damn, lady, you can sure handle yourself," he said with admiration. "If you'd lost your nerve and thrown up your hands, you'd be dead and I'd be a mental patient."

"I'm sorry." Shelby wept, her nerve broken from the combination of the near miss and the exquisite ardor of Justin's hard mouth. "I'm so sorry. I didn't even see you coming!"

The truck driver, a young man with red hair, just shook his head, barely able to get his breath. "Are you sure you're all right?"

"I'm fine," she said, forcing a trembling smile. "Thank you for stopping. It wasn't your fault."

"That wouldn't have made me feel any better," she was told. "Well, if you're sure, I'll be on my way." He looked at Justin, and almost offered to help, but the glitter in those black eyes wasn't encouraging.

"As my wife said, thanks for stopping," Justin said.

The younger man nodded, smiled and walked away with patent relief, wondering why a woman that pretty would marry such a desperado. He was glad she wasn't hurt. He wouldn't have relished having to face that wild-eyed husband unarmed.

Justin didn't say another word. He turned, carrying Shelby to the Thunderbird. He balanced her on his knee, opened the passenger door and put her inside very gently.

"What about my car?" she asked.

His black eyes met hers. "Damn your car," he said huskily. He slammed the door and went around to get in under the wheel. But he didn't start the car. He sat with his hands, white-knuckled, gripping the steering wheel for a long moment while Shelby waited for the explosion that she knew was about to come. Justin had been badly shaken and somebody was going to pay for it. Now that he was sure she was all right, she could imagine that he was loading both verbal barrels.

"Go ahead, give me hell," she said tearfully, searching in the glove compartment for a tissue. "I was driving too fast, and I wasn't watching. I deserve every lecture I get." She blew her nose. "How did you get here so fast?"

He still didn't speak. After a minute, he sat back in the bucket seat and fumbled a cigarette out of his pocket. He lit it with still-trembling hands, staring straight ahead.

"I followed you," he said curtly. "When I heard you gun the car out of the driveway, I was afraid you might try to take out your temper on the highway, so I tagged along." His head turned and his black eyes flashed at her. "My God, I paid for sins I haven't even committed when I saw you spin out."

She could imagine how it had been for him, having to watch. Even though he didn't love her, it would have been terrible.

"I'm sorry," she said inadequately, folding her arms across her breasts shakily.

His chest rose and fell with a huge, angry breath. "Are you, really?" he said. He was back in control now, and the cool smile on his face infuriated her. "Well, you can say goodbye to that damned sports car. Tomorrow, I'll go downtown with you and steer you toward something safe."

"What did you have in mind, a Sherman tank?" she asked with ice in her tone.

"A bicycle, if you keep this up," he corrected angrily. "I told you once before, Shelby, your reckless days are over."

"You're not going to order me around!" she shot at him through trembling lips and clenched teeth. "I'm not your ward!"

"No," he agreed with a mocking smile. "You're my wife, aren't you? My saintly, untouched wife who can bear anyone's hands except mine."

It was too much. She burst into tears again, turning her face to the window, burying her eyes in the soggy tissue.

"Don't," he groaned. "For God's sake, stop it. I can't stand tears!"

"Then don't look, damn you," she whispered, stomping her foot.

He swore roughly, digging into his pocket for his freshly laundered linen handkerchief. He thrust it into her trembling hands, feeling as if someone had kicked him.

"You'll make yourself sick. Stop it. You're all right. A miss is as good as a mile, isn't it?" he asked, his voice softer now, deeper. He touched her hair hesitantly. It was all coming back into focus, little by little. He frowned, because now he remembered something that panic had knocked out of his mind. She'd touched his face and whispered something, and she'd put her mouth against his to comfort him. What had she said . . . ?

"You called me darling," he said aloud.

She moved jerkily. "Did I? I must have been out of my mind, mustn't I?" She sniffed and mopped herself up. "Can we go home, Justin? I need something to drink."

"I could use a neat whiskey myself," he said heavily. His eyes searched over her wan, sad little face. "Are you sure you're all right?"

"I'm tough," she murmured.

"Tough," he agreed. "And reckless, stupid, impulsive—"

"You stop that!" she protested. Her pale green eyes glared at him, red-rimmed.

"You kissed me."

She went from white to rose red and averted her eyes. "You were upset."

"I've been upset before, but you never kissed me, Shelby." His dark eyes narrowed as he reached for the ignition switch. "Come to think of it, in all the years we've known each other, that's the very first move toward me you've ever made."

She leaned back against the seat, her arms folded. "Justin, my purse is still in the car," she murmured evasively.

He reached down to the floor, picked it up and put it in her lap. "You grabbed it before I lifted you clear," he said. "It came along for the ride."

"You aren't really going to shoot Abby's old car, are you?"

He reversed the car and then pulled in a perfect circle back the way he'd come. "It might get that gentle a treatment if it's lucky," he muttered.

"Justin! It wasn't the car's fault!"

"Sit back and relax now, Shelby. I'll have you home in a minute."

She ground her teeth together as he sped down the road at no less a speed than she'd been driving. "Pot," she muttered.

"Pardon?"

"Pot! The one that calls the kettle black! You're doing sixty!"

"It's a big car."

"What has that got to do with it?"

"Never mind." He smoked his cigarette, frowning thoughtfully. Things had been pretty clear in his mind until ten minutes ago. Now he began to wonder if he hadn't got things twisted. He'd assumed that Shelby found him repulsive all those years ago, that she still did. But her soft lips had been warm and eager, and for those few seconds she'd been absolutely ardent. Of course, she was frightened, he had to admit, and reaction did funny things to people. But if she was that concerned when he was upset, there had to be a little caring left in her.

He pulled up in front of the house and, despite her protests, carried her up to the door where he balanced her long enough to open it.

"No need to worry Maria . . ." he began, but no sooner had he got the words out than Maria came running down the hall. When she saw Shelby's white face, a stream of Spanish broke from her.

"I'm all right," Shelby told her. "The car went into the ditch, that's all."

Maria looked at Justin. That wasn't all, but she knew better than to make a fuss. "What do you want me to do, Señor Justin?" Maria asked.

"I'll get her upstairs. How about pouring me a neat whiskey and bringing up a brandy for Shelby?"

"*Si, señor.*"

"Why can't I have a neat whiskey?" Shelby asked.

Justin's dark eyes searched hers and he pulled her just a little closer as he went easily up the staircase with his soft burden cradled against his chest. "You're just a baby."

"I'm twenty-seven," she reminded him.

He smiled gently. "I'm thirty-seven," he reminded her. "And that's a pretty formidable ten-year jump I've got on you, honey."

The careless endearment made her flush. She lowered her eyes to his shirt. He'd changed earlier, before they ate. This one was Western cut and blue plaid. It suited him. It smelled of detergent and starch, smoke and cologne. She loved being in his arms. If only she could tell him that, and explain why she was afraid of him. But she couldn't.

He carried her into her room and put her on the bed, his eyes going hungrily over the way that damned red and white dress clung in all the right places. It wasn't low-cut, but it displayed her high breasts in the best possible way, and looking at them made him ache.

Shelby frowned at the expression on his face. "What's wrong?" she asked, fatigue in her soft voice.

He straightened. "Nothing. I'll have Maria bring up the brandy. You'd better have a hot bath and then I'll take you to the doctor. I want you examined, to make sure you haven't done any damage."

She sat up, her eyes like saucers. "Justin, I'm all right!"

"You're not a doctor and neither am I. You took a hell of a jolt and you were damned near in shock when I pulled you out of that car." His jaw set stubbornly. "You're going. Hurry up and get changed. Wear something—" he hesitated "—less sexy."

Her eyebrows arched. "I beg your pardon?"

He turned toward the door. "I'll phone the doctor while you take a bath."

She stared after him blankly. "I don't want to go to the doctor."

He just closed the door, ignoring what she did or didn't want. Taking control, as usual, she fumed. She wanted to throw things. She was all right, couldn't he see that? She burst into tears of frustrated temper and went into the bathroom. She felt as if her knees had been knocked out from under her.

After her bath, she dried her hair and put on a neat white blouse and gray skirt and brightened it with a gray and red scarf at her throat. She wondered why he wanted her to wear something less sexy, and then felt her heart skip at the realization that *he* must have found the red and white dress sexy. She smiled demurely. That was the first time since their marriage that he'd admitted to finding her attractive. If only she could be sure that he wouldn't lose control, it might have given her enough courage to do more than just kiss him.

She picked up the brandy snifter Maria had left with a teaspoon of brandy in it and sipped it quietly. She had kissed him, all right. He was going to worry that to death. But he'd been upset and she'd wanted so desperately to comfort him that her usual inhibitions hadn't built a wall between them. And the kiss had been delicious. Her mouth still tingled from the rough sweetness of his. And then she remembered why it had been so sweet. He'd let her make all the moves. He hadn't taken control away from her. She frowned.

A knock on the door interrupted her brooding. She opened it. Justin was already looking impatient.

"How do you feel?" he asked.

"I'm sore . . ." she began.

"The doctor's waiting. Let's go." He took the brandy snifter from her, put it on her dresser and escorted her out of the room.

The doctor he'd found was at the hospital emergency room. Shelby felt nervous and edgy, because she'd hardly been near a hospital since her wreck in Switzerland, except to Dr. Sims for her premarital examination. But this wasn't Dr. Sims. This was a nice young doctor named Hays, very personable and kindhearted, and obviously a little amused by Justin's irritated concern.

"You'll be stiff for a couple of days, but I'm sure your husband will be relieved to know that you've done no lasting damage," Dr. Hays said after he'd finished his examination and she'd answered the necessary questions. "Just one more thing—there's no possibility that you might be pregnant?" he asked quietly, made more curious by her blush and Justin's averted face. "An experience like this could be risky..."

"I'm not pregnant," she said huskily.

"Then you'll be fine. I'm going to give you some muscle relaxants in case you need them. You can take a non-aspirin analgesic for pain, and a little extra rest tomorrow might be beneficial. Of course, if you have any further problems, let me know."

Shelby thanked him and Justin muttered something before he escorted her out of the examination room and down the hall to pay the bill. By the time they were through and on their way back to the house, it was almost eight o'clock and dark outside.

Justin was quiet all the way home. Shelby knew why. It was the doctor's very natural question about pregnancy. It had embarrassed Justin and probably enraged him as well, because intimacy was such a bone of contention between them.

"You should have told him that we could get you in the *Guinness Book of World Records* if you got pregnant," he said through his teeth as he parked the car in the driveway and cut off the engine.

She turned her purse in her lap. Now that the tension was lifting, she only felt tired and sore. "What did you do with my car? It wasn't on the highway when we came past the intersection."

His black eyes shifted toward her and then away. "You don't want to talk about it, do you?"

"I'm frigid," she said dully. "Let's just leave it at that, unless you want a divorce."

"I want a wife," he said harshly. "I want kids." His jaw tautened as he lifted his cigarette to his mouth. "Oh, God, I want kids, Shelby," he said in a faintly vulnerable tone.

That was something they'd never talked about, except in the very early days of their association. She leaned her head back against her seat, nibbling her lower lip and stared down at her lap. "You probably won't believe it, but so do I, Justin."

He turned in his seat to look at her downcast face, his eyes dark and quiet. "How did you plan to get any without help?"

Her hands contracted on her purse. "I'm afraid," she said softly, because for once she was too tired to lie, to find excuses.

There was a long pause. "Well, childbirth isn't really the terror it used to be, from all I've heard," he said, getting the wrong end of the stick. "And there are drugs they can give you for pain."

She looked up at him, shocked. "What?"

It was incredible that he believed she was afraid to have a child. She just stared at him without moving.

"It doesn't have to be right away, either," he said doggedly, averting his gaze out the window, as if the subject embarrassed him. It probably did. Shelby remembered that he'd always found it difficult to talk about things like pregnancy and that he never did discuss intimate matters in mixed company. In his own way, he was as reticent as she was. It was one of the things she'd always loved about him.

She was trying to understand what he meant when he took another draw from the cigarette and put it out. There was a dull flush across his cheekbones and he wouldn't look at her.

"You could talk to the doctor about something to take," he said tersely. "Or I could use something. You don't have to get pregnant if you don't want to. I won't force you to have a child."

She went beet red and stared out her window, her hands trembling and cold as the intimacy of what he was saying finally got through to her. She cleared her throat. "I...could we go inside now?" she whispered. "I'm tired and I ache all over."

"It's hard for me to talk about it, too," he said quietly. "But I wanted you to know. To think it over. If that's why you won't let me touch you..."

"Oh, don't!" She buried her face in her hands.

He sighed roughly. "I'm sorry. I shouldn't have said anything." He got out and came around the car to help her out. "Did he give you any muscle relaxants or do I need to go to the drugstore for you?" he asked.

"He gave me some samples," she said. She walked alongside him up the steps, ashamed of the way she'd changed the subject and shied away from the discussion. She wanted to tell him what was wrong. But talking to Justin that way was so embarrassing.

"You go on up and have an early night," he said, as remote as if he'd been talking to a total stranger. "I'll have Maria bring you up some hot chocolate. Do you want anything to eat?"

"No, thank you." She paused at the foot of the staircase and smoothed her hand over the banister. She didn't want to go. Her eyes lifted to his across the hall and she looked at him with hopeless longing and anguished shame. "I shouldn't have married you," she whispered huskily. "I never meant to make you unhappy."

His jaw went taut. "I never meant to make you unhappy, either, but that's what I've done."

She hesitated. "You never told me what you did with the sports car," she said after a minute. "Can't I have it back?"

"Sure," he said, lifting his chin and pursing his lips. "We can have it made into an ashtray or a piece of modern art."

Her eyebrows shot up. "What do you mean?"

He shrugged. "It's about five inches thick and four feet long by now. A bit big for an ashtray, I guess, but framed, it would make one hell of a wall decoration."

"What are you talking about? What did you do with it?"

"I gave it to Old Man Doyle."

She turned her head slightly as the words registered. "He owns a junkyard."

He smiled faintly. "Sure does. He has a brand-new crusher. You know, one of those big machines that you use to push old cars into scrap metal..."

She flushed. "You did that on purpose!"

"You're damned right I did," he said with a glittery challenge in his eyes. "If I'd taken it back to the car lot, I couldn't be sure that you wouldn't rush right down there and buy it again. This way," he added, pulling his hat low over his eyes, "I'm sure."

"I still owe for it! It was a lot of money!"

He smiled pleasantly. "I'm sure you can explain it to the insurance company. Atmospheric pressure? Termites...?"

She was stuck for a reply when he turned and went into the kitchen.

She went up the staircase, smoldering. It had been an upsetting day all around, and it wasn't improving. Her mind whirled with questions and problems.

At first, she hadn't wanted to take the muscle relaxants, but she got sore as the night wore on. Finally she gave in, downing them with a sip of cooling hot chocolate. She put on her gray satin pajamas and climbed under the covers. Minutes later, she was asleep.

But then the dreams started. Over and over again, she could see herself in the sports car, but in Switzerland. She'd been speeding around the Alps with skill and ease until she was almost at the bottom of a mountain. She'd hit a patch of ice and all her experience at the wheel hadn't been able to save her. The car, that time, had rolled. And rolled. And rolled.

She was pitching down the side of the white mountain, sky and snow combining in a terrible descent. She waited for the impact, waited, screaming...

Hands lifted her from the pillow, gently shaking her.

"It's all right," someone said. "It's all right. Wake up, Shelby, you're dreaming."

She snapped awake as if a switch had been thrown in her brain. Justin was holding her, his black eyes narrow with concern.

"The car..." she whispered. "It was pitching down the mountain."

"You were dreaming, little one," he said. He smoothed the dark tangle of her hair away from her flushed cheeks and her shoulders. "Only dreaming. You're safe now."

"I always was, with you," she said involuntarily, leaning her head on his shoulder. She sighed heavily, relaxed now, secure. Her cheek moved and he stiffened, and she realized that she was resting on bare skin, not a pajama top.

The light was on and he was sitting beside her on the bed, his dark hair tousled. She almost lost her nerve when she lifted her cheek away from his muscular upper arm, but she breathed easily when she saw that he was only bare from the waist up. He was wearing dark silk pajama trousers, but his muscular chest was completely bare. Thick black hair curled down to the low waistband of the pajamas, and the very sight of him was breathtaking.

Shelby felt her breath catch at all that masculinity so close to her. She knew without being told that he wasn't wearing anything under those trousers, and it made her feel threatened.

"Did you take those pills the doctor gave you?" he asked quietly.

"Yes. They made the aching stop, but now I'm having nightmares." She laughed jerkily. She pushed back her thick cloud of hair, glancing up at him apprehensively. "Did I wake you?"

"Not really." He sighed. "I don't sleep well these days. It doesn't take much to wake me. I heard you scream."

She didn't sleep well, either, and probably for the same reason. She locked her arms around her knees, curling up to rest her forehead there. "Today's accident brought back the wreck I had in Switzerland," she murmured drowsily.

"I was concussed and I kept drifting in and out." She moved her forehead against the soft satin. "They told me I called for you night and day after they brought me to the hospital," she said without meaning to.

"Me, and not your lover?" he asked coldly.

"I've never had a lover, Justin," she said shyly.

"Sure. And I'm the king of Siam." He got to his feet, looking down at her half angrily. She was lovely in those satin pajamas. He'd never thought about what she wore to sleep in, but now he was sure he'd think of nothing else. The jacket was low-cut and he'd had a deliciously tempting glimpse of her firm breasts when she'd first come awake. They were small, he thought speculatively, but perfectly formed if their outline under that jacket was anything to go by. His eyes narrowed and he had to pull his gaze away, because he wanted to look at them with a hunger that made him go rigid.

He turned away. "If you're all right, I'll go back and try to sleep. I've got an early appointment in town at the bank."

She watched him go with a deep sadness. The distance between them grew all the time, and she was making him unhappier by the day. "Thank you for coming to see about me," she said dully.

He paused with his hand on the doorknob, his gaze concerned. "You'd die before you'd do it, I know," he said slowly. "But if you get frightened again, you can double up with me." He laughed coldly. "It's safe enough, in case you're worried. I won't risk my ego again with you."

He was gone before she could contradict him. She winced at the pain those words had revealed. She felt worse than ever, knowing how she'd hurt him.

And it was so unnecessary. All she had to do was tell him. For God's sake, she was twenty-seven years old! Yes, and sheltered to the point of obsession by her money-hungry father, who'd been afraid to lose her to a poor man. She'd never even been kissed intimately until the night they got engaged. She wondered if he knew that.

He probably didn't, she decided. She got out of bed and turned on the light, heading for the door. Maybe it was time she told him.

Chapter Six

It didn't occur to her until she was out in the hall, bare-footed, at Justin's door, that three o'clock in the morning wasn't the best time to share intimate secrets with a man who'd gone starving for physical satisfaction since his marriage. She hesitated, nibbling her lower lip. The light was still on in his room, but it was pretty quiet in there.

She frowned, wondering what to do, and brushed back her unruly hair with a sigh.

"He's not in there," came a soft, deeply amused voice at her back.

She whirled to find Justin behind her, holding a jigger of whiskey. "What are you doing out here?" she asked.

"Watching you prowl the halls. What were you planning to do, go in there and rape me?"

She burst out laughing. It bubbled up from some unknown place, and her eyes twinkled up at him. "I don't know how," she confessed.

He actually smiled. She was pretty when she laughed. She was pretty any way at all. He lifted the whiskey ruefully. "I thought it might help me sleep," he said.

"I'm afraid nothing's going to help me," she murmured. She shifted from one bare foot to the other, aware of his curious scrutiny and her own loud heartbeat.

"Do you want to sleep with me?" he asked.

She flushed. "That wasn't the only reason I came." She glanced up and then down again at his own bare, very big feet. "Did you know that nobody had ever kissed me intimately until you did?"

He blinked. "You came down the hall at three o'clock in the morning to tell me that?"

She shrugged. "It seemed pretty important at the time," she said. She looked up at him sadly, her pale green eyes searching his lean, craggy face, his sensuous mouth, the firm, hair-roughened muscles of his chest and stomach. "It's amazing," she murmured, her eyes fascinated by the bare expanse of brown muscle.

"What is?" He frowned, watching the way her eyes went over him. It was disturbing. Surely she knew that.

"That you don't have to chase women out of your room with a broom handle," she murmured absently.

His eyebrows arched. "Have you been into my brandy snifter?"

"I guess it sounds that way, doesn't it?" She raised her eyes to his. "Can I sleep with you, Justin? I'm still pretty shaky. If . . ." She cleared her throat and looked away. "If it won't bother you too much, I mean. I don't want to make things any worse for you than they already are."

"I'm not sure they could get worse," he said quietly. He searched her wide, soft eyes. "All right. Come on."

She followed him inside. She'd never been in his room before, although she'd been by it a number of times and had peeked in curiously.

The furniture was old. Antique, like that in the house she'd grown up in. She wondered if it went far back in his family, if he'd inherited it from his parents. She smoothed her hand over a long bedpost, admiring the slickly polished wood of the four-poster and the beige and brown striped sheets on the bed.

"I didn't think you liked colored sheets," she said conversationally. "Maria said you didn't."

"I don't," he said curtly. "Maria does. She swears that she lost all the white sheets and had to replace them."

"Well, these are nice," she murmured.

"Climb in."

He held the top sheet back and let her slide under it. "I'll adjust the air-conditioning if it's too cool in here to suit you," he offered.

"No, it's fine," she said. "I hate a hot bedroom, even in winter."

He smiled faintly. "So do I." He turned off the light and came back to the bed. The mattress lowered as he sat down, obviously finishing off his whiskey.

"You, uh, you do sleep in pajama bottoms?" she asked, grateful for the darkness that spared her blushes.

He actually laughed. "Oh, my God."

"Well, you don't have to make fun of me," she muttered, fluffing the pillow before she laid her head on it.

"I always thought you were a sophisticated girl," he said pleasantly. "You know, the liberated sort with a string of men on your sleeve and the kind of sophistication that goes with champagne and diamonds."

"Boy, were you in for a shock," she murmured. "Until you came along, I'd only dated one man, and the most he did was to make a grab for me and get himself slapped. My father was obsessed with keeping me innocent until he could sell me to someone who'd make him even richer. But you don't know that, of course, you think he's a saint.''

He switched on the light. His eyes were black and steady on hers, noticing the flush that covered her cheeks.

"Will you turn that off, please?" she asked tightly. "If I'm going to talk about such things, I can't look at you and do it.''

"Prude," he accused.

She glared at him. "Look who's talking."

He smiled ruefully. He cut off the lights, too. She felt the mattress shift as he lay back on it and pulled the sheet up over his hips.

"All right. If you want to talk, go ahead."

"My father never wanted you to marry me, Justin, despite the show he put on for you," she said shortly. "He wanted me to marry Tom Wheelor's racing stables so that he could merge them with his and get out of debt.''

"That's a hard pill to swallow, considering what I know about your father," he said, remembering that it was her father's money that had helped his family's feedlot. He wondered if she'd ever found that out, and almost said so when he heard her sigh.

She shifted. "Nevertheless, it's true. He was all set to ruin you if I hadn't gone along with him when he cooked up that story about my marrying Tom."

"You admitted that you'd slept with Tom," he reminded her. His tone darkened. "And I know how little you wanted to sleep with me."

"It wasn't because I found you repulsive," she said.

"Wasn't it?"

Before she could say another word, he'd rolled over. One lean arm went across her body, dragging her against him.

In the darkness, he sought her mouth with his and kissed her with rough abandon. Her hands went up against his hair-roughened chest, pushing at solid warm muscle, while his mouth demanded things that frightened her. His knee insinuated itself between both of hers and she stiffened and pushed harder, fighting him.

He let her go without another word and got up. His hand flicked the light switch. When he turned toward her, his eyes were blazing like forest fires, his face livid with barely controlled rage.

"Get out!" he said in a biting fury.

She knew that she couldn't say anything now that would calm him. If she tried to argue or smooth it over, she might unleash something physical that would scar her even more than his ardor had six years before.

She got out of the bed, her eyes apologetic and tearful, and did as he'd told her. She didn't look back. She closed the door gently and, still crying, made her way down the long staircase.

Justin's study was quiet. She turned on the light, went to the liquor cabinet, and with hands that shook, found a brandy snifter. She poured brandy into it and swished it around. She wanted to jump off the roof, but perhaps this would do instead.

The house was so quiet. So peaceful. But her mind was in turmoil. Why couldn't he understand that violent love-making frightened her? Why wouldn't he listen?

She'd pushed him away, that was why. She'd fought him. But if she hadn't, and he'd lost control... Her eyes closed on a shudder. She couldn't even bear the thought.

Her legs shook as she made her way to the sofa and sat down, her body bowed, her forehead resting on the rim of the glass. Tears blurred it. She sipped and sipped, until finally the sting of the liquor began to soothe her nerves.

When she realized that she was no longer alone, she didn't even look up.

"I know you hate me," she said numbly. "You didn't have to come all the way down here to say it."

Justin winced at the tears on her face, at the anguish in her soft voice. His pride was shattered all over again. But it hurt him to see her cry.

He poured himself another whiskey and sat down on the edge of the heavy coffee table in front of her. "I've been up there calling you names," he said after a minute. "Until it suddenly got through to me what you'd said, about never letting another man kiss you intimately."

"I'm a scarlet woman, though," she said bitterly. "I slept with Tom. I even told you so."

"You've just told me that your father lied about it." His black eyes narrowed. He took a sip of the whiskey and put the glass down. He knelt just in front of her, not touching her, his eyes on a level with hers. "I remembered something else, too. Just after you wrecked the car, you kissed me. You weren't afraid of me, and you weren't repulsed, either, Shelby. But you were making all the moves, weren't you?"

Her eyes lifted to his. So he'd made the connection. She sighed worriedly. "Yes," she said finally. "I wasn't afraid, you see."

"But up until then," he added, his shrewd eyes making lightning assessments, "I'd been pretty rough with you when we made love."

She flushed, avoiding his gaze. "Yes."

"And it wasn't revulsion at all. It was fear. Not of getting pregnant. But of intimacy itself."

"Give that man a cigar," she murmured with forced humor.

He sighed, watching her fondle the brandy snifter. He took it out of her hands and put it on the coffee table. "Get up."

Startled, she felt him lift her from the sofa. He put her to one side and stretched out on the cushions, moving toward the back. "Now sit down."

She did, hesitantly, because she didn't understand this approach.

He took one of her hands and drew it to his chest. "Think of me as a human sacrifice," he murmured dryly. "A stepping stone in the educational process."

Her lips parted on a sudden gasp as she realized what he was doing. Her eyes darted up to his, curious, shy. "But you...you don't like that," she said perceptively, because in the past he'd always made the moves, he'd never encouraged her to.

"I'm going to learn to like it," he said frankly. "If it takes this to get you close to me, I'm more than willing to give you the advantage, Shelby."

Tears stung her eyes. She bit her lower lip to stop its trembling. "Oh, Justin," she whispered shakily.

"Can you do it this way?" he asked softly, his eyes black and alive with tenderness. "If I let you, can you make love to me?"

The tears broke from her eyes and ran down her cheeks. "I wanted to tell you," she wept. "But I was too embarrassed."

"It's all right." He put his big hand over hers and traced the tiny blue veins in it. "I should have realized it a long time ago. I won't hurt you. I'll never hurt you."

She laughed through the tears. Amazing, that he should puzzle it out for himself. She smiled and bent hesitantly to his warm mouth and touched it with her lips.

Justin felt as if his heart were about to burst. God only knew why he'd never understood before. Obviously Wheelor had hurt her, and she'd drawn away from any further intimacy. He hated knowing that the other man had been her first lover, but he couldn't stand by any longer and watch Shelby beat herself to death emotionally over it. They had to start someplace to build a life together, and this was the very best way.

He felt her soft, shy mouth with a sense of wonder. She still didn't know a lot about kissing, and he smiled under her searching lips. He'd been celibate for a long time, but in his younger days, his lack of looks hadn't kept him from getting some experience. He knew what to do with a woman, even if discussing such things in public made him uncomfortable.

He didn't touch her. As he'd promised, he lay there with his body keeping him on the rack and let her soft mouth toy with his.

"Come closer," he breathed against her lips. "You're as safe as you want to be."

"It isn't hurting you?" she asked worriedly.

"When it gets that bad, I'll tell you," he promised, lying through his teeth, because it was already that bad.

She smiled, moving so that her soft breasts rested fully on his chest, her legs chastely beside his and not over them. There was a fine tremor in his lips when she bent again, but he still hadn't tried to pull her down or to make the kiss more intimate.

Her hands moved into his thick hair, ruffling it, and her lips traced patterns on his face, loving its strength. He was so sweet to kiss. She laughed with pure delight at the new freedom to touch him as she'd wanted to for so many lonely years.

His eyes opened and he studied her curiously. "What was that all about?"

"If you knew," she said, "how long I've wanted to do this..."

His jaw clenched. "You might have told me."

"I couldn't." She touched his broad chest. "It's so intimate a thing to talk about." Impulsively, she leaned down and brushed her mouth over the hard muscle of his breastbone. "Justin, I've missed you so much."

His chest rose heavily under the tiny caress. "I've missed you, too," he said huskily. "God, Shelby, I can't...!" He clenched his teeth.

She looked up. "It isn't enough for you, is it?" she asked hesitantly. "I guess I seem pretty green."

His eyes darkened. "I want to touch you," he breathed. "I want to put you on your back and slide that jacket out of my way."

Her body trembled over his. "If you lost control, it would be just the way it was upstairs," she ground out. "I get scared!"

"I swear to God I won't lose it," he said curtly. "Not if I have to run out into the night screaming."

She believed him. It was the most difficult thing she'd ever done, to trust him now. But she swallowed hard and moved gently alongside him and onto her back, watching him shift so that he was poised over her.

"Trust comes hard, doesn't it?" he asked softly.

"Yes." She searched his face quietly. "I could have died this afternoon. I keep thinking about it, and how insignificant things seem at the point of death. All I thought about was you, and what a sad memory I'd left you with."

"Is that what this is all about?" he asked with a smile.

"Not really." She studied his hard mouth. "I was hungry for you, when you let me kiss you. I wanted to know if I could stop being afraid. But upstairs, when you grabbed me, I just went to pieces."

"I'm not going to grab you this time." He bent, barely touching her mouth with his. He brushed it, bit at it, until her lips began slowly to follow his. He felt her breath quicken. And then his fingers began to trace patterns on the pajama jacket.

At first she stiffened, but his movements were very slow and undemanding, and his mouth was gentle. He lifted his head, feeling her begin to relax, and he smiled reassuringly. "Okay?" he whispered.

The tenderness was new. Her eyes smiled up at him. "Okay."

He looked down at her breasts and saw hard peaks forming where his fingers teased. He put his thumb over a hard tip and heard her gasp and felt her body shudder. He liked that reaction, so he did it again, and this time she arched a little.

"I like that," he said softly, holding her eyes. "Do it again."

She did, but only because she couldn't help it. "I feel . . . strange," she whispered. "Shuddery."

"So do I," he whispered back, and brushed his mouth lazily over her lips until they parted. "Do you want me to tell you what I'm going to do now?"

Her heartbeat went wild. "Yes," she said against his mouth.

He smiled. "I'm going to unbutton your jacket."

Her breath sighed out quickly against his lips as she felt his hard fingers flicking buttons out of buttonholes. Then the fabric was open down the middle and he was slowly easing it away. He drew it just to the curve of her breasts and looked into her eyes, registering the faint shyness there and the excitement that she couldn't hide.

"You're small," he whispered. His fingers drew along one smooth curve. "I like my women small."

She trembled at the way he said it, at the knowledge in his black eyes, at the experience in the fingers that traced up and over and then stopped short of that hard, aching peak. She shuddered when he did that. He did it again, and she gasped.

His nose brushed against hers. His breath mingled with her own, tasting smoky and warm. "Yes, you want it, don't you?" he mused softly. He traced her again and this time he didn't stop. His hand smoothed over her and down, taking the hard tip into his moist palm and pressing down over it.

She cried out. The sound seemed to shock her because she swallowed, moistening her lips with her tongue.

"You act," he whispered, moving the fabric aside sensually, "just like a virgin with her first man." He peeled the satin away from her breasts and looked down. His breath caught, because the creamy mounds and their hard mauve tips were shaped so exquisitely that they took his breath.

"Do you really not mind...that I'm small?" she heard herself whisper.

"Oh, God, no," he returned. His eyes held hers and his fingers traced her soft skin. "Will it shock you if I put my mouth on them?"

"Yes," she said, smiling.

He smiled back and bent his head toward her body. She arched up at the first touch of his lips on her breasts, thinking that in all her life, she'd never dreamed there could be such pleasure in being touched. Her hands tangled in his thick hair and held him against her while his light, brushing caresses made her tremble. She moaned and tears sprung to her eyes.

He felt her body tremble and understood why. It was the advantage he'd been waiting for. His lean, callused hands smoothed down her hips, over her flat belly. They caressed the satin away so expertly that she didn't mind, didn't care. His hands touched her as if she'd always belonged to him, and she loved the touch, the slow tenderness of his rough hands on her skin.

His mouth opened, moist, the suction on her breast making her draw up with pleasure. She felt her hands helplessly gripping his muscular arms, pulling at him. She was whispering something that she didn't understand, pleading with him for something she didn't even know about. She needed . . . something.

Her mouth bit at his shoulder. When he lifted his head and looked down at her, she could barely see him through a red haze. She thought he smiled as his mouth fastened on hers. Then she felt his tongue go into her mouth in slow, exquisite thrusts and her body went wild under his.

She pulled at him, her arms around his neck. She felt him against her, felt the hard, warm contours of his body and the heat of his rough skin against her soft skin. She realized dimly that his pajama trousers were gone, but the touch of him against her was so exquisite that she didn't really want him to stop.

"It's going to happen now," he whispered into her mouth as his knee eased between her long, trembling legs. "I won't hurt you. I won't rush you. You can still stop me in time, if you want to. We're going to do this with such tenderness that you won't be afraid of me. Now just lie still and trust me for another few . . . seconds . . ."

She was trembling and so was he, but she'd never wanted anything in her life the way she wanted to belong to him. This was Justin. He was her husband and she loved him more than her life. He'd been so patient, so tender, that she wanted to give him her body along with her heart.

"Justin," she whispered achingly, watching his face harden. She felt the first touch of him and jerked a little.

"Shh," he whispered back. He smiled at her, forcing himself to hold back. "I'm going to watch you," he breathed huskily. "I'll know the instant it happens if there's the first hint of pain."

It was incredibly intimate. The lights were on. But all she could see was his face. She could feel his breath, quick and hard on her face, she could see the pulse beating in his throat. But she wasn't afraid, not even of his weight on her body, crushing her down into the cushions. He was hers, and she was going to take him...

She felt the pain like a hot knife. She clutched at him and her eyes got as big as saucers. She cried out and tears ran down her face.

Justin's eyes darkened and the pupils grew and grew and she realized then that he was frozen like a statue over her. His lips parted. His breath blew out. He looked down at her incredulously. He moved again, and watched her clench her teeth even as he knew for certain why she was doing it.

"I'm sorry," she whispered. Her hands reached up. "Don't stop," she said. "It's all right, I think I can...bear it...!"

"My God!"

He drew back, struggling away from her to sit up with his back to her, bowed, his body shuddering wildly. "My God, Shelby!"

"Justin, you didn't...you didn't have to stop," she whispered, biting her lip. "It would have been all right."

He wasn't listening. His head was in his hands and he shivered. He reached for the whiskey glass that still had a swallow of liquid in it, and his hands shook so badly that he almost spilled it before he got it to his mouth.

He stood up and Shelby flushed and averted her shocked eyes from his blatant masculinity.

"I'm sorry," he said curtly. He reached for his pajama bottoms and got into them distractedly. Then he stood looking down at her until she went bloodred and tried to curl up.

But he wouldn't let her. He reached down unsteadily to pick her up. He cradled her in his arms and sat down in his armchair, holding her with marvelous tenderness, whispering endearments into her dark hair, holding her while the tears came.

When she stopped, he mopped her eyes with a tissue. Her cheek was against his broad, shuddering chest, nestled against the thick hair, and her breasts were lying soft against his stomach. She shivered at the intimacy of it, because she didn't have a stitch on.

"You're my wife," he whispered when he saw her embarrassment. "It's all right if I see you without your clothes."

She curled closer. "Yes, I guess it is. It's just . . . new."

"My God, yes, I know."

There was an unmistakable note in his voice. She looked up, giving him a sudden and total view of her pretty breasts. He had to drag his eyes back up to hers.

"My virgin bride," he whispered huskily. His fingers touched her breasts hesitantly, with something like reverence. "Oh, Shelby. Shelby!"

"I . . . Dr. Sims made me have some minor surgery, but he muttered about it when I wouldn't let him do a proper job," she said, hiding her eyes from him. "I guess it wasn't quite enough . . ." Her face went red.

"Why wouldn't you let him do it properly?"

"So that I could prove that I hadn't slept with Tom," she said simply.

"You little fool!" He tilted her eyes up to his. "If I hadn't stopped upstairs, or if I'd ever lost my head with you ... God, it doesn't even bear thinking about!"

She bit her lip, staring at his broad chest with its thick pelt of hair. "Justin...it would have stopped hurting," she began shyly.

"Like hell it would." He leaned back with a rough sigh. "I hate to be the bearer of bad tidings, honey, but you're going to have to go back and have the rest of that surgery."

"But..."

He tilted her eyes up to his. "A little pain is one thing, but you've got one hell of a lot of proof there," he said curtly. He shifted restlessly, noting her embarrassment and feeling just a little of his own at trying to explain things to her. He drew her head against his chest and bent to brush his mouth softly over hers. "Put your clothes back on while I top off your brandy snifter. The feel of you is making me hurt."

He got up and put her down on the sofa with only a cursory glance. While she fumbled her way back into her pajamas, he poured brandy into her glass and whiskey into his, and then went searching for a cigarette.

She knew her face was flaming. She'd never imagined that intimacy was so...intimate. But along with the shyness was a kind of excitement that went along with her new discoveries of Justin. He didn't lose control and go wild and hurt her. He was slow and patient and considerate. That made her blush even more.

"Who told you that men go nuts and hurt women when they make love?" he asked conversationally. "Because you

seemed to think that's what was going to happen upstairs."

She took the brandy snifter and watched him go back to
the armchair, where he sat and pulled up an ashtray. "You
did," she said hesitantly. "The night we got engaged, and
you lost control."

His eyebrows shot up. "Did I lose it that badly?"

"I thought so." She studied the snifter. "I knew I had
this problem, you see, and I'd already been told about the
surgery I'd have to have before my first time." She
shrugged. "I've been terrified of it ever since my fifteenth
birthday, when the doctor examined me for a female dys-
function. Some girls have a little discomfort, but he told
me it would be unbearable if I didn't have the surgery.
Then when you came on so strong, and I didn't think I
could stop you..."

"You didn't tell me any of this," he said quietly.

"How could I?" She sighed miserably. "Oh, Justin, I'm
twenty-seven and as green as a preadolescent! I can't even
talk about it now without blushing!"

"I thought you were repulsed by me," he said, his voice
deep with remembered pain. "I never dreamed... And
then you told me what you did about Wheelor, and my ego
shattered." His broad shoulders rose and fell. "I've been
a lot rougher with you than I ever would have been if I'd
known the truth. It hurt so damned bad to think that
you'd been with someone else, and when you flinched
away, it made me sick."

"At least now you know why I flinched away," she said
with a sigh.

He took a draw from the cigarette. "I want you damned
bad," he said without preamble.

She lowered her eyes to the carpet. "I want you, too."

"Then let's do something about it. Go see Dr. Sims. Have the surgery. Let's have a real marriage. The kind where two people sleep together, share together, make babies together."

Her face flamed, but she looked up. "You really do want children, don't you?"

"I want them with you," he said simply. "I never wanted them with any other woman."

"Then I won't need to...to take anything."

He smiled slowly. "No."

She got up, nervous and shy all over again. "I guess it wouldn't be a good idea for us to sleep together?" she asked, without realizing how wistful she sounded.

He got up, drawing her eyes as he towered over her. "Maybe it wouldn't, but we're going to. Even if we can't make love, I can hold you."

Her breath sighed out. "Justin, I'm sorry for so many things."

"So am I, but we can't go back." He bent and brushed a gentle kiss across her mouth. "We'll take it one day at a time. I won't rush you again."

She smiled at him. "Thank you."

He smiled back, but he didn't say anything. She watched him put everything away before he came back to her, turning out the light. He still had his cigarette in hand as they went upstairs together.

"Are you all right?" he asked her when they were in bed, and she was curled up beside him. "I didn't hurt you badly?"

"No," she whispered in the concealing darkness.

"I didn't frighten you, either?" he persisted, as if it mattered.

"Not at all," she assured him, going closer. He was warm and muscular and she loved the feel of him against her. "Not once." She nuzzled her cheek against him. "You're very tender."

"That's how lovemaking should be," he said quietly. "But I'm rusty, Mrs. Ballenger. I've been celibate for quite a while."

She held her breath. "A few months, you mean?"

"Um, not quite." He brushed his mouth over her forehead. "For about six years, Shelby."

She caught her breath. "My gosh! I didn't dream . . . !"

"It's a good thing," he murmured. "I guess you'd have run from me screaming if you'd known, thinking that a man who'd gone hungry that long would be ravenous and uncontrollable."

"But you weren't."

"You needed tenderness, so that's what you got. You won't always get it, after we've had each other a few times," he said flatly. "I don't like it that way all the time."

The mind boggled at what he did like and she realized that he'd been curbing his instincts, holding back, to make things easier for her. "Justin . . ."

"Shhh." He kissed her mouth softly. "Go to sleep. You're arousing me."

"I'm sorry."

He kissed her again and rolled over onto his stomach with a long sigh. "Good night, baby doll."

"Good night, Justin."

But she didn't sleep for a long time. There were a thousand questions buzzing around in her mind, and only a few answers. At least she'd gotten one big hurdle out of the way, and Justin still wanted her. That was something. Even if he couldn't love her, he might grow to have some kind of affection for her again. He couldn't blame her totally about the past, since he knew she was still innocent. Or

could he? It occurred to her then that he might still want
vengeance for the bitterness and humiliation he'd suffered. That was a sobering thought, and it kept her awake
for a very long time.

Chapter Seven

Justin could hardly believe what he saw when he woke up the next morning. He was so used to the dreams of Shelby ending at dawn. But here she was, with her long, dark hair on his pillow, her soft, elfin features relaxed in sleep, her mouth full and sweet and tempting.

He lay there, just watching her, for a long time. He'd been lonely without her. More lonely than he'd realized until they were speaking again. When they were dating, he'd dreamed of having Shelby in his bed, relaxed in sleep, and doing just this—watching her sleep. She couldn't know how precious she was to him, or that last night had been a revelation, a culmination of every longing he'd ever had, even though he hadn't been able to finish what he'd started. Just finding her virginal was a shock of pure delight.

He didn't even start to think about why she'd deceived him. He was too enraptured by the sight of her lovely face in sleep, by her dark head lying so trustingly on his pillow.

When she didn't stir, he smiled gently and bent to brush her lips with his.

He saw her long black eyelashes flutter and then lift. She sighed, saw him and smiled, a new softness in her pale green eyes.

"Good morning," she whispered.

"Good morning." He kissed her again. "Did you sleep well?"

"I've never slept so well in all my life. And you?"

"I could say the same." He pulled the sheet back over her, tucking it in. "You don't have to get up yet."

"Are you going to work this early?" she murmured with a sleepy glance at the clock.

"I have to fly up to Dallas, honey," he said, rising. "A new customer. I'll be home by dark."

"I don't have to be at work until nine," she said with a smug smile.

"I wish you'd give up that job," he said, frowning down at her.

"Justin, I like it," she protested, but not vehemently.

"I don't like having you so handy to Barry Holman," he murmured.

She stared at him. "Maybe he is a womanizer, but not with me," she told him. "He's a very nice man and he's good to me."

Justin turned away. It wouldn't do to have her know how jealous he was of her handsome boss. "I've got to get a shower."

She watched him rummage in his drawer for underwear and head toward the bathroom, her eyes hungry on his bare torso. It seemed so unreal, the intimacy that they'd shared the night before. She blushed just remembering it, but he was gone before he saw the scarlet flush on her cheeks.

She wondered if she should have told him about Tammy Lester and the way Mr. Holman seemed so interested in her. She might do that later.

But she dozed off while he was in the shower, and when she woke up again, he was dressed in a pale gray suit that clung lovingly to the powerful lines of his tall body, and he was straightening his red and gray striped tie in the mirror.

"Is Maria up this early to feed you?" she murmured sleepily.

"I'll have breakfast on the plane." He turned, digging into his pockets, and tossed a set of car keys on the bed beside her. "Take the T-bird to work. Your transportation problem will have to wait until tomorrow."

She sat up, holding the keys. "But how will you get to the airport?"

He cocked an eyebrow. "I wonder if my heart will take all this concern?" he asked.

Her soft eyes ran over him and then the night before came back with alarming clarity. She saw him the way he'd been downstairs with her, felt again the intimacy...

"My God, what a scarlet blush," he murmured, loving her reactions. "I suppose you'd get under the bed if I started reminiscing?"

"You bet I would," she said with her last bit of pride. Then she ruined it all by smiling and hiding her face in her hands. "Oh, Justin," she whispered, remembering.

He sat down on the bed beside her, drawing her forehead against his chest. He smelled of cologne, and just being close to him made her weak and giddy.

"Do you feel like going to work?" he asked then, tilting her eyes up to his. "You don't have to."

"I know." She sighed gently. "But I'm only sore. I was more scared than hurt in the first place."

"You weren't the only one," he murmured. "I've got five new gray hairs this morning, thanks to you."

She reached up and touched his neatly combed hair at the temple, where silver hairs were threaded through the black ones. "I'm sorry. I was running away, I guess. You seem to hate me from time to time."

"Sometimes I thought I did," he confessed, and he didn't smile. "Six years is a long time to brood. I believed you, about Wheelor." He slid his hand under her nape. The fingers contracted suddenly, not hard enough to hurt, but hard enough to pin her forehead to his jacket. "Why?" he asked in a deceptively soft voice. "Why lie to me about it? Wasn't breaking the engagement enough, without ripping my pride to shreds, as well?"

And there it was, she thought, the bitterness seeping through. He was never going to get over what she'd done, and the fact of her innocence physically didn't seem to make much difference. It certainly wasn't going to stop him from blaming her for the past, even if he wanted her desperately. He'd always wanted her, but that wasn't enough anymore. Her eyes went misty with sadness. He'd told her last night that he'd been six years without a woman. That showed how bitter he was, that he didn't even want women anymore. But he wanted her, and she could imagine that it made him forget the past when he was close to her. Years of celibacy would probably make a man forget a lot when he was in the throes of passion.

Her world crumbled. She closed her eyes with a small sigh.

"I told you why last night," she said. "It was Dad's idea."

"And I told you before, your father liked me. He did everything in the world to help me. That night he and Wheelor came to see me, he even cried, Shelby."

Her eyes lifted to his. "It all goes back to trust, and I know how little of that you have for me," she said. "Not that it's all your fault, Justin. I didn't help things by deliberately lying to you in the beginning. But you don't trust me at all."

His jaw tautened. "I can't," he said. He let go of her all at once and got to his feet, moving away. "I want you, you know that. But I can't let you close. A woman who'll betray a man once will do it twice."

"I'm still a virgin," she reminded him uncomfortably.

"That isn't what I meant. You lied to me. You sold me out." He took a deep breath and pulled out a cigarette. "I'm not even sure you wouldn't do it now, with that slick boss of yours." He glanced at her set face, his eyes glittering. "It's easy to see how little encouragement he'd need from you, and he's good-looking, isn't he, honey? There's nothing plain about him."

"You aren't plain," she muttered.

"How perceptive of you to know I was talking about myself," he snapped. "Stay out of trouble while I'm gone, and don't put your foot down on my accelerator."

"I won't touch your precious car, if you'd rather," she shot back, her green eyes flashing. "I'll take a cab, and let all of Jacobsville see me do it!"

He glared at her and she glared back. And all at once, he started to grin, then to smile, and finally laughter burst from his set lips and glittered in his black eyes.

"Hellcat," he murmured.

"Savage," she threw right back.

He tossed the cigarette into the big ashtray on his dresser and moved toward her purposefully. She threw off the covers and headed for the other side of the bed, but he was too quick. Before she was halfway over, he had her flat on her back and had pinned her with the length of his big, hard-muscled body.

"That's it, struggle," he encouraged with a groan. "My God, can you feel what's happening to me?"

She could. She stopped, her cheeks like red flags.

"Well, the world won't end," he said with soft amusement. "You know how I feel when I'm aroused, and last night we didn't have several layers of clothes between us."

"Stop!" She buried her face in his throat, clinging, trembling with embarrassment and excitement.

"You baby," he chided, but the words were tender. He rolled over onto his back, pulling her over with him, his dark eyes searching her pale ones as she poised over his chest. He looked down at the deep cleavage of her pajama jacket and the faint swell of her breasts above it where they were pressed against him. "Is this better?" he murmured.

"You're a horrible man, and I don't think I want to live with you anymore," she said, pouting.

"Yes, you do." He coaxed her mouth down to his by pulling a strand of her long, silky hair. "Kiss me."

"You'll rumple your suit," she said.

"I've got a lot of other suits, but I want to be kissed. Come on, I've got a plane to catch."

She gave in to the gentle teasing. All the arguing was forgotten the minute her soft mouth touched his hard one. She felt his hand sliding into her hair, pulling gently, and her lips parted to the soft, intense searching of his warm mouth.

"After you see the doctor, we'll have to wait a couple of days before we can finish what we started last night," he whispered into her mouth. "So don't start worrying about that and getting nervous all over again, okay?" His dark eyes searched hers. "I won't rush you, Shelby. This time, it's going to be exactly the way you want it."

She kissed his eyes, gently closing the eyelids, lingering on the thick lashes in a rage of tenderness. She wanted to whisper that she loved him more than her own life, that everything she'd done that had hurt him had been, in the beginning, only to protect him. But he didn't trust her yet, and she was going to have to bring him around before she could share her deepest secrets with him.

"Will you believe me when I say that I'm not afraid of you anymore?" she whispered against his lips.

"Honey, that's pretty hard to miss, considering the position we're in," he whispered back.

"What positi...Justin!"

He laughed as he flipped her onto her back and slid over her, nibbling warmly at her lips. "This position," he whispered. "Kiss me goodbye and I'll go."

"I've already done...that...several times," she whispered, the words punctuated with soft, clinging kisses.

"Do it several more and I'll work on getting my legs to support me," he murmured dryly. "My knees are pretty weak right now."

"So are mine." She linked her arms around his neck and bit his lower lip. "You're mine now," she said quietly, her eyes holding his. "Don't you go off and flirt with other women."

Her possessiveness made him ache. He slid his hands under her back and lifted her up, taking his time as he bent hungrily to her open mouth. He kissed her with growing insistence until his own body forced him to either stop or go on.

He rolled away reluctantly and got to his feet, taut with pride as he looked down at his handiwork. She was sprawled in delicious abandon on the sheets, her hair like a halo around her, her mouth soft and red and swollen from his kisses, her eyes dreamy with desire.

"If I had a photograph of you that looked the way you look now," he said huskily, "I'd walk around bent double every time I looked at it. I've never seen a woman as beautiful as you are."

"I'm not even pretty," she chided, smiling. "But I'm glad you like me the way I am. I like you, too."

He drew in a slow breath. "I'd better get out of here while I can. It helps to remember your condition."

She averted her eyes to the sheets, feeling nervous.

"You'd really have let me go on, wouldn't you?" he asked, his voice deep with feeling. "Even knowing how bad it was going to hurt you, you wouldn't have stopped me."

"I wanted you to know," she whispered.

"It took a lot of courage." He frowned, watching her. "Did it hurt you, when I accused you of being frigid?"

"A little," she said, trying to spare him.

He sighed angrily. "A lot, I imagine. Try to remember that I didn't know the truth, and don't hate me for it. There are a lot of things you don't know about me, either, Shelby." He turned then, retrieving his cigarette from the ashtray. "I'd better get a move on," he said after a cursory glance at the thin gold watch on his wrist. "No speeding," he cautioned from the door.

The remark intrigued her, but she knew he wasn't going to tell her any more than he wanted her to know. "All right. Have a good trip."

"I'll do my best."

He didn't say goodbye. He gave her one last glance and closed the door behind him. Shelby watched him leave with mixed emotions. Sometimes she wished she could read his mind, because that was the only way she was ever going to know how he really felt about her. She wondered if he knew himself.

She got up and dressed and drove the Thunderbird to the office, taking a minute to make an appointment that afternoon with Dr. Sims. By the time she got home, she was worn out, from the combination of an unexpectedly long day trying to keep peace between an irritable Mr. Holman and a venomous Tammy Lester, and having the rest of the surgery done—which was embarrassing as well as uncomfortable, because she had to tell Dr. Sims why she needed it.

But a cup of fresh coffee and a nice supper soothed her. She went upstairs to her own room, wishing she had the right to go straight to Justin's. But he hadn't said anything about the sleeping arrangements, so apparently he'd thought of last night as a temporary thing because of what had happened.

She went to sleep early. She didn't hear the car come in, or Justin's footsteps heading toward his own bedroom expectantly. She didn't hear the muffled curse when he found his bed empty, or the shocked silence when he found Shelby asleep in her own.

He closed the door firmly and went to his room, dreams going black in his eyes. He'd expected her to be waiting up, or at least sleeping in his bed. But she hadn't, and he didn't know if she'd just been uncertain about what to do or if she was putting a wall between them because of the argument they'd had that morning.

Shelby, blissfully unaware of what had happened after she was asleep, went down to breakfast the next morning full of hope. Only to find a cold, taciturn Justin at the table looking at her as if she'd just tried to shoot him.

She stopped suddenly in the doorway. Her long denim skirt swung around her calves, her hands going nervously to the blue cotton blouse and scarf she was wearing with it.

"Good morning," she said, faltering.

"Hell, no, it isn't," he said.

Her eyebrows arched. "It isn't?"

He lifted his coffee cup and sipped the rich black liquid. "I'll have one of the boys drive you to work," he said. "May I have the keys to the Thunderbird?"

She reached into her skirt pocket and put them beside him on the table, but he caught her hand before she could move away.

He looked up, his expression brooding. "Why did you go back to your own room?"

She sighed and then smiled. "Because I didn't know if you still wanted me to sleep with you," she said sadly. "You were half mad when you left, and you didn't say anything." Her shoulders lifted and fell. "I didn't want to impose."

"My God, honey, we're married," he said huskily. "You couldn't impose on me if you tried."

She stared down at the big, lean hand holding hers. Its warm strength made her tingle. "You've been very remote since we've been married."

"I think you're beginning to understand why, though, aren't you?" he asked softly.

She looked down into his dark, quiet eyes. She nodded. "You . . . want me."

"That's part of it," he agreed without elaborating. "Did you see Dr. Sims?"

Her blush gave him the answer even before she nodded.

He drew her down in the chair beside him. "I'll drive you to work," he said and pushed a platter of eggs toward her.

She smiled, but she didn't let him see her do it.

Justin had calmed down by the time they got to Jacobsville, but Barry Holman set him off again immediately when they reached the office. The handsome blond lawyer was outside on the street, looking all around, and to an onlooker, it might have appeared as if he was waiting impatiently for Shelby. To Justin, unfortunately, that's exactly what it looked like.

Holman's head lifted when Justin pulled the Thunderbird up at the curb, and his face lit up. He smiled with exaggerated pleasure and rushed to meet Shelby with a cursory nod to Justin, whose expression turned murderous.

"Thank God you're here," Barry enthused, opening the door for her. "I was afraid you were going to be late. How pretty you look this morning!" He knew about day-before-yesterday's mishap, of course, but Shelby was shocked by his attentiveness and was already beginning to wonder what ailed him as he helped her onto the sidewalk. "I'll take good care of her, Justin," he said, adding fuel to the fire, grinning at her smoldering husband.

Justin didn't answer him or speak to Shelby. He slammed the car door, his eyes glittering in Shelby's direction, and roared away down the street.

"What's wrong?" Shelby asked, mentally nervous about Justin's unexpected anger. Mr. Holman had certainly given Justin a bad impression of their working relationship.

"That woman has got to go," he said without preamble, waving his hands. "She's locked herself in my office and she won't let me in. I've called the fire department, though," he added with a smug glitter in his eyes. "They'll break the door down and get her out, and then she can leave. Permanently."

Shelby put a hand to her head. "Mr. Holman, why is Tammy locked in your office?"

He cleared his throat. "It was the book."

"What book?"

"The book I threw at her," he said irritably.

"You threw a book at Tammy!" she gasped.

"Well, it was a dictionary." He shifted with his hands in his pockets. "We had a slight disagreement over the spelling of a legal term, which I should know, Shelby," he added angrily, "after all, I'm a lawyer. I know how to spell legal terms; they teach us that in law school."

Shelby, who'd sampled some of Mr. Holman's expertise at spelling legal terms, didn't say a word.

He shifted again. "Well, I said some things. Then she said some things. Then I sort of tossed the book her way. That was when she locked herself in my office."

"Just because of the book," she probed.

He stared down at the pavement. "Uh, yes. That. And the broken glass."

Her eyes gaped. "Broken glass?"

"The window, you know." He moved sheepishly toward the curb, having spotted what he was searching for earlier. He picked up the torn dictionary with a faint grin. "Here it is! I knew it had to be out here somewhere."

Shelby was torn between laughter and tears when the fire truck came blaring down the street with its siren going and pulled to a screeching half at the curb.

"You didn't tell them why you needed them to come here, by any chance?" Shelby asked as she watched the firemen, because they'd come in a pumper truck and were very obviously unwinding a long, flat hose.

"No, come to think of it, I didn't. Hi, Jake!" Mr. Holman called to the fire chief with a big grin. "Good of you to come. Uh, there's not exactly a fire, though. I'm more in need of a different kind of help."

Jake, a big, burly man with a red face, came closer. "No fire? Well, what do you need us to do, Barry?" he asked, gesturing to the men to roll up the hose again.

"I need you to break down my office door with an ax," Mr. Holman said.

"Why?"

"I lost my key," Mr. Holman improvised.

"Then wouldn't a locksmith do you more good?" Jake continued. He was beginning to give Shelby's boss a strange kind of look.

Mr. Holman frowned thoughtfully. "Oh, no, I don't think so. It wouldn't make nearly the impression that an ax would."

Jake was looking puzzled.

"One of our... employees... has locked herself in the office and won't come out," Shelby explained.

"Well, my gosh, Barry, an ax banging the door down would scare her slam to death!" Jake said.

"Yes," Mr. Holman smiled thoughtfully. "It sure as hell would."

Just as Jake started to speak, Tammy Lester came out of the building, looking explosive, and went right up to Barry Holman and hit him as hard as she could.

"I quit," she said furiously, almost trembling with rage. "Sorry, Shelby, but you're back to being a one-woman office. I can't take one more day of Mr. God's Gift to Womanhood! And you can't spell, Mr. Big-Shot Attorney!"

"I can spell better than you can, you escapee from a high-school remedial spelling course!" he yelled after her. "And don't expect that I'll come running, begging you to come back! There must be hundreds of stupid women who can't spell in this town who need work!"

Jake was gaping at the normally calm attorney. So was Shelby. She was having a hard time trying not to laugh. That would only complicate things, of course. She eased past the fire chief and quickly went into the office to escape what was about to happen.

And sure enough, she'd barely gotten inside the carpeted office when Jake let Mr. Holman have it with both barrels. There was something about false alarms and potential arrests . . . at that point, Shelby closed the door and went to her computer.

She worried about the way Justin had reacted to Mr. Holman waiting on the street for her. It didn't look good, and Justin was already wildly jealous of the man. That didn't make a lot of sense, but then Shelby didn't know a lot about men. She assumed that it was only a surface jealousy, because Barry Holman was handsome and a womanizer and Justin was possessive and very territorial. She never once thought that it might be anything more than that.

Because it disturbed her, she phoned the house to explain to Justin what had happened. But Maria told her that he hadn't come back yet. She tried again at lunch, but he was out with a client. So she went back to work and forgot all about it, while Mr. Holman sputtered and muttered about Tammy for the rest of the day and finally closed the office an hour early because he wasn't getting any work done.

"Don't worry about making up the time," he told Shelby quietly. "We've got court next month, and you may have to put in some overtime getting out briefs and helping me with research." He glowered at the door. "I was going to let Miss Lester help with that, since she does seem to have a feel for legwork. But now that she's quit for such a stupid reason, you'll have to do it."

"Most secretaries would get nervous if their bosses threw books at them," Shelby pointed out.

"I didn't hit her, did I?" he asked mockingly. "I hit the window. That reminds me, you'd better call Jack Harper and get him over here tomorrow to put in another window-pane." He looked uncomfortable. "And, uh, you don't need to go into details about how it got broken. Do you?"

"I'll tell him an eagle flew through it," she agreed.

He glared and stomped off toward his car.

Shelby started toward where she usually parked her car when it dawned on her that she didn't have a car.

"Oh, Mr. Holman," she called without thinking, "could you drop me off at the feedlot? I haven't been able to get Justin, and he won't be here for another hour to pick me up."

"Sure. Come on."

He helped her into the black Mercedes and shot off down the road toward the Ballenger feedlot. "What happened to your new car?" he asked. "Engine trouble?"

She smiled wistfully. She hadn't told him about the sports car, even though he knew she had been driving Justin's car the day before. "Justin gave it to Mr. Doyle."

"He runs a junkyard," Mr. Holman reminded her.

"That's right, he does, and he has a brand-new car crusher." She sighed. "Justin said if I liked, he could have my sports car made into a nice wall decoration. It's about five inches thick . . ."

"What did he do that for?" the lawyer asked.

"He thinks I'm reckless," Shelby said. "I think he's planning to buy me something sedate. Like a Sherman tank."

Mr. Holman smiled. "I hope I didn't get you into any trouble this morning," he said belatedly as he turned off

on the long road that led to the feedlot. "I wasn't thinking. I was glad to see you because I knew that you could
talk her out of the office if the firemen didn't work."

"Tammy's really a nice woman," she said.

He glowered. "She's a pain."

"If you'd give her half a chance, she might surprise you.
She's very efficient."

He shifted against the seat. "I did notice that you're
pretty rushed. I didn't mean to rob you of her help."

She glanced at him. "You might consider asking Tammy
to come back. Maybe she's sorry, too."

He pursed his lips. "Maybe she is. I suppose I could
drop by her dad's house and just mention that she could
come to work tomorrow."

"It might be a better idea to call first," Shelby said, remembering Tammy's temper.

"I'll do that." He pulled up at the feedlot office and
grinned. "Thanks for being so understanding."

"My pleasure. No, don't get out. I can open the door all
by myself." She laughed. She got out, smiling at him, and
waved him away.

Behind her, Justin stood watching, a cigarette smoking
in his lean fingers, his height emphasized by the jeans and
chambray shirt and boots he wore around the feedlot. His
hat was pulled low over his black eyes and he looked dangerous.

Shelby turned and saw him and stopped suddenly. "Uh,
hi."

He lifted the cigarette to his mouth. "You're an hour
early."

"We had a problem at the office." She flushed, and that
made it worse. "I need a ride to the house."

"Calhoun's going that way," he returned. "He can drop
you off."

He went inside the building, leaving her standing in the sun with the sound of the cattle lowing and moving in the sprawling complex ringing in her ears.

Calhoun came out in a beige suit, scowling. "Justin is sitting behind his desk with his feet crossed, not doing a damned thing, and he dragged me out of a meeting to run you home," he said, stunned. "Not that I mind, Shelby. I'm just curious. Is he at you again?"

"When isn't he?" she said curtly. "Mr. Holman brought me out here. I guess Justin thinks I seduced him on the highway!"

"Shhh!" Calhoun put his finger to his lips and pulled her toward his white Jaguar. "Don't make him any worse than he already is. His secretary's already threatened to walk out!"

"He has that effect on so many people," she said with venom in her tone. "Overbearing, unfeeling, insensitive, insufferable...!"

"Now, now," he soothed. "You'll just work yourself into a lather, and it won't solve anything. He's only jealous. You're a woman. You ought to know exactly what to do about that."

She flushed and averted her face as he helped her into the front seat and got in beside her.

He glanced in her direction curiously, noting her scarlet blush. It amazed him how much alike Justin and Shelby were; both old-fashioned and full of hang-ups.

He started the car and cleared his throat. "Do you mind if I say something pretty personal, Shelby? Since we're related these days and all?"

She couldn't look at him. "That depends on what it is."

"Yes, I can imagine. You react just like Justin does," he mused. He pulled out onto the road and pressed down on the accelerator. "Well, it's this. My brother isn't exactly a lily, but in recent years he's been a hermit. He hasn't dated anybody. He's sort of rusty with women, is what I'm driving at."

"I could tell you what he is, if you weren't his brother," she muttered, clutching her purse.

"Shelby," he said patiently, "the best way to get a man's attention, and knock the fire off his temper, is just to hug him as hard as you can and let nature take care of the details."

She went scarlet. She knew that Calhoun was pretty much like her boss, a man who knew women well. But if she couldn't talk to Justin about intimacy, she certainly couldn't talk to Calhoun about it.

"He wouldn't like it," she said in a husky voice.

"He'd like it," he returned. He reached over and patted her shoulder gently. "He's so crazy about you that he can't see straight. You take my word for it, honey, he'll fold up like an accordion if you use the right approach. And that's all I'll say. How are you and the sports car getting along?"

She gaped at him. He didn't know? "Justin didn't tell you?"

"Justin doesn't talk much when he's at the office," he said pleasantly. "Mostly he works, and when he doesn't, he broods."

"I had a near-miss in the car, actually," she mumbled. "I spun out and almost hit a truck." She felt his stunned glance. "Justin took the car away and had it crushed."

"Good for Justin," he said unexpectedly. "That car was dangerous." He stared at her. "And you know better than most how dangerous."

She cleared her throat. "Switzerland was years ago."

"All the same, Justin was right. He wouldn't want to have to bury you so shortly after your wedding, you know."

"Wouldn't he?" she asked bitterly. "I think he hates me."

"I wish I could convince you what a joke that statement is." He pulled up in front of the house and smiled at her. "I dare you. Play up to him and see what happens. He's as unknowledgeable about women as you are about men, so keep that in mind. And don't, for God's sake, mention that I said so," he said under his breath. "The one time Justin and I really got into it, we both had to have stitches. Okay?"

"Okay." She opened the door and glanced back shyly. "You're a nice man."

"Of course I am," he said. "Ask Abby if you don't believe it." He grinned with the smugness of a man who knows how much he's loved. "See you."

"Tell Abby hello and give her my love."

He laughed and waved as he went down the road. Shelby thought about what he'd said and wondered if she might be able to get up enough nerve to take his advice.

If Calhoun was right, and Justin was as backward as she was, it might really be interesting to see what would happen. Then she remembered his ardor and wondered if Calhoun actually knew his brother at all. The Justin Shelby experienced on the sofa wasn't a man who didn't know what to do with women. Justin was pretty tight-lipped with everyone, and Calhoun might not know exactly how well informed his big brother was.

But the thought of tempting Justin was delicious, and now she had no more reason to be afraid of him. She knew that he could be tender and that he wouldn't lose control too soon. And now, thank goodness, there would be no more painful barrier to inhibit her. She smiled thoughtfully as she went up the steps, already making exciting plans for the night ahead.

Chapter Eight

It was well after dark when Justin finally came home from
the feedlot, looking worn and in a black temper. He spared
a glance at the dining room, where Shelby was eating her
lonely meal, and went upstairs without even a hello.

She sighed, wondering if there was worse to come. She
finished her dessert and was sipping coffee when he came
back downstairs. He'd obviously just showered, because
his hair was still damp around the temples. He was wearing a clean gray and blue plaid western shirt with gray
denim slacks, and his temper hadn't improved.

He sat at the head of the table and began to fill a plate
with lukewarm beef and gravy and buttered new potatoes.

"Maria could warm it up for you in the microwave,"
Shelby ventured.

"If I want Maria to do anything, I'll ask her," he said.

So it was going to be that kind of evening. She put her
napkin aside and straightened the skirt of the red and white

dress she'd worn deliberately because Justin had thought it sexy.

She wasn't quite sure how to reach him. He looked so unapproachable, just as he had in the earliest days of their relationship. She studied his hard face quietly. "Justin, if you're still angry about this afternoon, Mr. Holman closed the office an hour early, and I was already on the street when I realized I didn't have a car," she said. "He was kind enough to drop me off at the feedlot on his way home. He comes right by it, you know."

He looked up, black eyes glittering. "And you know how I feel about your damned boss."

She glowered at him. "Yes, I know, but I didn't think that you'd mind him giving me a ride home. He's a perfect gentleman when he's around me," she said shortly. "I've told you that until I'm blue in the face, Justin!"

"You might have phoned me," he returned. "I'd have come after you."

"I didn't even know if you were at the feedlot," she said. She put her fork down gently. "I didn't know if you'd come, either, after the way you roared off this morning without even saying goodbye."

He pushed his plate away, hardly touched. "He was waiting for you, pacing back and forth," he replied icily. "And then he practically carried you to the sidewalk. I damned near got out of the car and went for him then, Shelby. I don't like other men touching you."

If he expected her to be irritated by that flat statement, he was disappointed. The admission made her pulse skip. She stared at him, wondering if he even realized what he was admitting. She sighed wistfully, and smiled at him. "I'm glad."

He frowned. "What?"

"I'm glad you don't like other men touching me." She picked up her coffee and sipped it. "I don't like other women touching you, either."

He shifted in the chair. "We weren't talking about that."

She smiled, because he seemed to have forgotten what they *had* been talking about. She pushed back her long, dark hair and her eyes sparkled as they searched his. "Calhoun said you dragged him out of a meeting and made him drive me to the house."

He reached for a cigarette and looked uncomfortable. "I was pretty hot."

She wondered if it was his jealousy of her boss, or frustration. Calhoun had intrigued her by what he'd said about the way Justin would react if she made advances. She wanted to find out herself.

But thinking about it and doing it were entirely different things. Sitting there, looking at the taciturn, stern man across from her, she couldn't really imagine going over to him and sitting in his lap. It would have been lovely, though, to feel welcome if she reached out to him.

She colored delicately from her own thoughts and put her coffee cup down. "What about a car for me?" she asked.

"I forgot," he murmured. "We'll go tomorrow."

"All right."

He ignored the fresh apple pie in a saucer beside him and finished his coffee. "I got a new movie in the mail today," he remarked. "A black-and-white war movie, made in the early forties. I thought I might watch it."

"You'll enjoy that, I know."

He eyed her warily. "You could watch it with me. If you wanted to," he added carelessly, so she wouldn't know how badly he wanted her to.

But she sensed it. She smiled. "If I wouldn't be in your way, I'd like to. I like war movies."

"Do you?" He smiled slowly. "How about science-fiction?"

Her eyes lit up. "Oh, yes!"

He actually laughed. "I've got quite a collection of old ones, and a good many new releases."

"All we need now is some popcorn," she remarked.

"Maria!" he called.

The housekeeper came to the doorway. "*Si*, Señor Justin?"

He threw a request at her in rapid-fire Spanish, and Maria grinned and answered in kind. She laughed, made another remark, which caused Justin's cheeks to go a ruddy shade, and went back to the kitchen with a wink in Shelby's direction.

"What did she say?" Shelby asked, because her Spanish was sketchy at best and she didn't have Justin's facility for languages.

"That she'd make the popcorn and bring it in," he replied shortly. "Well, come on, if you're coming."

He got up and went out of the room, leaving her to follow.

The living room was cozy with only the end table lamp on. Shelby curled up on the sofa, barefooted, with the bowl of popcorn between herself and Justin. Maria stuck her head in long enough to say that she and Lopez were going to her sister's for the evening, and then the house was quiet except for the loud excitement of bombs going off and machine-gun fire as the Allies and the Axis fought it out all over again on the screen.

When they got down to the inevitable unpopped kernels in the bottom of the bowl, Justin moved it and took off his boots before he lit a cigarette, propping his long legs on the coffee table. As the movie ran on, Shelby found herself moving helplessly closer to him. Her hand slid hesitantly across to his free one, where it lay on the sofa. She started to touch it and then stopped, shy and uncertain.

He glimpsed the movement and turned his head. "Do you have to have permission to touch me, Shelby?" he asked, his tone deep and slow and gentle.

"I don't know," she replied. "Do I?"

"No." He watched her with patient amusement until she moved her hand toward his again and touched it, tingling at the warm strength of his fingers as they wound through hers and contracted.

She smiled shyly and turned her attention back to the movie again. She didn't see it or hear it, though, because Justin's thumb was rubbing gently against her moist palm. She felt the movement like a brand, burning her blood, making her hungry. Her lips parted as she remembered the last time they'd been on this sofa together, and what they'd done. She remembered the leather cool against her back, the weight of Justin's body over hers in an intimacy that could still color her cheeks scarlet.

"Do you like mysteries?" she asked, for something to say during a lull in the battle scene.

"Sure," he said easily. "I've got a few Hitchcock thrillers, and a copy of *Arsenic and Old Lace* with Cary Grant."

"I love that one," she mused. "I laughed myself sick the first time I saw it."

"How about John Wayne westerns?" he asked with a sly glance.

She laughed. "I've seen *Hondo* so many times, I can even growl along with the character's dog."

"So have I." He studied her for a long moment, admiring the way she looked in the red and white dress, liking the length of her dark hair. "We always did have a lot in common, Shelby. Especially guitar." He rubbed his thumb over the tips of her fingers. "Do you ever play?"

She shook her head. "Not anymore. I . . . lost the taste for it."

"So did I," he confessed, because after they'd broken it off, he couldn't bear the memories the guitar brought back. "Maybe we could practice together again sometimes."

"That would be nice." She smiled at him. He smiled back. And the television set seemed a long way off as the smiles faded and the look became long and intensely arousing.

His fingers contracted roughly on hers and he drew in a steadying breath. "Come here, sweetheart," he said softly.

She tingled all over at the way he said the endearment, because he hardly ever used one at all. He made her feel young and vulnerable. She slid closer with subdued eagerness and curled up against him with her head going to rest naturally on his hard shoulder.

"Don't go to sleep," he murmured dryly.

"I'm not sleepy," she said with a sigh. She smiled and nuzzled her cheek closer. "You smell spicy."

"You smell like a gardenia," he murmured. "It's a scent I never connected with anyone but you."

"It's the perfume I used," she said.

He took his hand away from hers and paused to put out his cigarette. Then he lifted her and turned her across him, so that she was lying in his lap with her head on his chest.

"If you'd rather watch something else, I don't mind," he said softly, knowing full well that the movie was the last thing on both their minds.

She couldn't have cared less what was on the screen, because all she'd seen since the beginning of the movie was Justin's hard profile. But she didn't say that.

"This is fine," she assured him.

"Okay."

He smoothed her long hair, holding her slender hand to his broad chest while he tried to pretend an interest in the movie. He was aware of Shelby now, of the scent of her, of the softness of her breasts pressed against his hard chest, of her warm hand touching him.

Her caressing fingers made his heartbeat quicken. He felt the first stirrings of desire in his powerful body and when he looked down and saw the hunger echoing in her soft eyes, he lost all efforts at pretence. Unhurriedly, he unsnapped the pearly buttons of his shirt and slowly drew Shelby's hand against thick hair and hard, warm muscle, coaxing her to touch him. While her fingers worked on his body, his mouth began to trace patterns on her forehead, her closed eyelids, her nose, her cheeks, her chin and throat.

She felt her breathing quicken as he drew her closer. His nose brushed against hers. His mouth began to search for her lips, and when he found them, the touch was explosive.

She heard his breath sigh out heavily as his mouth became demanding, intimate. His fingers slid into the thick fall of hair at her nape and arched her throat so that her mouth pushed against his, answering his hungry ardor.

Her heart went wild. Her quick, unsteady breathing suddenly matched his. She dug her nails helplessly into his hard chest, and he groaned against her lips.

"Sorry," she faltered.

He took her lower lip between his teeth and traced it with his tongue. "I liked it," he whispered, and his mouth

opened hers, very slowly, while he stretched his length
alongside hers. He sighed, and she felt the touch of his
body from head to toe while the kiss grew warmer and
slower and more intense. "Kiss me hard, Shelby," he
breathed huskily.

She reached up, her inhibitions wearing away under the
deep caresses. Her fingers slid into his thick black hair and
savored its coolness as her mouth began to answer his.

The movie blared away, the battle scenes loud in the
stillness, but neither of them heard. The kisses grew longer,
drugging, aching as Justin's hands worked at buttons and
snaps. Shelby felt his bare chest against her breasts without a protest. It was delicious, the touch of skin against
skin, just as it had been a few nights earlier. But this time,
the old fears were greatly diminished, because now she
knew that what he did wasn't going to hurt her. She knew
how gentle he could be, how patient.

She felt his hands sliding the dress away, tenderly
smoothing it down her long, trembling limbs. She caught
her breath and in the dim light of the lamp, he smiled at
her softly.

"It's all right," he whispered. "I won't go too fast. You
can still stop me, if you want to."

That gave her back the choice, and made everything all
right. She began to relax, letting her hands slide hungrily
over his hard, hair-roughened muscles. It was heaven to
touch him this way, to be given the freedom to learn him
with her hands. She looked up into his dark eyes with the
discoveries lying vulnerable in her soft eyes, and he smiled
down at her.

"Oh, Justin," she whispered huskily. "It's so sweet!"

He bent and lowered his mouth onto hers, feeling the
words sigh against his lips. He slid his hands gently over
her, feeling the ripple of her skin under them. She was like

satin to the touch, and he'd gone hungry for what seemed forever.

In the back of his mind, he knew there was no chance that he was going to be able to stop, but she didn't seem to be worried about that. She pulled him down to her and her mouth was suddenly as ardent as his, as uninhibited.

Still kissing her, he managed to get out of his own clothes, and then she was against him, trembling, while he slowed his pace and began to arouse her all over again with exquisite patience until he felt the passion shaking her slender body.

"Now," he whispered when she was crying with her need. He eased down, turning her face up to his with a caressing hand. "No. Don't turn away. I want to see."

She colored feverishly, but she looked up at him at the instant his body took possession of hers.

His lips parted. It was the most profound experience of his life. All the long years of loving her, needing her, and it was finally going to happen. She was his. There were no more barriers. He felt her accept him totally and his breath caught.

She stiffened just a little at the newness, the stark intimacy, but he slowed and hesitated.

"It's all right," he whispered tenderly, and bent to kiss her, coaxing her to relax, to let it happen. "Yes. Like that." He laughed jerkily at the ease of it, at the exquisite sense of oneness. "Oh, Shelby!"

Her face was bloodred, but she didn't look away. His face was taut with victory, his eyes glittering blackly with it. She reached up, her trembling hands going to his cheeks to bring his head down so that she could reach his mouth.

"Love...me," she whispered, her voice breaking as he moved and she felt the first sweet piercing pleasure. "Justin...love me!"

The words broke his control. He couldn't believe what he was hearing, much less what he was feeling. He went under in a wave of white heat, crying out as the force of the pleasure took his restraint and left him helpless in the drive for fulfillment.

Somewhere in the back of her mind, Shelby knew that she should be frightened by his lack of control. But his movements were causing a kind of silvery tension that made her body sing with pleasure. Ecstasy was just out of her reach, and she stretched toward it with her last thread of strength just as Justin caught her hips and pulled.

She felt the world go spinning down under her, and she cried out his name again and again and again . . .

He laughed. She felt his lips at her temples, on her cheeks, her mouth, in kisses that were as tender as they were comforting.

"The first time," he breathed, laughing again as his mouth covered hers, trembling. "My God, the first time!"

She opened her eyes, still shaking from the sudden descent from a kind of pleasure she'd never dreamed existed. She gazed up at him, fascinated by the way he looked. He seemed years younger. His hair was damp, his face sweaty, his eyes glittering with exultant pleasure. He was shuddering, his body heavy over hers, damp.

"Justin?" she whispered, disoriented.

"Are you all right, sweetheart?" he asked softly. "I didn't hurt you?"

"No." She blushed and lowered her eyes to the pulse in his throat.

"Look at me, you coward."

She forced her gaze up to his and he bent and brushed his mouth over her closed eyes.

"I . . . I never realized . . ." She couldn't find the words. She clung to him, hiding her face against his damp throat.

He turned, holding her warmly against him on the long leather sofa, sighing with exquisite pleasure at the way she held him. "So many lonely nights, Shelby," he whispered. "So many dreams. But even the dreams weren't this sweet." He pulled her closer. "Kiss me, honey."

She lifted her face to his, obediently putting her swollen lips against his. He trembled and eased her gently onto her back, so that they were completely joined. He looked into her eyes with a dark, soft question in his. She didn't answer him. She lifted her body against him, and he saw the words in her eyes. He bent, sighing unsteadily, and his mouth opened over her parted lips. He moved down, and she clung, and the world went again into shared oblivion.

He carried her upstairs a long time later, cradling her in his arms like the most precious kind of treasure. He put her into his bed and climbed in beside her, turning off the lights. He curled her against his tired body and sighed with haunted pleasure. She was asleep only seconds before he was.

Shelby felt a kiss brush her lips. "Justin," she whispered softly and opened her eyes.

He was sitting on the bed beside her, dressed in jeans and a chambray shirt, smiling. "I have to go to work," he whispered.

"No," she moaned, reaching up.

He eased the covers away and brought her across him, touching her soft breasts with exquisite tenderness while he kissed her. "We made love," he whispered.

"Several times," she whispered back, and then spoiled her new image by flushing furiously.

He nibbled her lips. "I didn't use anything," he said quietly, searching her eyes.

The blush got worse. "Neither did I."

He touched her lips with one lean finger. "I know. Is it going to matter, if you get pregnant?" he whispered.

"No," she moaned. "I want a child with you."

He caught his breath and bent to kiss her with aching tenderness, pleased beyond words at the way she said it, at the need he felt in himself, in her. "Did you sleep?"

"I'm still asleep," she whispered at his lips. "I dreamed it all, and I don't want to wake up."

"It wasn't a dream." He kissed her. "Have I hurt you?"

"Oh, no," she whispered quickly. "Not at all!"

His dark eyes sketched her face adoringly. "You'll sleep with me from now on," he said. "No more walls, no more looking back. We start here, now, together."

"Yes," she whispered, sighing, her heart in her eyes. "Don't go to work."

"I have to. So do you." He glowered down at her. "But no more rides with the boss, got that?"

"I'll call you. I promise." She reached up and kissed his cheek. "You can't possibly be jealous after last night."

His lean hand smoothed her breast. "Don't kid yourself," he said softly. "I'll be ten times as possessive now that I've made love to you. You're mine."

"I always have been, Justin," she said quietly, wondering at the way he was looking at her, at the heat of possession in his black eyes. Surely he was sure of her now?

He searched her eyes and then let his gaze run hungrily over her slender body. "Exquisite," he breathed. "All of you. I've never felt anything half as profound in my life as what I felt with you. I feel . . . whole."

Her heart skipped a beat, because that was how she felt. But she loved him, and he only wanted her. Or was it possible that he was finally beginning to feel something for her?

"I feel that way, too," she said.

He smiled. "But you were a virgin, honey," he mused, brushing his mouth over her nose. "I wasn't."

She glared at him. "So I noticed."

That glare made him feel all man and a yard wide. He bent and nipped her mouth with his teeth, softly arousing. "It was a long time ago, and it has nothing to do with you. For the past six years, I haven't even kissed another woman, and that's gospel. You don't have a damned thing to be jealous of."

She hugged him fiercely, her head against his bare chest. "I'm sorry."

"There's nothing to apologize for," he replied. He kissed her forehead with breathless tenderness. "I've got to go," he groaned. "I don't want to, but Calhoun's going to be out of the office all day, and I have to be there."

"I know." She rubbed her cheek against him. "Will you drop me off at work?"

"Of course. What do you fancy for breakfast?"

She looked up at him with the answer sparkling in her eyes. He laughed with pure delight, stood up with her in his arms and tossed her into the center of the bed, watching her scramble under the sheet with indulgent amusement.

"Not now," he murmured dryly at the blatant invitation in her eyes, even through her shyness. "Get dressed before all this stoic control melts."

"Spoilsport," she said, sighing.

"I don't want to overdo it," he said with sudden seriousness. "You're still new to this. I don't want to hurt you."

Her eyes softened. "And I was afraid of you." She shook her head.

"I can understand why. But you won't need to be, ever again." He turned away, stretching hugely. "God knows how I'll keep my mind on work, but there's always tonight," he added from the doorway with a slow grin. "What do you want for breakfast?" he repeated.

She smiled shyly. "Eggs and bacon."

"It'll be waiting."

He went out and she got up and got dressed, feeling as if her feet weren't even touching the floor when she walked.

He was at the table waiting when she got there. She'd put on a simple gray skirt with a pale blue blouse for work, and her hair was in a neat French twist. It was a sedate outfit, which was what she meant it to be. Since she knew how possessive Justin was, she didn't want to spoil their delicate new relationship by making it look as if she was taking special pains with her appearance to go to work.

He looked up when she came into the dining room, and he smiled at the image she projected.

"Very businesslike," he said with approval. He leaned back in his chair, the action pulling the shirt taut over his hard-muscled chest. He looked devastating that way, with the light shining on his black hair and emphasizing his deep tan. He wasn't a handsome man, but Shelby thought he was the most attractive man she'd ever seen.

"I'm glad you approve," she said, smiling at him.

He got up and seated her next to him, pausing to drop a warm, slow kiss on her mouth. His eyes searched hers, warm and soft and darkly glowing. "Pretty creature," he whispered. "Eat your eggs before I make a meal out of you."

She laughed with pure delight and dragged her eyes down to her plate. She could hardly believe the way things had changed in the past few days. Her eyes adored him. He was hers, now. For the first time, she felt really married. Finally they were on their way to a lasting relationship.

The following days emphasized it. She thought about Justin all day at work, and when they got home at night, there were no more arguments, no more barriers. He kissed her coming and going, and every night he made love to her and she slept in his arms. It was as close to heaven as she'd ever been, like a waking dream that never seemed to sour or end. They spent time together, riding, playing the guitar, watching movies on the VCR. It was a new beginning, and Shelby could almost believe that what they had was perfect.

But even as they drew close physically, even as they spent more time together, still Shelby could feel the emotional distance between them. Justin shared none of his deepest feelings with her. He never spoke of love, even when they were the most intimate. He didn't talk about the past or the future. It seemed to her as if he was doing his best to take it one day at a time, without bothering about tomorrow.

His reticence worried her. She was as much in love with him now as she had been in the very beginning, but Justin was adept at hiding what he felt. He had a poker face that she'd never been able to see through. He wanted her. That was obvious and delightful. But if there was more than desire in him, Shelby never saw it.

She kept on with her job, even though she knew that Justin wanted her to give it up. He was only fractionally less jealous of her boss, but he didn't make any more harsh remarks. Meanwhile, Barry Holman had talked Tammy Lester into coming back to work, and things were developing very nicely between them. Shelby expected a breakthrough any day, because they were already exchanging heated looks.

And there was another development at home, too. Over four weeks had passed since Shelby and Justin had been intimate for the first time, and there were growing signs that their intimacy might bear fruit. She hadn't mentioned her suspicions to him, but she was almost sure that she was pregnant. The thought made her delightfully happy. Having a child with Justin would make her happiness complete, and he'd said himself that he wanted children. It would be the final balm, to heal the breach that existed between them. And when the baby came, Justin might begin to care about her as well as the child.

She was curled up on the sofa when he came into the room, scowling. He'd just been on the phone and he looked preoccupied.

"Is something wrong?" she asked gently, sitting up straight. He looked very somber for a change.

He glanced at her and grimaced. "I've got to fly up to Wyoming for a few days. I've been asked to appear in court as a character witness for a friend of mine who's being sued." He sighed. "I don't want to go, but he'd do it for me. I think he's getting a raw deal."

He sat down beside her, drawing her close, while he smoked his cigarette and explained that the rancher was being accused of selling contaminated beef to a packing plant.

"You're sure he didn't do it?"

"I'm sure," he replied. He kissed her absently. "I wish I could take you with me, but I'm going to stay with Quinn Sutton. He's not much of a woman's man."

"I see. He's a grizzled old hermit," she teased.

He chuckled. "Actually, he's about my age and jaded. He lost his wife to another man about ten years ago and he never got over it. She had a child, a little boy. She left the boy behind and Quinn's raised him. I don't know what the boy will do if his dad goes to jail." He shook his head. "Hell of a mess."

"I hope he doesn't have to go to jail," she said. Her pale green eyes searched his face. "I'll miss you, Justin."

He wrapped her up tight and kissed her hungrily. "No less than I'll miss you, honey," he whispered. "I'll phone you every night. Maybe it won't take too long."

"It had better not. If you leave me alone at night too long, I'll run away with some sexy man," she teased, knowing there wasn't a sexier man alive than her husband.

But Justin, still unsure of her even after the weeks of exquisite pleasure, didn't realize what she meant. He held her, his chin on her hair, and stared quietly over her head, wondering if she was already beginning to tire of him. She was a beautiful woman, and he wasn't a handsome man. She seemed to enjoy sleeping with him, but he wanted much more than her slender body in the darkness. He wanted her to love him.

"Don't speed while I'm gone," he cautioned quietly.

She laughed softly. The small American car he'd bought her wasn't a speeding kind of automobile. He'd made sure of that first, but apparently he wasn't going to trust her completely.

"I won't," she promised. "And Maria and Lopez will be here at night, so you don't have to worry about me. I'll be fine. I'll just be lonely," she added, sitting up. Her eyes searched his. "Justin, you're worried. What about?"

He shifted. "Just business, honey," he said evasively. His eyes narrowed as they searched hers. "You aren't getting tired of marriage already, are you?"

She actually gasped. "What?"

"You heard me. I can't give you all that your father could. I just hope it's enough."

She reached up, bringing his face down to hers. "Oh, Justin, you're all I want!"

She kissed him, feeling the ripple run through his powerful body at the touch of her mouth against his. It still amazed her, that wild reaction she got when she kissed or touched him. He never said anything about it, but he seemed to love having her make the first move, having her reach out to him. She didn't do it often, because she was still the least bit shy with him. But it was getting easier. His response was encouraging.

He lifted her, turned her, and his mouth grew hungry. The passion between them never seemed to wane. If anything, it was even stronger now than it had been at the beginning. She held nothing back, and her lack of inhibition keyed a similar lack in him. He was still tender, but occasionally his ardor grew demanding and fierce, and at those times she knew a fulfillment that surpassed her wildest dreams.

"When do you have to go?" she whispered, trembling because his hands were under her soft blouse, touching her.

"Tomorrow."

"So soon?"

He lifted her, getting to his feet in one smooth, graceful motion. "We've got all night," he whispered over her mouth before he took it. "God, I want you! I want you all the time..."

She moaned under his hard mouth, loving his touch, needing the ardent sweetness of his arms. She clung to him as he opened the door and carried her slowly upstairs. If only she could tell him how much she loved him, share the delightful secret that she was hoarding. She wanted to. In fact, she started to. But as she opened her mouth to tell him, his lips began to probe hers tenderly. And as always, the spark of desire knocked every thought out of her mind except Justin, and the exquisite pleasure of loving him in the darkness.

He was gone when she woke up the next morning. She barely remembered feeling his mouth brush hers, hearing his whispered goodbye. But she'd been so tired, and she hadn't fully awakened. When she did, she wished then that she'd made him listen. She had an odd feeling that she should have tried harder, a premonition that their harmony was about to be disrupted. But perhaps it was only her condition and her uncertainty about Justin's feelings for her. Surely they were so close now that nothing could rebuild the old wall that had kept them apart for six years.

Chapter Nine

Court was in session, and there was more work than ever in the small office for Shelby and Tammy. Mr. Holman was working on two divorce cases, a land settlement, a suit for damages resulting from a highway car crash, and he was defending a local man who'd been charged with manslaughter. No sooner did Tammy get through researching one case than she had to start on the next. The land settlement involved complicated research in the county clerk's office, looking up plats and deeds. One of the divorces involved allegations of child abuse, and that required a deposition from an emergency-room physician who'd treated the child—Mr. Holman did that, of course, with the court stenographer. But Tammy had to get the medical records and take down potential testimony from a psychologist and check into the husband's criminal record. The car crash meant more delving into police records and interviewing potential witnesses, and the manslaughter charge looked like a full-time job in itself.

Shelby didn't envy the young woman her paralegal status. Tammy had been taking courses at night at a nearby junior college, and now it was paying off. Mr. Holman had already raised her salary and she was coping with things Shelby couldn't begin to understand. It was a good thing, Shelby thought, that she hadn't wanted that training herself. With her almost positive pregnancy, she wouldn't be able to work for many more months. She knew Justin was going to insist that she stay home the last month or so of her pregnancy. Secretly, she wanted that, too. She wanted the time to plan things for the baby, to get furniture and fix up a room for a nursery. She smiled, thinking about the look on Justin's face when she told him the news.

"I said," Mr. Holman interrupted her thoughts gently, "I'm afraid you're going to have to put in some overtime this week—you and Tammy. Civil court's in full swing, and superior court convenes next week. We don't have a lot of time to get our cases in order."

"I don't mind," Shelby assured him. "Justin's out of town, so I've got nothing to do in the evenings."

"His loss, my gain." The blond lawyer grinned. "Thanks, Shelby. I don't know what I'd do without you. I've got to run to the courthouse and then I'll be at Carson's Café for lunch. Back about one."

"Okay, boss."

He started out the door and collided with Tammy, who was rushing in. He caught her upper arms to steady her and she rested her hands on his chest to support herself. They looked at each other and froze there, a tableau that Shelby found oddly touching.

"You okay?" Barry Holman asked the young woman.

Tammy's full lips parted. "Yes," she breathed. She didn't look up, and she was blushing.

His hands contracted for a minute, then he let her go. "Be careful," he said softly, and smiled. "I don't want to lose you."

"Yes, sir," Tammy murmured huskily.

He let his glance drop to her mouth for one long instant, then he was gone, frowning and impatient all over again.

Shelby had to smother a grin. From fighting tooth and nail, the two of them had become shy and reserved and uncomfortable with each other. Tammy actually seemed to vibrate when the boss came into a room, and her face lit up like a neon sign.

"I, uh, have some notes to type," Tammy said, faltering.

Shelby smiled. "I'll go out and get us some lunch. What would you like?"

"Tuna-fish salad and crackers, and iced tea. Here. And thanks a million! I'll go tomorrow." Tammy grinned.

"That's a deal. I won't be long. Hold the fort."

Shelby went around the corner to the drugstore and found Abby bent over a greeting-card display.

"What are you looking for?" she asked her sister-in-law conspiratorially.

Abby chuckled, her blue-gray eyes lighting up. "A card for my gorgeous husband. His birthday is week after next," she reminded Shelby.

"How could I forget, when we're having the party for him?" Shelby replied. "Which reminds me, I was supposed to call you two days ago to go over the arrangements. I got busy..." She flushed. What had happened was that Justin had wrestled her down on the carpet when she'd picked up the phone to call Abby, and nothing had gotten done for the rest of the night.

"I gather that things are going well over at your place," Abby mused, watching the scarlet blush. "Calhoun says Justin sits around dreaming at the feedlot instead of working, and that he's got a photograph of you on his desk that he just stares at all the time."

Shelby laughed delightedly. "Does he, really?"

"You newlyweds." Abby smiled. "I'm glad it's working out for you. I knew it would. You two were always equal halves of a whole—even Tyler mentioned it that night you and Justin danced together at the square dance."

Shelby blushed. "I never dreamed it would work out like this, though," she confessed. "I've never been so happy."

"I imagine Justin feels the same." She studied Shelby's face curiously. "Why are you still working? Don't you want to stay at home?"

"Well, I didn't think it would be right to just walk off and leave Mr. Holman," Shelby confessed. "Tammy Lester's working out very well and sooner or later I'll go home. It's just that I wanted to try my wings. I've never been independent before. It's fun."

"So is marriage." Abby grinned. "I'm having a ball just being a housewife, as traitorous as that sounds coming from a modern woman. Was that Tammy I saw in the window this morning?" she added. "The shade was pulled down, but it was dark and there was a light behind her. She was leaning over Mr. Holman. She sure does look like you," she added. "Maybe not in person, but your silhouettes are really similar."

"It's probably because we both have long hair and we're tall and slender," Shelby said. "But she's stuck on the boss, and just between us, I think it's mutual. They started out hating each other. Now they're at the throat-clearing, foot-shuffling stage."

"Guess what comes next," Abby said wickedly.

Shelby laughed softly, averting her eyes. "Well, they'll get to that stage before much longer, I suppose. Calhoun doesn't know about the surprise party, does he?" she asked to divert the younger woman.

"Heavens, no, and he wouldn't drag it out of me at gunpoint, I promise. Justin phoned the other night and said he'd invited a couple of people who wouldn't be on my list. I don't guess he mentioned that to you?"

Shelby frowned. "Well...no. Who do you suppose he's invited?" Her green eyes flashed. "Surely he wouldn't invite any of his old flames...?" she mused to herself.

"I wouldn't worry too much about that," Abby murmured, because Justin had once confessed to her that he'd never been in Calhoun's league as a ladykiller. But Shelby didn't need to know that, and it was Justin's place to tell her when and if he wanted to.

"Then who?" she persisted.

"We'll have to wait and see. You might ask him when he gets back. Pity about Mr. Sutton, isn't it?" Abby sighed. "I met him and his son at one of those cattle conventions Calhoun and I went to month before last. He's not much to look at, very reserved, but bristling with masculinity, if you know what I mean. He looked right through me, and there was a woman who came on to him..." Abby shivered. "I used to think Justin was kind of remote when I first went to live with the Ballengers, but Mr. Sutton makes Justin look like an extrovert. He hates women."

"His loss," Shelby said with a faint grin. "Of course, he obviously has never encountered women of our caliber."

Abby burst out laughing. "Shame on you."

Shelby laughed, too. "Call me when you have time and we'll get those arrangements for the party finished. I've got to run. Tammy's at the office by herself."

"Okay. I'll just go through these cards again. Have a nice lunch."

"See you."

Shelby puzzled over what Abby had said all the way back to the office. She couldn't help but wonder whom Justin had invited that he hadn't told her about. She'd have to ask him.

He'd flown to Wyoming on Wednesday, and although he'd hoped to be back two days later, there had been complications and the hearing had been held over until Monday. He wasn't going to get back for the weekend.

"Oh, Justin," she moaned. "And I have to work late next week. We've got court."

"Quit that damned job," he said shortly. "A woman's place is at home, having children and keeping things straight."

A cold, deep voice in the background laughed and made a curt remark that Justin replied to.

"What was that?" Shelby asked curiously.

"Mr. Sutton thinks women are best when floured and salted and fried in lard," he mused.

"You can tell Mr. Sutton that men have to be marinated first," she shot back.

There was a murmur of voices and a deeply appealing laugh in the background. "Shame on you," Justin murmured. "I've got to go. This turkey goes to bed at nine, so I'll be left up in the dark if I don't hang up. Be good, sweetheart. I'll see you Monday evening."

"You can pick me up at work if I'm not here, okay?" she asked softly.

"Okay. Good night."

"Good night, Justin," she said softly and kissed the receiver before she put it back in the cradle. She missed him already until it was almost unbearable. She wanted him to come home so badly.

The next two days passed all too slowly, but Monday was hectic and she didn't have time to look forward to seeing her husband. It was one tangle after another. The phone never stopped and Tammy had to run to the courthouse twice to take information to Mr. Holman in court.

By the end of the day, Shelby wondered if she was ever going to get to go home. Mr. Holman came in needing letters typed and a new brief prepared. It was pages long, and even with the computer, it took Shelby a long time.

Meanwhile, Tammy was flitting around the office following orders while Mr. Holman got more and more impatient. Shelby knew there was going to be trouble from the way Tammy began gnawing on her lower lip and glaring toward the boss's office. At nine o'clock, he came to the doorway and made a sarcastic remark about a property-line measurement that Tammy had written incorrectly and the younger girl exploded.

"You expect miracles!" she told the angry blond man. "I'm working overtime, I haven't had supper, I've had to get down on my hands and knees to get some of this stuff for you, and you're yelling at me! I hate you!"

"You cream puff!" he threw back. "If you think this is hard work, try practicing law, honey!"

He gave her a smug smile and went back into his office.

"Oh, no, you don't, big shot," Tammy muttered. She followed him in, slamming the door.

There were raised voices. A chair scraped and something fell. Then there was a long, poignant silence that grew and grew. Shelby, sitting at her computer, smiled to herself. It looked as if that next step in the boss's courtship had just been taken.

But to the man sitting across the street in the black
Thunderbird, the two figures so closely silhouetted in the
window, against the thin shade, didn't look like Barry
Holman and Tammy. They looked to him like Barry Holman and Shelby. From her height to her long hair, it
looked like Shelby in that man's arms.

Justin felt his heart stop dead in his chest. He'd come
straight from the airport into town, desperate to see Shelby
again, so hungry for the sight of her that he'd taken a
chance on her still being in the office. Only to find…this.

He thought the wounding would never stop. It was killing him to see Shelby in that man's arms. It couldn't be—
but, then, it had to be. She'd teased him about finding another man if he stayed away too long. She wasn't a virgin
anymore; she was a sensual woman now. Perhaps the
hunger had gotten to her. It wasn't rational, but then, neither was jealousy, and he was eaten up with it. He wanted
to go in there and kill that man. He wanted to throw
Shelby out of his house, out of his life. He'd trusted her,
and she'd betrayed him, again.

He didn't want to believe it, but what else could he believe? That was Shelby in that window, Shelby with her
boss. He knew the sight of her too well to mistake her for
anybody else, and who else could there be, because there
was only one woman at the office and Shelby was the
woman!

He started the car and pulled out onto the street, his
dark eyes black with hurt, seeing the end of his dreams.
She'd been fire in his arms, loving him, holding him, giving him everything he'd ever wanted. But she'd betrayed
him in the past, and he'd forgotten that in their new closeness. He'd forgotten what she'd done to him before. She
hadn't slept with Wheelor, but she'd still betrayed him—
she'd thrown him over. And now history was repeating it-

self, and he didn't know what he was going to do. He drove home without even knowing how to get there, sick at heart and already grieving for Shelby all over again. How could she do that to him? How could she!

At the office, Shelby finally finished her chores and wondered whether or not to knock on Barry Holman's door. She decided against it. If they were in a clinch, it would be cruel to interrupt them.

She phoned the house and asked if Justin was there, but Maria said that he hadn't arrived yet. So she went out, leaving a note on her desk, got into her car and drove home. So much for Justin's promise to come and pick her up. But maybe he hadn't gotten home yet. She smiled, comforting herself with that thought.

She pulled into the driveway and left the car at the front steps, eager to see if he'd come in. She darted down the hall to his study, and there he was.

"Hello!" She laughed.

But the man whose black, cold eyes sought hers across the room didn't remotely resemble the tender lover who'd left for Wyoming last Wednesday. He was smoking a cigarette, and he looked as indifferent to her as a stranger might.

"You're late," he remarked.

"I...we had court," she said, faltering. "I told you I'd be working late."

"So you did." He took another draw from the cigarette. "You look worried. Is anything wrong?"

"I thought you might be glad to see me," she said with a hesitant smile.

He smiled back, but it wasn't pleasant. He was dying inside, but he wasn't about to let her see it. "Did you?" he asked carelessly. "I suppose you don't remember what you did to me six years ago. I'm sorry to disappoint you if you expected me to have fallen under your spell again. I haven't. What we had those few weeks was a small recompense for the anguish you gave me in the past. But I didn't realize you expected to build a future on it." He laughed coldly. "Sorry, honey. Once was enough. But don't think I can't live without you. You're like wine—I don't need to get drunk on you to enjoy the occasional sip."

She couldn't believe what she was hearing. She knew her face had gone quite pale. She was almost surely pregnant and Justin was telling her that he didn't want her anymore.

"I thought...you realized that I hadn't slept with Tom."

"Sure I did," he admitted. "But you broke the engagement all the same, didn't you, and told the whole damned world that I wasn't rich enough to suit you." His eyes glittered coldly. "Now it's my turn. I'm rich and I don't want you anymore, honey. Try that on for size."

She turned and ran, a sob breaking in her throat as she went helter-skelter up the staircase and into her old room. She locked the door and threw herself on the bed, crying helplessly. It was like a nightmare.

Several minutes passed. She'd thought, hoped, that Justin hadn't meant it. She'd listened and waited, hoping against hope that he might come after her, that he might reconsider what he'd said. But there were no footsteps on the staircase and she was finally forced to the conclusion that he wasn't going to follow her.

It didn't seem to bother him, either, that she'd gone to bed in her old room. She heard his footsteps much later going down the hall toward the bedroom they'd shared. The door closed and stayed closed.

Shelby didn't know what had gone wrong. When Justin had left for Wyoming, everything had been perfect for them. His emotional distance had disturbed her, but she'd been sure that he was beginning to feel something for her. Now, he was a stranger. The revenge she hadn't thought he wanted was now evident. He looked at her as if he couldn't care less about her, and what he'd said had cut her to the bone.

She finally slept, wondering how she was going to manage to go on. Exhausted, tears streaking her pale cheeks, she faced the loss of everything she'd ever loved. And Justin was first on that list.

Down the hall, the man who'd just returned from Wyoming was lying awake, too, missing the familiar sound of Shelby's breathing, the feel of her soft body against his in the darkness. He felt guilty and sick at the way he'd spoken to her, at the tears and hurt he'd caused. But he was hurting, too. He'd thought that Shelby loved him, and all along she'd only married him because she'd lost her home and security. She was playing him for a fool all over again, keeping a man in the background. The fact that it was her handsome boss only made it worse. Now he knew why she'd fought him about giving up her job. She was in love with her playboy boss, that was why she'd refused to come home. And now he'd seen proof of her disloyalty. He could hardly bear the pain. He didn't know how he was going to go on living with her after what he'd seen.

Just for a minute, he considered the possibility of confronting her with the truth. But what good would that do? He'd confronted her with Tom Wheelor, and she'd lied. She'd lied at the time, and she'd lied since. He'd been lured into a false sense of security. He'd really begun to trust her again. What a good thing that he'd gone into town unannounced tonight to bring her home. Now she couldn't fool him again. He'd seen the real Shelby, and he was disgusted with her. He knew she'd been a virgin when she'd married him, but now that he'd gotten her over the hurdle of her first time, probably she was enjoying a totally new relationship with her boss.

That was the last straw. With an angry sigh, he closed his eyes and forced himself to put her out of his mind.

The next morning, he went downstairs with a carefully schooled expression, determined not to let Shelby know that he was cut to the bone emotionally. He'd die before he'd show it.

Shelby was up early, too, drinking black coffee and nibbling halfheartedly at toast. She looked up when he came into the dining room, her eyes swollen from crying all night, her expression one of hopeful uncertainty.

"You didn't mean what you said last night, did you?" she asked. Her green eyes searched his. "Did you, Justin?"

He moved past her and sat down casually at the head of the table, pouring coffee into his cup from the carafe before he answered her. "I meant every word of it, Shelby," he replied. He helped himself to bacon, eggs and biscuits, as nonchalantly as if she were a business associate. "Have some eggs."

She couldn't bear the sight of them, much less the taste. Her appetite had long since gone, and she was already in danger of losing the tiny bites of toast she'd taken. She shook her head.

His dark eyes narrowed as he studied her. She looked worn. Her long hair was luxurious, but her face was pale and pinched, even with makeup.

"I'm not very hungry," she added.

"Suit yourself." He didn't show his own lack of appetite. He was quiet long enough to clean his plate, but he could feel Shelby's eyes and they made him uncomfortable.

"What kind of relationship do you have in mind for us now?" she asked with the shreds of her pride drawn around her.

He pushed his plate aside and sipped his coffee. "You're my wife," he said coolly. "You'll live in my house and I'll take care of you. But we'll have separate rooms, and separate lives, from now on."

Her eyes closed on a wave of sorrow and shame. And what about the baby I'm carrying, she wanted to ask. What about our child?

"Surely sleeping alone won't bother you now," he chided. "Since you've already satisfied your curiosity."

"It won't bother me," she said huskily. She couldn't finish her coffee. The smell of it made her stomach churn. She got to her feet very slowly. "I'll be late if I don't leave now."

His eyes flashed. "God forbid that you should be late for... work," he said.

She was too sick to notice the hesitation or the venom in his tone. She got out while she could, forcing herself not to show weakness. That was the one thing she couldn't afford at the moment.

She went to work and was violently sick in the bathroom the minute she got there. She mopped her face with wet paper towels and sat quietly at her desk until she got the nausea under control. It was going to take time to reconcile herself to Justin's new coldness. It was like having a glimpse of heaven and then being forced back to reality again. She didn't know why he'd taken this way to get back at her. It was going to be almost impossible for her to stay with him, but she had nowhere else to go. Not yet, at any rate. And certainly not until she was over the first phases of morning sickness and able to move around better than this.

When the boss and Tammy got to the office, she had the nausea under control temporarily. But the late hours were difficult for her, and her appetite was well and truly gone. As the days dragged by, just to put one foot in front of the other was an ordeal.

Abby came over one evening and they worked out the details for Calhoun's birthday party. Abby noticed the atmosphere and almost said something, but Shelby looked so bad that she bit her tongue and kept quiet. Obviously, something had gone wrong.

"You haven't forgotten Calhoun's party?" Shelby asked Justin as they had an increasingly rare meal together before the party.

He looked up from food he didn't even taste, his eyes quiet and somehow haunted for an instant before he blinked and removed the expression. She looked bad. Her color was terrible and she seemed weak and lackluster. He knew it was because of his coldness, but he couldn't help it any more than he could help his feelings of betrayal and hurt.

"I haven't forgotten," he replied. He leaned back in his chair and studied her. "You don't look well."

"It's been a long week, Justin," she said dully. "And a little unexpected. You don't need to worry," she said with a faint laugh. "I'm all right. I'm just fine, in fact. I've got a roof over my head and food to eat, and a job. I've got everything you promised me when we got married. I don't have a complaint."

She put her fork down and got up, swaying a little. She caught the back of the chair, praying that the sudden blackness would relent before she went down. It did, and she turned away from Justin's quick movement toward her.

"Are you all right?" The words were torn from him. He hated the way she looked. She made him feel cold with guilt. Amazing, when she'd hurt him, not the reverse.

"I told you. I'm fine." She left the room with her head high, and went upstairs without another word. They spent no time at all together now. If they had a meal at the same time, it was unusual. Afterward, he always went to his study and she went to her room. Maria noticed, but she and Lopez kept silent. With Justin in his present mood, it was safer that way.

The night of the party, Shelby rested before she dressed. She'd found a dark emerald velvet dress that she'd worn the year before. It had been a little too small when she and Justin married, but the weight loss made it just the right size. It was floor length, sleeveless, with an A-line skirt and a rounded neckline. She pinned up her hair and complemented the dress with a dainty emerald necklace that had been her grandmother's. She looked frail even with makeup, and she wished that things were different between her and Justin. Abby would surely have mentioned her brief happiness to Calhoun. When Calhoun came tonight and was able to see the distance between his brother and sister-in-law, he was bound to mention it to Justin. Shelby didn't think she could bear another confrontation.

She touched her stomach, wondering how much longer she should wait before she saw the doctor. They could tell at six weeks, she knew, and it was almost that. But the problem was going to be how to keep it from Justin in a small community like Jacobsville. Perhaps she could go up to Houston and have herself tested at a clinic.

Music was playing downstairs. She dabbed on a tiny bit of perfume and went downstairs, carefully holding onto the banister. She felt wobbly. The past week had been a terrible strain, due to overwork and Justin's unexplained cold attitude.

She spotted Abby and Calhoun when she got to the first landing. They were arm in arm, looking so happy that they broke her heart. Calhoun was big and blond and Abby was slender and dark. They made a handsome contrast, Calhoun in dark evening clothes and Abby in a pale blue silk that matched her eyes.

Shelby didn't see Justin until she got downstairs. He was dressed in a dinner jacket, and he looked very elegant. Shelby wondered if he planned to put on an act for their guests, or if he was going to be himself. She didn't dare look at him too closely. He might see the hurt and longing in her eyes.

She turned toward the door, where Lopez in his white jacket was just opening it to admit the newest guest. Shelby stopped dead at the sight of the man who stood nervously just inside the hall, shifting his feet as he searched the room for a familiar face.

Shelby's eyes flashed. She couldn't believe that Justin had had the audacity to invite him. It was Calhoun's birthday, and she knew Justin wouldn't expect her to make a scene.

But that didn't even register as she moved out into the hall, ignoring Justin, and picked up a very expensive antique vase on the way.

"Hello, Tom," she greeted Tom Wheelor with icy politeness. "How nice to see you again."

And without a break in her stride, she lifted the vase and threw it straight at Wheelor's balding head.

Chapter Ten

Shelby watched, fascinated, as the antique vase whizzed past Tom's left ear and crashed into the hat stand in the corner, knocking Justin's battered black Stetson to the floor.

"Shelby?" Tom asked, moving back a step.

She reached out for the flower arrangement Maria had painstakingly created for the hall table.

"Shelby, don't!" Tom whirled, his hands over his head, and ran out the front door.

Shelby took off after him, blind to the shocked looks from the other guests, including her wide-eyed husband.

"Insect," she raged. "Weak-kneed money man!" She let him get halfway down the stairs before she heaved the flower arrangement in its delft bowl. It connected. Tom almost lost his balance as he caught onto the balustrade with shards of pottery shattering around him.

He struggled the rest of the way down the steps and ran for his car. Shelby watched him go with fury in her eyes.

He'd been responsible, indirectly, for all her heartaches. How could he have the gall to come tonight, of all nights, and at Justin's invitation? Did Tom really think she'd forgotten his part in her anguish? She'd even told him at the time just what she thought of him.

She turned and went back up the steps. She didn't even look at Justin.

"Good evening," she greeted the guests, as if nothing at all had happened. "Happy birthday, Calhoun! We're so glad Abby let us throw this party for you." She went close and kissed his tanned cheek.

"Thanks, Shelby," Calhoun murmured.

"Shall we go in to dinner?" Shelby nodded to the others, mostly friends of Justin's and Calhoun's whom she barely knew. She took Justin's arm as if she feared his touch would burn her. She didn't look at him or speak to him.

"What the hell was that all about?" he asked when they were temporarily out of earshot of the others, heading into the elegantly arranged dining room.

She ignored his question. "How dare you invite that man here?" she asked instead. "How dare you bring him into our home, after the way he let my father use him to break us up?"

"I wanted to see if there were any embers left from the fire," he said with a cool smile.

"Embers?" She took a sharp breath. "You're lucky I didn't kill him. I'm sorry I didn't!"

"Temper, temper."

"You can go to hell, Justin, dear," she said with a smile as icy as his. "And take your moods and your taste for revenge and your cold heart with you."

His black eyes narrowed. "Still sticking to your story that your father made you break it off with me?"

"Why can't you believe me?"

"Very simple," he replied as the others filed into the room. "It was your father's money that pulled the feedlot out of bankruptcy. He footed the whole damned bill." His eyes registered her shock. "Surprised? It's hardly the act of a man who wanted to break us up, wouldn't you agree?"

Shelby knew her heart was going to beat her to death. She grabbed the back of a chair and almost went down, to Justin's surprise.

"Here, sit down, for God's sake," he muttered, easing her into her place. "Are you all right?"

"No, I'm not." She laughed shakily.

Abby, noticing Shelby's sudden pallor, sat quickly across from her. "Can I get you anything?" she whispered, glancing at the others.

"I'll be fine, if Justin will get away from me," she breathed, looking up at him with quiet rage.

He straightened, searching her furious eyes for a long moment. "My pleasure, Mrs. Ballenger," he said coldly, and turned his attention to their guests.

Shelby never knew afterward how she got through that dinner. She sat like a statue, answering questions, smiling, being the perfect hostess. But when she escaped upstairs to repair her makeup, Abby was two steps behind.

"What's happened?" her sister-in-law asked without preamble.

"For one thing, I'm pregnant," Shelby said stiffly.

Abby's breath sighed out, and her eyes softened. "Oh, Shelby! Does Justin know?"

"He doesn't, and you're not to tell him." Shelby sat down in her wing chair, easing her head back. "He's on the rampage again about the past. Just for a little while, things were going so well. Then he came back from Wyoming a stranger. He's been ice-cold ever since. How can I possibly tell him about the baby when he's acting like that?''

"It might soften his mood," Abby suggested.

"I don't need pity." She put her face in her hands with a tiny shudder. "It's never going to work, Abby. He can't leave the past alone. I don't know what to do. I can't live like this anymore."

The tears slid past her hands and Abby bent, hugging her, saying all the right things, while she wanted nothing more than to go downstairs and hit Justin in the knee with a stick.

"What are you going to do?" Abby asked when the tears diminished and Shelby was wiping her red-rimmed green eyes with a tissue.

"I'm going to cut my losses, of course," Shelby said wearily. "I'm going to Houston tomorrow. I have a cousin there who'll let me stay with her until I can figure out where I'm going. I'll phone her later. I just need a little time to think. I can't do it here."

"What about your job?" Abby persisted, grasping at straws to keep Shelby from doing something stupid.

"Tammy and Mr. Holman are getting along very well," Shelby said. "As a matter of fact, I think they're very likely going to get married in the not-too-distant future. Tammy will take care of everything. I'll phone her tonight, too."

"You can't walk out on Justin like this, without trying to talk to him," Abby said softly, choosing her words. "I don't know what's gone wrong, but I do know how Justin feels about you. Shelby, you didn't see him that night Calhoun took you home from the square dance. But he was heartbroken that he'd made you cry. He cares deeply about you."

"He has a wonderful way of expressing affection," Shelby said. "First he tells me that we'll live separate lives, then he brings that...that *man* here!"

"I think he got the idea that you weren't carrying a torch for dear Tom." Abby chuckled.

"Tom and my father were two of a kind, both out to increase their already substantial fortunes," Shelby said. She stared down at the crumpled wet tissue. "But what hurts the most is that my father funded Justin and Calhoun's feedlot, and I didn't know it until Justin told me tonight." She sighed. "No wonder he wouldn't believe what I said about Dad trying to break us up. My father surely fixed things for me. Justin will never believe me again."

"He might listen if he knew about the baby."

"He's not going to," Shelby said doggedly. "It's my baby, not his. He can go to hell."

Abby's breath sighed out. Shelby looked bad, and talking wasn't going to solve anything. "Let's not discuss this now. You need to get some sleep and give this more thought when you're not so tired. Why don't you go to bed? I'll play hostess for you. I'll tell Justin you've got an upset stomach or a headache."

"He's the only headache I've got," Shelby said wearily.

Abby stood up, about to leave, when the door opened and Justin came in. He looked odd. Drawn and quiet and frankly puzzled.

"There's a woman here. A Miss Lester," he added. "She says she works with you."

"She's our paralegal," Shelby said dully. She wouldn't look at him. "What does she want?"

"She's coming up the staircase now. You can ask her." He shifted uncomfortably. "How long has she worked with you?"

"Several weeks," Shelby said. She looked up as Tammy came sheepishly into the room, looking bright-eyed and radiant. "Hi," she said with a smile. "What are you doing here?"

"I couldn't wait until tomorrow to show you my ring. Look!" She extended her left hand, where a huge diamond sparkled. "He gave it to me tonight."

Shelby laughed and got to her feet unsteadily to hug the younger woman. "I'm so happy for you. I had a feeling this was coming the other night, when the two of you went into his office and there was such silence!"

Tammy grinned. "Yes. Well, we seem to have started a good deal of gossip in town, outlined as we were against the window shade." She flushed. "Neither of us were thinking about being observed. But since we're engaged, it will be all right."

Justin had gone white. Abby saw his face and frowned but Shelby hadn't noticed. She was still talking to Tammy.

"Where's the boss?" she asked.

"Outside in the car, waiting impatiently. We're on our way to his parents' house to break the news. He wouldn't come in because of the party, but I just had to tell you! Isn't it great?" Tammy laughed.

"It certainly is. Congratulations!"

"Thank you. I'd better run." She hugged Shelby again. "See you bright and early tomorrow, okay?"

Shelby wanted to tell her that she wasn't going to be there Monday, but she couldn't, in front of Justin. Her plans to leave had to be kept secret.

"Yes," she agreed. "See you tomorrow. Tell the boss how happy I am for him, too," she added with a laugh.

"Okay. And I'm sorry for interrupting," Tammy added with a shy glance at Justin and Abby. "But I couldn't help it! Good night."

She left. Shelby sat down heavily. "Thank goodness," she told Abby with a breathless laugh. "Now the office can get back to normal again. It's been incredible working there for the past few weeks."

"She looks like you," Justin said curtly.

"Yes, she does," Abby agreed. She looked at Justin. Suddenly she knew that Justin had seen Barry Holman and Tammy in that window shade, silhouetted, and he'd thought it was Shelby. Maybe if she got out, they could talk about it and settle their differences.

"I'd better get back downstairs. Sure you're okay now?" she asked Shelby.

"I'm fine," Shelby assured her. "Thanks, Abby."

"I'll make your excuses."

Justin watched her go, searching for the right words to undo the damage he'd done. Shelby looked so wounded, so fragile. He could have shot himself for that frailty. He'd caused it by jumping to conclusions, by not listening to her. He hadn't trusted her, and now he wondered if he could ever repair the damage.

"Shelby..." he began slowly.

"I don't feel well," she said without preamble. "I'd like to lie down."

"You've lost weight," he remarked.

"Have I really?" She laughed, and it had a hollow sound. "Please go away, Justin. I don't have a single thing to say to you. I don't even want to have to look at you after what you did to me. Inviting that man here...!"

"I had to know!"

She looked up at him as she got to her feet. Her eyes blazed angrily. "I told you the truth. You wouldn't listen. You never have. You prefer your own interpretation, so go ahead and enjoy it. I don't care what you think anymore."

He stiffened. His pride was going to take a few knocks before this was over, and he knew he deserved it, after the way he'd treated her.

"Why did your father break us up?"

"He wanted me to marry Tom," she said, turning away from him. "He didn't want a poor son-in-law. On the other hand, he didn't like to make enemies, not in a small community, so he let me be the scapegoat. You played right into his hands when you went into business for yourself. That gave him leverage, and he used it."

"Then why did he lend me the money?" he asked curtly. "For God's sake, it was that loan that eventually caused his downfall. It took me years to pay it back, but it wasn't in time to do him any good."

She stared at the bed, with her back to Justin. "It was a long time ago. You may find the past comforting, but I don't. I had great hopes for the present until you decided to start evening old scores. Now I just feel tired and I want to go to bed."

He opened his mouth, but the words wouldn't come. He didn't know what to say. "I...saw you. At least, I thought it was you. In the window of your office when I came to pick you up the night I got home from Wyoming," he confessed hesitantly.

She turned. Her eyes widened. "You thought you saw me kissing him?"

His broad shoulders lifted and fell. "You and Tammy have similar profiles, and you'd never told me there was anyone in the office with you."

Her chin lifted. "Thank you," she choked huskily, "for your sterling opinion of my character and morals. Thank you for believing that I could never betray you with another man."

His cheeks went ruddy. "You'd betrayed me once!" he shot at her. "You left me for another man."

"I never did," she said firmly. "Never! My father threatened to ruin you and made me say what I did. He promised to save you, but I never realized that he did it with his own money."

"You dated Tom Wheelor," he added.

"No; it broke my father's heart that I refused to marry Tom," she said with a cold laugh. "Life without you was the purest hell I ever knew. I tried to tell you, but you wouldn't listen. You *still* won't listen." Tears clouded her eyes. "Well, I'm tired of talking to you, Justin. You're too bitter and too much in love with the past to ever give up your grudges. I can't live like this anymore. You've hurt me more than you'll ever know, even though I have to admit that my own cowardice helped things along. But what I did, I did to protect you, because I loved you too much to let you lose everything. All I ever wanted was you. But you only ever wanted me one way, and now that you've—how did you put it?—satisfied your desire for me, even that's gone, isn't it?"

His teeth ground together on a wave of pain. "Oh, God, Shelby," he whispered huskily.

"Well, don't lose any sleep over it, Justin. Maybe we were doomed from the beginning. Without trust, we don't have anything." She brushed the loose strands of hair away from her face. "I thought there was a chance for us, before you went to Wyoming. But if you still can't trust me, then we don't even have a common ground to build on. I'm so tired, Justin," she said then, sitting on the edge of her bed. "I'm so tired of fighting. I just want to go to sleep."

He ran his hand through his thick black hair, watching her. "Of course," he said quietly. "Tomorrow we'll talk."

She wasn't going to be here tomorrow, but she wasn't about to tell him that. "Yes. Tomorrow."

He wanted to hold her. To talk to her. To confess that his coldness had been out of jealousy, because he didn't think such a lovely woman could ever really love him. He'd never thought it, and his own uncertainty about his attraction for a woman like Shelby was the biggest part of the problem. But she did look worn, and it would be cruel to make her evening any harder than he already had.

"Get some rest. If you need me, just sing out."

"You're the last person on earth I need, Justin," she said quietly.

He drew in a slow breath. "My God, I know that. I always was." His black eyes slid over her hungrily. "It never seemed to make any difference, though. I couldn't stop wanting you. I never will."

He went out the door without looking back, and Shelby lay down on the coverlet and cried for all the happy years she'd never have with him, for the child she was carrying that he didn't even know about. She cried for all of them, and fell asleep in her evening gown, lying on top of the covers.

Justin found her that way the next morning. He didn't wake her. She looked so fragile, with her black hair haloed around her sleeping face. She was pale and he felt the guilt all the way to his soul. He'd hurt her. She was the most precious thing in his world, and he'd done nothing but hurt her.

He took off her shoes and pulled the quilted coverlet over her, his black eyes adoring on her face. "I'd fight the world for you, little one," he said softly. "What an irony it is that I can't seem to stop hurting you."

She didn't hear him. He reached down and touched her cheek gently, tracing it up to her eyebrows. His dark eyes softened, became tender.

"I love you," he breathed huskily. "Oh, God, I love you so! Why can't I tell you?" He bent and brushed his mouth with exquisite tenderness over her lips, a light touch that wouldn't awaken her. He stood up again, sighing heavily as he studied her sleeping face. "You said that I didn't trust you. Maybe the truth is more than I don't trust myself. You need someone gentler than I am. Someone less abrasive and set in his ways. I always knew it, but I couldn't find the strength to give you up." He lifted her slender hand in his and savored its softness. He smiled wistfully. "It would serve me right if I lost you. But I don't think I could stay alive if I did."

He put her hand on the coverlet and after one last glance at her sleeping face, he turned and went out of the room. Perhaps later they could talk, and he would tell her all these things when she was awake and listening. If he kept holding back, he stood a very real chance of losing her.

Shelby woke an hour after he left and her mind registered her evening-gown-clad person along with the coverlet that had been put over her. She wondered if she'd done that, or if Maria had covered her. Well, it didn't matter. She had things to do and not much time to do them in.

She tried to phone Tammy, but Tammy must have left for the office. Well, she'd call her from Cousin Carey's house in Houston. She did phone Cousin Carey and ask if she could visit for a day or two, and an invitation was extended with flattering immediacy. She and Carey had known each other since grammar school and were friends as well as relatives. She promised to see her cousin later in the day, hung up and got a reservation on the midday flight out of the Jacobsville airport that was Houston-bound.

She packed a suitcase, taking only what she had to have, and prayed that her morning sickness would hold off until she could get away.

She sneaked downstairs, called a cab and was almost out the door when Maria came into the hall to announce breakfast and found Shelby with a suitcase and a cab waiting.

"*Señora!*" Maria exclaimed helplessly.

"I'm only going away for a couple of days," Shelby said, faltering. "Abby knows where I'll be. You mustn't tell Justin. Promise me!"

Maria grimaced, but she finally agreed. She watched Shelby climb into the cab and drive away. She'd promised not to tell Justin. She hadn't promised not to call Abby. She picked up the phone and quickly dialed Abby's number.

Justin was on the telephone when Abby came into his office, dressed in jeans and a plaid shirt, her hair uncombed and no makeup on. She closed the door and sat down in the visitor's chair, watching the expressions that crossed her former guardian's face as he abruptly ended the telephone conversation and hung up.

"What's wrong?" he asked, because she looked worried.

"Everything!" she muttered, frowning. "I was half asleep when Maria called. Shelby made her promise not to call you, so she called me instead. I've broken speed records getting here. And now that I have—" she sighed "—I don't know how to say this to you."

He'd stiffened at the mention of Shelby's name. He'd had a premonition about her. He knew how badly he'd hurt her, and she'd mentioned last night that she couldn't take any more.

"She's left me, hasn't she, Abby?" he asked quietly.

"Yes, she has. The question is, what are you going to do about it?"

He lit a cigarette with steady hands while his world collapsed around his ears. He stared at the desk. "I'm going to let her go," he said after a minute. "I've hurt her enough."

Abby's breath stuck in her throat. "Justin!"

He looked up, the pain in his eyes making them even blacker. "You don't know how I've treated her," he said. "I was jealous and scared to death of losing her..." He broke off to run his hand roughly through his hair. "What have I got to offer her? How do I keep her?"

"You might try telling her that you love her," Abby said simply. "That's all she ever wanted."

His jaw clenched. "She wouldn't listen, after last night."

"You saw Barry Holman and Tammy, didn't you?" Abby asked.

He stared at her blankly. "Yes."

"And instead of telling Shelby, and letting her explain, you went off the deep end."

He smiled faintly. "Bingo."

"Oh, Justin." She shook her head. "She's on her way to Houston."

"Maybe she'll find someone there who can give her what she needs," he said, feeling bitter that he'd ruined all his chances.

Abby was getting nowhere and if Justin didn't go after Shelby, things were going to fall apart. She bit her lower lip. She didn't want to steal Shelby's thunder, but Justin was being difficult.

"Justin... how do you feel about babies?" she asked.

He was only half listening, his heart lying like lead in his chest. "I like babies," he said absently.

"Good. Then why don't you go after Shelby and get yours back?"

At first Abby didn't think he'd heard her. His eyes swung around and he stared at her. "I beg your pardon?" he asked.

"I said, Shelby's pregnant. If you really want a baby, you'd better get to the airport before she carries yours off to Houston with her."

"What the hell are you talking about?" he exploded.

"Now, Justin . . . !"

But he was on his feet and the chair was on the floor. He grabbed onto the desk for support. His eyes were wild and there was a tremor in the lean hand holding his cigarette. "A baby? Shelby's pregnant, and she didn't tell me?"

Abby was uncertain about what to do, so she rushed out of the office and found Calhoun.

"Come on." She pulled at his big hand. "I need you."

He grinned. "Now, honey, this isn't the place . . ."

"Justin's in shock."

That wiped the smile off his face. He followed her into Justin's office. The older man was right where Abby had left him, still white in the face and looking as if he'd been stabbed.

"You need to take him to the airport," Abby instructed.

"Airport, hell, he needs a doctor. What did you do to him?" he asked in a half whisper.

"I told him Shelby was pregnant."

Calhoun whistled through his teeth.

"And that she was on her way to Houston."

"I can drive," Justin said unsteadily. He started toward the door, but his eyes were dilated and his hand shook as he tried to put out the cigarette, knocking the glowing tip onto the desk.

Calhoun got it into the ashtray and took his brother firmly by the arm. "Don't you worry, big brother, I'll get you there on time." He glanced at Abby. "Which terminal?"

She grimaced. "Jacobsville airport only has one terminal."

"You're a big help," Calhoun muttered. "Anyway, I think there are only a couple of flights to Houston during off-peak hours."

"She's pregnant," Justin said huskily. "She didn't tell me. She knew and she couldn't tell me. It's all my fault. I failed her."

"Everything will be all right," Abby said reassuringly.

"God, I hope so." Justin glanced at her. "Thanks, honey."

"Don't tell Shelby I told you," Abby returned. "It's her place to tell you, but I was afraid you'd let her go if I didn't."

He only nodded, and finally he moved away from Calhoun and went out the door. But he didn't argue when Calhoun gestured toward the Jaguar and got in under the wheel.

"What if the plane's already gone?" Justin asked, smoking like a furnace all the way to the airport.

"Then we'll get you a ticket to Houston." He grinned. "I'm going to be an uncle. Imagine that." He glanced at his taciturn brother. "And here I thought you and Shelby were living chastely."

"Shut up," Justin said, hiding embarrassment in bad temper.

"Whatever you say, big brother." He whistled to himself as he swung the car onto the highway and gunned the accelerator.

They reached the airport in record time. Justin was out the door almost before Calhoun stopped the car, half running to get into the terminal. They found the flight to Houston and Justin went to the ticket counter only to be told that the plane was scheduled to take off in less than five minutes.

Justin outdistanced Calhoun on his way to the concourse, his eyes fixed on the distant gate, his heart bursting with fear that she was going to get away before he got there. He broke into a run as the gate numbers got bigger, determined to make it in time.

Only another minute, he told himself, and he'd have her in sight. Then he could talk to her, he could make her understand how much he loved her.

He pushed past a group of departing passengers from the concourse and made it to the empty ticket counter just in time to watch the clerk pull down the Houston sign and replace it with one for another city.

"The Houston flight," Justin asked curtly. "Where is it?"

"It left about two minutes ago," the clerk said pleasantly. "It's taxiing out to the runway now."

Justin felt his heart stop. He moved around the desk to the window and looked out. Planes were taking off, and one of them had Shelby on it. Shelby and his baby.

He stood there, frozen, his heart shattering. It was his own fault. He'd driven her to this. But he didn't know how in hell he was going to live with it. He could only imagine the anguish that had caused her to run away.

Calhoun touched his shoulder gently. "How about something to eat? Then we'll get you a seat on the next plane."

"I don't even know where to look for her, do you realize that?" he asked huskily. "My God, Cal, I don't know where she's gone!"

"It will be all right," Calhoun said firmly. "We'll find her. I swear we will."

Justin turned away from the window. "Food be damned, I want a drink." He strode off toward the flashing Restaurant and Lounge sign down the concourse.

Calhoun followed, wondering how he was going to keep his big brother sober after his devastating letdown. Justin was shattered and Calhoun didn't quite know what to do for him. He'd said that they'd find Shelby, but he had no better idea of how to go about it than Justin did. It wasn't going to be easy to find one lone pregnant woman in a city the size of Houston. Especially if she didn't want to be found.

He stood out in the corridor, watching Justin go into the lounge and sit at a window table. He gave the waitress an order, and Calhoun sighed heavily. Well, maybe it would be a good idea if he went to the ticket desk and found out when the next plane left for Houston so he could get Justin a seat.

He was on his way down the concourse when a familiar face caught his eye. He stopped in the middle of the aisle and stared. He wasn't dreaming. That gray-clad woman with the small suitcase was Shelby, and she was coming straight toward him.

Chapter Eleven

Shelby felt the ground shake under her at the sight of Calhoun barring her path. She'd been certain Maria wouldn't say anything, but now she wasn't sure. Unless, of course, Calhoun was here to meet a client.

"Uh, hi, Calhoun," she said with a shaky smile.

He sighed. "Hi, yourself, Shelby." He noted the small suitcase she was carrying. "Going somewhere?"

She shifted restlessly. "Yes," she murmured. She stared at his suit instead of his face. "I'm leaving your brother."

"I know. Maria called Abby. Justin knows, too."

Shelby felt her face going pale, but a quick look around didn't produce Justin, and she sighed with relief. "He isn't with you, then?"

He took her arm gently. "I think it might help things along if you had a look at him. Come on, now, he won't bite."

"That's what you think," she muttered. "Where is he?"

"In there." He pulled her just inside the lounge entrance and nodded toward the corner, where Justin sat bareheaded and stooped with a bottle of whiskey and a shot glass in front of him. He was staring at the bottle obliviously while a forgotten cigarette sent up spirals of smoke from his free hand.

Shelby frowned. Justin didn't drink, as a rule. She remembered Abby saying something about him getting drunk the night of the square dance, but she knew it was a rare thing for him. He liked to be in control all the time. He didn't like having his mind fogged.

"What's he doing?" Shelby asked.

"Getting drunk, I imagine." Calhoun took the suitcase from her and looked down at her pale, fragile features. "Now, Shelby, would you say that he looks like a happy man?"

She grimaced. "No."

"Does he look like a man who's overjoyed that his wife has gone off and left him?"

She shook her head. In fact, he looked exactly the opposite. He looked defeated. Her pale green eyes ran over him lovingly, a soft sadness in their depths.

"I had to drive him here because he was shaking too bad to handle a car," he said quietly, nodding at her shocked expression. "He won't like remembering that, and when he's back together, I'm going to catch hell for having seen him in this condition. But I wanted you to know just how upset he is. That man loves you, honey. For years, you've been the only star in his sky. He's been alone all that time, and despite the fact that he's given you hell, I know he'd die for you. If you don't love him, the kindest thing you can do is to get out. But if you care about him, don't run away. Get in there and talk to him."

"I love him," she said simply. "But he believes bad things about me. He won't listen..."

"If you tell him how you feel, he'll listen. Believe it."

She looked up at him, weakening. "It's so hard..."

"Isn't life?" He bent and kissed her cheek gently. "Go on. Get it over. I'll sit in the concourse over there and look like a passenger and drink coffee. I'll look after your suitcase, too."

She smiled softly. "Thanks, Calhoun."

"My pleasure. Now go on."

She hesitated, but only for a minute. Calhoun was right. She was going to have to face Justin.

She walked nervously toward the table where he was sitting. As she got closer, she could see the paleness of his skin, the new lines that cut into his face.

"Justin?" she said hesitantly when she reached him.

He glanced up. Something flashed in his eyes as they went over her, tracing her body reverently. "You aren't here," he said quietly. "You left."

She bit her lip. He sounded as if he was talking to a ghost. "Not yet," she said gently. She eased into the chair beside his and stared at his lean hands. "I'm sorry to just run out like that. But I'd had all I could take."

"I know that," he said, his voice soft, tender. "I'm not blaming you. I never gave you a chance." He lifted the shot glass to his lips, but her fingers touched the back of his hand, coaxing him to put it down. He laughed hollowly. "I hate liquor, did I ever tell you? But it isn't every day a man loses everything he loves."

Tears moistened her eyes. She caught his hand and held it in both of hers, her face lifted, her expression open, loving. "You never said that you loved me, Justin," she whispered. "But I never stopped loving you. I never will. All I ever wanted was you."

His fingers contracted convulsively around hers. His black eyes glittered over his face. "Didn't you know, even without the words?" He breathed roughly. "My God, I'd have walked through fire if you'd asked me to. You were my world. I loved you..."

Her head nuzzled against his shoulder and she hated the crowded room, because she wanted nothing more in life than to throw her arms around him and hold him and kiss him and tell him all the things she'd never said before.

His arm went around her, holding her, and he drew in a shaky breath. "My God," he whispered at her forehead. "I thought you married me because you were alone and frightened."

"And I thought you married me because you felt sorry for me," she replied, letting the tears run freely down her face. "And all along, I loved you so."

His lean fingers brushed away the tears. He searched her misty eyes. "We've got to get out of here," he whispered. "I have to make you understand what I feel. I can't lose you now. Oh, God, Shelby, I'll die without you," he said huskily, and it was in his eyes, blazing out of them like black fire.

The tears came again. She got up, taking his hand. He went with her, holding her against him, even while he settled the tab, as if he couldn't bear to release her even that long.

Calhoun saw them come out of the lounge. He grinned knowingly and picked up Shelby's suitcase. "I'll drop you two off at the house," he offered. "Then I've got a meeting to get to."

They barely heard him. Justin looked completely oblivious, and Shelby was so close to him that she seemed a part of him.

He put them in the back seat and drove off, smiling smugly at his role in this reunion. Not that they seemed to notice him. They were too busy looking at each other.

He let them out at the front steps of the Ballenger house, setting the bag on the steps beside them. "I phoned Abby while you two were in the lounge. She said how about coming over to our place for supper? Maria's going to her sister's tonight, and Shelby sure isn't up to cooking."

"That would be nice," Justin said quietly. He clapped his brother on the shoulder. "Thanks."

"You'd do the same for me," Calhoun replied. He grinned. "In fact, you did, or have you already forgotten? See you at six. Goodbye, Shelby."

"Thanks, Calhoun," she said, smiling at him.

Justin picked up the suitcase and helped her into the house. Maria came running, a stream of Spanish echoing from her lips. Justin abruptly swung her up by the waist and planted a heartfelt kiss on her tanned cheek. She giggled when he put her down.

"Señor!" she chided. She was dressed up. "Lopez and I are leaving now, but I had to wait and make sure everything was all right. *Señor*, what about a meal this evening?"

"Calhoun's invited us over to eat with him and Abby," Shelby told her, and hugged her. "Thank you for calling Abby. I'll never forget what you did for us."

Maria grinned. "You would have found a way, *señora*." She laughed. "I only helped a little bit. Lopez and I must hurry. We will be back tomorrow, *señor*. I will cook you a magnificent breakfast!"

"We'll look forward to that. Godspeed."

Maria smiled and went down the hall into the kitchen, where Lopez was waiting.

Justin led Shelby into the living room, where Maria had a tray of coffee and small cakes waiting for them. After she sat down, he poured the coffee. But before he handed her the cup, he bent and kissed her with exquisite tenderness.

"I love you," he whispered softly, searching her eyes. "I always did, even if I couldn't find the right way to tell you."

She kissed him back. "That was all you ever had to say," she replied. "I loved you, too, Justin. But you never seemed to believe that I could."

He gave her coffee to her and sat down close beside her to sip his. "I was a poor man in those days, and I've never been much to look at," he confessed. "You came from a wealthy background, you were beautiful and pursued." He laughed. "I never felt like serious competition for men like Wheelor."

"Money and looks never counted for much with me," she said firmly. "You had qualities much more important." Her eyes searched his quietly. "But the important thing was that I loved you," she said. "Love doesn't depend on surface things or possessions."

He looked at her with undisguised hunger. "No. I don't suppose it does. I was unsure of you."

She smiled. "And now?"

"And now." He laughed softly. His free hand touched her face. The smile faded. "I've made you unhappy. I've hurt you and scorned you, all because I didn't trust you. But if I'd known how you felt, there wouldn't have been any doubts. None. Can you believe that, and forgive me for the way I've treated you?"

"I love you," she said simply. "Nothing else matters." She reached up and kissed him hungrily. "I understand why you thought what you did, Justin. It was my father's mischief-making, not anything either of us did that caused such heartache. But now it's enough that you love me. It's everything.''

He put down his cup and hers and drew her across his lap, holding her hungrily. ''I'd take back the whole six years, if I could,'' he whispered huskily. ''I'd do anything to make it up to you.''

''Justin . . . you've already made it up to me,'' she said with soft hesitation. She took his lean hand and pressed it slowly, gently, to her still-flat abdomen. She held it there and searched his eyes. ''I'm carrying your baby.''

He knew. But hearing it from her made it profound and infinitely touching. He caressed the softness gently and, bending, brought her mouth under his to kiss her with exquisite caring.

''Shelby,'' he whispered. He kissed her again. ''Shelby. You and a baby . . .''

''You aren't sorry?'' she whispered, softly teasing.

He smiled at her with pride and love in his dark eyes. ''I'm not sorry about anything. Are we having a son or a daughter?''

''I don't care, as long as we have a healthy baby.'' She reached up to hold him. ''And I'm quitting my job, in case I haven't mentioned it. I think Tammy and the boss are going to be very happy without me.''

''I'm going to be very happy with you, if this is what you really want,'' he said. He traced her lips with a long finger. ''I won't cheat you of outside interests, if you want them. I won't insist that you be only a wife and mother.''

''I won't be,'' she assured him, ''although that's going to be my most important job for a little while. Then I may take courses or do some volunteer work. But right now, the baby is my main concern.''

He laughed softly. ''How long?'' he whispered.

"I think I'm just at six weeks," she whispered back. "I'm going to the doctor next week to make sure."

"The first time we made love," he breathed, holding her eyes. "Wasn't it?"

She hid her face against him, laughing with shy embarrassment. "Yes."

"I'm good," he murmured dryly.

She pressed closer. "You're very good," she whispered and lifted her face.

He bent, easing his mouth down onto hers, caressing it. She relaxed against him, loving his touch, loving the strength of his body so close to hers. She sighed, and the sound went into his mouth, kindling a new and overwhelming desire.

Her hands slid around to the back of his head and he drew her hips against his, turning her, while his mouth became more and more demanding.

He wanted her. She knew the signs now, in ways she hadn't before. And she moaned, because he loved her and she loved him, and this time would be different than the other times. It would be the most poignant time of their lives.

"Do you want me?" he whispered against her lips. "Because I want you. Right here."

"The first time . . . was right here," she breathed, jerking a little when his hand eased between them to work at the pearly buttons down the front of her gray dress.

"It's handy." He chuckled, the sound rich and deep with love. "But there's always the carpet."

Her eyes searched his. "How kinky."

"Not at all. It's thick and soft . . . and there's no one to see us. And just to make sure . . ."

He got up, still smiling, and went to close and lock the door. He took off his shirt, watching the way her eyes went to the thick curling hair that arrowed down to the belt of his jeans. He liked the way she looked at him. Her eyes grew dark and soft and faintly sensuous.

He drew her up from the sofa, putting her hands on his chest, smoothing them over the warm, pulsating muscle. "Is it dangerous for the baby?" he asked softly.

She shook her head and pressed her lips against him. "Not if you're gentle. And when have you ever hurt me?"

"No regrets, Shelby?" he asked, hesitating.

She reached up to put her mouth against his. "Not even one."

His hands caught her hips and pulled them into his, moving her body with his so that she felt the force of his need. Her body reacted to it in a now familiar way and she reached up to get closer, signaling her hunger in subtle ways.

She kissed him until her lips grew swollen and tender, until her body began to feel the familiar hot shakiness that he aroused so easily in her.

He eased her down onto the carpet, sliding alongside her easily. He had her dress unbuttoned and her undergarments out of the way with lazy skill, and then she felt his mouth, and all her inhibitions went out the window.

She held his mouth against her, drowning in its moist caresses, loving the way he was with her. There had never been any fear of intimacy since their first time. Her body knew what kind of pleasure lay ahead, and now it reacted with delight, not apprehension.

For long, lazy minutes, he aroused her, not satisfied until she was trembling from head to toe and completely at his mercy. Only then did he undress himself, feasting on her soft curves and creamy skin while he discarded the rest of his clothing and lay back down beside her.

She looked up with misty eyes as he arched above her, catching his weight on his powerful arms, and she felt the exquisite tracing of his skin on hers as he eased down over her.

Her breath jerked at the first touch of him, and he laughed wickedly.

"It shouldn't shock you anymore," he whispered at her lips as he moved even closer. "You're an old married woman now."

"It isn't shock, it's...pleasure!" She clutched at him as he began to move. She buried her mouth against his shoulder, moaning again as his body merged so gently with hers. "Justin!"

"I love you," he whispered softly. "I've never really shown you how much, but now I'm going to. Lie still for me, little one. Let me take you straight into the sun." He eased his mouth over hers, and began to speak to her in husky whispers, in fluent Spanish. Love words. Descriptive words that he punctuated with slow caresses and tender tracings that made her weep with new pleasure. There was no holding back this time, no hidden worry, no barrier. He adjusted his movements to the needs of her body, taking his time, treating her with exquisite tenderness. And somewhere in the slow fire of it, she heard her voice cry out as she followed him into the whirlwind of fulfillment.

She couldn't stop trembling afterward. She clung to his shoulders, trying to keep her breathing steady, her heartbeat from shaking her. But he seemed just as affected, which made it less inhibiting.

"It's all right." He soothed her with his hands, kissing her face gently with lips that adored her. "It's all right. It's just the shock of coming down from such a height, sweetheart," he breathed. "I feel it, too."

"It's never been like this before," she whispered brokenly.

"But we never made love like this before," he whispered back. He lifted his head to search her dazed eyes. "Not this completely."

She touched his mouth with trembling fingers, lost in him, totally his. "I don't want to stop."

"Neither do I," he whispered softly. "We don't have to. We're alone in the house, with nothing else to do. We'll go upstairs and see if we can top what we've just had together."

He got up slowly, picked her up and started for the door.

"Justin, our clothes," she whispered, glancing back at the very evident turmoil of their garments leaving a visible trail.

He balanced her on his leg and unlocked the door. He opened it and started up the long staircase with her cradled against his damp, hair-roughened chest. "They'll still be there when we get back," he promised.

"But we don't have any clothes on," she protested.

He looked down at the pretty pink body in his arms with pure pride of possession. "I noticed."

"But Maria and Lopez..."

"...won't be back tonight." He put his mouth over hers. After a few seconds of it, she began to cling to him, loving the feel of him against her soft bareness. Loving, she thought while she could, was the most incredible pleasure. She kissed him back, all thought of arguing gone from her whirling mind.

It was longer the second time. He drew it out, his voice soft and slow, speaking partly in Spanish as he taught her new words and coached her in their enunciation. And all the while, he touched her, adored her with his hands and his eyes, whispered all she meant to him, how pleased he was about the baby they'd made. They reached heights they'd never scaled, and it was almost dark when they awoke in each other's arms.

"We slept," she murmured.

"No wonder." He grinned down at her, laughing when she blushed.

"I'm thirsty," she whispered.

"So am I." He got up, stretching lazily while her eyes adored his blatant nudity. "How about something cold and icy? And something to nibble on?"

"That would be lovely." She moved against the sheets, her eyes sultry. "Don't be long."

He chuckled. "I'll be back before you miss me."

He looked around for something to put on. His clothes were downstairs. Finally he went into the bathroom and came out with a huge colored beach towel with a giant frog on it. It was her bedroom he'd carried her to, and there was a noticeable shortage of male clothing.

"Damned flashy thing," he muttered, glaring playfully at her as he wrapped it around his hips. "You couldn't buy a plain one, I don't suppose?"

"I like frogs," she murmured.

He arched an eyebrow and, ignoring Shelby's giggles, went downstairs.

He filled two glasses with ice and sweetened tea from the refrigerator, made ham sandwiches, and put it all on a tray. He went out of the kitchen into the hall and paused at the foot of the staircase to adjust his slipping towel when the front door suddenly opened and Calhoun walked in.

He stopped dead, staring at his taciturn, very dignified brother standing in the hall with a giant frog towel wrapped around his lean hips. Justin was carrying a tray full of food and drink and he looked . . . strange.

"I thought you and Shelby were coming to supper," Calhoun began.

"Supper?" Justin echoed.

"Supper. It's almost seven. You didn't call and your phone seems to be off the hook. We were afraid something might have happened, so I came over to see about you."

Justin blinked. He'd taken the phone off the hook when he'd carried Shelby upstairs. He looked down at his towel. "Nothing's wrong. I was, uh, just taking a bath," he improvised, a little embarrassed at being caught in such a compromising situation even in his own home.

Calhoun noticed the open door of the living room and the trail of clothing. "In the living room?" he asked. "And since when do you wear dresses?"

Justin glared at him, his lips in a thin line. "I was sorting clothes at the same time. Then I got hungry."

"You were invited to supper."

"I got hungry first. I was going to have a bite to eat before I started getting ready." His complexion had gone ruddy by now.

Calhoun was grinning from ear to ear. "In the shower?"

"I was going to eat first," Justin said stubbornly.

"Where's Shelby?" Calhoun asked curiously.

Justin cleared his throat. "Upstairs. She was tired."

Just then, a plaintive voice came from upstairs. "Justin, are you ever coming back?" Shelby moaned. "I'm lonely."

Justin's face went scarlet. "I'll be right there!" he called tersely. He glared harder at Calhoun. "She's taking a shower, too."

Calhoun had to stifle laughter. He grinned knowingly at his older brother and turned on his heel. "When you finish your snack in the shower and get through sorting

clothes, come on over and we'll feed you." He glanced at
the towel. "Better put on some pants first, though, we
wouldn't want to shock Abby. Honest to God, Justin, a
frog?"

"It was the only damned thing I could find, and what's
it to you?" Justin demanded hotly.

"Oh, I think it suits you," Calhoun replied. "I like
frogs."

"We forgot the time," Justin said stiffly. "We'll be there
in about thirty minutes, if it's convenient."

"No rush." Calhoun grinned wickedly. "If you think
the living-room carpet is a good place, you ought to try it
in a whirlpool bath," he murmured, and got out quick,
because Justin looked torn between shock and homicide.

Justin carried the tray upstairs, his dignity bruised, and
put it on the bedside table.

"Ice tea! I'm parched." Shelby laughed and picked up
her glass to drink thirstily. "I heard voices."

"Calhoun came to see where we were," Justin muttered. "We were invited to supper, remember?"

"I didn't think about it," Shelby confessed.

"Neither did I. We can go in a half hour. Still want a
snack first?"

"Maybe we'd better wait. We can always have them for
a bedtime snack. I'll wrap them up and put them in the
refrigerator when I've dressed." She looked at her husband lovingly. "Calhoun and Abby are married, too," she
reminded him. "It's not so shocking to be caught spending the afternoon in bed with your wife, is it?"

He shifted. "No. But it's uncomfortable," he confessed with a wry glance. "Six years of celibacy makes a
man secretive, I guess."

"Six years." She reached up and kissed him very tenderly. "I thought I'd made you too bitter to sleep with

anyone else. But it wasn't that at all, was it, Justin?" she asked quietly.

He touched her fingers to his lips. "I didn't want anyone else," he said with a sigh. "I loved you too much. It was you or nobody."

She had to bite her lip to stem the tears. "That's how I felt. I tried so hard to protect you," she whispered.

"I was doing the same thing for you, when we got married. I suppose both of us went overboard, though."

"But no more." She smiled. "Now we'll use our protective instincts on our baby."

"That sounds like a good idea." He bent and kissed her. "We'd better get dressed and go see the in-laws, little mama," he murmured. "Before they come back."

"It was nice of Abby to invite us."

"Yes. I hope you feel up to what's coming," he added. "Knowing Calhoun, it's going to be a trying supper."

She laughed, hiding her face against him. "I love you."

"I love you, too, honey." He got up, frog and all. "Shelby, would you have told me about the baby if Calhoun hadn't gotten me to the airport on time?"

She nodded. "It was your right. I wasn't really leaving you, Justin, I just needed a little time to think things through. I'd have come back. I'm not equipped to live without you any more." She stared at him hungrily. "Were you coming after me?"

"Of course." He chuckled. "I figured I'd spend several months searching the city for you, but that wouldn't have stopped me. I felt bad about what I'd said and done. But it was because I loved you that I'd have gone looking for you, honey, not out of guilt."

"Yes. Now I know." She sighed lazily, so much in love with him that she felt near to bursting with it. "I could eat a horse."

"I'll phone Abby to cook one. Get up and get your clothes on, woman. I'm starving."

"Don't look at me. Not eating was your idea."

She got out of bed and he swung her up against him, his eyes full of tenderness. "It sure was. I take these spells from time to time." He bent and kissed her. "Will you mind?"

She linked her arms around his neck and held him closer. "I won't mind at all."

Outside the night sky grew even darker, and a few miles down the road, Abby was starting to reheat the meat and vegetables in her Irish stew one last time. She'd tried to tell Calhoun that champagne didn't really go with such a simple dish, but he was too busy chilling it to listen. So Abby just laughed, and got down her best champagne flutes. Maybe he was right at that. It did seem like a good night for a celebration.

*   *   *   *   *

TYLER

Diana Palmer

Chapter One

To Tyler Jacobs, the hot arid southeastern Arizona landscape still seemed about as welcoming as Mars, even after six weeks of working on the Double R dude ranch near Tombstone.

He was restless and vaguely depressed. He'd taken a day off to fly to Jacobsville for his sister, Shelby's, wedding to Justin Ballenger, a man she'd refused to marry years ago. Tyler was still puzzled by the courtship. They hadn't looked the picture of a happy couple, and he knew that Justin had been bitter toward Shelby for breaking their earlier engagement.

But it wasn't any of his business; he had to keep that in mind. And better to see Shelby married to Justin, who was old-fashioned enough to keep his marriage vows, than to see her mixed up with the local playboy attorney she worked for. Maybe things would work out for them. If the way Shelby had looked at Justin was any indication, they had to work out. She was obviously still deeply in love with him.

Abby and Calhoun had been at the wedding, too, and Tyler was relieved to find that his brief infatuation with Abby was over. He'd been ready to settle down and was unconsciously looking for the right kind of woman. Abby had fit the bill in every respect, but he wasn't nursing a broken heart. His eyes narrowed in thought. He wondered if he was capable of loving a woman. Sometimes he felt that he was impervious to anything more than surface interest. Of course, there was always the woman who could hit a man hard before he knew it. A woman like Nell Regan, with her unexpected vulnerabilities and compassion...

Even as the unwelcome thought touched his mind, his pale green eyes narrowed on a rider approaching from the direction of the ranch house.

He sighed, glaring through the endless creosote bushes. They dominated the landscape all the way to the Dragoon Mountains, one of Cochise's old strongholds back in the mid-1800s. The "monsoon season" had almost passed. Today it was on the verge of a hundred degrees, and damn what they said about the dry heat not being hot. Sweat was pouring down his dark olive complexion from the sweatband of his gray Stetson, soaking his Western-cut chambray shirt. He took his hat from his jet-black hair and drew his forearm over the wetness while he got his bearings. Out here one stretch of valley looked much like any other, and the mountain ranges went on forever. If elbowroom was what a man wanted, he could sure get it in Arizona.

He'd been out in the brush trying to round up some stray Hereford calves, while his worn leather chaps were treated to the double jeopardy of cholla and prickly pear cactus where the creosote wasn't so thick. Nothing grew around creosote. Having smelled the green bush, especially in the rain, he could understand why.

Before the rider got much closer, Tyler realized that it was Nell. And something was wrong, because she usually kept the length of the ranch between them. Their relationship had become strained unexpectedly, and that saddened him. It had seemed as though he and Nell would be friends at their first meeting, when she'd picked him up at the Tucson airport. But all too soon something had sent Nell running from him.

Perhaps that was for the best. He was earning a living, but not much more, and all his wealth was gone. He had nothing to offer a woman like Nell. All the same, he felt guilty if he'd hurt her, even inadvertently. She didn't talk about the past, and neither did anyone else. But Tyler knew that something had happened to make her wary and distrustful of men. She deliberately downplayed the few attractions she had, as if she was determined not to do anything that would catch a man's eye. Tyler had gotten close to her at first, because he'd thought of her as a cute little kid. She'd been so anxious to make him comfortable, sneaking him feather pillows and all kinds of little things from the house to make him feel at home. He'd flirted with her gently, teased her, delighted in her shy company. And then, like lightning, the housekeeper had made him see that the child he was playing with was really a twenty-four-year-old woman who was misinterpreting his teasing. From that night on, he and Nell had somehow become strangers. She avoided him, except at the obligatory square dance with guests twice a month.

Nell did seem to find him useful in one respect. She still hid behind him at those every-other-Saturday-night barn dances. The way she clung to him was the only crumb left of their easy first acquaintance. But it was vaguely insulting, too. She didn't consider him a threat in any sexual way, or she'd have run screaming from his presence. He'd made some hard remarks about Nell to his sister, Shelby, but he hadn't really meant them. He hadn't wanted anyone to realize how Nell was getting to him.

He sighed, watching her approach. Well, she wasn't dressed to fan a man's ardor, in those baggy jeans and blouse and slouch hat, and that was a good thing. He found her shyness and his odd sense of empathy for her disturbing enough without the added complication of an exquisite figure. He frowned, wondering what she looked like under that baggy camouflage. As if he'd ever find out, he thought, laughing bitterly. He'd already scared her off.

He wasn't a conceited man, but he was used to women. His money had always attracted the beautiful ones, and whatever he wanted, he got. And so, being snubbed by the stone girl stung his pride.

"Have you found those strays yet?" Nell asked with faint nervousness as she reined in beside him.

"I've only gone through five thousand miles," he murmured with soft antagonism. "Wherever they are, they're probably enjoying the luxury of enough water to drink. God knows, except in the monsoon season, they'd need a divining rod or second sight in this barren wasteland to find any."

Nell searched his hard face quietly. "You don't like Arizona, do you?"

"It's foreign." He turned his gaze toward the horizon, where jagged mountains seemed to change color as the sun shifted, first dark, then mauve, then orange. "This takes some getting used to, and I've only been out here a few weeks."

"I grew up here," she remarked. "I love it. It only looks barren. If you see it up close, there's all kinds of life."

"Horny toads, rattlesnakes, Gila monsters..." he agreed dryly.

"Red-winged blackbirds, cactus wrens, roadrunners, owls, deer," she corrected. "Not to mention wildflowers by the score. Even the cacti bloom," she added, and there was a sudden softness in her dark eyes, a warmth in her voice that was usually missing.

He bent his head to light a cigarette. "It looks like desert to me. How's your trail ride coming?"

"I left the guests with Chappy," she said with a sigh. "Mr. Howes looked as if one more bounce would put him on the ground. I hope he makes it back to the ranch."

Tyler smiled slightly as he glanced at her rigid figure in the saddle. "If he falls off, we'll need a crane to get him back on."

Nell grinned without meaning to. He wouldn't know it, but he was the first man in years who'd been able to make her smile. She was a somber, quiet woman most of the time, except when Tyler was around. Then she'd found out what he really thought of her....

"Tyler, could you take over the camp out for me?" she asked unexpectedly. "Marguerite and the boys are coming for the weekend, and I have to go into Tucson and get them."

"I can handle it, if you'll persuade Crowbait to cook," he agreed. "I'm not making biscuits again. I'll quit first."

"Crowbait isn't so bad," she defended. "He's—" her dark eyes narrowed as she searched for a word "—unique."

"He has the temperament of a cougar, the tongue of a cobra and the manners of a bull in heat," Tyler said shortly.

She nodded. "Exactly! He's unique."

He chuckled and took another draw from his cigarette.
"Well, boss lady, I'd better get those strays before somebody with an itchy trigger finger has beef for supper. I won't be long."

"The boys want to go looking for Apache arrowheads while they're here," she added hesitantly. "I told them I'd ask you."

"Your nephews are nice kids," he said unexpectedly. "They need a firmer hand than they get, though."

"Marguerite isn't the ideal parent for two high-strung boys," Nell said defensively. "And since Ted died, it's been worse. My brother could handle them."

"Marguerite needs a husband." He smiled at the thought of Marguerite. She was like the life he'd been used to—sophisticated and uncomplicated and pretty. He liked her because she brought back sweet memories. She was, in fact, all the things Nell wasn't. "But a dish like Margie shouldn't have much trouble finding one."

Nell knew her sister-in-law was beautiful, but it hurt somewhere deep inside to hear Tyler acknowledge Margie's good looks. Nell was only too aware of her own limitations, of her round face and big eyes and high cheekbones. She nodded, though, and forced a smile to her unlipsticked mouth. She never wore makeup. She never did anything to draw attention to her...until recently. She'd tried to attract Tyler, but Bella's comments had killed the notion. Tyler's subsequent behavior had buried it.

Now Nell knew better than to make eyes at Tyler. Besides, Margie was just his style, she thought bitterly. And Margie was interested, too.

"I'll go into Tucson, then, if you're sure about the camp out. And if you can't find those strays by five, come back in and we'll let your Texas friends look for them in the morning," she added, referring to two of the older hands who shared a Texas background with Tyler and had become fast friends of his in the six weeks he'd been in residence.

"I'll find them," he said carelessly. "All I have to do is look for a puddle of water, and they'll be standing on their heads in it."

"You already know not to sit in any dips or washes," she murmured. "Out here is even worse than in Texas. It can be raining twenty miles away and the sky can be clear, and before you know it, you're in a floodplain."

"We have flash floods where I come from," he reminded her. "I know the dangers."

"I was just reminding you," she said, and hated the concern that she'd unwittingly betrayed.

His eyes narrowed and he smiled unpleasantly, stung by her condescending attitude. "When I need a nursemaid, honey, I'll advertise," he said in a pronounced Texas drawl.

Nell steeled herself not to react to what was blatantly an insult. "If you have a chance tomorrow, I'd like you to speak to Marlowe about his language. One of the guests complained that she was getting tired of hearing him swear every time he saddled a horse for her."

"Why can't you tell him?"

She swallowed. "You're the foreman. Isn't keeping the men in line your job?"

"If you say so, ma'am." He tipped his hat with faint insolence, and she wheeled her mount too quickly, almost unseating herself in the process when she pulled on the bit too hard. She urged the horse into a trot and soothed him, stroking his mane as she apologized. She knew Tyler had seen that betraying action, and she felt even worse. She was the last person on the ranch who'd ever hurt a horse voluntarily, but Tyler had a talent for stoking her temper.

He watched her go, his cigarette smoking, forgotten, in his lean, tanned fingers. Nell was a puzzle. She wasn't like any woman he'd ever known, and she had quirks that intrigued him. He was sorry they'd become antagonists. Even when she was pleasant, there was always the reserve, the bitter holding back. She seemed to become rigid when she had to talk to him.

He sighed. He didn't have time for daydreaming. He had to find six little red-and-white-coated calves before dark. He turned his horse and moved into the thick brush.

Nell dawdled on her way back to the adobe ranch house. She wasn't anxious to have Marguerite around, but she hadn't been able to find an excuse to keep the redhead away. Tyler's remark about her sister-in-law still rankled. He found Marguerite attractive, and it wasn't because of Nell that Marguerite was finding reasons to spend time on the dude ranch. She wanted Tyler. She'd made it obvious with her flirting.

Marguerite was beautiful, all right. She was redheaded, green eyed, and blessed with a figure that looked good in anything. She and Nell got along fairly well, as long as neither of them looked back nine years. It had been Marguerite who'd helped put the scars on Nell's young emotions. Nell had never been able to forget what had happened.

On the other hand, it wasn't until Tyler came that Nell really noticed how often Marguerite used her. She was impulsive and thought nothing of inviting her friends out to the ranch for horseback rides or of leaving her two young sons in Nell's care.

Those actions had never bothered Nell very much until lately. Recently, Nell had been feeling oddly restless and stubborn. She didn't like the idea of Marguerite coming for two weekends in the same month. She should have said so.

Giving in to her sister-in-law had become a habit, the way of least resistance. But not anymore. She'd already given Marguerite some unmistakable signals that little Nell wasn't going to be walked over anymore.

Margie only came out to see the Texan, Nell was sure of it. She felt a sense of regret for what she might have felt for Tyler if he hadn't made his lack of interest so apparent. But that was just as well. Margie had made it obvious that she liked Tyler, and Nell knew she was no competition for the older woman. On the other hand, she was pretty tired of letting Margie use her for a doormat. It was time to say so.

Her sister-in-law and her nephews, Jess and Curt, were already packed and waiting when Nell parked the Ford Tempo at the steps of their apartment. The boys, red-headed and green eyed like their mother, made a beeline for her. At seven, Jess was the oldest. Curt was five and already a contender for a talking marathon.

"Hi, Aunt Nell, how about taking us to hunt lizards?" Curt asked as he clambered into the back seat a jump ahead of his taller brother.

"Never mind lizards, nerd," Jess muttered, "I want to look for arrowheads. Tyler said he'd show me where to look."

"I reminded him," Nell assured the older boy. "I'll go lizard hunting with Curt."

"Lizards make my skin crawl," Marguerite said. She wasn't quite as tall as Nell, but she was equally slender. She was wearing a green-and-white striped dress that looked as expensive as the diamond studs in her ears and the ruby ring on her right hand. She'd stopped wearing her wedding band recently—just since Tyler came to the ranch, in fact.

"Well, if I get a lizard, he can live with me," Curt told his mother belligerently.

Nell laughed, seeing her brother in the small boy's firm jaw and jutting chin. It made her a little sad, but it had been two years since Ted had died, and the worst of the grief had worn off. "Can he, now?"

"Not in my house," Marguerite said firmly. After her husband had died, Margie had taken her share of the ranch in cash and moved to the city. Margie had never really liked ranch life.

"Then he can live with Aunt Nell, so there."

"Stop talking back, you little terror." Marguerite yawned. "I do hope all the air conditioners are working this time, Nell. I hate the heat. And you'd better have Bella stock up on Perrier—there's no way I'm drinking water out of that well."

Nell got in under the wheel without any comment. Marguerite always sounded like a conquering army. It was annoying and sometimes frankly embarrassing to have Margie ordering her around and taking things for granted. Nell had taken it for a long time, out of loyalty to her late brother, and because the boys would suffer if she didn't. But it was hard going, and until just recently she'd taken a lot from Marguerite. It was only when Marguerite began making a dead set at Tyler that Nell had started talking back. And now that she'd gotten the hang of it, she rather liked not being talked down to and told what to do. She stared at her sister-in-law coldly while the boys argued in the back seat about who got the middle and who got a window seat.

"The ranch is mine," she reminded Marguerite quietly. "Uncle Ted is in charge until I turn twenty-five, but after that, I'm sole owner. Remember the terms of my father's will—my brother got half and I got half. Uncle Ted was executor. Then when my brother died, you got his share of the ranch in cash. As executor, Uncle Ted keeps control until I come of age. You don't give orders to me, and you don't get special consideration just because you're an in-law."

Marguerite stared. It wasn't like Nell to fight back so fiercely. "Nell, I didn't mean to sound like that," she began hesitantly.

"I haven't forgotten what happened nine years ago, even if you're trying to," Nell added quietly.

The older woman actually went bloodred. She looked away. "I'm sorry. I know you don't believe that, but I really am. I've had to live with it, too. Ted despised me for it, you know. Things were never the same between us after I had that party. I still miss him, very much," she added in a soft, conciliatory tone, with a glance in Nell's direction.

"Sure you do," Nell agreed as she started the car. "That's why you're dressed to the teeth and finding excuses to suffer the heat at the ranch. Because you miss Ted so much, and you want to console yourself with my hired help."

Marguerite gasped, but Nell ignored the sound. She pulled out into traffic and started telling the boys about the new calves, which kept the older woman quiet during the drive home.

As usual, when Bella saw Marguerite coming in the front door, the buxom housekeeper went out the back door on the pretense of carrying an apple pie over to the bunkhouse. On the way there she ran into Tyler, who looked tired and dusty and half out of humor.

"What are you doing out here?" he asked, grinning at the older woman with her black scowl.

"Hiding out," Bella said grumpily, pushing back strands of salt-and-pepper hair while her black eyes glittered. "She's back," she added icily.

"She?"

"Her Majesty. Lady Leisure." She shifted the pie. "Just what Nell needs, more people to take care of. That lazy redhead hasn't lifted a finger since poor Ted drowned in a dry wash. And if you knew what that flighty ex-model had done to Nell..." She flushed as she remembered who she was talking to. She cleared her throat. "I baked the men a pie."

"You baked me a pie," Nell muttered, glaring at her housekeeper as she came out of the back door. "And now you're giving it away because my sister-in-law is here. The boys like pie, too, you know. And Margie won't spoil her figure with sweets, anyway."

"She'll spoil my day," Bella shot back. "Wanting this, wanting that, make the bed, bring her a towel, cook her an omelet... She can't be bothered to pick up a shoe or carry a cup of coffee, no, not her. She's too good to work."

"Don't air the dirty linen out here," Nell said shortly, glancing at Tyler.

Bella lifted her small chin. "He's not blind," she said. "He knows what goes on here."

"Take my pie back in the house," Nell told her.

Bella glared at her. "She's not getting a bite of it."

"Tell her."

The older woman nodded curtly. "Don't think I won't." She glanced at Tyler and grinned. "You can have a slice, though."

He took off his hat and bowed. "I'll eat every crumb twice."

She laughed gleefully and went back inside.

"Aren't you late for the camp out?" Nell asked curiously.

"We canceled it," he replied. "Mr. Curtis fell into a cactus and Mrs. Sims got sick on the chili we had at lunch and had to go to bed. The rest figured they'd rather watch television."

Nell smiled faintly. "Oh, well. The best laid plans... We'll try it again on the weekend."

Tyler studied her quietly, his eyes narrowed in thought. "About this afternoon..." he began, holding Nell's surprised gaze.

But before he could say another word, the door behind Nell swung open.

"Why, Tyler, how nice to see you again," Marguerite said laughingly, pausing in the doorway.

"Nice to see you again, Mrs. Regan," he replied dryly, and there was a world of knowledge in the pale green eyes that swept lazily down her slender body. Marguerite couldn't take him in with that strategic pose. He knew too much. But it was amusing to watch her try.

Nell wanted to throw herself down in the dust and cry, but that wouldn't have done any good. She went back inside, giving up without a struggle.

Marguerite gave her a curious glance, but Nell didn't even look at her. If she wanted Tyler, she was welcome to him, Nell thought miserably. After all, she had nothing to give him herself.

Supper was a quiet affair, except for the boys squabbling over everything from milk to beans.

"Tyler is taking me riding tomorrow," Marguerite said, giving Nell an apprehensive glance. "You'll mind the boys, won't you?"

Nell looked up. She felt rebellious. Restless. "As a matter of fact, I can't," she said with a faint smile. "Take them with you. Tyler's already said he wouldn't mind helping them find arrowheads.''

"Sure!" Jess burst out. "I'd love to go."

"I'll go, too," Curt said.

Marguerite looked annoyed. "I don't want you along."

"You don't love us," Jess wailed.

"You never did," Curt seconded, and he started to cry.

Marguerite threw up her hands. "See what you've done now!" she accused Nell.

"I haven't done anything except refuse to be your doormat." Nell finished her potatoes. "I don't remember inviting you here," she replied coolly. "Don't expect me to entertain you or baby-sit for you."

"You always have before," Marguerite reminded her.

"That was before," Nell replied. "I'm not doing it anymore. You'll have to take care of yourself."

"Who's been talking to you?" Marguerite asked, fascinated.

"Nobody has," Nell replied. "I'm just tired of holding up the world. Why don't you get a job?"

Marguerite's gasp was audible, but.Nell had gotten up and left the table before she had time for any outbursts.

Tyler took Marguerite and the boys riding the next morning. Marguerite did look good in a riding habit, Nell had to concede, but the redhead was obviously out of sorts at having the boys along. Tyler hadn't fussed about taking the boys, either. He liked children. Nell smiled. She liked them, too, but it was Marguerite's job to be their mother, not Nell's.

She wandered out to the kitchen and picked up a biscuit, having refused breakfast because she hadn't wanted to hear Margie raising cain about the boys going along on her romantic ride.

"And what's eating you, as if I didn't know?" Bella asked.

Nell laughed. "Nothing at all."

"You've got Margie running for cover. Imagine, you talking back to her and refusing to be pushed around. Are you sick or something?" she added, her keen old eyes probing.

Nell bit into the biscuit. "Not at all. I'm just tired of being worked to death, I guess."

"And watching Margie flirt with Tyler, I've no doubt."

Nell glared at the older woman. "Stop that. You know I don't like him."

"You like him. Maybe it's my fault that things never got going between you," Bella confessed gently. "I was trying to spare you more heartache, or I'd never have said anything when you put on that pretty dress...."

Nell turned away. She didn't like being reminded of that day. "He isn't my type," she said gruffly. "He's Margie's type."

"That's what you think," Bella murmured dryly. She put her towel down and stood staring at the other woman. "I've wanted to tell you for years that most men are nice critters. Some of them are even domesticated. All men aren't like Darren McAnders," she added, watching Nell's face go pale. "And he wasn't even that bad except when he was pushed into getting drunk. He loved Margie."

"And I loved him," Nell said coldly. "He flirted with me and teased me, just like Tyler did at first. And then he did...he did that to me, and it wasn't even because he was attracted to me. It was just to make Margie jealous!"

"It was despicable," Bella agreed. "But it was worse for you because you cared about him, and you felt betrayed and used. It was a good thing I happened upstairs when I did."

"Yes," Nell said tautly. The memories hurt.

"But it wasn't as bad as you've always made it out to be, either," Bella said firmly, ignoring the shocked look she got from Nell. "It wasn't," she added. "If you'd ever gone out with boys or had a date, you'd understand what happened a lot better. You hadn't even been kissed—"

"Stop it," Nell muttered miserably. She stuck her hands in her jeans and shifted. "It doesn't matter, anyway. I'm plain and countrified and no man is ever going to want me, no matter what I do. And I heard what Tyler said that night," she added with a cold glare. "I heard every word. He said he didn't want a 'lovesick tomboy hanging on to his boots.'"

Bella sighed. "So you did hear him. I was afraid that's why he was getting the deep-freeze treatment lately."

"It doesn't matter, you know," Nell said with deliberate carelessness. "It's just as well I found out early that I was annoying him. I've been careful not to bother him since."

Bella started to say something, but obviously thought better of it. "How long is Her Highness here for?"

"Just until tomorrow afternoon, thank God." Nell sighed. "I'd better get cracking. We're going riding, and then this afternoon I've got a busload of shoppers to take into town. I thought I'd run them over to the El Con mall. They might like to get some real Western gear at Cooper's."

"The silversmiths are over near San Xavier," she was reminded. "And they could have some Papago fry bread for refreshments."

"*Tohono o'odham,*" Nell corrected automatically. "That's a real Papago word, meaning people of the desert. They changed it because they got tired of being called 'bean people' in Zuni."

"I can't say that," Bella muttered.

"Sure you can. *Tohono o'odham.* Anyway, the fry bread is a good idea if we have any time left from the shopping."

"Are any of the husbands tagging along?" Bella asked.

Nell pursed her lips. "Do you think I'd look this cheerful if the men were coming with us?"

"Stupid question," Bella said with a sigh. "I'd better get started on chow, or is Chappy laying on a barbecue tonight before the square dance? He never asks me, he just goes ahead with whatever he wants to do."

"Chappy did say something about a barbecue. Why don't you make a bowl of potato salad and some homemade rolls and a few pies to go with it?" She put an arm around Bella's formidable girth. "That will save you some work, too, won't it? Actually, I think Chappy's kind of sweet on you."

Bella flushed and glared at Nell. "He ain't, neither! Now get out of here and let me get busy."

"Yes, ma'am." Nell grinned and curtsied before she darted out the back door.

Nell went down to the stables to check on the mounts for the morning ride. Chappy Staples was alone there, and after all the years, Nell was still a little in awe of him. He was older than most of the men, but he could outride the best of them. He'd never said a thing out of the way to Nell, but she couldn't help her remoteness. It was the same with all the men, except Tyler.

"How is the mare this morning?" she asked the wiry man with the pale blue eyes, referring to a horse with a bad shoe.

"I had the farrier come over and take a look at her. He replaced the shoe, but she's still restless this morning. I wouldn't take her out if I were you."

She sighed. "That will leave us one mount short," she murmured. "Margie's gone riding with Tyler and the boys."

"If you can handle it alone, I'll keep Marlowe here and let him help me work the colt, and one of the guests can have his horse," Chappy said. "How about it?"

"That sounds great." She sighed, thanking her lucky stars that the foulmouthed Marlowe was being kept clear of her guests. If he kept it up, he'd have to go, and that would leave them a man short. Nell didn't like the idea of adding on new men. It had taken her long enough to get used to the ones she already had on the place.

"We'll start at ten," she told Chappy. "And we have to be back in time for lunch. I'm taking the ladies shopping about one-thirty."

"No problem, ma'am." He tipped his hat and returned to work.

Nell wandered back toward the house, deep in thought, almost running head-on into Tyler because she didn't see him until he rounded the corner of the house.

She gasped, stepping back. "Sorry," she said, faltering. "I didn't see you."

He glared down at her. "I was about to head off riding with Margie and the boys when I heard that I'm escorting Margie to the square dance tonight."

"Are you?" she asked, all at sea.

He lifted an eyebrow. "That's what Margie tells me. She said it was your idea," he added in an exaggerated Texas drawl that could have skinned a cactus at close range.

"I guess you wouldn't believe me if I told you I haven't said a word to her about it," she said resignedly.

"You throw her at me every time she comes out here, don't you?" he asked with a mocking smile.

She lowered her eyes and turned away. "I did once or twice, sure. I thought you might enjoy her company," she said in a subdued tone. "She's like you. Sophisticated and classy and upper crust. But if you'd rather she went with someone else, I'll see what I can do."

He caught her arm, noticing the way she tensed and froze. "All right. You don't have to make a federal case out of it. I just don't like having myself volunteered for guest escort services. I like Margie, but I don't need a matchmaker."

"No, you wouldn't," she said more sadly than she realized. "Will you let go of my arm, please?"

"You can't bear to be touched, can you?" he asked speculatively. "That was one of the first things I noticed about you. Why?"

Her heart went wild. He couldn't know that it was his touch lancing through her like white-hot pleasure that made her tremble, not a dislike of being touched by him. And that surprised her. "My private life is none of your business," she said firmly.

"No. You've made that very clear lately," he replied. He let her go as if her arm burned his fingers. "Okay, honey. Have it your own way. As for Margie, I'll work things out with her."

He sounded vaguely exasperated, but Nell was far too nervous to wonder about his tone of voice. A quick getaway was on her mind. When she was alone with him, it took all her willpower not to throw herself into his arms, despite all her inhibitions.

"Okay," she said, and shrugged, as if what he did were of no consequence to her. She went around him and into the house without looking back, unaware of his quiet gaze following her every step of the way.

Chapter Two

Nell avoided Tyler for the rest of the day, and she didn't go to the square dance that night. She excused herself right after the barbecue and went up to her room. She was being a coward, she thought miserably, but at least she wouldn't have to watch Margie flirt with Tyler.

But memories of Tyler wouldn't be put out of her mind. Her thoughts drifted relentlessly back to the very beginning, to his first few days at the ranch. From the moment she'd met him at the airport, he'd been gentle and kind to her, putting her at ease, making himself right at home in her company.

And not only with Nell—he'd won over the men and Bella just as quickly. Nell had warmed to him as she never had to any man, with the exception of Darren McAnders. But even though Darren had left deep scars on her emotions, Nell knew instinctively that Tyler wouldn't harm her. Before she realized what was happening to her, she was following him around like a puppy.

She grimaced, remembering. She'd alternated between sighing over him and trying to find ways to make him more comfortable. She didn't realize how her eagerness to please him might seem to other people...or even to Tyler. She was in awe of him, the wound of McAnders's long-ago rejection forgotten.

There was a square dance the second week he was in residence. Nell hadn't put on a dress, but she did make sure her long hair was clean and neatly brushed, and she didn't wear her slouch hat. As usual when there were strangers around, especially male ones, she drew into herself. Tyler made a convenient hiding place, and she got behind him and stayed there.

"Scared?" he'd teased gently, not minding her shy company. She was a little sunflower, a child to cosset. He hadn't asked her age, but he assumed she hadn't made it out of her teens yet. She didn't threaten him in any way, and he could afford to be kind to her.

"I don't mix well," she confessed, smiling. "And I don't really trust men very much. Some of the guests...well, they're older men and their wives aren't interested in them. I guess any young woman, even one like me, is fair game to them. I don't want trouble, so mostly I stay away from dances." Her dark eyes sought his. "You don't mind if I stick back here with you?"

"Of course not." He leaned against one of the posts that supported the loft and busied his fingers braiding three strands of rawhide he'd found. "I haven't been to a barn dance in a long time. Is this an ongoing ritual here?"

"Every other Saturday night," she confided. "We even invite the kids, so everybody gets to join in. The band—" she indicated the four-man band "—is a local group. We pay them forty dollars for the evening. They aren't famous, but we think they're pretty good."

"They are," he agreed with a smile. He glanced down at her, wondering what she'd think of the kind of party he was used to, where the women wore designer gowns and there were full orchestras or at least string quartets and jazz quintets to provide the music.

She twisted a strand of her hair in her fingers nervously, watching the married couples dance. There was a wistful expression in her eyes. He frowned as he watched her.

"Do you want to dance, Nell?" he asked gently.

She blushed. "No. I, well, I don't dance," she confessed, thrilling to the thought of being in his arms. But that might not be a good thing. He might see how attracted she was to him. She felt helpless when his hand accidentally brushed hers. She wasn't sure she could handle a dose of him at close quarters without giving away her growing infatuation for him.

"I could teach you," he volunteered, faintly amused at her reticence.

"No, I'd better not. I don't want to..." She was going to say that she didn't want to have to explain to the male guests why she wouldn't dance with anyone but Tyler. It was too hard to make him understand that her flesh crawled at the thought of being handled by strange hands. But she coveted *his* touch, and that was new.

"Okay, tidbit. No need to worry the point." He smiled. "But I think I'm about to be abducted, so what will you do while I'm away?" he asked, indicating a heavyset middle-aged woman who was heading toward him with a gleeful smile.

"I'll just help out at the refreshment table," she said, and excused herself. She watched him being led onto the dance floor and she sighed, wishing she was the one dancing with the long, tall Texan. But she was uncertain of herself. It was better if she didn't rush things. Much better.

After that evening, he became her port in a storm. If there were business meetings or problems that she had to discuss with the men or male guests, she always made sure Tyler was included. She began to think of him as a buffer between herself and a world that frightened her. But even as she relied on him, she couldn't help feeling an attraction that was making it impossible for her to go on as she had. She wanted him to notice her, to see her as a woman. It was the first time in years that she'd wanted to show off her femininity, to look the way a woman should.

But as she stared at herself in her mirror one morning, she wanted to cry. There wasn't even good raw material to work with. She'd seen photos of movie stars who looked almost as bad as she did without their makeup, but she didn't have the first idea how to make herself look beautiful. Her hair, while long and lustrous, needed shaping. Her eyebrows almost disappeared because they were so sun bleached. She had a good figure, but she was too shy to wear revealing clothes. Maybe it wasn't a good idea to go overboard, anyway, she told herself. It had taken years to get over her bad experience and the brutal honesty of the first man she'd set her cap at.

Finally, she'd braided her hair into two long pigtails and looped Indian beaded holders around them. That didn't look too bad, considering that her paternal grandmother was a full-blooded Apache. She only wished her face looked as good as her hair did. Well, miracles did happen. Maybe someday one would happen for her. And Tyler did actually seem to like her.

She tried a hint of lipstick and put on her newest jeans—the only ones she had that really fit properly—with a pullover knit blouse. She smiled at her reflection. She really

didn't look too bad, she thought, except for her face.
Maybe she could wear a gunnysack over it....

Then Bella called her to lunch before she had time to
worry anymore.

She bounced into the dining room with more energy
than she'd had for weeks. She felt reborn, full of new, shy
confidence. She was blooming.

The rain had come to the desert, making the guests uncomfortable and ranching dangerous. The men were
working overtime keeping cattle and horses out of the dry
washes that could kill so suddenly and efficiently when
they filled with unexpected rainwater. The past three days
had brought a deluge, and two of the guests were giving up
and going home. The other eight were going to tough it
out. Nell had smiled at their stubbornness and was determined to make life as pleasant as possible for them.

The guests were having their meal half an hour later than
Nell, Tyler and Bella in the huge oak-decorated dining
room with its heavy chairs and table and comfortable
lounge furniture.

Tyler hadn't shown up, but Bella was bustling around
putting platters of food on the table when she got a glimpse
of the mistress of the house and almost dropped the tray
she was carrying.

"That you, Nell?" she asked hesitantly, her gray head
cocked sideways.

"Who are you expecting?" Nell asked, laughing. "Well,
I won't win any beauty contests, but don't I look better?"

"Too much better," Bella said gently. "Oh, honey,
don't do it. Don't set yourself up for such a hard fall."

Nell stopped breathing. "What?" she asked.

"You take him things for the cabin," Bella said. "You
sew buttons on his shirts. You make sure he's warm and
dry when it rains. You're forever making him special things

in the kitchen. And now this transformation. Honey, he's a sophisticated man who was, until just recently, very rich and well traveled." She looked worried. "I don't want to smash any dreams, but he's used to a different kind of woman. He's being kind to you, Nell. But that's all it is. Don't mistake kindness for true love. Not again."

Nell's face went bloodred. She hadn't realized that she was doing those things. She'd liked him and she wanted him to be happy. But it didn't look like that—of course it didn't. And her new appearance was going to put him in a very embarrassing situation.

"I like him," Nell faltered. "But I'm not...not chasing him." She turned and ran upstairs. "I'll change."

"Nell!"

She ignored Bella's remorseful wail and kept going. But she wouldn't come back down for dinner, despite the pleading from the other side of the door. She felt raw and hurt, even though Bella had just meant to be kind. Nell was going to have to watch her step. She couldn't afford to let Tyler think she was chasing him. God forbid that she should invite heartache again.

Downstairs, Tyler and Bella had been sharing a quiet meal. He studied the old woman curiously.

"Something bothering you?" he asked politely.

"Nell." She sighed. "She won't come down. She fixed her hair and changed clothes, and I..." She cleared her throat. "I said something."

"Nell could use a little self-confidence," Tyler said quietly. "That wasn't kind of you to knock her down when she was just getting started."

"I don't want her to get hurt again," Bella moaned. "You just mean to be kind, I know that. But that child has never had any affection, except from me. She doesn't know what it is to be loved and wanted. Her father lived for Ted. Nell was always an afterthought. And the only other time she was interested in a man, she got hurt bad." She sighed again. "So maybe I'm overprotective. But I just didn't want to see her throw herself at you because you pay her a little attention."

"I never thought she was," Tyler said, smiling. "You're wrong. Nell's just being friendly. She's a cute little kid with pretty brown eyes and a nice way about her. I like her and she likes me. But that's all it is. You don't have to worry."

Bella eyed him, wondering if he could be that blind. Maybe he could. "Nell is twenty-four," she said.

His black eyebrows arched. "I beg your pardon?"

"Well, how old did you think she was?" the woman asked.

"Nineteen. Eighteen, maybe." He frowned. "Are you serious?"

"Never more so," Bella told him. "So please don't make the mistake of putting her in patent leather shoes and ruffled pinafores. She's a grown woman who's lived alone and been slighted all her life. She's just ripe to have her heart torn out by the roots. Please don't be the one to do that to her."

Tyler hardly heard her. He'd thought of Nell as a cute kid, but maybe he'd gotten everything wrong. Surely she didn't see him as a potential romantic interest? That was just too farfetched. Why, she wasn't even his type. He preferred a much more sophisticated, worldly woman.

He picked at his food. "I didn't realize," he began, "that she might be thinking of me in those terms. I'll make sure I don't do anything to encourage her." He smiled at Bella. "I sure as hell don't want a lovesick tomboy grabbing me by the boots every time I walk by. I don't like being chased, even by attractive women. And Nell is a sweet child, but even a blind man couldn't accuse her of being beautiful.''

"Have some more beef," Bella said after a minute, grateful that Nell was still up in her room and not likely to hear what he'd said.

Of course, as fate would have it, Nell had started back down the hall and was standing just outside the door. She'd heard every word, and her face was a pasty white. She just barely made it back to her room before the tears that she'd pent-up escaped.

Maybe it had been for the best that she'd found out early what Tyler really thought of her. She'd gone a little crazy because of the attention he'd paid her, but now that she knew what he really felt about her, she'd keep those stupid impulses under better control. Like Bella said, she'd mistaken kindness for interest. And she should have known better. For God's sake, hadn't she learned her lesson already? She had nothing that would attract a man.

So she'd dried her eyes and put back on her comfortable clothes, and later she'd gone down to supper as if nothing at all had happened. Neither Bella nor Tyler realized what she'd overheard, and she hadn't told them.

But after learning how Tyler felt, Nell's attitude toward him changed. She was polite and helpful, but the light that had been in her eyes when she looked at him had gone out. She never looked directly at him and she never sought him out. The little attentions vanished, as did her shy adoration. She treated him like any other ranch hand, and what she really felt, only she knew. She never talked about him again, even to Bella.

But tonight, in the silence of her room, she still ached for what might have been. It seemed very likely that she wasn't cut out for a close relationship with a man, much less with Tyler Jacobs. But that didn't stop her from being hurt by

what had happened. It had been the first time in years that
she'd made an effort to look like a woman. It would be the
last, too, she vowed. She rolled over and closed her eyes.
Minutes later, she was asleep.

A couple of weeks later, the sun was out, thank God,
because the recent rains had been catastrophic. Bookings
had been canceled and the ranch's finances had suffered.
But now they had all eighteen rooms filled, most of them
double occupancy. The ranch catered to families with
children, and family fun was emphasized, with hayrides
and trail rides and barbecues and square dancing. They did
a lot of repeat business. Mr. Howes and his wife had been
regulars for ten years, and although Mr. Howes spent a
great deal of his time falling off his horse, it never seemed
to deter him from trying to keep his girth in the saddle.
And despite the fact that Mrs. Sims had been infuriating
her ulcer with Crowbait's homemade firehouse chili for the
past five years, she kept trying to eat it. She was a widow
who taught school back East during the year and vaca-
tioned for a week at the ranch every summer.

Most of the regulars were like family now, and even the
husbands didn't bother Nell because she knew them. But
there was always the exception, like the very greasy-looking
Mr. Cova who had a plain, loving wife whose affection he
seemed determined to abuse. He was always watching Nell,
and she looked forward to the day when they left.

"You could have Tyler speak to Mr. Cova, if things get
too rough," Bella mentioned as she was setting the buffet
table for lunch.

"No, thanks," Nell said quietly. "I can take care of
myself."

She turned, almost colliding with Tyler's tall form as he
appeared quietly in the doorway. She mumbled an apol-

ogy and dashed past him without a word. He watched her irritably for a minute before he swung himself into a straddling position over one of the kitchen chairs and tossed his hat onto the table. His lean, dark hands lit a cigarette while he nursed a warm regret for the friendliness he'd once shared with Nell. He felt as if he'd hurt her somehow. Her quiet sensitivity disturbed him. She touched a chord in him that no other woman had ever reached.

"You're brooding again," Bella murmured dryly.

He smiled faintly. "It's just that Nell's changed," he said quietly, lifting the cigarette to his chiseled lips. "I thought we were going to be the best of friends. But now, when I come into a room, she can't leave quick enough. She sends me messages through Chappy. If I need to see the books, she has somebody bring them to me." He shrugged. "I feel like a damned leper."

"She's just nervous around men," Bella soothed. "She always has been—ask Chappy."

Tyler's green eyes shifted and met hers. "It wasn't like this at first. I couldn't turn around without bumping into her. Do you know why things changed?"

Bella shrugged. "If I did," she said, choosing her words carefully, "she wouldn't thank me for saying anything. Although she sure is quiet these days."

"Amen. Well, maybe it's just as well," Tyler murmured absently. He took a draw from his cigarette. "What's for lunch?"

"Open-faced roast beef sandwiches, homemade French fries, salad, homemade banana pudding and iced tea and coffee."

"Sounds delicious. By the way, I've added two new men on the payroll to help do some work on the equipment and renovate the stable and the barn. That's going to have to be done before we finish haying, as I'm sure you know."

Bella whistled through her teeth. "Nell isn't going to like that. She hates having to deal with new men."

He scowled at her. "What happened to her?"

"I can't tell you that. She'll have to."

"I've asked, but all I got was the runaround."

"She's a secretive person. Nell doesn't talk about herself, and I won't." She smiled to soften the words. "Trusting someone doesn't come easy to that child."

"Trust is difficult for most of us." He tilted his hat over his eyes. "See you."

The barn, like every other building on the place, leaked in heavy rain, but when it was sunny like today, it was cozy and plenty warm enough. Nell was kneeling beside a small Hereford calf in a rickety stall filled with green-gold hay, stroking its head.

Tyler stood in the hay-filled aisle watching her for a long moment, his eyes narrowed in thought. She looked like Orphan Annie, and maybe she felt that way. He knew what it was like to live without love, to be alone and alienated. He understood her, but she wouldn't let him close enough to tell her so. He'd made a mistake with Nell. He didn't even know what he'd done to make her back off and treat him with such cool indifference. He missed the way things had been at their first meeting. Her shy adoration had touched him, warmed him. Because of Nell, he felt a kind of emptiness that he didn't even understand.

He moved closer, watching the way she reacted to his approach, the way her dark eyes fell, her quick movements as she got to her feet and moved out into the aisle. As if, he thought irritably, she couldn't bear being in an enclosed space with him.

"I thought I'd better tell you that I've hired two men, temporarily, to help with some repairs," he said. "Don't panic," he added when he saw the flash of fear in her eyes. "They're not ax murderers, and they won't try to rape you."

She blushed furiously and tears burned her eyes. She didn't say a word. She turned and stormed out of the barn, hurting in ways she couldn't have told him about, old memories blazing up like bonfires in the back of her mind.

"Damn it—!" he burst out angrily. He was one step behind her. Even as she reached the barn door, he caught her arm firmly to stop her. The reaction he got shocked him.

She cried out, twisting sharply away from him, her eyes wide and dark and fearful.

He realized belatedly that what had frightened her was the anger in his face, the physical expression of it in his firm hold on her. "I don't hit women," he said quietly, moving back a step. "And I didn't mean to upset you. I shouldn't have made that crack about the new men. Nell..."

She swallowed, stuffing her hands into her jeans while she fought for composure. She hated letting him see the fear his violence had incited. She glanced away from him and her thick black lashes blocked his view of the emotion in her dark eyes.

He moved closer, looming over her. His lean hands slid into the thick coolness of her hair at her ears and tilted her face up to his.

"Stop running," he said curtly. "You've done it for weeks, and I can't take much more. I can't get near you."

"I don't want you near me," she said, choking on the words. "Let go."

Her words stung his pride, but he didn't let her see. "Tell me why, then," he persisted. His gaze was level, unblinking. "Come on."

"I heard what you said to Bella that night," she said, averting her eyes. "You thought I was just a kid, and when she told you how old I really was, you... you said you didn't want a tomboy hanging from your boots," she whispered huskily.

He saw the tears before he felt them sliding onto the backs of his hands. "So that was it." He grimaced. He hadn't realized that Nell might have heard him. His words must have cut her to the quick. "Nell, I never meant for you to hear me," he said gently.

"It was a good thing," she said, lifting her chin proudly as she fought down embarrassment. "I didn't realize how... how silly I was behaving. I won't embarrass you anymore, I promise. I liked you, that was all. I wanted you to be happy here." She laughed huskily. "I know I'm not the kind of girl who would appeal to a man like you, and I wasn't throwing myself at you." Her eyes closed on a wave of pain. "Now, please, will you let me go?"

"Oh, Nell," he groaned. He pulled her close, wrapping her up in his arms, his dark head bent to her honey-brown one under the slouch hat. He rocked her, feeling the pain in her as if it hurt him, too. His eyes closed as he swung her in his arms, the close contact easing the tears, easing the pain. She wept silently at the sweetness of it, even while she knew that she couldn't expect any more than this. A few seconds of pity mingled with guilt. Cold comfort for a lonely life.

She let herself rest against him for one exquisite moment, loving the wiry strength of his tall body, the leather and tobacco smells that clung to his soft cotton shirt, the sound of his heartbeat under her ear. This would be something to dream about when he left. But now, she had to be strong.

She pulled away from him and he let her go. She knew that there was no hope for her in his life. Margie was more like him—she was sophisticated and good-looking and mature. They'd hit it off like a house on fire, and Nell had to keep that in mind and not let her heart get addicted to Tyler. Because Margie wanted him, Nell was sure of it. And Margie always got what she wanted.

She drew in a shaky breath. "Thanks for the comfort," she said. She even forced a smile. "You don't have to worry about me. I won't make things hard for you." She looked up, her brown eyes very soft and dark, shimmering with a hurt that she was trying so hard to keep from him.

Tyler felt something stir in him that knocked him in the knees. She had the most beautiful, sensual eyes he'd ever seen. They made him hungry, but for things that had no physical expression. She made him feel as if he'd been out in the cold all his life, and there was a warm fire waiting for him.

Nell felt that hunger in him, but she was afraid of it. His eyes had become a glittering green, and they were so intent that she flushed and dropped her gaze to his chest. He made her weak all over. If he looked at her like that very often, she'd have to go off into the desert forever. She felt as if he were taking possession of her without a physical move.

She stepped back, nervous, unsure of herself. "I'd better go inside."

"About those new men—they're only temporary. Just until we get through roundup." His voice sounded oddly strained. He lit a cigarette, surprised to find that his fingers were unsteady. "They'll be here in a few weeks."

She managed a shy smile. "Well, I'll try not to treat them like ax murderers," she promised nervously. "I'm sorry about the square dance. About leaving you to deal with Margie." She lifted her shoulders jerkily.

"I don't mind. But don't make a habit of it, okay?" he asked, smiling to soften the words. He reached out and tugged a lock of her long, unruly hair. "I'm feeling a little raw right now, Nell. I've lost my home, my job... everything that used to matter. I'm still trying to find my feet. There's no place in my life for a woman just yet."

"I'm sorry about what you lost, Tyler," she said with genuine sincerity, gazing up at his hard, dark face. "But you'll get it all back one day. You're that kind of person. I can't see you giving up and settling for weekly wages."

He smiled slowly, surprised at her perception. "Can't you? You're no quitter yourself, little Nell."

She blushed. "I'm not little."

He moved a step closer with a new kind of slowness, a sensual kind of movement that made Nell's heart stop and then skip wildly. She could barely breathe, the manly cologne he wore drifting into her nostrils, seducing her. "You're not very big, either," he mused. He touched the very visible pulse in her soft neck, tracing it with a long, teasing finger that made it jump. "Nervous, honey?" he breathed.

She could hardly find enough breath to answer him. "I... I have to go inside."

His head bent so that his green eyes were looking straight into her dark ones while that maddening finger traced a hot path down her throat and up to her jaw. "Do you?" he asked in a husky whisper, and his breath touched her parted lips like a kiss.

"Tyler..." Odd, how different her voice sounded. Strained. Almost frantic.

His eyes fell to her mouth, and he wanted it suddenly and fiercely. His chest rose and fell quickly, his eyes glittered down at her. He almost bent that scant inch that would have brought her soft, full mouth under his. But she was trembling, and he couldn't be sure that it wasn't from fear. It was too soon. Much too soon.

He forced himself to draw back, but his hand gripped her shoulder tightly before he let her go. "See you later," he said with a slow smile.

She cleared her throat. For one wild second, she'd thought he meant to kiss her, but that was absurd. "Sure," she said huskily. "See you."

She turned and went into the house on wobbly legs. She was going to have to get her imagination under control. Tyler was only teasing, just as he had in the beginning. At least he still liked her. If she could control her foolish heart, they might yet become friends. She could hardly hope for anything more, with Margie around.

Chapter Three

A couple of weekends later, Margie and the boys were back at the ranch. Curt and Jess were up at the crack of dawn Sunday, and Nell noticed with faint humor that they followed Tyler wherever he went. That gave Margie a good excuse to tag along, too, but the woman seemed preoccupied. She'd tried to get a conversation going with Nell earlier, although Nell hadn't been forthcoming. It was hard going, listening to Margie try to order her life for her. Margie apparently hadn't noticed that her sister-in-law was a capable adult. She spent most of her time at the ranch trying to change Nell into the kind of person she wanted her to be. Or so it seemed to Nell.

"I do wish you'd let me fix your face and help you buy some new clothes," Margie grumbled at the breakfast table. She glared at Nell's usual attire. "And you might as well wear a gunnysack as that old outfit. You'd get just as much notice from the men, anyway."

"I don't want the men to notice me," Nell replied tersely.

"Well, you should," she said stubbornly. "That incident was a long time ago, Nell," she added with a fixed stare, "and not really as traumatic as you've made it out to be. And don't argue," she added when Nell bristled. "You were just a child, at a very impressionable age, and you'd had a crush on Darren. I'm not saying that you invited it, because we both know you didn't. But it's time you faced what a relationship really is between a man and a woman. You can't be a little girl forever."

"I'm not a little girl," Nell said through her teeth. She knew her cheeks were scarlet. "And I know what relationships are. I don't happen to want one."

"You should. You're going to wind up an old maid, and it's a pitiful waste." Margie folded her arms over the low bodice of her white peasant dress with its graceful flounces and ruffles. "Look, honey," she began, her voice softening, "I know it was mostly my fault. I'm sorry. But you can't let it ruin your whole life. You've never talked to me or to Bella. I wish you had, because we could have helped you."

"I don't need help," Nell said icily.

"Yes, you do," Margie persisted. "You've got to stop hiding from life—"

"There you are," Tyler said, interrupting Margie's tirade. "Your offspring have cornered a bull snake out in the yard. Curt says you won't mind if he keeps it for a pet."

Margie looked up, horrified.

Tyler chuckled at the expression on her face. "Okay. I'll make him turn it loose." He glanced at Nell, noticing the way she averted her eyes and toyed nervously with her coffee cup. "Some of the guests are going to services. I thought I'd drive them. I'm partial to a good sermon."

"Okay. Thanks," Nell said, ignoring Margie's obvious surprise.

"Did you think I was the walking image of sin?" Tyler asked the prettier woman. "Sorry to put a stick in your spokes, but I'm still just a country boy from Texas, despite the life-style I used to boast."

"My, my." Margie shook her head amusedly. "The mind boggles." She darted a glance at Nell, sitting like a rock. "You ought to take Nell along. She and her hair shirt would probably enjoy it."

"I don't wear a hair shirt, and I can drive myself to church later." Nell got up and left the room, her stiff back saying more than words.

She did go to church, to the late morning service, in a plain gray dress that did nothing for her, with no makeup on and her honey-brown hair in a neat bun. She looked as she lived—plainly. Bella had driven her to town and was going to pick her up when the service was over. It would have been the last straw to go earlier with Tyler's group, especially after Margie's infuriating invitation at Tyler's expense.

So the last person she expected to find waiting for her was Tyler, in a neat gray suit, lounging against the ranch station wagon at the front of the church when services were over.

"Where's Bella?" Nell asked bluntly.

Tyler raised a dark eyebrow. "Now, now," he chided gently. "It's Sunday. And I'd hate to let you walk back to the ranch."

"Bella was supposed to pick me up," she said, refusing to move.

"No sense in letting her come all this way when I had to come back to town anyway, was there?" he asked reasonably.

She eyed him warily. "Why did you have to make two trips to town on Sunday?"

"To pick you up, of course. Get in."

It wasn't as if she had a choice. He escorted her to the passenger side and put her in like so much laundry, closing the door gently behind her.

"You're killing my ego," he remarked as he pulled out onto the road.

Her nervous hands twisted her soft gray leather purse. "You don't have an ego," she replied, glancing out at the expanse of open country and jagged mountains.

"Thank you," he replied, smiling faintly. "That's the first nice thing you've said to me in weeks."

She let out a quiet breath and stared at the purse in her hands. "I don't mean to be like this," she confessed. "It's just—" her shoulders lifted and fell "—I don't want you to think that I'm running after you." She grimaced. "After all, I guess I was pretty obnoxious those first days you were here."

He pulled the station wagon onto a pasture trail that led beyond a locked gate, and cut off the engine. His green eyes lanced over her while he lit a cigarette with slow, steady hands.

"Okay, let's put our cards on the table," he said quietly. "I'm flat busted. I work for your uncle because what I have left in the bank wouldn't support me for a week, and I can't save a lot. I've got debts that I'm trying to pay off. That makes me a bad prospect for a woman. I'm not looking for involvement...."

She groaned, torn by embarrassment, and fumbled her way out of the car, scarlet with humiliated pride.

He was one step behind, and before she could get away he was in front of her, the threat of his tall, fit body holding her back against the station wagon.

"Please, you don't have to explain anything to me," she said brokenly. "I'm sorry, I never meant to—"

"Nell."

The sound of her name in that deep, slow drawl brought her hurt eyes up to his. Through a mist of gathering tears she saw his face harden, then his eyes begin to glitter again, as they had once before when he'd come close to her.

"You're all too vulnerable," he said, and there was something solemn and very adult in his look. "I'm trying to tell you that I never thought you were chasing me. You aren't the type."

She could have laughed at that statement. He didn't know that years ago she'd run shamelessly after Darren McAnders and almost begged for his love. But she didn't speak. Her eyes fell to the quick rise and fall of his broad chest under the well-fitting suit, and she wondered why he seemed so breathless. Her own breathing was much too quick, because he was close enough that she could feel his warmth, smell the expensive cologne that clung to him.

"I'm nervous around men," she said without looking up. "You were the first one who ever paid me any real attention. I guess I was so flattered that I went overboard, trying to make you happy here." She smiled faintly, glancing up and then down again. "But I never really thought it was anything except friendship on your part, you know. I'm not at all like Margie."

"What do you mean by that crack?" he asked sharply.

She shivered at his tone. "She's like the people in your world, that's all. She's poised and sophisticated and beautiful..."

"There are many different kinds of beauty, Nell," he said, his voice softer than she'd ever heard it. With surprised pleasure she felt the touch of his lean fingers on her chin as he lifted her face up to his eyes. "It goes a lot deeper than makeup."

Her lips parted and she found that she couldn't quite drag her eyes away from his. He was watching her in a way that made her knees weak.

"We'd better go...hadn't we?" she asked in a husky whisper.

The timbre of her soft voice sent ripples down his spine. He searched her dark eyes slowly, finding secrets there, unvoiced longings. He could almost feel the loneliness in her, the hidden need.

And all at once, he felt a need spark within him to erase that pain from her soft eyes.

He dropped his cigarette absently to the ground and put it out with a sharp movement of his boot. His lean hands slid against her high cheekbones and past her ears.

"Tyler...!" she gasped.

"Shh." He eased her back until she was resting against the station wagon, with his chest touching her taut breasts, and all the time his eyes searched hers, locked with them, binding her to him.

Her nervous hands, purse and all, pressed against him, but not with any real protest, and he knew it. This close, she couldn't hide her hunger from him.

"But..." she began.

"Nell." He whispered her name just as his lips brushed against hers. It wasn't a kiss at all. It was a breath of shivery sensation against her mouth, a tentative touch that made her stand very still, because she was afraid that he might stop if she moved.

His fingers toyed at her nape as they removed the hairpins and loosened her hair, and all the while his mouth was teasing hers, keeping her in thrall to him. He closed one of her hands around her hairpins and ran his fingers slowly through the mass of honey-streaked hair he'd loosened, enjoying its silky coolness.

"Open your mouth a little," he whispered as his teeth closed gently on her lower lip.

She blushed, but she obeyed him without pause.

His own mouth parted, and she watched it fit itself exactly to the contours of her lips. Her eyes glanced off his fiery ones, and then the sensation began to penetrate her shocked nerves, and she gasped as her eyes closed in aching pleasure.

He murmured something deep and rough, and then she felt the length of his hard body easing down against hers while birds called in the meadow and an airplane flew overhead and the sun beat down on her head. She moaned in sweet oblivion.

He felt her tremble, heard the first cry from her lips. His mouth lifted just enough for him to see her face, and he was startled by the pleasure he found there. Her eyes opened, black pools of velvet. His hands slid gently down her back to her waist, and he realized that breathing had become an Olympic event.

"My God," he whispered, but with reverence, because not once in his life had he felt this overwhelming tenderness for a woman.

"You . . . you shouldn't hold me . . . like this," she whispered back, her voice shattering with mingled fear and need.

"Why not?" He brushed his nose against hers while he spoke and managed a faint smile for her.

She colored. "You know why not."

"No, I don't." His mouth covered hers slowly, and he felt her yield, felt her submission like a drug as he drowned in the softness of her body and the sweetness of her mouth. He relaxed, giving in to his own need. His hips slowly pressed against hers, letting her feel what she probably already knew . . . that he was feverishly aroused by her.

She stiffened and gasped, and without warning he felt her ardor turn to fear as she pushed at his chest in flaming embarrassment.

He drew away gently, releasing her from the soft crush of his body. His eyes searched her scarlet face, noting the way she kept her own eyes hidden.

"You haven't done this before," he said with sudden conviction.

"Not . . . not voluntarily, no," she replied with forced lightness. She gnawed on her lip. "I'm sorry. It's . . . it's a little scary." And she blushed again, even more.

He laughed softly, delighted. His mouth pressed gently against her forehead. He nuzzled her face with his. "I suppose it would be, to a quiet little virgin who doesn't chase men."

"Please don't make fun of me," she whispered.

"Was that how it sounded?" He lifted his head, touching her mouth with a slow, tender forefinger as he watched her. "I didn't mean it to. I'm not used to innocents, Nell. The world I came from didn't accept them very readily."

"Oh. I see."

"No, you don't, honey. And that's a good thing. It isn't my world any longer. I'm not sure I even miss it." He toyed with a long, silky strand of her hair. "You're trembling," he whispered.

"I'm . . . this is . . . it's new."

"It's new for me, too, although I imagine you don't believe it." He brushed the hair back from her face, and his green eyes searched her dark ones. "How long is it since a man kissed you . . . really kissed you?"

"I don't think anyone ever did, and meant it," she confessed.

"Why?"

"I don't attract men," she faltered.

"Really?" He smiled but without mirth as he caught her by the waist and pulled her to him. She flushed and tried to pull away, but this time he held her firmly.

"Tyler!" she protested, flustered.

"Just stand still," he said quietly, but he let her hips pull away without an argument. "You're twenty-four years old and damned ignorant about men. It's time you had a little instruction. I won't hurt you, but I can't kiss you from a safe distance."

"You shouldn't," she pleaded, looking up. "It isn't fair to... to play with me."

His dark eyes didn't blink. "Is that what I'm doing, Nell?" he asked softly. "Am I playing?"

"What else could you be doing?"

"What else, indeed," he breathed as his head bent. He pulled her up to meet the hard descent of his mouth, and he kissed her with passion and a little anger, because she was arousing him in ways she couldn't have dreamed. He couldn't stop what was happening, and that irritated him even more. Nell was the last woman in the world he should be kissing this way. He had no right to get involved with her when he had nothing to offer. But her mouth was sweet and gentle under his, softly parting; her body, after its first resistance, melting into his. He lifted her against his chest, drowning in the long, sweet, aching pleasure of the most chaste kiss he'd ever shared with a woman. His body fairly throbbed against her, but he kept himself in full control. This was an interlude that couldn't end in a bedroom; he had to remember that.

He groaned finally and listened to reason. He put her back on her feet, his hands gripping her soft arms hard as he held her in front of him and struggled for both breath and sanity.

Nell was dazed. Her eyes searched his glittery ones, and she could feel the fine tremor in his hands as he held her. He was breathing as roughly as she was. He wanted her. She knew it suddenly and without a doubt. With a sense of shock, she realized how much a man he really was.

"I need to sit down," she said shakily.

"I'm just that unsteady myself, if you want the truth," he said on a rough sigh. He opened the door and let her into the station wagon before he slid his long legs inside and got in under the wheel.

He lit a cigarette and sat quietly, not speaking, while Nell fumbled her hairpins into her purse and dug out a small brush to run through her long, disheveled hair. She would have liked to check her appearance in a mirror, but that would look suspicious. She didn't want him to know how desperately sweet that interlude had been for her.

She put the brush back into her purse and closed it and stared down into her lap. Now that it was all over, she wondered how he felt. Would he think she was that starved for affection that she'd have reacted the same way to any man? She glanced at him nervously, but he seemed oblivious to her presence. He was staring out the windshield, apparently deep in thought.

In fact, he was trying to breathe normally. It was unusual for him to feel so shaken by such an innocent kiss. He couldn't remember the last time a woman had thrown him off balance. But Nell seemed to do it effortlessly, and that bothered him. Loss of control was the last thing he could afford with a virgin. He had to put on the brakes, and fast. The question was, how was he going to do that without making Nell think that he was little more than a playboy having fun?

He turned his head and found her watching the landscape without any particular expression on her soft face.

"We'll be late for lunch," Nell remarked without looking at him. She couldn't. She was too embarrassed by her reaction to his kiss.

He searched for the right words to explain what had happened, but Nell was far too unsophisticated for that kind of discussion. She seemed remarkably naive in a number of ways. He imagined her own abandon had been as embarrassing to her as his lack of control had been disturbing to him.

Better to let things lie, he supposed, for the time being. He started the station wagon without another word and headed for the ranch.

Margie got the boys ready to go early in the afternoon, and Tyler volunteered to take them back to Tucson. That seemed to thrill Margie, and it was a relief to Nell, who'd dreaded being alone with her sister-in-law. Margie had a way of dragging information out of her, and Nell didn't want to share what had happened with Tyler. It was a secret. A sweet, very private secret, which she was going to live on for a long time.

"You're not brooding again, are you?" Bella asked that evening as they washed supper dishes.

Nell shook her head. "No. I'm just grateful for a little peace. Margie was on her soapbox again about gussying me up." She sighed. "I don't think I'd like being a fashion plate, even if I had the raw material. I like me the way I am."

"Frumpy," Bella agreed.

She glared at the housekeeper. Nell's soapy hands lifted out of the water. "Look who's talking about frumpy!"

Bella glared back. "I ain't frumpy." She shifted her stance and shook back her wild silvery-black hair. "I'm unique."

Nell couldn't argue with that. "Okay, I give up. I'm frumpy."

"You could do with a little improvement. Maybe Margie isn't the terror we think she is. You know, she does care about you, in her way. She's only trying to help."

"She's trying to help herself into a relationship with Tyler," Nell corrected.

"She's lonely," Bella said. Her knowing eyes sought Nell's suddenly vulnerable face. "Aren't you?"

Nell stared at the soapsuds. "I think most people are," she said slowly. "And I guess Tyler could do worse. At least Margie makes him smile."

"You could, if you'd get that chip off your shoulder."

"I got hurt," Nell muttered.

"That's no reason to bury yourself. You're just twenty-four. You've got a lot of years left to be alone if you don't turn around pretty soon. You don't gain anything if you're afraid to take a chance. That isn't any way for a young woman to live."

Nell's mind had already gone back to the morning, to Tyler's warm mouth so hungry against her own, to the feel of his lean, strong body against hers. She colored at the sweet memory, and at that moment, she knew she was going to die if she could never have it again.

But Tyler didn't want her. He'd said that he didn't have room in his life for a woman—more than once. She had to keep her head. She couldn't run after him. Not when she was certain to be rejected.

"Bella, maybe I'm meant to be an old maid," she murmured thoughtfully. "Some women are, you know. It just

works out that way. It's the beautiful women who marry—"

"I ain't beautiful and I married," Bella reminded her
with an arrogant sniff. "Besides, looks fade. Character
lasts. And you got plenty of that, child."

Nell smiled. "You're a nice lady."

"I'm glad you like me. I like me, too, just occasionally.
Now wash off that spot, Nell, so we don't get food poi-
soning. When you have your own house and kitchen,
you'll have to do all this without me to remind you."

Nell had to stifle a giggle. Bella could be imposing, but
she was an angel.

Tyler threw himself into his work for the next couple of
days, and Nell hardly saw him. He came to meals, but he
was looking more and more haggard, and he was coughing. Since the Sunday he'd picked her up at church, they'd
hardly spoken. He'd been polite but remote, and Nell began to think he was avoiding her. She understood the reason for it—he didn't want to get involved. He was
probably afraid she'd read too much into those warm
kisses. Well, she told herself, there was no need for him to
worry. She wasn't going to throw herself at him. She just
wished she could tell him so, again. But it was too embarrassing to contemplate.

All the same, she couldn't stop being concerned about
him. He did look bad. Inevitably, there came a day later in
the week when he didn't show up for supper.

Bella went down to the foreman's cabin to find out why.
She'd asked Nell to go, but Nell had refused instantly.
Another confrontation with Tyler was the last thing she
needed now.

Bella came back a half hour later looking thoughtful.
"He don't look too good," she remarked. "He's pale and

he says he's not hungry. I hope he's not coming down with that virus that went through the bunkhouse last week.''

"Is he all right?" Nell asked too quickly.

"He says a night's sleep will do him good. We'll see."

Nell watched her amble off to the kitchen and had to force herself not to go rushing down to the cabin to see Tyler. He was the epitome of good health. She knew because he'd told them that he was never sick. But there was always a first time, and he'd worked like a horse since his arrival.

Sometimes it seemed that he was working off more than the loss of his ranch back in Texas. Perhaps there'd been a girl he'd wanted who hadn't wanted him when he lost everything. That put a new perspective on things and Nell started worrying even more. She hadn't thought of him having a girlfriend. But he was a handsome man, and he was experienced. Very experienced, even to her innocent mind. There had to have been women in his past. He might even have been engaged. She groaned. She didn't like to consider the possibility that he might have kissed her because he was missing some woman he'd left behind in Texas. But it might be true. Oh, if only there was some way to find out!

She paced the living room floor until Bella complained that she was wearing out the rug. She went up to bed, where she could pace uninterrupted.

But the more she paced, the more confused things got. In the end, she undressed, put on her soft long gown and climbed into bed. Minutes later she was blessedly asleep, beyond the reach of all her problems.

The next morning, Nell's first thought was of Tyler. She dressed in jeans and a yellow knit top, looped her long hair

into a ponytail, and ran downstairs with her boots barely
on.

"Have you been to see Tyler?" she asked Bella.

The older woman scowled at her from a pan of biscuits
she was just making up. "I will as soon as I get these biscuits in the oven...."

"I'll go."

Bella didn't say a word. But she grinned to herself as
Nell went tearing out the back door.

The foreman's cabin was nice. It was big enough for a
small family, but nothing fancy. Nell knocked on the door.
Nobody answered. She knocked again. Still nothing.

She paused, wondering what to do. But there was really
no choice. If he didn't answer, he was either asleep, which
was unlikely, or gone, which was equally unlikely, or too
sick to get up.

She opened the door, glad to find it unlocked, and
peeked in. It was in good order for a bachelor's establish-
ment. The Indian rugs on the floor were straight, and there
were no clothes thrown over the old leather couch and
chair.

Her heart beat wildly as she eased farther into the living
room. "Tyler?" she called.

There was a soft groan from the bedroom. She followed it, half-afraid that she might find him totally un-
clothed. She looked around the door hesitantly. "Tyler?"

He was under the covers, but his hair-matted chest was
bare, like his tanned, muscular arms. He opened his eyes
briefly. "Nell. God, I feel rough. Can you get Bella,
honey?"

"What for?" she asked gently, moving closer.

"To call a doctor," he said wearily. "I haven't slept and
my chest hurts. I think I've got bronchitis." He coughed.

"I can call a doctor," she said gently. She felt his forehead. It was burning hot. "Just lie there and don't move. I'll bring you something cold to drink, and then I'll get the doctor. I'll take care of you."

He caught her eyes, searching them strangely. It felt odd, the sensation her words had sent through his body. He'd never had to be taken care of, but it occurred to him that there was nobody he'd rather have nursing him than Nell.

"Be right back," she said, hiding her concern under a faint smile. She rushed out, all the antagonism gone in the rush of concern she felt for him. He had to be all right, he just had to!

Chapter Four

Nell got Tyler a cold soft drink from his small refrigerator and helped him get a few swallows of it down before she rushed back to the main house to phone the doctor.

Bella stood listening in the doorway while Nell described the symptoms to Dr. Morrison and was told to bring Tyler in to his clinic as soon as she could get him there.

She felt insecure when she hung up. "I'll bet he thinks it could be pneumonia," Nell told the older woman worriedly. "And I guess it could be. He's coughing something terrible and burning up with fever."

"I'll go get Chappy to help you get him into the station wagon," Bella said. "Or I'll go..."

"No, that's all right," Nell replied. "Chappy can come with us. We'll have to postpone the daily shopping trip with the guests, but Chappy can drive the Simses and the others to the mall as soon as we get back."

"He'll hate that." Bella chuckled.

"I know, but somebody's got to look after Tyler."

Bella almost strangled herself trying to keep quiet. She could have looked after Tyler, but it was pretty obvious that Nell had already assigned that chore to herself. And Bella wasn't about to interfere. "That's right," she said, grinning. "I'll get Chappy."

But as they went out the door together, they noticed immediately that the station wagon was missing. So was the pickup truck.

"Where's he gone?" Bella yelled to Marlowe, who was leading a saddled horse out of the stable.

"Chappy had to run into town to pick up that stomach medicine for the sick calves. He's been gone a half hour, so he should be back anytime."

"Where's the pickup?" Nell called.

Marlowe shrugged. "Sorry, ma'am, I don't know."

"Great," Nell muttered. She glanced at Bella. "Well, send Chappy down to the cabin the minute he comes back. I just hope he's not inclined to linger at the vet's office."

"I'll phone the vet and make sure," Bella replied. "Don't worry. Tyler's tough."

"I guess he is." Nell sighed. She forced a smile and quickly went down the path to the cabin.

Tyler was sprawled against the pillows asleep when Nell got back to him. She sighed, wondering how on earth he was going to dress himself.

"Tyler?" she called gently, touching his bare shoulder lightly. "Tyler, wake up."

His eyes opened instantly, a little glazed from sleep and fever. "Nell?" he murmured, shifting under the covers.

"Dr. Morrison wants me to bring you to his office," she said. "We have to get you dressed."

He laughed weakly. "That's going to be harder than you think. I'm as weak as a kitten." A sudden bout of coughing doubled him up and he grimaced at the pain it caused him. "Damn! It feels like I've got a broken rib."

Nell's heart sank. It was almost surely pneumonia. Her mother had died of it, and it held hidden terrors for her because of the memory.

"Can you dress yourself?" she asked hesitantly.

He sighed jerkily. "I don't think so, Nell."

"Chappy isn't here," she said thoughtfully. "But there's Marlowe, or Bella—"

"No," he said shortly. He glared up at her with fever-bright eyes. "As strange as it may seem to you, I don't like the thought of having myself dressed by yahoos and grinning old women. No way. If you want me dressed, honey, I'll let you help. But nobody else. Not even Chappy."

That was surprising. She hadn't thought men minded people looking at them. But then, Tyler wasn't like other men.

She hesitated. "Okay. If you can get the—" she cleared her throat "—the first things on, I guess I can help with the rest."

"Haven't you seen a man without clothes?" he asked with faint humor.

"No. And I don't really want to," she said nervously.

"You may not have a choice." He started coughing again and had to catch his breath before he could speak. "Underwear and socks are in the top drawer of the dresser," he said. "Shirts and jeans in the closet."

She paused, but only for a minute. The important thing was to get him to the doctor. She had to remember that and put his health before her outraged modesty. Since he wouldn't let anybody else help, she didn't have a choice.

As quickly as possible, she laid out everything he was going to need. But when he started trying to sit up, he held his chest and lay right back down again.

"God, that hurts, Nell," he said huskily. "It must have been the dust. We got into a cloud of it a few days ago bringing back some straying cattle, and I inhaled about half an acre, I think. I've had a lot of congestion, but I thought it was just an allergy. Until this morning, anyway."

"Oh, Tyler," she moaned.

"Should have worn my bandanna," he murmured. "That's why the old-timers wore them, you know, to pull up over their faces in dust storms and such."

"How are you going to dress?" she wailed.

He gave her a knowing look. "You mean, how are you going to dress me," he replied. "If it helps, it isn't something I'd choose to saddle you with. I don't even like stripping in front of men."

She colored. "I don't think I can," she whispered.

"It won't be that bad, I promise," he said softly. "Pull the sheet up over my hips and slide my briefs up as far as you feel comfortable. I think I can manage it from there."

The blush got worse as she picked them up. "I'm sorry," she muttered, fumbling the briefs over his feet and ankles. "Old maids aren't very good at this sort of thing."

"Neither are old bachelors." He coughed, groaning. "Come on, Nell, you can do it. Just close your eyes and push."

She laughed involuntarily. "That might be the only way." She eased them up, her hands cold against the warm, hard muscles of his thighs. She couldn't help but feel how well made he was, how powerful. She got them just under the sheet and her nerve gave way. "Is that…far enough?" she asked huskily.

"I'll manage." He eased his hands under the sheet and tugged and then lay back with a rough sigh. "Okay. The rest is up to you, honey."

She slid his socks on his feet. He had nice feet, very well proportioned if a little big, and even nice ankles. His legs were as tanned as his face and arms, and it almost had to be natural, because he certainly hadn't been sunbathing the past few weeks.

"This is the first time in my adult life that I've ever been dressed by a woman," he remarked weakly as she eased his undershirt over his head and pulled it down over his broad, hair-matted chest.

"They tell me there's a first time for everything," she returned, but her eyes were on the rippling muscles of his chest. She could feel the warmth of his skin, feel the thick abrasiveness of the hair that covered the broad expanse until it wedged down to his undershorts. When she reached under his arms to pull the undershirt down over his back, her face was almost pressed to his skin, and she had to grit her teeth not to kiss him there. The most unwanted sensations were washing over her body like fire. This wasn't the time or the place, she had to remind herself. He was a sick man, and she had to get him to a doctor. Besides all that, it was suicidal to feel that way about a man who'd already warned her off.

"You look like boiled lobster," he remarked. "It wasn't as bad as you thought, was it?"

"No, not really," she agreed with a thin smile. She helped him into his chambray shirt and snapped the cuffs and then the snaps down the front of it. "It's just new."

"Didn't you ever have to dress your brother?" he grinned weakly.

"No. Ted was much older than I was," she said. "And he went away to school, so we didn't spend a lot of time together. Dad and Mom worshiped him. He was their world. I guess I was more or less an accident. But they tried not to let me feel left out."

"My father never wanted kids at all," Tyler remarked. "He did his damnedest to break my spirit, and he almost did break my sister's, Shelby. But we survived. It's ironic that the ranch had to be sold. He'd have sacrificed both of us to hold on to it."

She unfolded his jeans. "You'll have your own ranch one day," she said gently. "And you won't break your children's spirits to keep it, either."

"If I have children," he replied. "Some men never marry. I may be one of them."

"Yes. I guess you might." She eased his jeans onto his long legs and pulled them up as far as she was able. They were tight and the material was thick, and it took most of her strength just to get them to his upper thighs. She knew that he'd never be able to pull them the rest of the way, not with his chest hurting so badly.

"If you can lift up, I think I can get them over your hips," she said through her teeth, and she didn't look at him as she eased the sheet away and tried not to blush at the sight of his undershorts.

"Sorry, little one," he said huskily. "But I do hurt like hell."

"I know," she said gently. "I'm not a child, after all," she said for her own benefit, as well as his. "Here goes."

She closed her eyes and pulled and tugged until she got the jeans over his hips. But she balked at the zipper, going hot all over.

"Fetch my boots, will you, honey?" he asked. He saw her hesitation and understood it. "I can manage this."

She almost wept with relief as she went to the closet to get his dress boots. She'd seen them there when she'd found his shirts and jeans. They were Tony Lama boots, exquisite and expensive, black and gleaming like wet coal.

"These are going to be hard to get on you," she said worriedly.

"You push and I'll push," he said. "They're not all that tight."

"Okay."

Between them, they worked the boots onto his feet. Then Nell got a comb and fixed his disheveled hair. And all the while he lay there against his pillow, his feverish eyes watching her, studying her in a silence that was unnerving.

The roar of a car arriving interrupted the tension. "That must be Chappy," Nell said. She caught her breath. "Tyler, you won't tell him that I..."

"That you helped me dress?" He smiled gently. "I won't tell anyone. It's between you and me, and no one else," he said, and the smile faded into an exchanged look that was slow and intensely disturbing. Nell's heart ran wild until she dragged her eyes away and got up to let Chappy in.

Between them, they got Tyler into the back seat of the station wagon, where he could lie down, and to Dr. Morrison's office.

The nurse helped Tyler to the examination room, while Chappy paced and Nell chewed on a fingernail. It took a long time, and she was expecting Tyler to come out with the nurse, but Dr. Morrison came to the doorway and motioned for Nell to follow him.

He beckoned her into his office, but Tyler was nowhere in sight.

"He'll be fine," he told her, perching himself on the corner of his desk, "but he's got acute bronchitis."

"I was so afraid that it was pneumonia," Nell said, slumping into a chair with relief. "That pain in his chest—"

"That pain in his chest is from a pulled muscle, because he's coughed so much," he said with a tolerant smile. He folded his arms across his chest. "I want him in bed until the fever goes. He can get up then, but he can't work for a full week. And then I want to see him again. I've written him two prescriptions. One's an antibiotic, the other's an expectorant for the cough. Give him aspirin for fever and keep him in bed. If he gets worse, call me."

"Did you tell him all this?" she asked.

"Sure. He said like hell he'd lay around for a week. That's why I wanted to talk to you."

She smiled. "Thanks. He's working wonders out at the ranch. I'd hate to bury him on it."

"He seems pretty capable to me," he agreed. "Mind that he doesn't sneak out and start back to work before you realize it."

"I'll tie him in his bed," she promised.

"Bombard him with fluids while you're at it," the doctor added as he got up and opened the door. "He'll be as docile as a kitten until that antibiotic takes hold, then look out."

"I'll post guards at his door," she said with a grin. She felt lighter than air. Tyler was going to be all right. The relief was delicious. "Thank you!"

"My pleasure. He's all yours."

She smiled as she went out. If only that were true.

She called Chappy to help her get Tyler out to the station wagon, but only after she'd whispered to the receptionist to send the bill out to the ranch. She had a feeling that Tyler wouldn't appreciate having her pay his medical bill, but that was something they could argue about when he was back on his feet.

All the way home, she wondered how she was going to manage getting him undressed again. But he solved that problem himself. When they got into the cabin, he sighed and murmured, "Don't worry, Nell. I think I can manage getting out of this rig by myself."

"I'll go up to the house and get Bella to make some chicken soup for you," Nell said quickly, and darted out the door. It was easier than she'd imagined.

She sent Chappy back to town to get the prescriptions filled, because it had seemed more sensible to bring Tyler home first. She gathered the few things she might need and told Bella where she was going.

"He's not much of a threat in his present condition, I guess," Bella said, and nodded, ignoring Nell's outraged glare. "You can sleep on his sofa. But if you need me, I'm here. I can sit with him while you sleep if he gets worse in the night."

"You're a doll," Nell said.

"I have a secret Florence Nightingale streak," she corrected. "Wanted to be a nurse, once, but I faint at the sight of blood."

"They say some doctors do the first time they see an operation," Nell replied. "But I'm glad you wanted to cook, instead. You're kind of special to me."

Bella beamed, unaccustomed to the praise. "I'll have that carved on my tombstone one day. Meanwhile, you fill Tyler full of that juice I gave you and don't let him rope cattle out the window."

"I won't. Thanks, Bella."

The older woman shrugged. "I'll bring the chicken soup when it's made. I'll put some in a thermos for you."

"It'll be welcome by then. And some coffee, too, please. I don't know if Tyler has a coffeepot, but I kind of doubt it."

"He carries his around in a thermos," Bella said surprisingly. "I fill one up for him every morning and every afternoon."

"Okay. I'll get going before he escapes. See you later."

She found Tyler asleep again, apparently back in the altogether under the single sheet that covered him. Nell watched his face for a long moment, seeing the lines erased in sleep, the masculine beauty of his mouth. Just the sight of him was like a banquet to her eyes. She had to tear herself away. While he slept, she might as well make herself useful by tidying up his kitchen.

She put the juice Bella had sent in the small refrigerator, and then she washed the few dishes and cleared the counter. With that done, she checked to make sure he was still asleep before she went to the bookcase in the living room to find something to read.

Apparently he was a mystery fan, because he had plenty of books by Sir Arthur Conan Doyle and Agatha Christie on the shelves. There were some biographies and some history books about the old West, and even a book about ancient Rome. She chose a work on the Apache tribe and sat down to read it, glancing curiously at the photograph atop the bookcase. It was of a young woman with long dark hair and green eyes and a rather sad expression on her beautiful face. Beside it was a smaller photo of the same woman in white, standing beside a tall, fierce-looking man in a suit. That, she decided, had to be Tyler's sister, Shelby. Nell knew Shelby had gotten married recently, because Tyler had gone to Texas for the wedding. That man was probably her new husband. He wasn't much to look at, but perhaps he had saving graces, Nell decided.

She didn't see any other photos. That had to be a good sign. If there had been a special woman in his life, surely he'd have a picture of her. Or maybe not. If he'd lost her to someone else, he might be too bitter to keep a picture of her in a prominent place.

Feeling gloomy, she went back to the book and started reading.

Bella brought chicken soup, and Chappy brought medicine. Tyler was still asleep, but when the visitors left, Nell took his medicine, a glass of juice and a bowl of soup into the bedroom on a tray. The medicine was important, and he needed nourishment. He hadn't eaten anything all day.

She sat down gently on the bed beside him, her eyes going helplessly over his broad, bare chest and his face. "Tyler?" she said softly. He didn't stir. She reached out and hesitatingly laid one slender hand on his chest, thrilling to its hard warmth. It was the first time she'd touched a man this way, and despite the circumstances, it was blatantly pleasurable.

"Tyler, I've got your medicine," she said.

He sighed and opened his eyes slowly. "I hate medicine," he said weakly. "How about a steak?"

"Dream on. Right now, it's going to be chicken soup and encouragement. I brought you a tray."

"What time is it?"

"Almost dark," she replied. "Chappy took the guests to town to shop, and now he's holding court at the supper table. I can hear him telling tall tales through the kitchen window, and everybody's laughing."

"He tells a mean story," Tyler agreed. He breathed heavily and touched his side, encountering Nell's warm hand as his own worked its way up his chest. "You're cool," he murmured.

"Only because you have a fever," she said, thrilling to the touch of his fingers on her soft skin. "Here. Let's get some medicine into you, and then you can have soup and juice. Are you hungry?"

"Half-starved," he said. "But I don't have much appetite."

She gave him the antibiotic with a swallow of juice, and then ladled the cough syrup into his mouth.

"That tastes terrible," he muttered.

"Most medicine does," she agreed. "Can you manage to sit up while you eat?"

"Under protest." He let her prop him up with pillows and dragged himself into a sitting position. The sheet lay loosely over his hips, but she caught a glimpse of underwear, not bare skin, as he moved. "That's for your benefit," he said dryly, smiling at her color. "I drew the line at pajamas, but I wouldn't outrage your modesty too much this way."

"Thank you," she said shyly.

"Thank you," he replied. "You're stuck with me, I gather. Didn't Bella rush to play nurse?"

"She did, but I headed her off. Crowbait would have to do the cooking if she came down here, and the whole outfit would quit on the spot."

"He's not that bad," he said. "The military would love to get their hands on him. Imagine, a cook who can make a lethal weapon of an innocent biscuit."

"Shame on you," she said.

He sighed and grimaced. "I guess my biscuits aren't much better, so I don't have a lot of room to talk. Nell, I'm sorry to cave in on you like this...."

"Anybody can get sick," she said easily, and began to feed him the soup without thinking about how much feeling that simple act betrayed. "It's amazing how many people come out here from the East, thinking that their allergies will go away overnight. What they don't realize is that the dust can be as bad as pollen, and that the soil itself harbors plenty of allergens. Just listen to Mr. Davis sneeze and wheeze on trail rides, if you don't believe me.''

"Well, it's the first time in my life I've had bronchitis, but I'll buck it," he said quietly. "And I'll be back at work day after tomorrow."

"No, you won't," she replied. "Dr. Morrison said you couldn't get out of bed until the fever's gone, and you can't work for a week."

He eyed her warily. "Did he tell you that?"

"He sure did," she said with a mischievous grin. "So don't try to get around me. If you do, I'll call my uncle, and then where will you be?"

"Out of work and sick, I guess," he said wearily. "Okay. I'll stay put. Under protest, you understand."

"I understand. You'll get through it. Have some more soup."

He might get through it, she thought, but would she? He slept through the night without waking, although she checked on him every hour or so until she was forced to curl up on the couch and sleep.

The next day was pretty much the same. She fed him and gave him his medicine, and he slept most of the day and all night through. But the following day he felt much better and nothing suited him. The breakfast Bella had sent over was too everything. Too hot, too much, too salty, too filling and too starchy. He didn't want to stay in bed, he had to start planning for winter, and he had to get the cattle operation in hand. That meant more work than ever, in between getting the calves ready for the fall sale. He didn't like the medicine, he hated the confinement, and Nell was beginning to wear on him, too, come to think of it.

She glared at him from red-rimmed dark eyes framed by long disheveled honey-brown hair, in the rumpled yellow knit shirt and faded jeans she'd slept in. She hadn't even bothered to put on her boots, having met Chappy at the door for the breakfast tray.

"If I wear on you, that's just too bad, Mr. Jacobs," she said shortly. "Somebody's got to keep you penned up, and everybody else is too busy. It's just the second day. The antibiotic's taking hold, and you want to fight tigers. Great. But fight them while you're asleep, please. I don't like people committing suicide on my ranch."

"It isn't your ranch yet, according to your uncle," he reminded her curtly.

"It will be," she said with cool determination. "Now you just lie down and get well."

"I don't want to lie down. I want to go to work. Hand me my clothes," he said firmly, nodding to where Chappy had draped them over his straight chair.

"Oh, no, I'm not going through that again," she said, reddening. "And you're not able to dress yourself yet—"

"Like hell I'm not able!" He pulled himself painfully into a sitting position, drew in a deep breath and tried to get his feet on the floor. He grimaced and groaned and lay back down, turning the air blue on the way down.

"Damn it, damn this disease, and damn you, too!" he swore furiously.

"Thank you. What a kind thing to say to someone who's given up regular meals and sleeping to wait on you for two days," she said icily.

"I didn't ask you to!"

"Somebody had to!" she shot back. She stuck her hands on her slender hips and glared at him. He looked all too good that way, lying back against pillows with crisp white cotton pillowcases. His chest was still bare, and his black hair hung down over his forehead, straight and thick. He looked exquisitely masculine, and the sight of his half-clothed body wasn't doing Nell's nerves any good.

"All right, thank you," he said. "You're an angel in disguise and I'll remember you in my will. Now will you get out of here and let me go back to work?"

"You can't work for a week—Dr. Morrison said so," she replied for the tenth time in as many minutes. "And he wants to see you again to make sure you're on the road to recovery. He told me not to let you on a horse."

"I don't take orders from women," he said shortly. "I work for your uncle, and I answer only to him. You don't and never have told me what to do."

"Will you listen to reason?" she demanded, passing over that bit of insolence.

"Sure. If you'll get me my pants."

"Well, I won't."

"Then I'll get them myself," he said shortly.

She folded her arms across her chest with a smile. She knew he had on his underwear, so he wasn't going to frighten her off. "Okay. Go ahead," she invited.

She didn't realize her mistake until he gave her a hard glare and abruptly threw off the sheet. Her face went from pale pink to scarlet red in seconds as he gingerly slid his long powerful bare legs over the bed and stood up. Without a stitch of clothing on.

Chapter Five

Nell was grateful that she didn't faint. What she did do was flush from the neck up and, after one long, shocked glance, turn and run out of the room.

Tyler immediately felt like a heel. He sat back down, his bad temper forgotten, and pulled the sheet over his hips. "Nell," he called gently.

She didn't answer him. She was staring out the living room window, with her arms folded tightly across her yellow shirt, trying to decide whether to stay or go. If he was going to be that difficult, she didn't know how she was going to cope. The sight of him had set her back a bit. Due to her experience with Darren McAnders when she was young, she'd led a pretty sheltered life. But she lived on a ranch, and because of that, she knew all about the technicalities of reproduction. But a nude man was a new experience. And a nude Tyler was...extraordinary. She was still shaking when she heard him calling her, more insistently.

With a deep breath, she turned and gritted her teeth and walked back to the doorway, pale and subdued.

"I'm sorry," he said tersely when he saw her face. "I won't do that again."

She shifted a little. "If you're that determined to kill yourself, I can't stop you. But for your own sake, I wish you'd do what the doctor wants."

His green eyes searched her frozen features. "I'll do damned near anything to get that look off your face. Including," he added wearily as he lay back down, "staying in the bed."

He looked tired. Probably he was, and she wished she'd been older and more sophisticated so that she wouldn't have made such a fool of herself. He made her feel about thirteen.

"Can I get you anything?" she asked.

"I could do with some more juice," he said. "And if you'll dig me out some fresh underwear, I'll put it back on again."

She felt hot all over and tried to hide her reaction to him as she got him a glass of juice and then took a pair of briefs from the dresser. As she put them beside him, he caught her wrist and pulled her down onto the bed, holding her there firmly while he looked at her.

"How can you be twenty-four years old and so damned innocent?" he asked quietly. "Especially with all the people who pass through here in a year's time?"

"I don't mix with people very much," she said. Her eyes slid helplessly over his broad, bare chest. "I socialize only to the extent that I have to, and since most people who come here keep to themselves except for organized activities, I don't have many problems. If I had my own way, this would be just a cattle ranch and I wouldn't take in paying guests. But the dude ranch part is paying for the cattle operation, so I don't have much choice."

"Do you date?"

She kept her eyes down. "No, I don't have time."

"So many secrets between us, Nell," he said, caressing her hand lightly. "Too many."

"You told me you weren't interested in involvement. Well, I'm not either," she lied.

"Really? Or is it that you don't think you attract men?"

She remembered when she'd said that and what he'd done about it on the way home from church. Her lips parted as she remembered the hungry kiss they'd shared, and she had to fight not to throw herself down against him and beg him to do it again.

"I can't attract men," she replied tersely.

"You're a pretty woman," he said. "You downplay your attractions, but they're there. Why don't you buy a new dress, have your hair done and put on some makeup for the next Saturday square dance?" he murmured, reaching up to tug on a long lock of her hair. "And I'll teach you to dance."

Breathing grew harder by the minute. She felt nervous and insecure, and the slow tracing of his long fingers on her hand and wrist was beginning to stir her blood.

"It's not practical," she said inanely, because she could hardly think at all.

"Why not?"

"Because...because you're..." She bit her lip. "You're just bored, Tyler, and when you're back on your feet again, when you're working for yourself again... Oh, I'm just muddling it."

"You think I'm playing."

She sighed. "Yes."

He took her hand and pulled it to his chest, pressing it hard over the hair-covered expanse where his heart was beating like a bass drum. "Nell, am I callous enough to play with a virgin?" he asked softly.

Of course he wasn't, but she couldn't keep her thoughts clear. The effect he had on her was incredible, and she was hungry for an affection she'd never had from a man.

"It doesn't matter," he said huskily, pulling on her hand. "Come here."

"Tyler, you're sick—"

"I don't have any fever, and I feel like a new man." He eased her across him until she was on her back in the bed with his lean bare torso above her, his green eyes glittering down at her. "I've never seen a woman with less self-confidence than you have, Nell," he said. "There's nothing wrong with the way you look or the way you are."

"Tyler, you're scaring me," she whispered. Her hands went to his chest, and part of her tried to protest. This was bringing back terrible memories of another man she'd loved, or thought she loved, and his harsh, hurtful treatment of her. But Tyler wasn't McAnders, and the look on his face was intoxicating. He wanted her. Not as a substitute for another woman, but for herself.

"No, that won't work," he said gently. His lean hands cupped her chin and held her face tilted up to his. "I'm not going to be rough with you, not ever. And anything we do together will be because you want it."

That was as new as her proximity to him, and she began to relax. There was nothing threatening about him. He seemed fully in control and lazily indulgent.

"Yes, that's it," he said as he felt the tension draining out of her body. "I'm not going to hurt you."

As he spoke, his dark head bent. She felt his mouth whispering over her eyelids, closing them, brushing her

nose, her chin, and then settling softly over her mouth.
Her breath seemed suspended while he found just the right
pressure, the right mingling of tenderness and expertise to
make her lips part for him. And while he kissed her, his
lean hands slid under her blouse at the back, and she
thrilled to the faint roughness of their touch on her bare
skin.

He was addictive, she thought dizzily, enraptured by the
warmth of his caresses. She didn't think she could have
pulled away to save her life. Every touch was more exciting than the one before. His mouth became a necessity.
Without its warm crush she was sure to die.

Shyly, she flattened her hands against his chest and let
them experience the thickness of hair, the strong padding
of muscle beneath it. His breath caught against her mouth,
and her eyes opened, questioning.

"I'm sorry, I didn't mean to..." she began quickly.

"It feels good," he said, smiling down into her shocked
face. "I can drag that sound out of you the same way."

Her body coiled inside, like a kitten anticipating being
stroked. She felt herself tremble and wondered at the
mental pictures that were flashing sensually through her
mind. His hands on her, touching her...there. Her lips
parted. "You...you can?" she whispered, which wasn't
what she wanted to say at all, but she was too shy and inexperienced to put it into words.

Tyler, with his greater experience, knew immediately
that she was going to welcome whatever he wanted to do.
It went to his head, making his thoughts spin with new
possibilities. His hands had already told him that Nell had
been hiding her light, physically at least, under a barrel. He
needed the intimacy with her as he'd needed nothing else
in his life, although he still didn't quite understand the way
she affected his senses.

"Yes," he breathed, bending again to her mouth. "I can."

As his lips toyed with hers, his hand went to the fastening of her bra. Subtly, almost without her knowing it, he released the catch and slid his fingers slowly, exploringly, under her arm to the soft edge of her breast.

She trembled, but she didn't pull away or protest, and his blood ran hot and fast through his veins. He wanted to look at her. He wanted to see her eyes when he touched her.

He lifted his head. The glitter of his eyes unnerved her at first, until she felt again the light tracing of his fingers against her skin. The sensations piled on each other until she went hot all over with the need to make him put his hand on her, to touch her. Her body was more demanding than her mind, because it tried to twist toward him, to force a contact he was deliberately denying her.

"Ty...ler?" she whispered brokenly.

His free hand was under her nape. It moved caressingly in her thick hair while his gaze searched her huge, hungry eyes. "Shh," he whispered gently. The hand under her arm moved again, tracing, and she arched, shuddering, while her big eyes pleaded with him. "It's all right," he whispered. "It's all right, honey."

And all the while, his fingers were driving her mad. She felt as if every single cell in her body was drawn as tight as a rope, as if the tension was going to break her in half. Her nails contracted on his muscular upper arms and dug in, and when she realized it, she was shocked at her own action.

"I'm...sorry," she whispered jerkily, caressing the red crescents she'd made in his skin. "I'm sorry, I... couldn't...help it."

"You haven't hurt me," he said gently. "You know that I'm doing this deliberately. Do you know why?"

"No," she whimpered, jerking as his fingertips edged a little farther onto her breast.

"It's very much like a symphony, little one," he whispered softly, and he managed a smile. "It starts slowly, softly, and builds and builds and builds to a crescendo. When I finally give you what you're pleading for, Nell, you're going to feel a kind of pleasure that I can't even describe to you."

Her teeth ground together, because the tension was growing unbearable. "But...when...?"

"Now." His mouth covered hers and his hand moved, at last, at last, at...last! It covered her breast, swallowing up the hard tip, giving her the tiny consummation her body had begged for.

And it was like fireworks. She cried out into his mouth, shuddered, arched with the anguished fulfillment. Her hand found his through the cloth of her shirt and pressed against it, holding it prisoner. She sobbed, and the hand at her neck contracted as his mouth grew feverishly hungry. For long, fiery seconds, the sounds of their breathing were audible in the quiet room.

"It isn't enough," he bit off against her mouth. While he held her, his hand began to unbutton her shirt. He lifted his head and looked into her eyes. "I won't go farther than this, I promise you," he said huskily. "But I...need...to look at you."

Her eyelids felt heavy. She couldn't work up the effort to protest. What he'd just given her was like honey, and she was helpless with pleasure. She wanted more. She wanted his eyes on her.

It was extraordinary, she thought, watching him divest her of her shirt and bra. Extraordinary, that look in his eyes, on his face, as he eased her down against the pillows and sat gazing at her taut, swollen breasts.

"Ty," she whispered. "There was a movie I watched once, and it was just a little racy. But the man...he did more than touch her. He put his mouth..."

"Here?" he whispered back, brushing her taut breast with the backs of his fingers, his eyes intent on hers.

She jerked involuntarily with pleasure. "Yes."

"Do you want that, with me?"

She colored, but she was beyond pretending. "Oh, yes...!"

His mouth eased down over the soft flesh, smoothing her skin, sensitizing it. The sensation was beyond anything she'd ever imagined. She made little whimpers that sent his mind whirling out of control. He groaned against her breast and gathered her up close, giving in to the need to taste her, to pleasure her.

She didn't hear the knock the first time it came. But the second time it was louder. She lay still, listening, and felt Tyler stiffen above her.

He caught his breath slowly, glancing through the open bedroom door toward the living room with glazed eyes and a mind that was still in limbo.

"Mr. Jacobs, I brought your mail. I'll slide it under the door."

It was Chappy's voice, and thank God he went away quickly. Nell colored furiously as she imagined what would have happened if Chappy had just walked in.

Tyler looked down at her quietly, letting his bold gaze go from her eyes to her swollen mouth to the alabaster skin of her breast.

"Are you all right?" he whispered softly. "I didn't frighten you?"

"No." She was looking at him as intently as he was studying her, measuring memory and imagination against the sweet reality of what they'd done together. "Not at all."

He touched her breast tenderly and smiled at her. "It was good," he whispered.

"Yes."

He eased down on his elbows and slowly drew his chest over her sensitized breasts, watching her shiver and gasp with the delicious sensation of it. "This is good, too," he breathed, bending again to her mouth. "I want you, Nell."

She tensed as his mouth brushed hers, and he smiled against her trembling lips.

"I'm not going to do anything about it," he reassured her. "Kiss me, and then you'd better get out of here."

She slid her arms up around his neck and gave him her mouth in a kiss as sweet and wild as the ones before. But seconds later he drew away and rolled over, taking her with him. He lay on his back, shuddering a little with a need he couldn't fulfill.

"You might as well get rid of the baggy britches and loose blouses," he murmured, holding her bare breasts against his broad chest. "I'll never fall for the camouflage again, after this."

"Am I too big?" she whispered, because it mattered if she was.

He brushed the hair away from her mouth. "No. You're just right. All of you." He brushed a warm kiss against her lips and loosened his arms. "You'd better get your things back on. I'm weak, but I'm still capable. I don't want this to get out of hand."

She touched his face, her fingers cold and nervous, tracing its hard contours, fascinated with him. "You can't imagine what it was like for me," she whispered. "I...well, it wasn't what I thought it would be."

He smiled. "Not even after you saw that racy movie?" he murmured dryly.

She swallowed, remembering when she'd told him about it and what had followed. "Well, no. Seeing and experiencing are different."

"Indeed they are." He helped her to sit up and spent a long minute looking at her before he gathered up her bra and blouse and proceeded to help her back into them. "No," he said when she tried to stop him. "You dressed me. Now it's my turn."

So she sat still and let him dress her, delighting in his gentle touch, in his obvious pleasure in her.

"You can't stay here tonight," he said. "I hope you realize why."

"Yes. I know why."

He buttoned her up to the throat and smoothed back her long disheveled hair. "I would like very much to take your clothes off and pull you under this sheet with me and love you up to the ceiling," he said seriously. "I could do that, despite your innocence. But I'd hate myself for abusing your trust, and you might hate me for backing you into a corner. I don't want anything to spoil what's building between us. I don't think you want that, either."

She linked her fingers into his as he toyed with her hair. "No. I don't want anything to spoil it, either," she whispered.

He drew her hand to his mouth and kissed it gently. "I won't sleep. I'll remember how it was while we were loving each other in this bed, and I'll ache to have you here with me."

She trembled at his description of what they'd done. It had felt like loving, even if he only meant that in a physical sense. Her warm eyes searched his, and her face was radiant with shared pleasure, with hope, with new dreams that seemed to be turning into reality.

"I never dreamed it would be this way," she said absently.

"How did you think it would be?"

"Frightening," she confessed without telling him why. McAnders had made it into a terrifying thing, a violent act that would have hurt if he'd succeeded. But what she'd experienced with Tyler wasn't terrifying. It had been beautiful.

"And it wasn't?" he persisted gently.

"Not frightening, no," she said with a demure smile. "A little scary, but in a nice way. So many sensations..."

"For me, too, Nell," he said somberly. His eyes held hers. "That was no casual diversion, and don't you forget it. I'm not a playboy."

"You're not a monk, either," she said. She smiled shakily. "I may be innocent, but I'm not stupid."

He sighed, smoothing her closed fingers with his thumb. "If you want the truth, yes, I've had women. But always women who couldn't or wouldn't consider marriage or anything permanent. And never for money. Lovemaking is too beautiful to reduce to a quick coupling that only satisfies a casual hunger."

She couldn't speak. She hadn't expected him to say anything like that, and it occurred to her that she didn't really know him very well. "I'm glad you think of it that way," she said.

"Don't you, honestly?" he asked.

"With you I do," she said after a minute. McAnders's angry handling was fading away like a bad dream. Now when she thought about physical expressions of affection, she was always going to feel Tyler's hands on her body.

He touched her lips with a long forefinger. "Go away," he said softly. "I want you terribly, Miss Regan."

She smiled tenderly. "I'm very glad of that. But I'll go."

She got up from the bed, her eyes possessive as they ran over his taut body.

"Would you like an anatomy lesson?" he asked with a dry smile. "I could pull this sheet away and teach you volumes about men."

She averted her eyes, her cheeks scarlet. "I'll just bet you could," she muttered, because she remembered how his body had changed when hers came into contact with it. "And stop making fun of me because I'm not clued in."

"I happen to like you that way, believe it or not," he mused. "Come back in the morning. We can have another argument."

"I don't really want to argue with you."

"The alternative could get us into real trouble."

She laughed because he sounded so morose and dryly amused all at once. Her face changed with the sound, brightened, went soft and radiant.

"You are lovely when you laugh," he said huskily. "And if you don't get out of here right now, I'm going to throw off this damned sheet and come after you."

She let out a low whistle and headed for the door. "The mind boggles," she murmured as she glanced over her shoulder and smiled at him. "Sleep tight."

"Oh, that's funny," he agreed. "A real screamer. I'll have to remember to put it in my memoirs."

"I won't sleep, either," she said softly, and left him reluctantly.

She went out the door smiling, her heart so light that it could have floated before her. She'd never been so happy in all her life. The most unexpected things happened sometimes. They'd argued and she'd been sure that there was no hope, and now he'd kissed her so hungrily, handled her so gently that she was building daydreams again. This had to be the real thing, she told herself doggedly. He'd told her he wasn't playing, so it had to be for real. It had to be!

And all of a sudden, she started thinking about the past, about a man who'd teased her and kissed her lazily once or twice, a man she'd thought she loved. And that man had betrayed her trust and tried to force her into bed, all because he'd wanted her bright, beautiful sister-in-law. It didn't bear thinking about. Surely history wasn't going to repeat itself with Tyler. Nell closed her eyes in faint fear. She couldn't bear the thought of that.

If Bella noticed that Nell's lips were swollen and her hair wildly disheveled and her face full of a new radiance mingled with fear, she kept it to herself. But she was less abrasive than usual as Nell helped with the dishes, and she was smiling when the younger woman went up to bed.

Nell awoke the next morning after a sleepless night to hear a furious commotion going on down in the kitchen.

She hurriedly dressed in jeans and a neat checked shirt, left her hair down around her shoulders and went to the kitchen for breakfast. She caught the tail end of a conversation that sounded curious at best.

Bella was still raging at someone. "...can't imagine what possessed him! Of course he didn't know—he isn't a mean kind of man. But we've got to get him out of here!"

"Can't be done." That was Chappy's voice, slow and measured. "Old Man Regan gave him the power to hire and fire. Even Nell can't override him in something like this. It's just a damned shame that one of you women didn't think to tell him!"

"Well, it ain't the kind of thing you talk about to outsiders," Bella grumbled.

"He was up and moving about last I looked. Should I go talk to him?"

"Hold off a few minutes. Give me time to think."

"Okay. Tell me when."

A door slammed. Nell hesitated before she went on into the room. When Bella saw her, she turned beet red.

"Nell! I wasn't expecting you this early," she said with a toothy grin that was as false as fool's gold.

"I heard you," Nell said. "What's going on? Is it something to do with the new men? They're supposed to show up today." She gnawed her lower lip. "I guess we can send them on over to Tyler. He was much better yesterday. He can't work, but he can still delegate—"

"You'd better sit down," Bella began.

"Why? Has he hired Jack the Ripper?" Nell grinned. She felt great. It was a beautiful day, and she wanted to get this over with so that she could see Tyler. Her whole life had changed overnight. Everything was beautiful.

"Worse." Bella took a deep breath. "Oh, there's just no use in pussyfooting around. He's hired Darren Mc-Anders."

There was a hush like death in the room. Of all the things Nell might have expected to hear, that was the last. She did sit down, heavily, with her heart in her throat. Nightmares were rushing in on her, old wounds were opening.

"How could he?" she asked huskily. "How could he give that man a job here? I thought Darren was working on a ranch in Wyoming."

"Obviously he came home, and it seems he thought nine years had healed old wounds."

"Not mine," Nell said, her dark eyes flashing. "Not ever. He used me. He hurt me, scared me out of my mind.... Well, he isn't going to work here. Tell Chappy to fire him."

"You know Chappy can't do that. Neither can you," Bella said. "You'll have to go and tell Tyler what happened."

She went white. After what she and Tyler had shared the day before, the thought of telling him about what McAnders had done to her was sickening. Not only that, she'd have to tell him all of it. That McAnders had flirted with her and teased her, just as Tyler had done. That he'd made a little light love to her, and she'd gone off the deep end and thrown herself at him. It had never been all Darren's fault—even in the beginning. Nell hadn't been able to talk to Bella or Margie, to tell them how much at fault *she'd* been. But she'd loved Darren, or thought she had, and she'd assumed from his affectionate advances that he felt the same way. She'd had the shock of her young life when he'd come into her room, expecting her cooperation to help get Margie out of his blood, and found her unwilling and apparently scared to death. He'd had some harsh things to say, and he'd been drinking. She still didn't know if he'd have gone far enough to force her, because her screams had brought Bella and Margie running. Surely Darren didn't think Nell was still carrying a torch for him and would welcome him back? He had to know how she hated him.

"Tell Tyler what happened," Bella said. "He'll understand."

Nell wasn't at all sure that he would. She thought of approaching Darren, but she couldn't bear to talk to him. Nine years hadn't erased her shame and fear of him, or her embarrassment for her own behavior that had led to such a tragic confrontation.

"I'll try," Nell promised as she went out the back door. She wasn't going to confess, she knew that. But maybe there was another way.

She knocked on Tyler's door, shaking in her boots. He called for her to come in, and she found him in the kitchen, frying eggs.

He glanced at her with a strange reserve, as if he'd forgotten the day before or didn't want to remember it. "Good morning," he said quietly. His eyes slid over her and quickly away, back to what he was doing. "Do you want some breakfast?"

His coolness robbed her of courage. He didn't seem like the same man who'd kissed her half to death. Perhaps he was ashamed. Perhaps he regretted every kiss. Or perhaps he was just afraid she might throw herself at him. Shades of the past fell ominously over her head.

"I'm not hungry." She took a deep breath. "One of the new men you hired is Darren McAnders. I want you to let him go. Right now."

His black eyebrows arched. He moved the pan from the burner and shut off the stove before he turned slowly to face her. "I don't think I heard you right."

"I said I want you to fire McAnders right now," she returned stiffly. "I won't have him on this ranch."

"How many available cowboys do you think I can find at roundup time?" he asked shortly. "I'm already a man short, even with McAnders, and he comes highly recommended by the Wyoming outfit he was working for. He's steady, he doesn't drink, and he knows what to do with a rope. And you want me to fire him before he's even started? You little fool, he could sue us to hell for that and bring down half the government on our heads!"

"You won't do it?" she asked coldly.

"No." He glowered at her. "Not without cause. If you want him fired, tell me why," he said, and his eyes were oddly intent.

She tried. She started to speak. Her sweet memories were turning black in her mind, and she was already mourning for what might have been. Tyler looked formidable. He also looked fighting mad. She'd gone about it all wrong. She should have tried honey instead of vinegar, but it was too late now. He'd see right through that tactic, anyway.

"We're old enemies," she said finally. "That's the best I can do by way of an explanation."

He smiled mockingly and there was a new coldness in his tone. "Now that's interesting," he said. "Because Mc-Anders told me this morning that you were old friends. Very close friends, in fact."

Chapter Six

Nell just stood, staring blankly at Tyler while she tried to decide what to say. His tone was enough to convince her that he was well on the way to believing that she'd lied to him. God knew what Darren had said about the past, but it had made a terrible difference in Tyler's attitude toward her. She could feel the distrust in him, and it chilled her.

"You don't have to agonize over an explanation," Tyler said when he saw her hesitation. It was obvious that McAnders had meant something to her. "But don't expect me to fire a man because he's one of your old flames," he added mockingly. "That isn't reason enough."

She didn't say another word. He was looking at her as if he was prepared to disbelieve anything she said. He didn't know her well enough to see that she'd never have asked him to fire a man out of some personal grudge. It went much deeper than that. McAnders was an unpleasant part of her past, a constant reminder of her own lack of self-control, her vulnerability. Tyler had shown her that physical desire wasn't the terrible thing she'd remembered. But that was over before it began, all because she couldn't bring herself to tell him the truth.

"Nothing else to say?" he asked.

She shook her head. "No, thank you. I'm sorry I disturbed you."

Tyler scowled as she left. She was subdued now when she'd been fiery-tempered before. What was McAnders to her? Was she still in love with him and afraid of succumbing? Or was it something more? He wished he'd made her tell him. Now, he had a terrible feeling that he might have left it too late.

Nell was keyed up and frightened of her first confrontation with Darren. It came unexpectedly that same day, at dusk, when he was passing the back porch as she went out the door.

She looked up and there he was. Her first love. Her first crush. Until Tyler had come along, her only crush. Darren McAnders had been in his early twenties nine years ago. Now he was in his early thirties, but he hadn't changed. He had dark auburn hair, threaded with gray at the temples now, and blue eyes. He was a little heavier than he had been. But it was his face that drew Nell's attention the most. He'd aged twenty years. He had lines where he shouldn't have had them, and the easygoing smile she remembered was gone completely.

"Hello, Nell," he said quietly.

She didn't flinch, although she felt like it. He brought back memories of her own stupidity and its near-disastrous consequences. He was walking proof that her self-control was a myth, and she didn't like it.

"Hello, Darren," she replied.

"I suppose you've given the word to have me thrown off the place by now," he said surprisingly. "Once I knew you still lived here, I was sure I'd made a mistake in hiring on without telling your new ramrod the truth.'' He frowned slightly, pushing his battered hat back on his head. "You don't mind that I'm here?''

"Of course I mind,'' she said coldly, and her dark eyes flashed. "I mind that I made a fool of myself over you, and that you used me because of Margie. But if you don't mind the memories, then neither do I. Keep your job. I don't care one way or the other.''

He searched her face for a long moment, and then what he could see of her body in her usual clothing, and a kind of sadness claimed his expression. "You might not believe it, but I had a lot of regrets about what happened. It's been heavy on my conscience all these years.''

He looked as if it had, too, and that was the most surprising thing of all to Nell. She didn't speak because she couldn't think of anything to say.

He took a slow breath. "How is Marguerite?'' he asked finally.

She'd suspected that Marguerite's widowhood had some place in McAnders's decision to take a job at the ranch. Even nine years hadn't dimmed his passion for Margie. Nell wondered how Margie would react.

"She's doing very well,'' Nell replied. "She and her sons live in Tucson. They come out here for an occasional weekend.''

"I heard about your brother,'' he remarked. "I'm sorry. I always liked Ted. I hated betraying his trust that way.''

"He never knew how you felt about her,'' she said. "Now if you'll excuse me...''

"You've changed,'' he said suddenly. "I wouldn't have known you in that getup.''

She flushed with mingled temper and embarrassment as she remembered the close-fitting outfits she used to wear to try to catch his eye. "I guess not," she said tightly. "We all change with age."

"Not as much as you have." He grimaced. "Oh, Nell," he said softly. "Ted should have shot me for what I did to you. He should have shot me dead."

And he turned on his heel and walked away before she could reply. That wasn't the Darren McAnders she remembered. He was no longer the cocky, arrogant young man who'd alternately teased and toyed with her. He was older and far more mature, and the teasing streak seemed to have been buried. All the same, it was too soon to start trusting him, and Margie was going to have a fit when she heard that he was back on the ranch.

Bella had the same feeling, because after supper was cleared away she mentioned that it might be a good idea for Nell to call and tell Margie about their new hand.

"I won't," Nell said firmly. "She'll find out soon enough. She and the boys are coming this weekend."

Bella sighed. "Going to be fireworks," she said.

"Then she can complain to Tyler. I didn't hire him."

"Nell!"

She jumped. Tyler's deep voice carried even when he didn't raise it, but it was clearly raised now, and irritated as he came down the hall toward the kitchen.

"Is that you, or did somebody stick a pin in a mountain lion?" Nell asked with more courage than she felt.

He didn't smile. He was bareheaded and grim, and there were several bills held in one lean hand. "We've got to talk," he said.

Nell glanced apprehensively at Bella, but the older woman began to whistle as if she hadn't heard a word. Nell put down the dishcloth and followed Tyler back down the hall to the front room that served as an office.

The desk was cluttered, and it looked as if Tyler had been at the books for at least a couple of hours. He'd been going over the ranch's finances for several weeks now, in his spare time, trying to make sense of Nell's hit-or-miss bookkeeping system. Apparently he'd just figured it out, and he didn't like what he saw.

"These—" he indicated a new set of books "—are the new books. I've boiled everything down to credits and debits. From now on, every purchase comes through me. If you want a needle and thread, you'll have to have a purchase order. This—" he held up a book of purchase orders "—is a book of them. It's going to be locked in the desk, and I have the only key."

"Why?" she asked.

He motioned her into a chair and perched himself on the corner of the desk to light a cigarette. "The way things have been run here, any cowboy could go to the hardware store and charge butane or vaccination supplies or go to the feed store for feed or salt and charge it without any authorization." He handed her the bills he'd been carrying. "Read a couple of those."

She frowned curiously, but she did as she was told. "A pair of spurs," she murmured, reading aloud, "a new saddle..." She looked up. "I never authorized those."

"I know you didn't." He smiled faintly. "That's the problem with giving carte blanche to the cowboys."

"Who had the saddle and spurs on here?" she demanded.

"Marlowe."

"You ought to fire him."

"I already have," he said. "Good thing I hired on two new men instead of one." He eyed the tip of his cigarette. "I saw you talking to McAnders. Is there still a problem?"

She didn't feel comfortable discussing it with him. "There won't be one. Darren and I will work things out."

That sounded ominous to him. As if she had ideas about recapturing the past. He scowled at her, his green eyes almost sparking with bad temper. "As long as you keep your dalliance after working hours, I don't care what you do."

She felt something inside her dying. He couldn't know how badly he was hurting her with his indifference. She supposed he wouldn't care if he did. She lowered her eyes to her jeans. "Have you told the men about the purchase orders?"

"I told the crew in the bunkhouse at supper. I'll tell the married hands in the morning. There are going to have to be other changes, as well." He picked up the ledger and went through it. "For one thing, we're going to have to cut back on the activities that require cowboy participation. It's getting time for roundup, and I'll need every man I've got. This open range may be fine for a big outfit, but it's hell on one this size. We'll spend the better part of a week just getting the saler calves into holding pens."

"We can borrow Bob Wyler's helicopter, if you want to," Nell said. "He always helps out that way, and he supplies the pilot, too."

"For what kind of payment?" Tyler asked narrowly.

Nell grinned involuntarily. "For a case of Bella's strawberry-rhubarb preserves," she said.

He chuckled, too, in spite of himself. "Okay. That's a deal. But can you manage the trail rides without Chappy?"

"I managed well enough before Ted died," she said. "I can do it again. What else?"

"This is the worst of it. We're spending a fortune on having a golf pro on the payroll for visitors who want to tee off on the Western Terrace greens. That's fine for the big dude ranches, but we're operating on a shoestring here. I can show you on paper that only one out of every ten guests avails himself of this service, but the pro collects his fee just the same."

"That was Ted's idea," she said. "I've just let it drag on. You may have noticed that most of the people who come here aren't really very athletic." She blushed and he laughed.

"Yes, I've noticed." He searched her dark eyes slowly, and little sparks of attraction seemed to leap between them before he drew his gaze down to his cigarette. "Then I'll take care of the pro. As for this daily shopping trip into Tucson, is that mandatory?"

"We could cut back to every other day," she compromised. "I realize that it's pretty hard on the gas budget, what with the van being used for transportation. I guess the city tour is hard on the budget, too."

He nodded his dark head. "That was going to be my next question. Can we subcontract the tours out to an existing agency in town?"

"Sure! I know a terrific lady who'd love the business, and her fees are very reasonable."

"Okay. Give her a call and work something out."

"You've been working," Nell remarked, nodding toward all the ledgers and paperwork.

"It's been a long job. But I didn't want to make specific recommendations until I had a handle on how the ranch was run. You haven't done a bad job, Nell," he said surprisingly. "Except for a few places, you've budgeted to the bone. You've only continued old policies. But we're going to change some of those and get this place operating in the black again."

"You sound encouraging."

"It's a good little operation," he replied. "It shouldn't be hard to make it a paying one. Anyplace you think you may need more help?"

She thought for a minute, trying not to notice the way his jeans clung to his long, powerful legs, or the fact that the top three buttons of his red-checked shirt were unbuttoned over that tanned expanse of hair-covered chest. She remembered all too well how it had felt to touch him in passion.

"I'd like to have someone come with me on the trail ride while that man from back East is here," she confessed with a faint smile. "His wife is rather cold-eyed, and she seems to have some insane idea that I'm chasing him."

Tyler's eyes went narrow. "Yes, I saw how he tried to come on to you at the square dance. They leave Thursday, don't they?" He saw her nod. "I'll go on the next two trail rides with you. Chappy can keep things in order for Bella while we're out."

"Thanks."

"Unless you'd rather I let McAnders go with you?" he added with a mocking smile.

She wanted to protest, but that would be a little too revealing. She swallowed. "Whatever suits you," she said. "It doesn't matter to me."

Which wasn't the answer he wanted. He put out his cigarette with faint violence. "McAnders can go with you, then," he said. "I've got enough work to do without playing nursemaid."

The words were meant to sting, and they did. She got up, avoiding his eyes as she went to the door. "Thanks for all you're doing," she said over her shoulder.

"My pleasure. Good night."

"Good night."

She didn't see him alone after that. There was always some reason to have other people present or to put off discussions until she could arrange for reinforcements. But that didn't stop Tyler from cutting at her verbally at every opportunity.

What hurt the most was that Darren McAnders didn't mind accompanying her on trail rides, and seemed even to enjoy her taciturn company. He began to smile again, as if being with her brightened his life. She didn't understand why, and she understood even less Tyler's new antagonism.

But the fire hit the fan on the weekend, when Margie and the boys arrived by taxi.

Nell had just come back from the trail ride, with Darren McAnders at her side. Marguerite, immaculate in a white linen suit, stepped out of the cab she'd recklessly hired in Tucson, with her long reddish-gold hair wafting in the breeze, and looked straight up into Darren McAnders's stunned face.

"Darren!" she exclaimed, missing her step.

She went down on her knees in the dust, and Darren vaulted out of the saddle to pick her up, his hands strong and sure on her upper arms, his eyes intent on her flushed face.

"Margie," he said softly. "You haven't aged. You're as beautiful as ever."

"What are you doing here?" Margie gasped. She glanced at Nell, even more shocked to find Nell apparently voluntarily in Darren's company.

"He's our newest hand," Nell told her. "Tyler hired him."

"Doesn't he know?" Margie asked, and then flushed when she saw Darren's rueful smile. "Oh, I'm sorry. It's just that..."

"The past is only a problem if we let it be," Nell said stubbornly. "Darren and I are getting along very well. Aren't we, Darren?" she asked.

He smiled ruefully. "As well as could be expected. Nell's been very generous. It was this job or welfare, and I couldn't have blamed her if she'd thrown me off the place. It's as much as I deserved."

Margie searched his face slowly and then glanced up at Nell, sitting still on her horse. "It took a lot of courage for you to come back here, Darren," she remarked, even though she was looking at Nell, waiting, questioning.

"I found out that running away doesn't solve much," he said enigmatically. He glanced past Margie. "Are these your boys?" He asked the question softly, and his eyes echoed that softness as he looked at them. "Curt and Jess, aren't you? Your Aunt Nell's said a lot about you."

They piled out of the car like marauding pirates and stared at him enthusiastically. "Did she, really?" Curt asked. "Did she say nice stuff? Me and Jess are lots of help around the ranch—Tyler says so. We help him find snakes and lizards and stuff and keep them from eating up Aunt Nell's cattle!"

Aunt Nell's eyes widened with amusement. "Did Tyler tell you that?"

"Well, not really," Jess murmured. "But it sounds good, don't it?"

"Doesn't it," Margie corrected absently. She was just beginning to get her self-confidence back after the shock of seeing Darren. "Boys, we'd better get inside." She paid the driver, and Nell got off her horse to help with the luggage, but Darren was one step ahead of her.

"I'll take care of this if you can manage the horses, Nell," he said with a hopeful glance in her direction.

She knew he'd never gotten over Margie. It didn't surprise her that he was anxious to renew that acquaintance. What Margie felt was less easy to perceive. But it certainly wasn't like the older woman to lose her step and pitch headfirst into desert sand.

"Sure," Nell agreed easily. "I'll take them to the barn. Margie, I'll see you and the boys in a few minutes."

"That's fine," Margie said absently, but she was looking at Darren as if she'd been poleaxed.

Nell was faintly relieved. With Darren around, maybe Margie wouldn't bat her eyelashes so luxuriously at Tyler. Not that it mattered anymore. Tyler had certainly made it clear that he wasn't interested in Nell. He avoided her like the very plague.

She led the horses to the barn, where Chappy took the reins with a curious glance at her rigid features.

"You okay?" he asked.

She smiled. "I'm fine." She glanced around. "Where's Caleb?"

Caleb was the big black gelding that Tyler always rode. Asking for the horse's whereabouts was a little less obvious than inquiring about Tyler's.

Chappy saw right through her. "He's out riding the boundary fence we put up around the holding pens."

She blinked. "He hates riding fence."

"He overheard two of the boys talking about the way McAnders hangs around you since he's been here," the wrinkled cowboy said with a twinkle in his pale blue eyes. "He set them to cleaning out the stables, and he went off to ride fence. I don't reckon anybody will mention such things around him again, once word gets through the outfit."

She bit her lower lip. "Why should he care?"

Chappy started to lead the horses toward the stable, where two sweating, swearing cowboys were mucking out the stalls and pitching fresh hay. "You need glasses," he said dryly.

Nell drifted back to the house slowly, her eyes everywhere on the horizon, looking for a glimpse of Tyler. Things had been strained between them. That, and McAnders's presence, were making her life miserable. Not that she minded Darren being around. He'd changed so much from the shallow, careless man she'd known. She felt no remnant of the old crush she'd had on him, nor any sense of bitterness. He was like a friendly stranger whom she began to like, but nothing more.

If only she could go to Tyler and tell him that. But despite his odd behavior this afternoon, he hadn't said anything that would lead Nell to believe he had any lasting affection for her. In fact, he'd said more than once that there wasn't any place for a woman in his life right now. And the thought of throwing herself at another man, after the misery her encounter with Darren had brought her, was unwelcome. Tyler might be kind about it, but she knew he wouldn't appreciate having her "hang on his boots," as he'd mentioned to Bella.

She sighed. She knew so little about men. If only she could talk to Margie, perhaps she could find a way out of the corner she'd painted herself into.

She went into the house to help Bella get supper on the table before the guests were called onto the elegant patio to eat. The wooden tables each had umbrellas and sat beside an Olympic-size swimming pool, which did a lot of business during the day. All meals were taken here, with Bella and Nell setting a buffet table from which guests could choose their portions. All around were palo verde trees, along with every conceivable form of cactus known

to the desert Southwest. It was amusing to watch the guests
from back East ask about the flower garden mentioned in
the brochure and then see it for real. The native plants were
surrounded by rock borders, and their arrangement was
both mysterious and compelling. In bloom, the cacti were
beautiful, like the feathery palo verde with its fragrant
yellow blossoms.

"You aren't eating?" Nell asked when Margie sat down
a good distance away from the guests while, as a special
treat, the boys had their meal in the bunkhouse with the
cowboys.

Margie shook her head. She'd changed into designer
jeans and a red tank top, and she looked elegant and
moody. "I'm not hungry. How long has he been here?"

"A few days," Nell said. "Tyler hired him."

"And you let him stay?"

"Not voluntarily," Nell said after a minute. "I tried to
bulldoze Tyler into letting him go, but he wouldn't. He
wanted to know why." She lowered her eyes. "I couldn't
tell him."

"Yes. I understand." She sat up suddenly, leaning her
forearms on the table. "Nell, it isn't terribly bad, is it?
Having him around?"

The intensity of the question was interesting. Nell smiled
faintly. "No, it isn't terribly bad," she said gently. She
studied the pale, beautiful features. "You still care about
him, don't you?"

Margie stiffened. She actually flustered. "I . . . well, no,
of course not. I didn't really care about him!"

"Ted has been dead for a long time," Nell said quietly.
"And I'm sure he never meant for you to live without love
forever. If you're asking me how I feel about Darren, he's
very much like a nice stranger." She smiled gently. "I guess
you and Bella were right about what happened. I blew it

all out of proportion because I didn't have any experience to measure it against. I didn't exactly invite what happened, but I'd led him to believe that I wanted him without realizing it."

"It was my fault, too," Margie admitted. "But I never meant you to be hurt." She looked at the table instead of at Nell. "I cared about him. Not in the way I loved Ted, but in a different way. But I was married, and despite the way I teased him, I never would have had an affair with him."

"I know that," Nell said.

Margie smiled at her sadly. "I've spent a lot of years trying to make you over in my image, haven't I? Being bossy, taking you for granted. But I meant it in the nicest way. I wanted to help. I just didn't know how."

"I don't need help," Nell told her dryly. "And I'm not going to try to recapture the past with Darren Mc-Anders."

"And Tyler?" Margie fished. "Where does he fit in?"

That question threw her again. Was Margie infatuated with Tyler? Was her interest in Darren only pretended so that she could find out how Nell felt about Tyler? Nell started drawing into herself again, defensively. "Tyler is my foreman, nothing more. He doesn't give a hang about me in any way," Nell said tautly. She got up from the table. "I'm not hungry, Margie. I think I'll go watch TV."

"Okay. I've got to go get the boys."

"They're already on the way," Nell remarked with a bitter smile, and gestured to where Tyler was coming with both boys by the hand. They were laughing and so was he. Margie was gazing at the group with such naked hunger that Nell turned away. "See you later," she said, but Margie wasn't really listening. Her whole attention was focused on Tyler. Actually, it was focused on Darren, who was right behind Tyler, but Nell didn't see the second man. She was sure now that Margie was using Darren as an excuse to mask her feelings for Tyler.

Nell went inside and threw herself into housecleaning until she was nearly exhausted, getting rooms ready for the boys and Margie. When she came back downstairs, she was surprised to find Tyler in the living room, already watching the news.

He looked tired. Dead tired. He'd showered and changed, but he had an oblivious kind of expression on his face that brightened a little when he saw Nell come into the room.

"Can I get you a lemonade?" he asked, hoisting his.

"Not a brandy?" she mused.

"I don't drink. I never have."

She sat down in the armchair across from him, feeling her way. "Why?"

He shrugged. "I don't know. I don't like either the taste or the effect, I guess." His green eyes went over her like hands, and she flushed, because memories were glittering there. It was shocking to remember exactly how intimate he'd been with her, for all the distance that had been between them since then.

"I don't drink, either," she said absently. "I'm frightfully old-fashioned."

"Yes, I know," he said softly, and the memories were there again, warm and overwhelming. His eyes caught hers and held them relentlessly. "How do you feel about McAnders?"

She sat up straight. She had to hide her real feelings from him, so she said, "I'm not sure."

"Aren't you? You seem to spend enough time with him lately," he accused quietly.

"You spend plenty around Margie," she shot back.

He smiled mockingly. "Yes, I do, don't I? But you don't seem to spend much time considering why."

"It's obviously because she attracts you," she said haughtily. "I'm not blind."

"Oh, but you are," he said quietly. "More blind than you know."

"I can spend time with anyone I please," she continued coldly.

"Have you been intimate with McAnders?" he asked suddenly.

She gasped. Her face went bloodred as she remembered what had happened that night, what Darren had tried to do to her.

Tyler saw the expression, but he took it for guilt, and something inside him exploded. No wonder Nell had eyes for McAnders. He'd been her first love, and now he was back and he wanted her, and she'd let him touch her in all the ways Tyler had. Maybe even more. His eyes glittered at her furiously.

"How could you do that?" he asked bitterly.

She blinked. "Do what?"

He threw up his hands and paced angrily. "And all the time I thought—" He stopped short, turning. "Well, if it's McAnders you want, consider him yours. I'll run the business end of the ranch and take care of the livestock. But don't make the mistake of running after me if McAnders dumps you," he added venomously. "I don't want another man's castoff."

Nell gasped with outrage. "You lily-white purist!" she threw at him. "How many women have you cast off, if we're going to get personal?"

"That's none of your business," he said shortly.

"Well, Darren is none of yours." She clenched her hands, hating his arrogance.

He wanted to throw things. He hadn't realized until then just how deeply Nell was under his skin. He had to face the possibility that a man from her past was about to carry her off, and he didn't know what to do to stop it. She'd got the wrong end of the stick about Margie. He liked Margie, yet he saw right through her antics. But Nell was so insecure that she couldn't see the forest for the trees. Considering that insecurity it was a miracle that she could even contemplate a relationship with Darren McAnders. But she might love him....

He sighed heavily. "Fair enough," he said finally and with a long, quiet stare. "Do what you please, Nell. I won't interfere. As you say, your life is your own."

He turned to go and she felt sick all over at the way things were working out. She didn't care about Darren. She wanted to call him back and tell him the truth, but something stopped her. She couldn't tell him, she couldn't face his contempt when he knew that she'd invited Darren's advances, that she'd chased him all those years ago and brought it on herself. So she let him go, watching with sad eyes as he left the room only to run into Margie in the hall.

Nell heard him laughing and caught a glimpse of Margie's rapt expression. She couldn't bear it. She was going to lose him to Margie, and she couldn't bear it. She went back into the living room, forcing herself not to cry.

She'd let Tyler think she'd been deliberately intimate with Darren, and that was a lie. She sat down on the sofa, remembering what had happened all those years ago. She'd been mistaken about McAnders's feelings back then, and she'd become obsessed with him after he'd paid her a little attention. She recalled how she'd teased him until one night she went a little too far. Margie had given a party and that evening Nell had flirted with McAnders, who'd been rejected by Margie and had had too much to drink. McAnders had come to Nell's room and found her asleep in her scanty gown, and since she hadn't locked her door, he'd thought she was waiting for him. He'd climbed into bed with her and, despite her protests, he'd been about to seduce her when Bella had come to her rescue.

But that had been years ago, long before she knew Tyler. He hadn't been talking about the past, though. He'd asked her if she'd been intimate with Darren, and he was talking about the present.

The impact of the realization hit her between the eyes like a hammer. Now she'd done it! She'd inadvertantly let him think that what she'd shared with him she'd also shared with Darren. She'd stung his pride by letting him think that she could go straight from his arms into Darren's and without a twinge of conscience.

She got up, shaking with reaction, and wondered if she could go after him, explain.

But before she got to the door, Curt and Jess came careering down the hall, and she looked past them to where Tyler was holding Margie's arm, escorting her laughingly out the front door.

It was too late now to smooth things over, she knew. She'd left it just a few seconds too long. She'd lost him.

Chapter Seven

"Hi, Aunt Nell," they chorused. "Can we watch that new science fiction movie on the VCR?"

"Sure. Go ahead," she said with forced tolerance, but her heart was breaking. "Where'd your mother go?"

"Uncle Tyler's taking her into town," Curt volunteered disinterestedly as he searched for the right videocassette. "I sure like Uncle Tyler."

"Yeah, me too," Jess agreed.

So it was "uncle" already, Nell thought, groaning inwardly. She made some brief excuse and left the room before the boys could see the tears forming in her eyes.

After that day Nell started avoiding him again. Not that it was necessary. Tyler cut her dead every time he saw her, his eyes hard and accusing, as if she'd betrayed him somehow. Nell began to wilt emotionally.

Margie and the boys left, but she and Tyler had seemed to spend a lot of time together during that visit, and Margie had been very nervous and standoffish around Darren. So any hope Nell had that her sister-in-law might be interested in her old flame was washed away almost immediately. It was Tyler Margie wanted, and Nell didn't have a chance anymore. Not with Tyler nearly hating her for what he thought she'd done. As if she could have borne the touch of any man's hands but his; it seemed impossible that he didn't know that.

After Margie left, a morose Darren McAnders began to seek Nell out to talk about the way Margie had avoided him. He was hurt, just as she was, and their common pain brought them together as friends. She even found an odd kind of comfort in his presence.

It was an odd turn of events all around, she thought as she walked with Darren to the corral fence to see two new mares Tyler had bought. Darren was turning out to be a friend.

"You're looking moody lately," Darren remarked as they watched Chappy work one of the unbroken mares on a lunging rein. He glanced at her and smiled mischievously. "And the boss is explosive. The men are betting on how long it's going to be before he throws a punch at somebody just to let the pressure off."

She flushed. "It's complicated," she said.

He propped a boot on the lowest rail of the corral fence. "It's pretty funny for me to be offering you a shoulder to cry on, when I was your worst enemy at one time. But times have changed and so have I. And if you need somebody to listen, here I am, honey."

She looked up at him tearfully. He was different, all right. A new man altogether. She managed a smile.

He smiled back and pulled her against him to give her a friendly, totally platonic hug.

But Tyler happened to be looking out the window in the bunkhouse and he saw them. And what was a platonic hug didn't look that way to a man already trying to cope with emotions he was feeling for the first time in his life, and eaten up with unfamiliar jealousy, to boot. Tyler let out a string of range language, turned and stormed off to where he'd tied his horse. He swung up into the saddle and rode away without the slightest idea of where in hell he was going.

The square dance was the following Saturday night, and most of the present guests were leaving on Sunday to make room for a new group of people. A one-week stay was about standard for most of them. By that time they were sore enough and rested enough to go home and cope with their routines. Margie and the boys showed up Saturday afternoon, and the older woman thrust a huge box at Nell, with a mischievous smile.

"For you," she said with dancing eyes. "Open it."

Nell eyed her curiously, but she put the box on the dining room table and opened it, aware of Bella's frank interest as she did.

It was a square-dancing outfit. A red-checked full skirt with oceans of petticoats and a pretty white Mexican peasant blouse in cotton, both of which had probably cost the earth. Nell just stared at it without speaking. It was the prettiest set she'd ever seen.

"For me?" she asked Margie blankly.

"For you," came the smiling reply. "And don't put your hair up in a ponytail, will you?"

"But, Margie, I can't dance," she began.

"Wear that and someone will be sure to teach you," Margie promised.

So Nell wore the new outfit and brushed her long honey-colored hair until it shone thick and gleaming around her shoulders. Margie taught her how to put on a thin coat of makeup, and they were both surprised at the results. Nell

lidn't look like Nell anymore. She wasn't beautiful, but
she was certainly attractive enough to make a man notice
her.

Margie was wearing a similar outfit, the difference being that Margie could do anything from a square dance to
a samba. Nell was too aware that she herself had at least
two left feet.

Once she tried to ask Margie about Tyler, but she lost
her nerve. Margie was so beautiful, and she had a way of
making every man she met want her. If Tyler fell victim to
her charm, who could blame him?

Nell couldn't help but wonder, though, why Margie had
bought her a dress. Did she possibly sense that Nell cared
about Tyler, and was trying to help her get over him by
attracting Darren? But surely Margie didn't think she was
interested that way in Darren, because she'd already denied it.

Downstairs, Bella made a big fuss over Nell's new image, and Nell had a feeling it was to make up for the last
time she'd dressed up and Bella had been worried about
Tyler getting the wrong idea. But this time praise was certainly forthcoming.

The band could be heard tuning up in the barn, which
had been cleared out for the dance. Bella grinned.

"Well, at least Tyler hasn't complained about that forty
dollars we have to pay the band twice a month," she said
dryly.

"Give him time." Nell sighed. "Lately he complains
about most everything. I hear he even made Chappy take
back a rope he bought without permission."

"In case you haven't heard," Bella told Margie, "Tyler
is in a snit lately. He walks around glowering at people and
talking to himself."

Margie lifted an eyebrow at Nell, who flushed angrily.

"I don't have anything to do with it," Nell said shortly. "Maybe he's missing your company."

Margie exchanged glances with Bella and smiled mischievously. "Well, that's possible, of course." She eyed Nell's averted face. "Shall we go find out? Bella, you're sure you can manage the boys? They're in their pajamas, waiting for that story you promised to read them."

"Sure, me and the boys will do fine." Bella picked up a book and started toward the staircase. "Don't you worry about us."

"What are you going to read them?" Margie asked.

Bella turned and grinned wickedly. "All about the pirate raids in the Caribbean, in gory detail."

Nell gasped, but Margie laughed. "Good for you."

"Won't they have nightmares?" Nell asked.

Margie shook her head. "They love that sort of thing. I'm told that most boys do—it's normal. Their young worlds are made up of monsters and battles."

"Isn't everybody's?" Bella chuckled. "Have fun."

Nell didn't have a wrap, and it was a chilly night, but she tried not to notice the goose bumps as she and Margie walked down to the barn. Things were already in full swing, and Nell noticed that Margie's eyes were restless, as if she were looking for someone. She sighed, thinking that Margie was apparently going to single out Tyler for the evening. Nell had once been certain that Darren was the recipient of Margie's affections, but she must have been wrong.

The guests were already dancing, with Chappy calling the square dance with gleeful abandon and clapping his hands as he stood at the microphone in front of the band. Tyler was standing to one side, near the refreshment table, braiding three strands of rawhide carelessly while he glared at the dancing. He had on jeans and a blue-plaid

Western shirt, and with his black hair neatly combed and his face freshly shaven, he made Nell's heart race. He was the handsomest man she'd ever seen.

"There you are!" Margie grinned, taking possession of his arm. "How are you?"

"Fine." Tyler looked past her at Nell, glared even more at Nell, then turned his attention back to Margie. "You look like a dream, honey," he said in a tone that would have attracted bees.

"Thank you," Margie purred. She glanced at Nell. "Doesn't Nell look nice?" she added.

Nell colored and Tyler didn't say a word. He caught Margie's hand in his. "Let's get in the circle," he told her, and dragged her off without noticing the surprise in her face.

Nell moved back out of the circle of dancers and sat down in one of the chairs, feeling alone and rejected and uncomfortable. It was there that Darren found her. He was wearing a black shirt and red bandanna with his jeans, and he looked almost as handsome as Tyler but in a totally different way.

"Hi, pal," he said, smiling at Nell. "Hiding out?"

She shrugged. "I don't dance," she said with a rueful grin. "I never learned."

He cocked an eyebrow. "No time like the present," he remarked. The band had just changed to a slow, dreamy tune, and he held out his hand.

But she shook her head. "I'm not really in the mood."

He turned to look at the throng of dancers, and his face hardened when he saw Margie dancing with Tyler. He moved beside Nell to lean against one of the posts with folded arms, glaring at what he saw.

"He doesn't waste much time, does he?" he asked under his breath.

"They come from the same kind of world," Nell said
quietly. "They've spent a lot of time together since he
came here, and the boys love him."

"The boys don't exactly treat me like a plague victim,"
Darren said coldly. "Well, faint heart never won fair lady,
Nell."

She smiled up at him. "In that case, good luck."

He smiled back. "Don't let him see you looking like
that," he advised. "You'll blow your cover."

She sat up straighter. "God forbid."

He winked at her and moved into the dancers to tap Tyler curtly on the shoulder, nod and sweep Margie into his
arms.

Tyler moved off the floor. He gave Nell a cursory glance
before he picked up the rawhide strands he'd left on the
corner of the refreshment table and began to braid them
again.

"Lost your escort, I gather," he said coolly without
looking down at her.

"What's the matter? Is the competition too much for
you?" she shot back with uncharacteristic venom.

He blinked at the unfamiliar heat in her tone. His green
eyes glanced over her composed features. "I thought that
was your big problem, honey," he said. "Although you're
dressed for it tonight."

"This old rag?" she said with a vacant smile. "Until just
recently, it was the kitchen tablecloth."

He didn't smile. His eyes went to Margie and Darren,
dancing like shadows, oblivious to the world.

"It's a nice crowd," Nell remarked when the silence between them lengthened.

"So it is." He finished the braid and tied it off.

"How are roundup plans coming?"

"Fine."

She took a deep breath. "My goodness, you'll talk my ear off."

"Will I?"

"You might offer to teach me to dance," she said shyly and not without reservations. Inside she was shaking as she tossed off the light remark. "You said once that you'd like it if I wore a dress, and you'd show me how."

His green eyes met hers like bullets. "Most men get poetic when they've been without a woman for a few months," he said with blunt insolence. "But you take things to heart, don't you, Nell?"

She felt the color run up her neck like fire. "I...I didn't mean..."

"Sorry, honey, but my taste doesn't run to tomboys," he said mockingly. "You might as well stick with your current favorite, if you can hold on to him. He seems to have a wandering eye."

She stood up. "That was unfair."

"Was it?" His eyes narrowed. "As for your offer, I don't want to dance with you, now or ever. And you might as well throw that—" he indicated her dress "—in the trash if you bought it to catch my eye. I'm not interested in you."

She felt the world caving in around her. She looked up at him like a small, wounded animal, tears glistening in her eyes.

She couldn't even fight back for the pain his careless words had caused. She'd had such hopes. But then, he'd made no secret of his interest in Margie. She'd been crazy to pit her charms against her sister-in-law's!

"I'm sorry!" she whispered, but her voice broke. Without another word, she turned and ran out of the barn, her skirts flying against her legs as she darted onto the porch, into the house and up the stairs. She didn't stop until she was locked in her room, and the tears came like rain.

Tyler had watched her go with anguish. He hadn't expected that reaction, especially since she'd been sitting with McAnders. Well, maybe it was the sight of Margie dancing with her lost love that had set her off that way, and not what he'd said to her at all. He had to hold on to that thought. If he started believing that what he'd said to Nell had put those tears in her eyes, he wasn't sure he could stand it.

Nell had cried herself to sleep. She woke up dry-eyed and miserable, wondering how she was going to bear it if she had to see Tyler again. Margie had come by her room last night as if she wanted to talk, but Nell had feigned sleep. She didn't know what Margie had to say, but it was probably a lot of sighing memories of Tyler and the dance, and Nell didn't want to have to listen to her.

She was only sorry that she'd shown Tyler how he'd hurt her. She never should have lost control that way. She should have thrown herself into the spirit of the dance, laughed and danced with Darren and given Tyler the cold shoulder. But she wasn't the kind of woman who could carry off that kind of charade. She wore her poor heart on her sleeve, and Tyler had crushed it.

She was surprised to find Tyler in the dining room when she went downstairs to breakfast, especially after the way they'd parted the night before.

"I want to talk to you," he began slowly.

"I can't imagine about what," she replied. She did look up then, and her dark eyes were almost black with cold rage.

"About last night," he said shortly. "I didn't mean what I said about your outfit. You looked lovely."

"Thank you," she said, but without warmth. "Last night that would have meant a lot."

"I got tired of watching you with McAnders," he admitted shortly.

She wasn't sure she'd heard him right. "Watching me with him?" she probed.

"Watching you throw yourself at him," he said with a mocking smile. "That's what it was, wasn't it? Dressing up in that fancy rig, putting on makeup. I hope he appreciated all your efforts."

She took a deep breath and felt her entire body bristling as she glared at him with her dark eyes flashing. "To be perfectly honest, I hadn't aimed my charms at Darren specifically. But thanks for the idea. Maybe I will 'throw myself' at Darren again! At least he told me I looked nice and offered to teach me to dance!"

"He felt sorry for you!" Tyler burst out without choosing his words.

"Doesn't everybody?" she shouted. "I know I'm not pretty! I'm just a stupid little tomboy who can't tell the right man from a hole in the south forty! And I'm glad he felt sorry for me—at least he didn't make fun of me!"

"Neither did I!"

"What would you call it?"

Bella came ambling into the room, her eyes like saucers, but neither of them noticed her.

"I got the wrong end of the stick!" he tried to explain.

"Well, why don't you get hold of the right end?" she invited. "And I'll tell you exactly where you can put it and how far!"

"Nell!" Bella burst out, shocked.

"If that's how you feel, we'll drop the whole subject," Tyler said through his teeth. One lean hand was almost crushing the brim of his hat, but he seemed to be beyond noticing it.

"Good! Why don't you go out and ride a horse or something?"

"You won't even listen . . . !"

"I did listen!" Nell raged, red faced. "You said I might as well throw my clothes in the trash as wear them to impress you, that you weren't interested and that I took things to heart . . . !"

"Oh, God!" he groaned.

"And that it was just abstinence that was responsible for everything!" she concluded fiercely. "Well, that works both ways, cowboy! And you can get out of my dining room. You're curdling my eggs!"

His face was like rock, and his eyes blazed up like green fires. "Damn your eggs! Will you listen?"

"I will not, and I'm not eating the damned eggs. Here, you can have them, and welcome!" And she flung the plate at him, eggs and all, and stalked out of the room.

Tyler stood there, quite still, with egg literally on his face, his shirt, his jeans. A piece of egg had even landed in his hat.

Bella cocked her head warily as she waited for the explosion. He glared at her for a minute and deliberately stuck the hat on his head.

"Would you, uh, like some bacon to go with your eggs?" she asked.

"No, thanks," he said calmly. "I don't really have anyplace left to put it."

He turned and walked out, and Bella was hard put not to collapse with hysteria. Imagine, Nell actually shouting at anybody! That young lady was definitely getting herself together, and Tyler was going to be in for some hard times if Bella didn't miss her guess.

The cold war had truly begun. Nell sent messages to Tyler by Chappy during roundup and she never went near the holding pens. The most she did was to call Bob Wyler about the helicopter and make arrangements with the transport people to get the calves to the auction barn. Otherwise, she busied herself with the guests, who were enjoying the warm autumn climate and especially the cookouts and trail drives that Nell led herself.

Her confidence was beginning to grow, except where Tyler Jacobs was concerned. She felt like a new woman. She discarded her old wardrobe and bought a new one. This time, she bought jeans that fit and tops that clung. She had her hair trimmed and shaped. She began to wear makeup. And she learned from Margie how to gracefully get out of potentially disturbing situations with male guests without hard feelings. She was beginning to bloom, like a delayed spring flower blossoming before winter.

Margie began spending more and more time at the ranch, and every time Nell looked out, she saw her sister-in-law with Tyler. Darren grew moody and frankly angry, and began cutting at Margie every time he saw her. She cut back. It got to the point that they were avoiding each other like the plague, but Tyler seemed to benefit from that, because Margie spent most all her time with him. He enjoyed it, too, if the expression on his face and in his eyes was anything to go by. The boys had even started teasing them about their preoccupation with each other. But it was a loving kind of teasing, because the boys were crazy about Tyler. Darren had captured at least some of their attention during the frequent visits, though, because they began to seek him out to show them about horses and cattle and tell them stories he'd heard from his grandfather about the old days in the West. That irritated Margie, but she couldn't make them stop following Darren around. And Tyler wouldn't. That, too, was puzzling to Nell.

Meanwhile, Tyler was becoming more and more unapproachable. He glared daggers through Nell when she was looking, and watched her hungrily when she wasn't. Bella knew, but she kept her mouth shut. It wouldn't do to interfere, she reckoned. Things had a way of working out better without meddling from interested bystanders. She'd learned her lesson.

Roundup ended and the calves brought a better than expected price at auction, which pleased Uncle Ted no end. He praised Nell for the way things were going at the ranch and then asked with elaborate carelessness what she thought of his foreman.

Nell made an excuse to get off the phone without answering the question. It was too hard thinking up nice ways to tell her uncle that she thought his foreman would be best barbecued.

She'd no sooner hung up than the phone rang again. She picked it up. The voice on the line was a woman's and unfamiliar.

"Is this Nell Regan?" she was asked hesitantly.

"Yes."

"I'm Shelby Jacobs Ballenger," came the quiet reply. "I was hoping that I might be able to speak to my brother."

Nell sat down. "He's gone into town to pick up some supplies," she said, remembering the fondness Tyler's voice had betrayed when he mentioned his only relative, his sister, Shelby. "But he'll be back within the hour. Can I have him call you?"

"Oh, dear." Shelby sighed. "Justin and I are leaving for Jacobsville in just a few hours. We're just in Tucson on a quick business trip, and I was hoping that we could see him." She laughed self-consciously. "You see, he's been worried about me. Justin and I got off to a rocky start, but things are wonderful now and I wanted him to see us together, so that he'd be sure I was telling him the truth."

"Why don't you come down here," Nell offered impulsively. "We're only about thirty minutes out of Tucson. Have you a car?"

"Yes, Justin rented one for his meeting. It would be all right? You wouldn't mind having two strangers barge in on you?"

"You're not a stranger," Nell said with a smile. "Tyler's talked about you so much that we all feel as if we know you. We'd love for you to come. Bella can make a cake—"

"Oh, please, don't go to any trouble."

"It's no trouble, really. You just come on down." And she proceeded to give Shelby directions. Although God only knew why she should go to so much effort to give Tyler a nice surprise when he'd been simply horrible to her. It must have been a touch too much sun, she decided after she'd hung up.

"Tyler's sister, coming here?" Bella grinned from ear to ear. "I'll go bake a nice chocolate cake. You tidy up the living room."

Nell glowered. "It's already tidy."

"Good. Then lay a tray and make sure the silver's nice and polished."

Nell threw up her hands. "Botheration!"

"It was your idea to have them come down," she was reminded. Bella smiled with sickening superiority. "What a sweet surprise for Tyler. And here I thought you hated him. Slinging scrambled eggs all over him, yelling at him..."

"I'll just see about that silver," Nell murmured, and got out of Bella's sight.

A little more than half an hour later, a rented limousine pulled up at the sidewalk and two people got out. Nell recognized Shelby Jacobs Ballenger almost at once, because she looked so much like her brother. She was lovely, very slender and tall and elegant with her dark hair in a French twist and wearing a green silk dress. She was no surprise, but the tall man with her was. He was very masculine, that was apparent, but he wasn't handsome at all, and he looked as if he didn't smile much. Nell felt immediately intimidated and tried not to show it when she went to the door to greet them.

"You have to be Nell." Shelby smiled. She reached forward and hugged the younger woman warmly. "It's so nice to meet you. I'm Shelby, and this is Justin." She looked up at the tall man, her expression full of love.

He smiled back at her for an instant and then diverted his lancing dark gaze to Nell. "Nice to meet you."

Nell nodded, tongue-tied, she was glad that she'd put on clean jeans and a nice blue-checked blouse and brushed her hair. At least she didn't look scruffy.

She led them into the living room and Bella came in to be introduced, carrying a coffee tray laden with the necessities and a platter of fresh chocolate cake.

"My favorite," Justin murmured, grinning at Bella. "Thank you, but what are they going to eat?" he asked with an innocent glance at the women.

The ice was immediately broken. Nell relaxed visibly and sat down to pour coffee.

"When Tyler comes, waylay him and send him in, but don't tell him why," Nell called to Bella.

"I'll tell him you want to give him some more eggs," Bella said smugly and left the room.

Nell's color intrigued Shelby, who stirred cream into her coffee absently and began to smile. "Eggs?" she probed.

Nell cleared her throat. "We had an, er, slight misunderstanding."

"Eggs?" Justin asked, looking dryly interested.

It was getting more uncomfortable by the second. "I sort of lost my temper and threw my breakfast at him," Nell confessed. She looked at Shelby pleadingly. "Well, he insulted me first."

"Oh, I can believe that." Shelby nodded, smiling. "I'm not going to put all the blame on you."

"How's he fitting in here?" Justin asked as he leaned back against the sofa with his coffee cup in one hand.

"He fits in fine with the men," Nell said restlessly. Justin's dark eyes were piercing, and they didn't seem to miss much.

Shelby was watching her just as closely, and with a faintly amused smile. "You know," she said, "you don't seem anything like Tyler's description of you at my wedding."

Nell cleared her throat. "Am I better or worse?" she asked.

"If you answer that, I'll disown you," came Tyler's deep voice from the doorway.

"Ty!" Shelby got up and ran into his arms, to be swung high and kissed while he smiled in a way Nell had never seen him smile. It made her see what she'd missed, and it made her sad.

"Good to see you again," Justin said, rising to shake hands with Tyler before he drew Shelby close to his side.

That simple gesture told Tyler how things were between the recently married couple. Justin looked at her with open possessiveness, and Shelby stayed as close to him as she could get. Apparently they'd solved their difficulties, because no couple could pretend the kind of explosive emotion that crackled between them like electricity. Tyler relaxed, sure of Shelby's future. That was one load off his mind. He'd been worried about the marriage's rocky start.

"We thought we'd call you before we left Tucson," Shelby explained while they drank coffee and ate chocolate cake. "But Nell invited us down to see you before we fly home to Texas."

"Nice of her, wasn't it?" Justin asked with that smug, lazy smile that made Tyler's neck hair bristle.

"Nice," Tyler said shortly. He didn't look at Nell, who was sitting in an armchair while he shared the sofa with Shelby and Justin.

"Don't strain yourself thanking me," Nell said with venomous politeness. "I'd have done the same thing for anyone."

Tyler's green eyes glittered at her across the coffee table. "I'm sure you would, you tender-hearted little thing."

He said it with deep sarcasm and Nell stiffened. "I used to have a tender heart all right," she told him flatly, "but I wore it out on men."

"That's right," he invited, "put all the blame on us. Men can't put a foot right where you're concerned, can they?"

"They can if they have a woman to lead them," Nell said, and smiled icily.

"Let me tell you, I won't live long enough to let a woman lead me anywhere! Furthermore..." He stopped, clearing his throat gruffly when he noticed the attention he was getting from the visitors. He smiled. "How are things back in Jacobsville?" he asked with pleasant interest.

It was to Justin's credit that he didn't fall on the floor laughing when he tried to answer that. Meanwhile, Shelby smiled into her coffee and exchanged a highly amused glance with her husband. They didn't need a program to see what was going on. It looked very much to Shelby as if Tyler had met his match, and not a minute too soon.

Chapter Eight

Shelby and Justin stayed for another half hour, giving Tyler some interesting news from back home. Justin's brother, Calhoun, and sister-in-law, Abby, had flown to Europe for a belated honeymoon, and a neighbor had bought Geronimo, Tyler's prize stud stallion.

"I'm glad Harrison got him," Tyler murmured, his face faintly bitter because the remark reminded him of all he and Shelby had lost. "He was a good horse."

"He'll be well taken care of," Shelby added. "I'll make sure of it." She smiled at her brother. "Don't brood over it, will you? We can't do anything about the past."

Justin saw storm clouds coming and quickly headed them off. "I hate to cut this short," he said with a glance at his thin gold watch, "but we've got to go, honey."

Shelby clung to Justin's hand as they stood up, releasing it for just a minute while she hugged Tyler and then Nell. "Thanks for letting us come, Nell. Ty, try to write once in a while, or at least call and let us know you're alive."

He smiled at his sister. "I'll do my best. Take good care of her, Justin."

"Oh, that's the easy part," Justin said, and his expression as he smiled at his wife was loving and possessive and very sexy. Justin might look formidable, but Nell had a feeling he shared with Shelby a side of himself that no one else would ever see. That was what marriage should be, Nell thought. Not that she was ever going to have a chance at it.

She walked to the door with Tyler to see Justin and Shelby off. It was already dusk and getting darker by the minute. In the distance, the guest houses were all alight and there was the sound of a guitar and a harmonica playing down at the bunkhouse. Nell wrapped her arms around herself, reluctant to leave Tyler, but too nervous of him to stay.

She turned, only to find his hand sliding down to grasp hers.

"Not yet," he said, and there was a familiar deep note in his voice.

She should have had more willpower, but things had been strained between them for too long already, and the touch of his hand on hers made her weak.

"Come for a walk with me, Nell," he said quietly, and drew her along with him down the path that led to his cabin.

Even as she went along, she knew that she shouldn't go. He was leading up to a confrontation. But the night was perfumed with flowers, and the stars were above them, and silence drew around them like a dark blanket. His hand in hers was warm against the chill of the desert night, and she moved closer, feeling the strength of his body like a shield at her side. She sensed his sadness and bitterness, and all the hostility fell away from her. He needed someone to talk to; that was probably all he wanted. She understood that. She'd never had anyone who she could really talk to, until Darren McAnders had come back and become her friend. But she'd much rather have talked to Tyler. She couldn't do anything to change his past, but she could certainly listen.

He stopped at the corral fence and let go of her hand to light a cigarette while they listened to the night sounds and the silences.

"I like your sister," she said softly.

"So do I. She and I have been close all our lives. All we ever really had was each other when we were growing up. After our mother died, our father became greedy and grasping. He was hell to live with most of the time, and he wasn't above blackmail."

"Have she and Justin known each other a long time?" she asked curiously.

"Years." He took a draw of the cigarette, and his smile was reflected by the orange glow from its tip. "Six years ago they got engaged, but Shelby ended it. I never knew why, although I'm sure my father had a hand in it. Justin wasn't wealthy and Dad had just the right rich man picked out for Shelby. She didn't marry anyone as it turned out. Then when we lost everything, Justin went to see her because she had no one—I'd just come out here to work. And the next thing we knew, they were married. I thought he'd done that for revenge, that he was going to make her life miserable. She didn't seem very happy on their wedding day." He glanced down at her. "But I think they've worked things out. Did you notice the way they look at each other?"

Nell leaned against the fence and kept her face down. "Yes. They seem to be very happy."

"And very lucky. Most people don't get a second chance."

She lifted her eyes. "If that's a dig at me because I've avoided you since the square dance..."

"I was jealous, Nell," he said unexpectedly. He smiled faintly at the stunned expression on her face that was barely visible in the dim light from the house. "Jealous as hell. I'd seen you and McAnders in a clinch, and then you dressed up for him, I thought, when you'd never dressed up for me. I just blew up. I didn't really mean the things I said to you, but you wouldn't listen when I tried to explain."

"Jealous of me?" She laughed bitterly. "That'll be the day. I'm a tomboy, I'm plain, I'm shy—"

"And sadly lacking in self-confidence," he finished for her. "Don't you think that a man could want you for yourself? For the things you are instead of how you look?"

"Nobody ever has," she said shortly. "I'm twenty-four and I'll die an old maid."

"Not you, honey," he said softly. "You're too passionate to live and die alone."

Her face went hot. "Don't throw that up to me," she snapped, her eyes flashing. "I was...I was off balance and you're too experienced for me, that's all."

"Experienced, hell," he said shortly. "There haven't even been that many women, and you weren't off balance—you were starved for a little love."

"Thanks a lot!"

"Will you just shut up and listen?" he demanded. "You never would give me a chance to say anything about what happened, you just slung scrambled eggs at me and stomped off in a fury."

"I was entitled to be angry after what you said to me," she reminded him curtly.

"Oh, hell, maybe you were," he conceded tautly. "But you could have let me explain."

"The explanation was obvious," she replied. "Darren was poaching on what you considered your territory."

He smiled in spite of himself. "You might say that."

"Well, you don't have to worry about Margie," she said after a minute. "I mean, it's obvious that she's crazy about you. And the boys like you...."

"What are you talking about?" he asked pleasantly.

"Nobody could blame you for being attracted to her," she went on. "And I'm sorry if I've made things difficult for you—I didn't mean to. You've lost so much. You should have somebody to care about. Somebody who'll care about you."

"Coals of fire," he murmured, watching her as he smoked his cigarette. "Do you want me to be happy, Nell?"

"I want that very much," she said, her voice soft in the darkness. "I haven't meant to be difficult. It's just..."

"You don't have a scrap of self-confidence, that's just what it is," he said for her. "That's a shame, Nell, because you've got a lot going for you. I wish I knew why you had this hang-up about men."

"I got hurt once," she muttered.

"Most people get hurt once."

"Not like I did." She folded her arms across her breasts. "When I was in my middle teens, I had a terrible crush on one of the cowboys. I plagued him and followed him around and chased him mercilessly. To make a long story short, he was in love with a woman he couldn't have, and

n a drunken stupor he decided to take me up on my of-
er." She laughed bitterly. "Until then, I had no idea that
romance was anything except smiling at each other and
maybe holding hands. It never actually occurred to me that
people in love went to bed together. And what made it so
bad was that physically I didn't feel anything for him. I
guess that's why I panicked and screamed. Bella came and
rescued me and the cowboy left in disgrace."

Tyler had listened intently. The cigarette burned away
between his fingers without his noticing. "It was Mc-
Anders," he guessed with cold certainty.

"Yes. He was in love with Marguerite, but I didn't know
it until he tried to make love to me. I realized that night
what a terrible mistake I'd made." She smiled halfheartedly. "So then I knew that I couldn't trust my instincts or my judgment anymore. I stopped wearing sexy
clothes and I stopped running after anybody."

"One bad egg doesn't make the whole carton spoil," he
said.

"That's true, but how do you find the bad egg in time?"
She shook her head. "I've never had the inclination to try
again."

"Until I came along?"

She flushed. "I told you, I was only trying to make you
feel welcome. You paid me a little attention and it flattered me."

"Where does McAnders fit into this now?" he asked. "I
gather that you were fairly intimate with him before Bella
came to the rescue, but how about today? Did you go from
me to him?"

She shifted restlessly. "No," she said under her breath.

He brightened a little. "Why not?"

She had to remember that he was interested in Margie,
not her. He might feel a little sorry for her, but he didn't

want her for keeps. She straightened. "He still doesn't appeal to me physically."

He wondered if she realized what she was giving away with that remark. If she didn't want McAnders she probably didn't really love him. But he was going to have to make her see that, and it wouldn't be easy.

"I appealed to you physically, once," he said gently, his voice deep and drugging in the still night. He moved closer, his fingers lightly touching her face, her loosened hair. His warmth enveloped her, his breath was like a faint breeze, moving the hair at her temples, making her heart race. "If McAnders hadn't shown up, I might have appealed to you in other ways. We didn't have enough time to get to know each other."

She put her hands slowly, flatly against his shirtfront, hesitating as if she thought he might throw them away. But he caught them gently and pressed them to the soft cotton of his shirt.

"You wouldn't want to, now," she said, and her voice shook. "Margie's here half the time."

"And, of course, you think I'm madly in love with her."

"Aren't you?" she asked stubbornly.

"I'm not going to tell you that," he said. He lifted her chin. "You're going to have to come out of your shell, little one, and start looking around you. You can't learn to swim if you keep balking at the water."

"I don't understand."

"Very simply, Nell, if you want me, you're going to have to believe that I can want you back. You're going to have to believe in yourself a little and start trusting me not to hurt you."

"Trust comes hard," she said, although what he was saying was more tempting than he realized. She did want him, terribly, but she was playing for keeps. Was he?

"It comes hard to most people." He smoothed the hair away from her face. "It depends on whether or not you think it's worth the chance. Love doesn't come with a money-back guarantee. There comes a time when you have to trust your instincts and take a chance."

She shifted restlessly, but he wouldn't let go of her hands. "Why?" she asked abruptly. "You said you wanted me, but at the same time you said you weren't interested in any relationships with women."

"I said a lot, didn't I, honey?" he murmured dryly.

She searched what she could see of his dark face. "I'm not the kind of woman you could care about," she said miserably.

"My whole life has turned upside down, Nell," he told her. "I'm not the same man I used to be. I don't have wealth or position, and about all that's left is my good name and a lot of credit. That makes me pretty vulnerable, in case you've missed it."

"Vulnerable, how?" she asked.

"You might think I was interested in you because you're a woman of property."

"That'll be the day," she murmured dryly. "There's no way I can see you chasing a woman for her money."

His quiet eyes pierced the darkness, looking for her face. "At least you know me that well," he said. "But part of you is afraid of me."

"You want Marguerite," she moaned. "Why bother with me?"

"Margie sends out signals. You could learn to do that, too," he said conversationally. "You could waylay me in the office and kiss me stupid, or buy a new wardrobe to dazzle me with."

She blushed and her heart jumped into her throat. "Fat chance when you made Chappy take back a rope he bought," she reminded him to lighten the tension that was growing between them.

He grinned. "Buy a new dress. I promise not to fuss."

"Margie bought me a new dress and you made me feel dowdy when I wore it," she said.

"Yes, I know." He sighed. "I keep trying to apologize, but you don't hear me."

Her heart was running wild; while he spoke his hands had gone to her hips and pulled them slowly to his. She tried to step back, but he held her there very gently.

"No," he said softly. "You can't run away this time. I won't let you."

"I have to go inside," she said. Panic was rising in her at the intimacy of his hold. It was bringing back dangerously sweet memories.

"Frightened, Nell?" he asked quietly.

"I won't be just another conquest!" she groaned, struggling.

"Stand still, for God's sake." He gasped suddenly, and his powerful body stiffened. "God, Nell, that hurts!"

She stopped instantly. Her color was rising when she felt what he was talking about and realized that she was only complicating things.

"Then you shouldn't hold me like this," she whispered shakily.

He took a steadying breath and his hands contracted on her waist. "We've been a lot closer, though, haven't we?" he asked at her forehead, brushing his lips against her skin. "We've been together without a scrap of fabric between your breasts and my chest, and you pulled my head down and arched up to meet my mouth."

She buried her embarrassed face in his shirt, shaking with remembered pleasure. "I shouldn't have let you," she whispered.

"Then Chappy came to the door and broke the spell," he murmured at her cheek. "I didn't want to answer it. I wanted to go on loving you. But I guess it was a good thing he came along, because things were getting out of hand, weren't they? We wanted each other so much, Nell. I don't really know that we could have stopped in time."

He was right. That didn't make her guilt any easier to bear. "And that would have been a disaster, wouldn't it?" she asked, waiting stiffly for his answer.

"I'm an old-fashioned man, honey," he said finally. His hands smoothed down her back, holding her against him. "I wouldn't ask you to sleep with me, knowing that you're a virgin. You aren't that kind of woman."

She bit her lower lip hard. "I've got all these hang-ups..."

"Most of which we removed that day in my bed," he reminded her. "But your biggest hang-up, little Nell, is your mental block about your attractions. You're the only person around here who doesn't see what a dish you are."

"Me?" she asked breathlessly.

"You." He bent to her mouth and brushed it with his. "You've got a warm heart," he whispered, bending again. The kiss lingered this time, just a second longer. "You're caring." He kissed her again, and this time he parted her lips briefly before he raised his head. "You're intelligent." His mouth teased, brushing hers open breath by breath. "And you're the sexiest woman I've ever made love to..."

He whispered the words into her trembling lips before he took them, and this time he didn't draw back. His tongue began to penetrate her mouth in slow, exquisite thrusts. This was a kind of kiss Nell hadn't experienced before, not even that day in Tyler's cabin, and she was afraid of it.

She tried to draw back, but his lean hand at her nape held her mouth under his.

"Don't fight it," he whispered coaxingly. "I won't hurt you. Relax, Nell. Let me have your mouth. I'll treat it just as tenderly as I'd treat your body if you gave yourself to me, little one," he breathed, and his mouth whispered down onto hers.

The words in addition to the expert teasing of his tongue shook away every last bit of her reserve. She melted into the length of him, trembling with the fierce hunger he was arousing in her body. She moaned helplessly and felt his mouth smile against hers. Then he deepened the pressure and the slow thrust of his tongue into the sweet, soft darkness of her mouth.

But what about Margie? she wanted to ask. How can you hold me like this when you want her? She couldn't have asked him that to save her life, because he was working magic on her body. She wanted him. Tomorrow she could hate herself and him for leading her on, for toying with her. But tonight she wanted nothing except the sweet pleasure of his mouth and his hands and a few memories to carry through the long years ahead.

She felt his hands at the back of her thighs, pulling her shaking legs closer so that her hips were grinding into his, so that she knew how aroused he was. She didn't protest. Her hands found their way around him, to his back and down, returning the pressure shyly even as the first shudder of desire ripped through her and dragged a cry from her lips.

He lifted his head abruptly. His eyes glittered and he was trembling a little; his heartbeat was rough against her breasts. "Come home with me. I'll sit with you in that big leather armchair by the fireplace, and we'll love each other for a few minutes."

She was crying with reaction. "It's so dangerous," she pleaded, but it was no protest at all, and he had to know it.

"I've got to, Nell," he whispered, bending to lift her so gently into his arms. He turned, carrying her the rest of the way to his porch in the darkness. "I've got to, sweetheart."

Her arms went around his neck, and she buried her face in his warm, pulsating throat. "I can't...I can't sleep with you," she whispered.

"I'd never ask that of you," he breathed ardently. He caught her mouth hungrily with his while he fumbled the door open with one hand and carried her into the dark stillness of his cabin.

He kicked the door shut and moved to the big armchair, dropping into it with his mouth still hard and sure on her lips.

There was no more pretense left. He was hungry and he wasn't trying to hide it. He fought the buttons of her blouse out of his way and deftly removed it and the lacy covering beneath. His mouth found her warm breasts, and he nuzzled them hungrily, nibbling, kissing, tasting while she shuddered and arched her back to help him.

"So sweet, Nell," he groaned as his lips moved on her. "Oh, God, you taste like honey in my mouth."

Her hands touched his cool dark hair, savoring its clean thickness while she fed on the aching sweetness of his mouth. "Oh, please!" she moaned brokenly when he lifted his head to breathe. "Tyler, please...!"

He held her quietly while he tore open the snaps of his own shirt and dragged her inside it, pressing her breasts against the hair-covered warmth of his chest, moving her sensually from side to side so that her breathing became as rough and torturous as his own.

His mouth ground into hers then, rough with need, his restraint gone, his control broken by the sounds she was making against his lips, by the helpless movement of her body against him, silky and bare and terribly arousing.

His lean hands caressed her soft, bare back, holding her to him so that he could feel the hard tips of her breasts like tiny brands on his skin.

"Nell," he groaned. His mouth slid away from hers and into her throat, pressing hard against the wildly throbbing artery as he drew her up close and held her, rocked her, until the trembling need began to drain out of her.

"I ache all over," she whispered with tears in her voice. She clung closer. "Tyler, this is scary!"

"This is desire," he breathed at her ear, and his arms contracted. "This is the raw need to mate. Don't be afraid of it. I'm not going to take advantage of something you can't help. I want you just as much as you want me."

She shuddered helplessly. "It must be...so much worse for you," she whispered.

"A sweet ache," he confessed huskily, and his mouth brushed her cheek, her throat. "I don't have a single regret. Do you?"

"I shouldn't admit it."

He chuckled, delighted with her headlong response to him, with her helpless hunger. "Neither should I. But wasn't it good, Nell? Wasn't it delicious?"

"Oh, yes." She sighed, nestling closer with a tiny sound deep in her throat. "I want to stay with you all night."

"I want that, too, but we can't."

"I could just sleep with you," she murmured drowsily.

"Sure you could. Platonically. And nothing would happen." He turned up her face and kissed her mouth hard. "You know as well as I do that we'd devour each other if we got into a bed together. We're half-crazy to be together already, and I've barely touched you."

She pulled back a little. "You call that barely touching?" she asked, awed.

"Compared to what I'd do to you in bed, yes."

She hesitated, but he read the thought in her mind and chuckled helplessly.

"Shall I tell you?" he whispered softly.

"You wouldn't dare."

But he would. And he did, sensuously, whispering it into her ear while he touched her, lightly caressed her, brought every nerve in her body to singing, agonizing pleasure.

"I never dreamed...!" she gasped, hiding her face in his chest when he finished.

"You needed to know," he said gently. "You're still very innocent, despite what happened in your teens. I want you to understand that what you and I would share wouldn't be painful or frightening. Physical love is an expression of what two people feel for each other so strongly that words aren't enough to contain it. It isn't anything to dread."

"Certainly not with you it wouldn't be," she said tenderly. She touched his hard face, loving its strength, its masculine beauty. "Tyler...I could love you," she whispered hesitantly.

"Could you, honey?" He bent, brushing his mouth with exquisite softness against her lips. "If you want me, Nell, come after me."

"That isn't fair," she began.

"It's fair," he said. "For your own peace of mind, you need to regain the confidence you lost because of what happened with McAnders. Oh, I could back you into a corner and force you into a decision, but that would rob you of your right to choose. I won't do it for you. You have to do it, alone.''

Her worried eyes studied his profile. "You said you didn't want a lasting relationship...." she said again.

He turned his head and looked down at her in the dimness of the unlit room. "Make me want one," he challenged. "Vamp me. Buy some sexy dresses and drive me crazy. Be the woman you can be. The woman you should have been.''

"I'm not attractive," she argued faintly.

His hand swept slowly, lovingly, over her breasts. "You're beautiful, Nell," he said huskily. "Firm and soft and silky to touch.''

"Tyler..."

"Come here," he groaned. He stood up with her in his arms and let her slide down his body, bent to kiss her hungrily before his hand shot out and fumbled with a light switch.

"No!" she protested, but it was too late. The soft light flooded the living room, and Tyler caught her hands before she could cover herself. He gazed down at her with an intent masculine appreciation of her attributes, which brought a wave of color up her neck and into her face. His chest rose and fell heavily, and his expression showed that he was having a monumental battle with his conscience to do nothing more than look.

"I'll live on this for a while," he breathed, lifting his eyes to hers.

Her lips parted as she stared back at him, all too aware of the tense swelling of her breasts, of their hard arousal, which he could see as well as feel.

"It embarrasses you, doesn't it?" he asked softly, searching her eyes. "I can see how lovely you are, how aroused I've made you. It's like letting me see you totally nude, isn't it? But you've seen me that way already, Nell. Remember?''

She lowered her eyes to his bare chest. "I couldn't forget if I tried. I thought you were perfect," she whispered shyly.

"I feel just that way about you. I love the way you look without your blouse. I'd give everything I have to carry you into my bedroom and love you in my bed. But as things stand, that's a decision I can't make." He let go of her hands and gazed at her one last time before he forced himself to turn his back and light a cigarette. "You'd better dress, sweetheart. I want you desperately right now, and I'm not quite as controlled as I thought I was."

She stared at his back for an instant, thinking of pressing herself against him. But she knew what would happen, and it would be her fault. She sighed softly and went to find her blouse and bra.

He got into his shirt and buttoned it and smoked half his cigarette before he turned around again. His eyes were dark with frustrated hunger as he looked at her. "We can't do much of that," he said with a tender smile. "It gets worse every time."

"Yes." She smiled back. "Oh, I want you so," she whispered helplessly.

"I want you, too." He held out his hand, and she put hers into it without hesitation. "I'd better walk you home."

"All right."

He went with her up the path in the darkness. He didn't speak and neither did she, but she clung to his hand and felt as if they'd become lovers in every sense of the word. There would never be, could never be, anyone after him.

She felt that with a sense of faint despair, because she still didn't know where she stood with him.

He stopped at the front steps and turned her. His face was clearly visible in the light pouring out the window from the front room.

"No more pretense, Nell," he said softly. "If you want me, show me."

"But men don't like being chased," she whispered.

"Try it and see," he challenged with narrowed eyes. "You've got to believe in yourself before other people will."

"You won't mind?" she asked. "You're sure?"

He bent and put his mouth warmly against hers in a brief kiss. "I won't mind."

"But what about Margie?" she groaned.

"You'll find out about that all by yourself when you start putting your life back in order," he said simply. "It's right under your nose, but you just can't see it."

"Tell me," she whispered.

"No. You work it out. Good night, Nell."

Impulsively she moved closer and lifted her mouth. "Would you . . . kiss me again?" she whispered.

He did, half lifting her against him, and so thoroughly and hungrily that when he let her down again, she gasped.

"I like that," he said roughly. "You might try it again from time to time. Sleep well."

"You, too." She watched him turn and walk back the way they'd come, lighting a cigarette on the way. His stride was moody and thoughtful, but as she turned to go in, she heard him whistling a light, cheerful tune in the darkness. She smiled, because it was a popular love song. She knew that she might be reading too much into what they'd done, but her heart was on fire for him. Maybe he didn't really care that much about Margie. Maybe she could worm her way into his affection if she tried. But it was going to take some hard thinking before she risked her heart again. She needed time.

Chapter Nine

Nell worried all night about Margie and Tyler and what she was going to do. Her own insecurities haunted her.

She went downstairs, her thoughts murky and still without concrete answers. She half expected Tyler to be there again, waiting for her, but he wasn't.

Bella bustled in with breakfast and sat down beside Nell. "Too early for the new arrivals to be up and hungry, so you and I can have ours in peace," she said, pouring two cups of coffee. "Tyler's having his in the bunkhouse."

"That's nothing unusual, is it?" Nell sighed. "He always seems to be eating down there lately."

"I don't think he's felt very welcome here in recent days," Bella told her bluntly. "Pity, because he sure is a nice fella and you could do worse."

"It isn't me he wants," Nell said curtly, glaring at the older woman as she helped herself to a fresh biscuit and buttered it. "It's Margie."

Bella sipped her coffee. "Did he tell you that?"

"No. But he didn't deny it, either."

The older woman spooned scrambled eggs onto her plate and reached for bacon. "Nell, I steered you wrong when Tyler came here. I should have encouraged you to dress up and act like a young lady. I should have realized what kind of man he was. But I didn't, and I've helped complicate things. I'm sorry."

"You didn't do anything," Nell said. She glowered at her eggs. "I'm not the kind of woman a man like Tyler needs. I'm just a country tomboy. I don't even know how to dance."

"Stop running yourself down," Bella said gruffly. "Listen, child, just because Darren McAnders couldn't see past Margie to you is no reason for you to bury yourself in baggy britches forever. You're young and pretty, and if you tried, you could be everything Tyler needs. Don't forget, he isn't a rich man anymore. He doesn't need a social butterfly, he needs a woman who can help him build a new legacy for his children."

"Margie can work," Nell said halfheartedly.

"Oh, sure, like she does when she's here?" Bella scoffed. "Fat chance. Tyler would be out of his mind after the first week and you know it. She'd never cook supper—she'd be too busy trying on dresses in town or gossiping on the telephone."

"She's pretty and flamboyant."

"A sensible man doesn't want a wall decoration, he wants a flesh-and-blood woman."

"I guess I'm flesh and blood," Nell agreed.

"And a hard worker, a good little cook, and a companion who listens more than she talks. You're a jewel," Bella concluded. "You should think positively. At least you've made a start. You're wearing clothes that really fit, and you've put away that horrible slouchy hat and let your hair down. You look like a different Nell.''

"I decided that you and Margie were right about what happened with Darren," she conceded. "I overreacted because I didn't know what a man was like when he was hungry for a woman. Well, not then, at least."

Bella's eyes widened. "And now you do?" she asked with a slow, wicked smile.

Nell felt the flush working its way up her neck. She reached blindly for her coffee and turned it over onto the tablecloth and herself.

"Oh, my, what little fumble fingers." Bella chuckled.

"I meant to do that," Nell protested as she got to her feet, brushing at a tiny spot on her blue-checked Western shirt and her new jeans. She glared at Bella. "I just hate coffee. And I don't fumble!" she added.

Then she turned around and tripped over the chair and fell flat on her face.

Bella doubled over laughing while Nell, bruised and furious, disentangled herself from the chair. She was turning the air blue when she saw a pair of boots come into view past her nose.

"She don't fumble," Bella explained to the boots, and walked off into the kitchen.

Nell scrambled to her feet, assisted by a familiar lean strong hand.

"Having trouble?" Tyler asked pleasantly.

She did fumble then, nervous with him and still uncertain of her ground. She looked up into his dark face, wondering at the secret pleasure it gave her just to stare at him.

"I was looking for a contact lens," Nell said, flustered.

"You don't wear contact lenses," he pointed out.

She cleared her throat. "That doesn't mean that I can't look for one if I want to."

He smiled slowly. "Whatever turns you on," he said dryly.

She brushed back her unruly hair. "What can I do for you?" she asked abruptly.

"You can come on the camp out trail ride with me this afternoon," he said. "Chappy's tied up with those new mares, so I told him we'd take the greenhorns out today."

She colored. "You and not Darren?"

He pursed his lips. "That's right. Is that a problem?" he added quietly.

She was still feeling her way, but telling the truth might be a good start, she decided. "No, it's not a problem," she said. "Darren has been a good friend. But I'd rather be with you."

He smiled slowly because her face flamed when she said it, and her shyness made her even more delectable to him. She was a pretty woman when she didn't dress like a baggy orphan.

"I'd rather be with you, too, sunshine," he said softly.

Her heart soared. Heaven must be this sweet, she thought dazedly. She smiled at him, her dark eyes like brown velvet.

Bella came through the door and broke the spell. Nell excused herself as the housekeeper giggled wickedly, and went out into the hall to get her hat. She did her usual chores, feeling as if she were walking on air, and the day was all too long until it was time to pack the bedrolls and the cooking utensils and the food that Bella had provided and head out for an overnight camp out. The Double R Ranch was one of the few left that did it for real, complete with bedrolls and rough accommodations and no luxuries. Only a few hardy souls were willing to rough it the way the old-time cowboys had.

There were six people in the party, three couples. Four of that number were good riders already, and they weren't afraid of snakes or coyotes or rolling into the camp fire in their sleep. It was a beautiful day, with the ragged mountains ringing around the flat grassy plain, and Nell felt on top of the world as she rode along at the head of the group with Tyler at her side. She kept looking back to make sure she wasn't losing any of their small parade.

"They're doing fine," Tyler told her as he lit a cigarette with steady hands. "Don't worry so much."

"Two of them have never even seen a real horse before," she reminded him.

"The Callaways?" He grinned, referring to a newly married, middle-aged couple who were, to put it politely, well fed. "No, but you've taught them how to stay on, at least, and they're getting the hang of it. Just relax."

She tried, but being a mother hen had become a habit, and she had a bad feeling about doing this camp out without Chappy and the chuck wagon that usually came along with a bigger crowd.

And sure enough, things did begin to go wrong suddenly. They rode for an hour and then turned back toward the ranch house and stopped about a mile out to make camp just before dark.

Mrs. Callaway, a pleasant cheerful little blond lady, came down off her horse too suddenly and caught her blouse on the pommel. There she hung, two inches above the desert floor, while the horse shook his head and pranced restlessly.

Tyler leaped forward to lift Mrs. Callaway while Nell soothed the horse and extricated the blouse.

"Are you all right, Mrs. Callaway?" Nell asked anxiously when the red-faced little woman had stopped shaking in her concerned husband's arms.

"Oh, I'm fine," she said with a grin. "What a story to tell the folks back home!"

Nell relaxed, but Mrs. Callaway's experience was only the beginning. Her husband went to help Tyler and the other men gather brush to make a fire and unearthed a long, fat, very unsocial rattlesnake.

He let out a war whoop, which startled Mrs. Donnegan, who backed into a cactus and let out a war whoop of her own. By the time the rattlesnake was disposed of by Tyler, and Mrs. Donnegan had her cactus spines removed by Nell, everybody was ready to eat. Tyler had a roaring fire going and had passed out wieners and buns and marshmallows and sticks for the guests while he brewed up a pot of black coffee.

"I really hate coffee," Mrs. Harris remarked. She was the only sour note in the bunch, a city woman who'd come to the desert only because her husband had coaxed her into it. She hated the desert, the cactus, the heat, the isolation—she hated everything, in fact. "I'd rather have a soft drink."

"No problem," her husband said. "We'll ride down to the ranch and get one."

"On that horse?" Mrs. Harris wailed, her black eyes going even blacker. "I hurt in places I didn't even know I had!"

"Then you can drink coffee, can't you, sweetheart?" her husband continued.

She pouted, but she shut up. The Callaways sat close together, sharing condiments for the hot dogs while they munched on potato chips and carried on a casual conversation with the other guests on a variety of newsy subjects.

Nell enjoyed the quiet wonder of night on the desert as she never had, especially when Tyler started telling their guests about the surrounding territory and something of its history. She hadn't realized how much he knew about southeastern Arizona, and some of it she hadn't even known herself.

He talked about places like Cochise Stronghold, where the famous Apache chief was buried. There was a marker there, he added, telling that Indian Agent Tom Jeffords, a friend of Cochise, was the only white man privileged to know the exact spot of the chief's burial. The Apaches had run their horses over the ground and dragged it with brush behind them to conceal forever the place where Cochise rested.

There was also the famous Copper Queen Hotel in Bisbee, a landmark from old copper mining days in the Lavender Pit, where guests drank French champagne and were entertained by famous singers.

Farther south was Douglas, where Agua Prieta lay just over the border in Mexico. Pancho Villa had raided the border town, and a hotel in Douglas bore the marks of his horse on its marble staircase, which could still be seen today.

"You know a lot about this part of the state, Mr. Jacobs," Mr. Callaway remarked. "Do you come from around here?"

"No. I'm from south Texas." He smiled. "Near Victoria. My people founded a little place called Jacobsville, where I was raised."

"I love Texas," Mrs. Callaway said, sighing. "I guess you have cactus and mesquite and sagebrush...."

"Actually, it's more like magnolias, live oaks and dog-wood trees," Tyler mused. "West Texas has those plants you're thinking about."

She blushed. "Sorry."

He laughed out loud. "Don't feel bad, a lot of people don't realize just how many different geographic sections there are in Texas. We've got everything from beach to desert to mountain country and plains. Texas had the op-tion of becoming five separate states if it wanted to. But nobody ever did."

"I can see why," Mrs. Callaway said. "I've heard that you can drive from sunup to sunset and never leave Texas."

"That's very nearly true," he agreed.

"I suppose you'll go back there one day?" the small woman asked.

Tyler looked at Nell, his eyes narrow, thoughtful as they caressed hers until she caught her breath. "Maybe. Maybe not," he added softly, and smiled at Nell.

She felt lighter than air all over again, invincible. She laughed delightedly. "Anybody want more marshmal-lows?"

They roasted marshmallows until nobody could stuff another one into his mouth, and then they laid out the bedrolls and settled down for the night, while the orange flames of the camp fire drifted lazily back and forth in the faint wind. It was cold on the desert at night. The guests had been told that and were prepared.

Nell moved her sleeping bag close to Tyler's, to his se-cret delight, and with a shy glance at him as he rested with his saddle for a pillow, she settled down beside him.

"Comfortable?" he asked, his voice deep and soft in the firelit darkness as he turned on his side to watch her.

"Yes." She gave in to the need to look at him, to memorize the lines and curves of his face, his body. She felt a kind of possessiveness toward him that she didn't really understand. "Do you miss Texas, Tyler?" she asked hesitantly.

"I got pretty homesick at first," he conceded. "But there's something about this desert that gets into your blood. It's full of history, but the cities are forward-looking, as well, and there are plenty of conservationists around who care about the land and water resources. Yes, I miss Texas. But I could live here, Nell," he said, smiling at her.

She wanted so badly to ask him if it was just because he liked the land, but she couldn't get the words to form properly. She blurted out, "With Margie?"

His eyebrows lifted. "Did I say with Margie?"

"No, but..."

He reached out a lean hand and touched her fingers where they lay cold and trembling on her stomach. His covered them, warmed them and made her tingle from head to toe. "I told you, Nell, you're going to have to figure it out for yourself. I won't tell you how I feel about Margie, or how I feel about you, for that matter."

"Why?" she asked more plaintively than she knew.

"Because I want you to understand a little more about trust than you do, honey," he replied. "There's a part of you that draws back and shies away from me. Until you get it worked out, I'm not going to influence you one way or the other."

She sighed. "I guess maybe I'll work it out, then."

"Want to come closer?" he coaxed with a warm smile. "You're pretty safe, considering how we're surrounded by curious eyes."

She yielded to the temptation to be close. Inching her way, she moved her sleeping bag right up against his and turned on her side to rest beside him, with her head pillowed on one of his hard arms.

"That's better," he said softly. He eased forward a fraction of an inch and brushed her warm lips gently with his, savoring their faint trembling, their helpless response. "You might keep something in mind," he whispered.

"Oh? What?" she breathed against his lips, and her eyes opened straight into his.

"You aren't wearing makeup or a fancy dress," he whispered quietly. "And I'm not drawing back because you don't appeal to me the way you are."

Her fingers touched his face, loving its strength. "I'm not pretty," she said.

"You are to me," he said. "That's all that matters in the long run, if you'd open your eyes and see what's right under your nose."

"I see you," she said, her voice achingly tender as she adored him with her eyes.

"That's what I mean," he replied. He drew her closer. The saddle protected their faces from prying eyes, and he bent slowly to press his mouth hard against hers. "I want you, Nell," he said into her parted lips as he bit at them.

She wanted him, too. Her body was already on fire, and all he was doing was kissing her. She nibbled helplessly at his teasing mouth, and her hand smoothed into his thick hair, trying to draw him down.

"No," he breathed. "You can't have my mouth that way, not tonight. I can't lose my head with you, honey. There are too many witnesses."

"What if we were alone?" she moaned under her breath. She slid her arms around his neck to press her breasts against his hard chest.

"Nell...damn it." He shuddered. He lifted his tormented eyes to the camp fire. It was dying down and he needed to get up and put some fresh wood on it. The other campers were in their sleeping bags and turned toward the fire in a semicircle, which he and Nell were behind. No one could see them. He realized that now, and his powerful body trembled with the need to ease Nell onto her back and slide his leg between both of hers and show her how much he wanted her. He could feel her skin against his, the silken warmth of her breasts hard tipped under his broad chest, the cries that he could tease out of her throat while he seduced her body slowly and tenderly and penetrated its virginal purity....

He groaned. His fingers on her arms hurt, but she didn't mind. Something powerful and mysterious was working in him, and she was too hungry to be afraid of it. This was Tyler, and she loved him with all her heart. She wanted memories, all that she could get, to press to her mind in the years that would follow.

"What is it?" she asked.

He looked down at her. In the dim light he could see her soft eyes, he could feel her quickened breathing. His hand moved with quiet possession over her blouse and smoothed around her breast until he found the hard tip. He watched her bite her lip and jerk toward him, trying not to cry out lest someone heard her.

"This is not sane," he whispered as the arm under her nape contracted with desire. "Of all the stupid places to make love...."

"Touch me," she whispered brokenly.

His breath was audible as the words shattered his control and made him vulnerable. "Oh, Nell, you can't imagine what I'm thinking." He laughed huskily as his hand
slid to the buttons of her blouse and began to lazily unfas-
ten them. "You can't imagine what I want to do to you."

"Yes, I can," she whispered back, "because you told
me, remember?" Her eyes met his searchingly. "You told
me every single detail."

His powerful body trembled as he reached the last button. "Yes. And I dreamed it that night. Dreamed that I
took you under me and felt your body like a field of flowers absorbing me so tenderly." He was whispering, but the
tone of his voice drugged her. His fingers slid under the
fabric and stopped with delighted surprise when he found
nothing except soft warm skin.

Her lips parted. "I've never done this before," she
whispered unsteadily. "Gone without...without what I
usually wear, I mean."

He could have jumped over the moon. His fingers
delved farther under the soft fabric and found a hard tip
that brought a pleasured gasp from her lips when he
touched it. "Lie still, honey," he whispered, his voice as
unsteady as her own as he peeled away the cotton. "And
for God's sake, don't cry out when I put my mouth on
you...."

She had to bite her lower lip almost until it bled to manage that, because his lips were hungry and demanding.
When he took her inside the warm darkness of his mouth,
she felt tears well up from her closed eyes because it was
like a tiny fulfillment in itself. She writhed helplessly, her
nails biting him, her mouth as hungry as his, while the stars
boiled down around them in white-hot flame.

He drew back first, and suddenly fastened her blouse with trembling hands before he rolled away from her and got to his feet.

She lay there, on fire for him, her eyes watching him as he moved near the camp fire. Her body trembled with a need she'd never felt before. She wanted him, she wanted him!

His back was arrow straight as he began to build up the fire. He stood there for a while, and by the time he came back to his bedroll, her heart was beating normally again and she could feel the tension easing out of her body. But when he climbed into his sleeping bag, the tension came back all over again.

"Tyler," she whispered achingly.

"It passes," he whispered back. "I'm sorry, little one. I didn't mean to take you that far. It's impossible, in more ways than one."

She felt for his lean hand and curled her fingers into it trustingly. "I know. But it was sweet, all the same. I love it when you touch me like that. I'm not even embarrassed to tell you so."

His fingers contracted. "Then I don't mind telling you that I almost couldn't pull back." His head turned and his eyes searched hers in the blazing orange reflection of the fire beyond them. "One day I won't be able to stop. What then?"

Her lips parted. "I don't know."

"You'd better start thinking about it," he said bluntly. "Because things are getting totally out of hand. Either we part company or risk the consequences."

She lowered her worried eyes to the steady rise and fall of his chest. "I... don't want to lose you," she said, burying her pride.

He brought her hand to his mouth. "That would be harder than you realize. Do you still want me, or is it easing off?"

She flushed. "It's easing off," she whispered back.

"At least now you understand why I get short-tempered from time to time, don't you?" he mused.

"Yes." She nuzzled her face against his arm. "What are we going to do?"

"What are *you* going to do?" he said, rephrasing the question. "The ball's in your court, honey. Make your move."

"But what do you want?"

"You."

"Just my body?" she asked softly.

"All of you."

She took a slow breath. "For how long?" she asked bravely.

"I told you, Nell. Love doesn't come with a money-back guarantee—if you do love me. What you feel might be infatuation, or just your first sensual experience making you vulnerable to me."

She searched his face, trying to see if he really believed that. "Is that what you think?"

"Not really. Why don't you tell me what you feel?"

She hesitated, and despite what she did feel, she couldn't lower her pride enough to tell him. She moved her fingers closer into his, feeling his own part and accept them in a warm, strong clasp.

"That reserve is the biggest part of our problem," he murmured. "You won't give in because you don't think I want you."

"I know you want me," she corrected.

"But not how badly, or in what way," he returned. "You're still locked up in the past, afraid of being hurt again."

"I know you wouldn't hurt me," she said unexpectedly, and her eyes were eloquent. "I never knew that a man could be so gentle."

He brought her fingers to his mouth. "That seems to come naturally with you," he said softly. "I've never felt as tender with a woman until now."

She moved her head on his arm. "Tyler, is it just physical with you?"

"If it was," he replied with a dry smile, "would I give a damn about your old-fashioned ideas on chastity? Would I even try to pull back?"

She felt her cheeks burn, and then she laughed self-consciously. "No. Of course not."

"Take it from there and think about it. Now we'd better get some sleep. We've already talked and...other things...for more than an hour."

"It didn't seem that long," she said shyly.

"For me, either, Nell." He let their clasped hands relax between them and closed his eyes. "After tonight," he murmured drowsily, "you'll never be able to deny that we've slept together."

"No, I won't." She curled a little closer and closed her own eyes. Her last thought before she fell asleep was that she'd never felt more secure or happy in all of her life.

She woke at dawn to the delicious smell of percolating coffee and bacon and eggs being fried. Tyler was already hard at work on breakfast, with a little good-intentioned help from a couple of the guests. Everyone ate quietly, enjoying the silence of the desert at dawn and the incredible colors of the sky on the horizon.

"I've never seen anything so beautiful," Mrs. Callaway said with a sigh, nestling close to her husband.

"A living art gallery," Tyler agreed, smiling at Nell. "With a new canvas every minute of the day. It certainly is beautiful." *Like you,* his eyes were telling Nell, wooing her.

She sighed, her heart in her eyes, in her smile, in her rapt attention. His gaze locked with hers while he smoked his cigarette, and the exchange lasted long enough to make her blood run wildly through her veins and her knees get weak.

They rode back to the ranch a few minutes later, and Nell helped Tyler get the horses unsaddled, unbridled and put back in their stalls.

"I've never enjoyed anything more," Nell told him honestly, and laughed uninhibitedly. "It was wonderful."

"I thought so myself," he murmured. He leaned against a closed stall, and his green eyes glittered over her. "Come here," he challenged from deep in his throat.

Her heart raced. She didn't hesitate. She went straight to him and deliberately let her hips melt into his, her legs rest against the powerful strength of his own.

She raised her face for his kiss, blatantly inviting, without fear or inhibitions or reservations.

"Now I want an answer," he said solemnly. "I want to know what you feel for me. I want to know where I stand. You're going to have to trust me enough to tell me."

"That isn't quite fair," she argued. "I have to lower my pride, and you won't lower yours."

"I'm not the one with all the hang-ups," he reminded her. "Any good relationship has to be built on absolute trust to be successful."

"Yes, I know. But..." She avoided his gaze.

He tilted her face up to his. "Take a chance, Nell."

She took a deep breath, gathered her courage and started to speak. And just as she opened her mouth, a familiar voice called, "Tyler, darling, there you are! The boys and I arrived yesterday evening, and we're going to spend the week—isn't that nice?"

Nell moved away from Tyler as Margie came laughing into the stable and threw her arms around him. "Oh, you darling man, how have I managed to live all these years without you? Nell, isn't he wonderful? I'm so happy! Tyler, have you told her our news?" she prompted, her face radiant.

"No, he hasn't," Nell said, turning away. "But he doesn't need to, now. I can guess. See you later. I need a bath and a change of clothing."

"Nell," Tyler called after her, but she wasn't listening. She kept going into the house, with her dreams around her ears. Only a blind fool wouldn't know what Margie had hinted at. She and Tyler had something going, it was just plain obvious. And how could he have touched Nell so hungrily only last night, knowing that Margie was going to be here, waiting for him? Nell could have thrown things. Once again she'd been taken in by her own stupid, trusting nature. Well, this was the last straw. She was going to call Uncle Ted and tell him he could keep the ranch forever—she was going to leave and find something else to do. And as far away from Arizona and Tyler Jacobs as she could get!

Chapter Ten

"What do you look so unhappy for?" Bella asked Nell. "Didn't you enjoy the camp out?"

"It was all right," Nell said with deliberate carelessness. She didn't want to remember what she and Tyler had done together. Margie had spoiled everything. Whatever Tyler had been going to say would never be said, and it looked as though Margie had pulled out all the stops and was going after him headlong.

"Hand me that mixer." Bella nodded toward the appliance she was going to use on a cake mix. "That Mrs. Norman was back in here again complaining about the menu. She's another Mrs. Harris, but at least Mr. Harris is here. Mrs. Norman doesn't like the way I cook. And besides all that, she thinks the entertainment stinks and there's nothing to do but ride horses."

Nell's eyes bulged. "Did you tell her that this is a dude ranch? People come here to ride horses?"

"I told her that and plenty more." Bella looked at the younger woman sheepishly. "She's packing to leave. She says she's going to tell the whole world what a miserable operation we've got here. Oh, and we don't even have a tennis pro," she added.

"Tyler fired him, along with the golf pro," Nell reminded her. "He said they weren't paying their way."

"You mad at me?" Bella asked.

Nell put her arms around the older woman. "I love you. If people say cruel things about your cooking, they deserve to be sent packing. I think you're terrific."

Bella smiled and hugged her back. "That goes double for me. But I'll apologize all the same, if you want me to."

"No. Mrs. Norman may leave, with my blessing. In fact," she said, moving toward the door, "I'll even refund her money."

"Tyler won't like that," Bella called after her.

"Tyler can eat worms and die," Nell muttered.

"So that's it," Bella said to herself, and giggled once Nell was out of earshot.

Mrs. Norman had finished packing. She had her full-length mink coat wrapped around her thin body and her black eyes were flashing. "I am leaving," she told Nell, who was waiting outside the apartment when the older woman came out with her nose haughtily in the air. "You may have someone bring my luggage and call me a cab."

"With pleasure," Nell said, and even smiled. "If you'll stop by the office, I'll gladly refund your money."

Mrs. Norman eyed her suspiciously. "Why?"

"You don't like it here," Nell said. "There's no reason you should pay to be made miserable. The cooking is terrible, there's nothing to do..."

Mrs. Norman actually squirmed and pulled the mink coat closer, despite the fact that it was ninety degrees outside and she was already sweating. "That won't be necessary," she said. "Money is the least of my problems." She averted her eyes, then suddenly blurted out, "I'm allergic to horses and the dust is choking me. All my husband's friends go to dude ranches, and he sent me here because he didn't want to take me to Europe with him." She lifted her chin proudly, even though it trembled. "It's just that...that this room...is so empty," she finished, choking the words out. "I'm so alone."

She broke down into tears and Nell did what came naturally. She took the weeping woman in her arms and just stood holding her and rocking her and murmuring soft words of reassurance.

"There's nothing wrong with the food," Mrs. Norman said with a hiccup. Mascara ran like black tears from her huge, hurting eyes. "It's delicious. And the people are nice, too, but they're all couples. My husband only married me as a business proposition—he doesn't even like me. He never tried to make our marriage anything else."

"You might consider that men don't read minds," Nell told her gently, and even as she said it she smiled inwardly at the irony of telling this sophisticated woman anything about men, when her own love life was so confusing and unfamiliar. "Your husband might think you didn't want to go with him."

Mrs. Norman pulled away self-consciously and dried her eyes with a pure white linen handkerchief. Then she smiled a little shakily. "I'm sorry, I never go to pieces like this." She blew her nose. "Actually, he asked me if I wanted to go, and I laughed at him. He's not a handsome man, but I...I do love him." She glanced at Nell. "Can I make a long-distance call to Europe and have it charged to my account?"

"Of course you can!" Nell smiled. "He might even decide to come back home."

Mrs. Norman smiled back, suddenly looking ten years younger. "I'll do it right now." She took off the mink coat. "That's my security blanket," she added ruefully, draping it over one arm. "I hate the damned thing, it makes me sneeze, and it's too hot to wear it anywhere except during blizzards in Alaska. I'll just make that phone call." She went inside the apartment, and before she closed the door she turned to look at Nell. "Thank you," she said sincerely.

Nell couldn't get over what had just happened. She felt on top of the world; she'd just learned a valuable lesson about human nature, and she might have helped save a marriage.

It wasn't a good time for Tyler to come around the corner of the apartment block, glaring into space.

He stopped, looking at her. "Are you lost?" he asked.

"Not lately." She put her hands in her back pockets and studied him quietly. "You look peaked."

"Do I? Why did you go rushing out of the stable?" he demanded.

She lifted her eyebrows. "Three is still a crowd, isn't it?"

"You thought I might have been waiting breathlessly for you to leave so that I could seduce Margie in one of the stalls?" he said with a cold tone to his deep voice.

Put that way, it sounded ridiculous. "Well, I guess not. But she was waiting for you."

"She had some good news. You won't get to hear it, of course," he continued. He lit a cigarette and threw her a mocking smile. "Margie and I don't think you deserve to hear it. You jump to conclusions on the shabbiest evidence, and you won't listen to explanations. You're still running away from involvement."

"I've had some hard knocks in the past," she defended herself.

"I know all about that," he said. "I wormed the rest of it out of Margie, and I'm sorry about what happened to you. But I thought you and I were on the way to something more important than a few stolen kisses—yet I still can't get close to you."

She flushed, remembering the trail ride. "I wouldn't exactly say that," she faltered.

"I'm not talking about physical closeness," he said curtly. "I can't get close to you emotionally. You back away from me."

"I have good reason to!" she shot back.

"Not with me, you don't," he said, his voice deep and quiet as he watched her. "I'm not asking you to move in with me, or even to spend the night with me in a nonplatonic way. I want you to trust me, Nell."

"But I do trust you," she began.

"Not in the way that counts." He drew in a slow breath. "Well, I've had all I can take. I won't run after you, honey. If you want anything more to happen between us, you'll have to make the first move. I'm not going to touch you again. You're going to have to decide."

He moved away without another word, leaving Nell to stand there and watch him leave with her heart down around her ankles.

Mrs. Norman left in a delighted flurry that afternoon. Her husband had been thrilled to hear from her, and he'd decided to come home and meet her in Vermont for a second honeymoon. Nell had driven the older woman to the airport and had been fervently hugged before Mrs. Norman ran like a teenage girl to catch her plane.

At least someone was happy, Nell thought miserably. But it sure wasn't her. She still didn't understand why Ty-

ler was trying to make her chase him. It didn't really make
sense. He was the man, and the man was supposed to make
all the moves, not the woman; at least, not in Nell's old-
fashioned world.

Of course, Tyler was old-fashioned, too. That was the
hard thing to reconcile. And with his attitude, it didn't really make sense that he'd be hanging around Nell when he
wanted Margie. And he had to want Margie. Every man
did. Margie was beautiful and cultured and sophisticated,
just the right kind of woman for a man like Tyler.

During the next few days, Margie kept very much to
herself. She smiled at Nell as if nothing were wrong, but
she spent a lot of time where the men—especially Tyler—
were, and she kept the boys with her. She seemed to understand that her presence irritated Nell, and she did everything she could to make it bearable for the younger
woman, right down to sleeping late and going to bed early.

Nell was actually looking for an excuse for a confrontation, because there was a lot she wanted to say to her
sister-in-law. But Margie made that impossible, and even
Tyler interfered if it looked as though Nell might find an
opportunity. So the days went by with Nell getting more
frustrated by the minute. What she didn't know was that
Darren McAnders had been furious that Margie was
spending time with Tyler, and had begun to make his
presence felt and heard while Tyler and Nell were away on
the camp out. He and Margie had it out that very evening
while the camp out was in full swing. The argument shortly
began to have results. When no one was looking, Mc-
Anders picked Margie up and carried her off to a quiet
spot under the big palo verde tree near the apartments.
And there he kissed her until she couldn't stand up or
protest. Then he began to tell her how he felt and what he
wanted. When he finished, she was smiling. And the next

kiss was instigated by her. But they kept their secret, because Margie didn't want to spring anything on Nell until Tyler had a chance to patch things up with his lady. Margie was getting impatient, though. Tyler and Nell seemed to have reached an impasse.

Nell went on teaching the daily riding lessons and avoided going to the dinner table until she was sure it was too late for Tyler to be there, if he'd decided to eat at the big house, that was. He spent more and more time in the bunkhouse or his own cabin.

Nights got longer and Nell's temper got shorter. Until Tyler had come along, she'd never known that she even had a temper, but he seemed to bring out the beast in her.

It was like being half a person. She strained for glimpses of him; she spun beautiful daydreams about him. Her eyes followed him everywhere. But she kept to herself, and spoke to him only when he asked her something directly. Which was all she could do, because he was still spending time with Margie. Actually he was chaperoning her with McAnders so that Bella wouldn't figure out their secret and spill the beans too soon, but Nell didn't know that and she didn't trust him.

Tyler was brooding, too. He almost gave up. Nell seemed more unapproachable now than she ever had, and she was retreating by the day. He wondered if he was ever going to be able to reach her again.

Texas seemed so far away. He remembered how he'd taken Abby Clark out on a date and how sweet it had been to dance with her. But it was nothing compared to the feel of Nell's body in his arms, her soft, shy mouth under the crush of his, welcoming him. She had a big heart and he wanted it, but Nell didn't seem to want him back.

She thought he was stuck on Margie, and that was a real laugh. Margie reminded him too much of the world he'd had to give up, of all he'd lost. He was going to need a woman who wasn't interested in frills and fancies, a woman who'd be willing to work at his side and help him start over. Nell was just right, in every way, and he cared about her deeply. The problem was getting her to believe he loved her when she had such poor self-image. She couldn't or wouldn't believe that she was infinitely desirable to him. And until he could break her out of that self-ordained mold, he was never going to reach her.

His green eyes glittered as he saw her riding back in from the trail ride with Darren McAnders at her side. Damn McAnders. Why couldn't he stop interfering?

He watched them dismount. McAnders took Nell's mount by the bridle and led both horses into the stable, with a grin and a cheerful greeting to Tyler.

Tyler didn't acknowledge it. He stood glaring at Nell for a long moment, and then he strode toward her.

She watched the way he walked, so tall and easy, which was deceptive. He was all muscle, and she knew the power in that exquisitely male body, the sweetness of being held by him while he brought her every nerve alive. He had on a beige shirt that emphasized his dark coloring, made his green eyes even greener. He came close and she felt the tension grow between them almost instantly.

"Having fun?" he asked.

She didn't like his tone. It was insulting. "No, I'm not," she replied tersely. "I hate running a dude ranch. I'm scared to death that a rattlesnake is going to bite somebody or a horse is going to run away with a greenhorn rider or that we're going to lose somebody out on that desert and find them several days later. I hate budgeting, I don't like the need to cut out half of our recreational facilities, and if I have to hear one more remark about how desolate and disgusting my desert is, I'm going to scream!"

"I just asked if you were having fun," he pointed out. "I didn't ask for a rundown on world economy."

"Don't mind me," she said mockingly. "Pat yourself on the back."

He did, and her face flamed with bad temper.

"Why don't you go back to Texas?" she muttered.

"Oh, I like it here," he told her. "Dust and rattlesnakes grow on a man."

Her eyes narrowed. "Don't you start," she dared.

His eyebrows lifted. "What a nasty temper you're in, little Nell. Why don't you go and eat something bland and see if it'll take the pepper off your tongue?"

"I'm going to tell my uncle how you're ruining the place," she threatened.

"He won't listen," he said with a lazy grin. "He's too busy depositing the money we've been making lately."

She took a sharp breath. "That's it, go ahead, put all the blame on me!"

"Mind you don't split a blood vessel with all that temper, honey," he said.

"Don't call me honey!"

"How about vinegar?"

She aimed a kick at his shin, but he was faster. He caught her up in his arms and carried her toward the corral, where the horses' watering trough was sitting innocently.

Through her kicking and cursing, she noticed where he was headed and clung to his neck.

"You wouldn't dare," she snapped.

He chuckled. "Of course I would."

Her arms tightened. "I'll take you with me."

"Promises, promises," he breathed huskily, and his mouth lowered so that it almost touched hers. "Will you, indeed?"

The threat of his lips made her heart race. She felt her breasts pressed against his chest; she smelled the leather and tobacco scent of his body mingling with the cologne he wore. She felt the strength of the arms under her and a kind of feminine delight in his maleness grew within her.

"Will I what?" she breathed. Her nails scraped gently against his nape as unfamiliar sensations trembled through her.

"Don't tease," he whispered. "If I start kissing you now, we're going to have the biggest audience this side of Denver."

Her lips parted. "I'm not teasing," she said softly.

His face hardened. "No? Then tell me how I feel about Margie."

She felt the spell shatter. "I don't know," she muttered. "Anyway, it's none of my business."

"The hell it isn't. You blind little bat!"

And with a suddenness that put her between shock and fear, his mouth went down on hers savagely for one long instant before he took advantage of her helpless reaction and threw her, bottom first, right into the horses' trough.

Chapter Eleven

Tyler had strode off in a black temper by the time Nell dragged herself, dripping and swearing, out of the horses' trough. A couple of the men were watching, and she gave them her best glare as she sloshed off toward the house. It didn't help her dignity that they were laughing behind her.

She stormed into the house and upstairs to shower and change her clothes before anybody got a good look at her and guffawed some more. Then she returned downstairs, cooler but still fuming, and dialed her Uncle Ted's number with fingers that trembled in her haste. And all the while she wanted to fling Tyler and Margie down a mine shaft.

"Hello?" A deep, masculine voice came over the other end.

"Hello, yourself. I don't want to run this ranch anymore," she said without preamble. "I don't care if it means I lose everything, I won't stay at the same place with that foreman of yours!"

Uncle Ted was getting a new lease on life. His man-hating niece was suddenly losing her temper, something sh never did, and over a real live man! He could have jumpe for joy. He knew it had been a good idea to send Tyler Ja cobs out to the Double R.

"Now, now," Uncle Ted soothed, "I can't let you throw away your inheritance, Nell. No, you'll just have to sta there and work things out, I'm afraid."

"I can't!" she wailed. "Look, I'll sign everything ove to you—"

"No." He hung up.

She stared at the dead receiver as if it had sproute flowers. Talk about finality! He hadn't even said good bye.

She slammed the receiver down with a bang and glare at it. "I hate you!" she raged. "I think you're an over bearing male chauvinist, and just because you're rich doesn't give you the right to try and run people's lives fo them!"

She was screaming by now, and Curt and Jess, standing unnoticed in the doorway, were watching her with saucer size eyes. They motioned to their mother, who joined th rapt audience.

"I don't want him here," she fumed at the telephone. " never did! I don't understand why you wouldn't give me a chance to straighten things out by myself before you stuck your big nose into my business. It's my ranch, my father left it to me and Teddy, and he never meant for you to dangle it over my head like a guillotine!"

"What's a guillotine?" Jess whispered to his mother.

"It's stuff you put on your joints when you have rheumatism," Curt whispered.

"Hush!" said their mother.

"Well, you can just tell him to go back to Texas, or I'll go there and live myself and he can have the ranch! I hate him, and I hate you, and I hate Margie, too!"

"It must be the insecticides in the groundwater table affecting your brain," Margie said, shaking her head.

Nell whirled, aghast to find three pairs of eyes staring at her. She stared back, speechless.

"Aunty Nell, why are you talking to the telephone?" Curt wanted to know.

"I was talking to your Great-Uncle Ted," she said with mangled dignity.

"Wouldn't you communicate better by talking into the receiver?" Margie mused.

Nell glared at her. "I haven't congratulated you yet. I'll make sure I send you a suitable gift when the time comes."

"How sweet of you, Nell." Margie sighed. "He's sooo handsome, and I can't believe he really loves me."

"We love him, too," the boys chorused, grinning. "And we can come and live here now—"

Nell screamed. She actually screamed. She did it and then stood stock-still, astonished that the sound had really come from her throat.

"I love you, too." Margie added fuel to the fire, making a kissing motion with her lips. "We'll be one big happy family."

"Like hell we will!" Nell burst out, and tears fell from her eyes. "I'm leaving, right now!"

"Leaving for where?" Margie asked.

"I don't know and I don't . . . care." She hiccuped from stuffy tears. "Oh, Margie, how could you!"

"Boys, go and find a new lizard to scare me with," Margie told her sons. She shooed them out and closed the door.

"I want to leave," Nell wailed.

"After you listen to me," Margie said. "Now dry up fo
a minute. How do you feel about Tyler?"

Nell tried to avoid the question, but Margie wouldn'
budge. She drew in a shaky breath. "I...love him," sh
bit off.

Margie smiled. "Do you? A lot?"

"Yes."

"But you think that he's the kind of man who plays witl
one woman at the same time he's courting somebody
else?"

Nell blinked. She turned her head slightly, and her great
dark eyes fixed on Margie's face. "Well, no, actually, h
isn't," she admitted. "He's kind of old-fashioned abou
things."

Margie nodded. "That's right. You're doing very well
darling. Keep going."

"If he'd been going to marry you, he'd have told m
himself," Nell ventured. "He wouldn't have let me fin
out by accident from someone else."

"Yes. And?"

Nell drew in a slow, exquisite breath. "He'd never play
around with an innocent woman unless he was serious
about her. Unless he was playing for keeps."

Margie smiled gently. "And you were going to cuss ou
Uncle Ted and run away."

Nell dried her tears. "I've been such a fool. I was scared,
you know, Margie."

"We're all scared. Commitment isn't easy, even when
people love each other." She went close to Nell, smiling.
"I'm going to marry Darren. Will you be my maid o
honor?"

Nell burst out laughing. "Oh, Margie, of course I will!"
She hugged the older woman fervently, laughing and crying all at once. "I'm so sorry for the things I said. I was so

ealous, and my heart was broken! But now I think I'm going to be all right, after all."

"I know you are. Wouldn't you like to take a nice, refreshing walk?" she added. "You might walk down by the holding pens. The scenery there is really something."

"Nice, is it?" Nell probed.

"Dark and handsome, to coin a phrase." Margie grinned. "But it may not last long, so you'd better hurry."

"I'll do that. But first, can you lend me a dress? Something very feminine and lighter than air and suitable for a woman to chase a man in?"

Margie was delighted. "You bet I can. Come on!"

It was a dream of a dress in creamy spring green with a full, flowing skirt and a pretty rounded neckline and puffy sleeves. Nell felt like a young girl again, all heart and nerves as she brushed her long, clean hair and put on makeup and a little perfume.

Nell smiled, thinking how sweet it was going to be to make her first move toward Tyler, to flirt openly with him, sure of herself at last.

She slipped on a pair of soft shoes and tore down the staircase and out the door toward the holding pens. It seemed to take forever to get there, and she was breathless from her haste when she finally reached them.

The pens were empty now, with roundup over, but Tyler was leaning back lazily against the fence with a cigarette in his fingers, his long legs crossed and one arm propped on the second fence rail. His hat was pulled low over his eyes so that Nell couldn't quite see them through the shadows, but he looked approachable enough.

"Hello," she said nervously.

He nodded. His green eyes glittered over her possessively before he turned back to the horizon and took a draw from his cigarette. "Lose your way?"

"Not this time." She went closer and stood beside him to look over the pasture. "Do you make a habit of throwing women into water troughs? Because if you do, we're going to have a rocky life together."

He couldn't believe he'd heard that. He turned, his eyes hungry on her face, his pulse racing. She'd dressed up and fixed her face and hair, and she looked radiant. "No, don't make a habit of it," he replied. "But at the time I'd had about all I could stand. Nell, I'm thinking of going back to Texas."

"Running out on me?" she asked with pure bravado. "I'll come after you."

He touched his forehead unobtrusively to see if he was dying of fever or having hallucinations. "I beg your pardon?"

She gathered up her shaken nerve. "I said, I'll follow you back to Texas."

He finished the cigarette and ground it out under his boot, taking so long to speak that Nell felt her knees getting ready to buckle in case she'd gotten it wrong and he didn't care.

"No doubts?" he asked suddenly, and his eyes met hers with a fiercely sensual impact.

It was hard to get enough breath to answer him, because he was even closer now, and she had to fight not to put her body right against his and hold on for dear life. "No doubts, Ty," she whispered. She looked up at him and went for broke. "I love you."

His eyes closed for an instant and then opened on a heavy exhaled breath. "My God." He drew her into his arms and held her there, rocking her hungrily from side to side, with his lips on her cheek, her ear, her neck, and finally, crushing into the warmth of her soft mouth.

She held on to him with all her strength, loving the furious beating of her heart, the weakness he engendered in her body, the warm wonder of knowing that he cared about her, too. She sighed under his devouring mouth and lifted, fractionally, while he searched her eyes with all the barriers gone.

"Did Margie tell you that it isn't me she's going to marry?" he asked quietly.

"Not really," she hedged, because it was a dangerous time to go into all the details.

He frowned. "She didn't talk to you?"

"It was more a case of her making *me* talk. And I worked it out by myself." She smiled tenderly at him. "If you were going to marry Margie," she began quietly, "you'd never have touched me, not even out of pity."

He didn't move for a minute. Then he began to stroke her bare arms very gently with his warm, work-roughened hands. "It took you a long time to realize that," he said deeply, and his heart sang because of the look in her eyes.

"Yes," she said with a faint grin. "Of course, I didn't work it out at first. After I got out of the horses' trough and dried off," she said with a glare that didn't faze him, "I called Uncle Ted and yelled at him and told him what he could do with the ranch and that I was leaving forever. He just hung up on me. I guess I'll have to call him back and apologize."

"I wouldn't just yet," Tyler advised. "He's probably laughing too hard. I get the idea that before I came along, you never yelled at anybody."

She nodded. "There was never any reason to." She sighed, looking hungrily at his dark face. "Oh, I want you," she whispered, letting down her pride. "I want to live with you and have children with you and grow old with you."

"And what do I want, do you think?" he asked, leading her on.

It didn't work. She just smiled. "You want me, of course."

He burst out laughing, the sound full with joy and delight. He lifted her up against his chest to kiss her with exquisite tenderness. "I'm sorry about the horses' trough. I'd waited and hoped, and we were almost there, and then Margie came along after the camp out and set us back several weeks. She didn't mean to. Her news, of course, was that she and McAnders were engaged. But when you took off, she decided to keep the secret a while longer."

"I'm sorry about that," she murmured. "I didn't think I could compete with her. I never dreamed that you could feel for me what I felt for you. It was like wishing for the moon."

"Not anymore, is it?" he mused, and brushed his mouth sensually across hers.

"Not anymore," she agreed huskily.

"When were you sure that I didn't want Margie?"

"When I remembered that you'd made the sweetest kind of love to me, without asking me to go all the way with you," she whispered, and for the first time, she kissed him with shy hunger. "And a man like you wouldn't do that unless he had something permanent in mind. Because I'm still a virgin," she breathed into his mouth. "And you're an old-fashioned man. You even said so."

"It took you long enough to remember it," he murmured dryly. He nuzzled her cheek with his, floating warm from the touch of her body against his, the clasp of her soft arms. "I love you, Nell," he whispered huskily. "And I do want you for keeps. You and a houseful of children and the best future we can make together."

"I love you, too," she whispered fervently.

"You grew on me," he mused, lifting his head to search her soft eyes. "But long before that time I was sick and you nursed me, I knew I'd lost my heart. I wasn't able to think about another woman after that."

"I'm very glad. I loved you from the beginning, although I was afraid to. You see, I thought you were just being nice to me because you felt sorry for me."

"I liked you," he said simply. "And when you started avoiding me, it was like a knife in my heart."

"I didn't think you could care about someone like me," she said quietly. "Then after you began to talk about my low self-image and my lack of confidence, I started thinking about things. I guess none of us is perfect, but that doesn't mean we can't be loved. It doesn't have much to do with beauty and sophistication and money, does it? Love is more than that."

"Much more." He framed her face and bent slowly to her mouth. "I'll cherish you all my life. I don't have a lot to give you, but you can have my heart."

She smiled against his mouth. "I'd rather have that than anything else in the whole world. I'll give you mine for it."

He smiled back. "That," he whispered before he kissed her, "is a deal."

A long time later, they walked back to the house hand in hand, and Margie and the boys and Bella stood on the porch, anxious to find out what had happened.

"Well?" Bella demanded, out of patience. "Is it going to be a wedding or a farewell party?"

"A wedding." Nell laughed and ran forward to hug Bella and Margie and the boys. "And we're going to be so happy together."

"As if anybody could believe otherwise," Bella said, sniffing. "Well, I'll go cook supper. Something special." Her eyes narrowed in thought. "And a cake...."

"You snake in the grass, leading me on like that!" Nell accused Margie. "Making me so jealous that I couldn't stand it!"

"I knew it would either open your eyes or close them for good." Margie smiled. "You could have gone on forever the way you were, untrusting and alone. I thought you needed a chance."

"Well, thank you," Nell said. She glanced at Tyler's radiant expression and then back at Margie as the other woman started to speak.

"I love Darren so much, Nell. Are you going to mind having us both on the place? Because he insists that he's going to support me."

"I don't have any problem at all with that," Nell said at once.

"I called Uncle Ted back after you went out to meet Tyler," Margie said with a secretive smile. "He said if you and Tyler got married, he'd turn over control of the ranch early—as a wedding present."

Tyler didn't say anything, and Nell went close to him. "Look," she said, "it isn't much of a ranch right now. It's lost a lot of money and times are still pretty bad. You are getting nothing but a headache, so don't look on it as a handout."

That took the bitter look off his face. "Then I guess you and I are going to have the challenge of building it up again," he said finally, and his hard features relaxed. He had to start back somewhere, and he loved Nell. The two of them together, working to build a future and a family. Yes, that sounded good. He smiled down at her. "Okay, honey. We'll give it a try."

"And Darren and I can live in the cabin with the boys," Margie suggested. "Or we can build a house close by. I think I'd rather do that. I still have a nest egg, and so does

Darren—he's been saving for years. We'll do that. Your foreman will have to have someplace to live."

Tyler glanced amusedly at Nell. "I thought we might offer it to Chappy. He's been here a long time, and he bosses everybody around anyway. What do you think?"

Nell laughed. "I think it's a great idea!"

"So do I," Margie agreed. "Well, shall we go inside and call Uncle Ted one more time?"

Nell slid her hand into Tyler's, and they followed the others back inside. Tyler looked down at her just before they went through the open door. The look on his face made Nell catch her breath. The awe and wonder of love blazed from it as surely as the Arizona sun warmed the desert. Nell's own face reflected a love for her long, tall Texan that would last forever.

*　　*　　*　　*　　*

*Look for Diana Palmer's
next LONG, TALL TEXAN,
appearing for the first time
in Silhouette Desire—
coming to you in March 1995.*

Silhouette Books
is proud to present
our best authors, their best books...
and the best in your reading pleasure!

Throughout 1994, look for exciting books
by these top names in contemporary
romance:

DIANA PALMER
Enamored in August

HEATHER GRAHAM POZZESSERE
The Game of Love in August

FERN MICHAELS
Beyond Tomorrow in August

NORA ROBERTS
The Last Honest Woman in September

LINDA LAEL MILLER
Snowflakes on the Sea in September

When it comes to passion,
we wrote the book.

Silhouette®

HE'S MORE THAN A MAN, HE'S ONE OF OUR

MAIL-ORDER BROOD
Arlene James

Leon Paradise was shocked when he discovered that his mail-order bride came with a ready-made family. No sooner had he said his vows when a half-dozen kids showed up on his doorstep. Now the handsome rancher had to decide if his home—and his heart—were big enough for Cassie Esterbridge *and* the brood she'd brought into his life.

Look for *Mail-Order Brood* by Arlene James.
Available in August.

Fall in love with our **Fabulous Fathers!**

Silhouette
R O M A N C E™

FF894